Wallace Family Affairs
Volume II Part 1
Sometimes Love Isn't Enough

Carey Anderson

ISBN: 061583065X
ISBN-13: 9780615830650

DEDICATION

This story is dedicated to my loved ones who indulged in my imagination with me. I appreciate your time, I could never thank you enough.

Join me on Facebook – Carey "The Writer" Anderson

Twitter - @CareyTheWriter

Blog - http://careyanderson.blogspot.com

Website – http://www.careythewriteranderson.com

Cover Design by Cover Couture
Photo Copyright: GlebStock / shutterstock
Photo Copyright: Jaroslaw Pawlak / shutterstock
Photo Copyright: boykung / shutterstock
Photo Copyright: Exotic Destinations / shutterstock

ACKNOWLEDGMENTS

I would like to thank my baby-girl who is my life's ultimate expression of a dream realized. Thank you for sacrificing mommy time so that I could have the time to work some things out on paper.

I would like to thank my Soul Sistah #1 who has been my captivated audience since middle school. Without your love, support, encouragement, and FIRE I never would've completed Volume I or II, etc. Thank you for bringing me laughter when I couldn't get outside of my head.

I would like to thank my Sister-In-Law for taking time out of your busy family life to humor me with a read through of my latest thoughts and expressions. (SS1 & SIL THANK YOU for the trip to St. Helena where we spent the day lost in my imagination. I will never forget it, and it was exactly what I needed. THANK YOU!)

I would like to thank my dear cousin for reassuring me that my little hobby was relatable and entertaining. You are definitely a speed-reader, thank you for taking time out of your busy life to be entertained by my imagination.

I would like to thank last but not least Mrs. Laverne Dyes! Mrs. Dyes the day that you read my short story to my class changed my life. Thank you for giving me a positive outlet for all the angst going on in my life. You have forever changed my life, I am so thankful to have ever known you.

Chapter 1

Momma said her brother needs to come stay with us. Daddy wasn't happy about it. They argued about it for a long time. Daddy said it was rude for him to ask knowing that they have daughters. Momma said he's her brother and family shouldn't matter. I think momma just wants her family to like her again. Her momma doesn't like us. Her momma never hugs us or even speaks to us. She always looks at us like we're some kind of a science project. I hate the way she touches my hair. She acts like its something she never seen before.

Grand momma doesn't like Daddy just because he's white. When he used to come with us to her house she would roll her eyes whenever he spoke and then act like she didn't hear him. My Daddy would be extra nice to her and she didn't care. She would yell at my Momma and say stuff like "after all the things the white man has done to us, you go and willingly be his house nigger!" Momma would cry, she would tell her momma she couldn't help who she fell in love with. But grand momma didn't care. That was the last time I saw her, I was seven. That's when I realized that my Daddy was white and my momma was black. That's when I realized how people looked at me like I was different.

My Daddy said your skin doesn't matter it's how you treat people that matters. I remember him hugging my Momma and telling her that we were a family, and that she needed to be around people who accepted her for who she was. He always told Momma how beautiful she was. I would see him just stare at Momma like she was the most beautiful lady ever.

At school the kids are so mean, well most of them. They called me white girl, or they called me mix girl, or whatever they felt would make them laugh that day. They would laugh when I turned red, and throw stuff at me. Rosalind was my best friend; she would stand up for me, and tell people to leave me alone.

One day Momma and Daddy were arguing in the morning, it made me so sad I thought Daddy was gonna leave. My big sister Jade made my lunch that morning and made sure we all left on time. Momma wouldn't stop yelling at Daddy, and he was so mad he walked outside. He put his workbag in his truck, and then he turned it on to warm it up. My big brothers Timothy and Malachi stayed with the truck while Daddy went back inside to talk to Momma. A long time ago, Daddy turned on the truck and he went back inside. When he came out the truck was gone. So now he has my brothers sit with the truck. Timothy goes to work with Daddy on the weekends, he is in high school, and Malachi is in middle school. Timothy is going to be a big man who draws buildings and then people build them. Momma and Daddy are so proud of him. They tell Timothy all the time how smart he is, and how he's gonna go real far. Malachi is real smart too, he doesn't know what he wants to be yet, but I tell him he can be anything!

Jade and I walked to school and I cried all the way. Jade told me everything would be fine and to stop crying. I thought she was mad at me until she hugged me, and told me it would be ok. I was in a bad mood though, and when Patrice pulled my hair at recess I got so mad! I punched her and kicked her. Patrice had pulled my hair to make fun of me to the other girls from our class. Rosalind was in the bathroom so she thought she would pull my hair and I would just cry. It surprised her when I punched her. I didn't give her a chance to hit me back. I went crazy on her. The yard teacher broke us up and took us to the office. The secretary Ms. Thomas gave Patrice some ice for her eye while we waited for the Principal.

The Principal Ms. Boyd was very disappointed to see me in her office for fighting. This was my first time being in her office for trouble. Normally I was there for awards and special stuff. Ms. Boyd would always tell me how pretty I was, and how she wished she had my hair. I wished I could give it to her, cause most girls didn't like me because of it. Patrice got suspended cause she was always in trouble. Ms. Boyd said she would let me go with a warning, because I was such a good student normally.

When I got back to class everyone was looking at me differently. That's when I realized I had to fight in order for people to leave me alone. I told Rosalind what happened and she gave me a high five. After that day I was always fighting at school. I was pretty tough, no one could beat me or at least I thought. I didn't go looking for trouble, but if somebody messed with me or said something that hurt my feelings I was fighting.

Momma would yell at me every time she had to pick me up for getting suspended, but it wasn't my fault. Sometimes she would whoop me so badly that Daddy would argue with her about my bruises. She would say she didn't hit me that hard and it only showed cause I was light skinned. Daddy would say that's not why. Jade would put witch-hazel on my bruises, and cocoa butter on my scars. Jade would tell me to just ignore those stupid girls, but they didn't mess with her like they messed with me. Jade looked more like momma then I did. I looked more like daddy. Some girls were mean to Jade too, but not like they were to me. Momma would tell me I didn't have to prove nothing to nobody, but she didn't understand. At school I was the different one, nobody ever came up to her and asked her "what are you"? Like I wasn't human or something. Nobody ever slapped her just for the joy of seeing their handprint on her face. I tried to stop fighting to make her happy, and it worked for a while. But then....

My Uncle Preston came on a Friday. Even though Momma and Daddy had argued about it, Daddy looked real happy to see Preston. Momma was so happy to have her little brother with us. The first night she and Preston stayed up real late talking about when they were little and all the fun they had. Preston brought up their daddy and how he died. They got real quiet. Jade and I were listening at our door. It sound like Momma was crying, but we didn't know why.

Eventually we went to bed, in the morning Jade got up to make everybody some pancakes. I told her I would be her helper. We still had our nighties on when we went in the kitchen. Preston was sleeping on the hideaway bed in the couch. He got up when he smelled breakfast cooking. He came in the kitchen in pajama pants and no shirt.

"What cha doing?" He said smiling.

"Making breakfast." I said.

He just sat there for a while watching us. Then when Jade bent over to get the griddle from under the cabinet he asked, "how old are you guys?"

"I'm getting ready to be twelve, and Amber just turned ten."

"You guys got boy friends?"

"Eeewwllll!" I said.

"Daddy said no boyfriends right now." Jade said.

"Do you always do what your daddy says?"

I didn't like the way he asked the question. "YES!" We were good girls!

Then Timothy came in the kitchen, "smells good!"

Preston was sitting on a stool with his legs open. When Timothy turned to walk out the kitchen, he turned red and he looked at Preston.

Preston put his hands up, "it's the morning what can I say?"

"GET AWAY FROM MY SISTERS!" Timothy yelled.

Preston got mad and stood in Timothy's face. "WHAT YOU GONNA DO? WHITE BOY!"

Timothy punched Preston, but Preston put him in a crazy hold. Timothy was so mad. Malachi came running out the room. When he got to the kitchen Preston kicked him and Malachi looked so shocked. But then he punched Preston and kept hitting him until he fell down. Then Timothy and Malachi kept beating him up. Momma and Daddy came out in their robes. Everybody was yelling I couldn't tell what was going on. Jade and I got sent to our room, when I tried to tell Momma that we were only trying to make breakfast. She got mad at me and slapped me. Then she told me to get in my room. Jade hugged me and we cried together. We were in our room for a long time. My stomach hurt cause I was so hungry. Momma and Daddy came in our room to talk to us. Momma said that the fight was a big misunderstanding. And that from now on we couldn't come out of our room until we were dressed. Momma got mad at me when I asked how were we gonna take showers. She said we had to take them at night. She said we were blossoming young ladies and we had to conduct ourselves that way from now on. Timothy and Malachi didn't like Uncle Preston anymore, and he didn't like them. They would always fight after that. Uncle Preston would always stare at us especially Jade. He would be real nice to her, and tell her how pretty she was.

One day Ms. Thomas told me I had to walk home alone cause Jade went home early cause she was sick. When I got home Momma wasn't home and Jade was laying on her bed crying. She wouldn't tell me what was wrong though. Momma put ground beef in the sink to thaw. There was spaghetti sauce and noodles on the counter. Normally Jade made dinner, but since she didn't feel well I told her I would make dinner. Uncle Preston came in the kitchen and watched me. He kept telling me how pretty I was. He kept calling me red bone, I liked my new name. When I couldn't reach the bowl for the salad I was gonna make, he came to help me. He kept rubbing his body on me as he reached for the bowl. He looked at me and smiled and then he gave me the bowl. I didn't understand what just happened, but that little voice in my head said it wasn't right. He went and sat back down though and I finished making dinner. Jade came out of our room when Timothy and Malachi came home. They asked her what was wrong and she just said she didn't feel good. That's when Jade started being quiet.

After that day uncle Preston kept telling me how pretty I was and how I needed to have a boyfriend. There was a boy in my class who everybody said had a crush on me, but he was always shy and quiet. I asked Quincy if he wanted to be my boyfriend, and he shook his head yes. I kissed him like my uncle showed me, and Quincy blushed. If he wasn't so dark I guess he would've turned red like I did. But Quincy didn't want to be my boyfriend anymore after a week. He said his momma said he couldn't have a white girlfriend. I told him I wasn't white, but he said no cause his momma told him no. I was so sad when I got home I was gonna tell Preston about it but he wasn't there. Momma was home early from work with a headache, she asked me what was wrong. Not thinking anything of it, I begged her not to tell Daddy that I had a boyfriend. Then I told her everything. I told her how Uncle Preston taught me how to kiss. How he showed me what she and Daddy did when we heard the bed in their room. My Momma sat there and listened to everything, she looked mad. I told her how he told me it was a secret and not to tell anybody because they just didn't want me to know about the good stuff yet. I asked her if she was mad at me for telling her and she said no. Then she went in the room and talked to Jade. When she came out the room Momma was crying. Daddy came home and they went in their room. Daddy was screaming but he wasn't screaming at Momma. Timothy and Malachi came home, they asked us what was going on, but I didn't know what to say. Momma called the police, and then Uncle Preston came home. Momma started screaming at him and hitting him. He pushed Momma down, and then my Daddy came out of nowhere. When he hit Preston you heard it. Preston tried to fight Daddy, but he was no match. My brothers sat back and watched. The police came and took Uncle Preston away; Jade and I had to go down to the police station. A nice police lady asked me to show her on a doll everything my uncle did to me. I didn't want to, but Momma told me to show her. I cried and cried as I showed her, Momma cried too. The police lady cried as well and then she told me I was gonna be safe from now on. That night Momma scream at grand momma over the phone! I could tell she was hurt cause grand momma didn't care that uncle Preston hurt us. She said a lot of mean things to Momma, and then Momma cursed her. She screamed words we're not supposed to use at her momma. She told her she was dead to her, and that they were all dead to her.

Chapter 2

"Who's the new boy?" Rosalind said

"I don't know but he's cute!" All the girls stared at the new kid Benjamin. He was so cute with his curly black hair and cocoa brown skin. Normally Ms. Thomas brought the new student to class but today Ms. Boyd personally escorted Benjamin and his father to our class. Benjamin's daddy was so handsome. He looked even better than his son. We didn't know who to look at. Benjamin or his daddy.

In a couple days we got another new student and his name was Damien. Damien had hazel eyes like mine and all the girls kept telling him how pretty his eyes were. I found it interesting that they told me my eyes were ugly and how they were gonna pluck them out, and then tell him his were pretty. When Damien said he liked me all the sudden girls wanted to fight me again. Momma was finally starting to act happy again. I didn't want to make her sad by fighting, so I did my best to avoid fighting.

Now that Jade was in Middle school, and I was in the sixth grade, I walked half way home with Rosalind, then two blocks by myself. This particular day Tamiko and her friends waited for Rosalind and I to separate and they followed me home talking about how badly she was gonna beat me up. She wouldn't leave until she took my hair home with her she yelled. When I got home I was surprised Momma was home. She called me in her room; she was mad which made me scared.

"Why are those girls following you?"

"Tamiko is mad because the new boy Damien likes me."

"She wants to fight you over a boy?"

"Yes, but I didn't because you told me not to."

"COME HERE!" She took me in the bathroom. She put Vaseline on my face and all over my arms and legs. She tightened up my ponytail. Then she grabbed me by my shoulders, she looked me in the eyes. "You go out there! You start with the baddest one and work your way down! You better not get beat up either! Otherwise you're gonna have to deal with me!" Then she pushed out the bathroom.

My heart was pounding out of my chest. Momma came and sat on the porch to watch. I followed Momma out the door, I couldn't let Tamiko hit me, Rosalind fought her before and she said Tamiko hits very hard. I hit her as hard as I could in the stomach. The fear of my Momma made me a monster! I beat Tamiko up so bad no one else wanted to fight. Her friends helped her up and then they slowly walked down the street.

Momma had tears in her eyes. I thought she was mad at me. She hugged me and told me that I did well, and that she was proud of me. She told me the story about her Daddy. She said her daddy grew up on a reservation, and she described him as no good. She said he was always cheating on her momma. She said one day a bunch of white men came to her house and beat her daddy up so bad that he later died from his wounds. He was messing around with one of their wives. She said her mother moved them to San Francisco and taught her brothers and sister to hate white people.

When my Momma started taking classes at the community college she met my Daddy. She said he liked her from day one, but she did not like him. She said she rolled her eyes at him all the time and she wouldn't give him the time of day. But he was always real nice to her, and one day she decided that they could be friends. But she wouldn't dare tell her momma or her sister or her brothers. Then one day a white guy at their school thought it would be funny to pour milk over her head as she sat under a tree reading her book. She said Daddy saw her arguing with the guy and then he saw the guy slap her, and he told her to shut up. She told me that my Daddy lost it and beat the guy senseless. She told me my dad used to practice boxing with his brothers.

She still tried to not like my Daddy, but he went through so much behind liking her that she couldn't help but fall for him. She was scared to tell her mother about my Daddy because she knew she wouldn't approve. Her mother wanted her to date and eventually marry this boy from her neighborhood, but she didn't like him. And once she started liking my Daddy she wouldn't even talk to the guy. Momma said Daddy's family has always loved her and accepted her for who she was. That's when she knew all white people weren't the way her mother said they were. Momma ran away with Daddy and they got married then they moved to Oakland. She said it hurt her to see those little girls doing what her mother only accused white people of doing. She told me ignorance knows no color lines.

Then she told me that I didn't have to identify myself to anyone. I'm a child of love, and I don't have to prove myself to anyone. She told me not to go looking for a fight, and to try to avoid it as much as I could but if I had no other choice I had to defend myself, and I wasn't allowed to let just anyone beat on me. Then she hugged me and told me that I was her beautiful baby. For the first time I felt beautiful.

The next day at school everybody heard about my fight with Tamiko.

"It's about time somebody beat her up." Rosalind said giving me a high five.

Tamiko and I ended up becoming friends.

Damien on the other hand was just looking for someone to do it to. Talking to him made me think of my uncle, so I didn't like him anymore. Rosalind and Benjamin on the other hand were quite smitten with each other. They held hands all the time and at our sixth grade graduation ceremony they kissed behind the stage when they were alone. I wanted to kiss somebody but nobody ever really liked me. Most times they called me white girl, or they just wanted to do it to me.

My Uncle Jeff moved to Oakland, Daddy was so happy his brother moved to our city. We ended up buying a house right around the corner from them. Fortunately I didn't have to switch schools and my cousin Sophia who was the same age as me started going to my school. She only attended the last two weeks of school with us, but it was still so much fun. She would come to my house after school since her mother and father both worked.

That summer my parents threw Timothy a huge graduation party. Rosalind came to the party and we showed Sophia the latest dance moves. Jade was in the corner with her nose in a book. Eventually she took a break and danced with us a little bit, after we begged and pleaded, but then she went back to her book. We told Malachi how Jade wasn't having any fun, so he made Jade put her book down and dance.

Malachi's friend Sonny was there, he always got quiet whenever Jade was around. I told her before that I thought he had a crush on her. But Jade was not interested, she wanted to get good grades and make Momma and Daddy proud.

"Why don't you ever wear your hair down?" Sophia asked

"It gets so tangled and it hurts to comb it out." I said

"Why don't you perm it?" Rosalind asked

"Momma won't let me. She said I don't need it."

"Why don't you press it?" Rosalind said

"That hurt too! And my ear got burned." I said rubbing my ear at the memory.

"We're going to middle school, we need to make sure we look the part. In middle school I think we should wear our hair down. We got all summer to figure it out."

Chapter 3

Preparation for middle school was so much fun. When we went school shopping we had a lot of fun. Malachi used his money from his summer job to buy his clothes. He was so proud of himself. Momma was proud of him too.

For Jade and I, Momma said we were going shopping with Auntie Lauren and Sophia. Auntie Lauren and my Momma were so excited to pick stuff out for us. Last year Momma got so irritated with Jade as she didn't want anything really girlie or standout cute. Sophia and I wanted everything. Jade brought a book with her; she rarely took her nose out of it. Plain jeans, plain shirts, plain shoes, and plain everything, that's what Jade, wanted. We were done with Jade's clothes in less than thirty minutes. Now Sophia and I were very girlie. Momma and Lauren were so tickled with us, until I went too far. I wanted earrings that Momma said were too much for a thirteen year old. I guess I was having a moment where I forgot who my Momma was. I copped an attitude and right there in the middle of the store Momma slapped me. I was so embarrassed that I was quiet for a long time. Momma went right back to talking like nothing just happened.

"I thought my momma was the only one like that." Sophia whispered

Auntie Lauren looked at Sophia, "what did you say?"

Sophia swallowed hard. "I was just saying..." She started fidgeting with her hands and twirling her foot. "I was just saying that I thought you were the only one." Then she braced herself to be hit.

"Are you trying to be smart?" Auntie Lauren said

"No ma'am!" Sophia said putting her eyes on the floor.

"You better watch yourself!" Auntie Lauren said, and then she looked at Momma. "Annette can you believe these kids?"

Then they decided that we needed to eat, so we went to a nearby pizza shop, Malachi met us for lunch. Momma and Auntie Lauren sat at their own table, and we had own teenager table. All of us talked about our ideas of what the next school year was gonna be like. Jade wanted to make the honor roll again. Malachi wanted to be the top athlete just like Timothy. Timothy soared in everything, he was the all-star athlete, he was on the honor roll, and all the girls liked him. Timothy got a full scholarship to Stanford. My parents couldn't have been prouder. Malachi was his own person, he was just as smart, but he wanted to have his own time to shine. He wasn't sure what he wanted to do after high school, but he had time to figure it out. Meanwhile he and Daddy bought a car from the junkyard. They rebuilt the engine together. Malachi was excited to have a car even though he still had a few weeks until his sixteenth birthday. After he bought his school clothes he was gonna save up to get his car painted. Daddy told him he would split the cost with him. I said I was excited to be at a new school with new people. Plus Sophia, Jade, and Rosalind would be there. It was gonna be sweet.

Away from Malachi and Jade, Sophia and I talked about how we hoped we met cute boys. I really wanted a boyfriend, but I knew better than to mention it to them. Sophia brought mousse and we practiced putting it on my hair. It made my hair crunchy, but I loved the way it made my hair look. My hair had darkened some but when I wet it and then put the mousse on it it looked a lot darker and it was curly instead of a puffy mess. Momma liked it too. She just told me to keep my headbands on so that I didn't try to look too grown. But I wanted to look grown, but I feared her more than my want so I did as I was told. We offered to do Jade's hair but she declined.

The morning of the first day of school I was up so early that I was up with Daddy and Timothy.

"Well don't you look pretty."? Daddy said

"Yea look at you! You look nice. I can't believe you're going to middle school. It seems like yesterday Momma was telling us she was gonna have a baby, now look at you."

"Tim, I'm not a baby!" I said pouting

He put his hands up in defeat, "I know! I know!" Then he kissed my forehead. "Have a good day at school chipmunk."

I made a pot of oatmeal in hopes that the smell would wake Jade up. Sophia came over as Daddy and Timothy left. We tried our hardest to be quiet. Eventually Jade got up, she took her time eating breakfast and then brushing her teeth. We were dying! Finally Momma got up, she put fire under Jade by saying, "hurry up". With those two words Jade moved super fast. Sophia and I smiled at each other. We weren't the only ones afraid of our mommas. Momma dropped Malachi off first then she drove us to school. We sat quietly in the backseat, inside I felt like I was gonna burst. When we got to school there were so many kids.

"I will pick you guys up right here at three o'clock, that should give you plenty of time to talk to your little friends."

"Yes" I said

Through clinched lips she said, "yes WHAT!"

"Yes Momma." Jade and I said at the same time.

"Yes Auntie" Sophia said as well.

I was so happy to see a rainbow of colors in my fellow students. We spotted Rosalind and Benjamin right away. Jade took us to the wall outside of the office. There were papers on the wall A - B Mr. Booth, C - D Ms. Connor, and so on. Jade explained that we were assigned homerooms by our last names. She said we'd get our class schedules in this class. Rosalind and Benjamin were in the same homeroom, she was Smith and he was Seaver. We were Wallace's so we had the same class. Then we walked back out to the cafeteria area. Jade saw some of her friends; I didn't know she had friends. She never talked about her friends or even talked to them on the phone. But they were definitely her speed; they talked about all the books they read over the summer. They got really excited about one book, and Sophia and I looked at each other. We sat down a couple benches away from them. When the bell rang we followed Jade to homeroom. Mr. Thornton was our homeroom teacher. He welcomed us to a new school year. He passed out our class schedule and our locker locations and combinations, and then as long as we promised to talk quietly he'd let us discuss our schedules. Sophia and I had PE and Home Ec together. I had Mr. Thornton for history, Ms. Blevins for English, Ms. Cobb for science, Mr. Harris for math, Ms. Strickland for PE, and Ms. Reed for Home EC. Sophia and I agreed to a location for lunch and then we went or separate ways. When we walked into Ms. Blevins' class she asked us to stand a long the wall. As she called our names she told us where to sit. The desks were arranged in clusters of fours. "Amber Wallace", then she pointed to a seat by the door. I took the final seat in our four cluster. There was a girl named Cassondra, a boy named David, and boy name Gerald but he told us to call him Jerry. David looked at me like he had a crush on me, but he was kind of shy and didn't say much. Cassondra told me she liked my hair and my dress. I knew we would be friends. Her hair was short and dark brown, she had a perm, and it looked like a lot of her hair broke off. She had big women breast so she kind of hunched over to not poke them out. I thought it was odd that she was wearing a turtleneck at the end of summer, but I didn't ask any questions. Tamiko was in my class too; she waved hi to me when I walked into the class. Ms. Blevins introduced herself to us, and explained how the class would go. She said she didn't give homework on Fridays but if we missed assignments during the week the weekend was our last opportunity to make up missed assignments. She said tardiness was unacceptable and her door closed at the time of the bell. If we were late we need a slip from the office to get into her class. She warned us that she was the only person allowed to open the door at all times. Cassondra and I had all but two classes together. I had all advance classes, except for my PE and Home EC class. She didn't have advanced math, and she had Ms. Tipper for PE. At lunchtime Sophia and I invited her to join us. We introduced her to Rosalind and Benjamin. Then we noticed David eating alone so we invited him to eat with us too. Benjamin was happy there was another boy with us. David was a even brown like momma; they were so brown you could almost see red in their complexion. David had a low fade. Sophia invited a girl named Christen to sit with us too. Christen had a long blonde ponytail. She kind of breathed through her mouth and she spoke on everything like she was an authority. But that was our little group.

One day on a rainy day in PE we sat on the gym floor waiting for our teachers to assign the teams for volleyball. Since we were forced to be in the gym due to the inclement weather Ms. Tipper and Ms. Strickland combined the classes. As Sophia, Cassondra, and I talked about the shoes I was begging my mother to get me. Brenda who was sitting with two other girls says loudly, "so what are you?" I kept talking cause I didn't realize she was talking to me. "Are you Mexican or something?" That's when I realized she was talking to me. Her question made me mad, but I was trying to be peaceable.

Then one of her friends said, "Mexicans don't turn colors like that."

"Eeewwllll are you black?" Brenda asked

In seconds I was off the floor and in her face, "YOU GOT A PROBLEM WITH THAT?"

"I was just asking chill out!"

"I don't appreciate how you asked the question! What are you?"

Mr. Turner saw me in Brenda's face and he ran over while his class of boys finished their push-ups. "Come on ladies, calm down." The boy class stopped and they all looked in hopes to see a girl fight. Sophia and Cassondra told me to calm down and they pulled away. As they pulled me away, I noticed a boy in his class who continued to stare even after everyone else stopped looking. I was still very mad, and I only calmed down when Ms. Strickland threatened to call home. In the locker room Brenda's friends made her apologize to me. She seemed even a little scared of me. I accepted her apology and then I told her she needed to watch the way she spoke to people.

After class that boy was standing close by the locker room. He didn't look like he was waiting for anybody just standing around. He just kept looking at me with very serious eyes. We hurried to the cafeteria and sat at our table. That boy came in the cafeteria and he sat at the far end of our table. He kept his hood on his head, which made it very hard to see him. His skin was black and with the hood he almost disappeared.

"Do you know who he is?" I asked our group as he kept staring at me.

"That's Malcolm" Christen said, "he's an eighth grader so I don't know why he's here. He's very smart, but he's also very mean. Last year my brother told me he had a fight with this one boy cause he called him blackie. He put that kid in the hospital. Everybody learned real fast not to talk about him." Then she shook her head, "I don't know why he has to be so sensitive."

"You don't understand what it's like. People look at you or Sophia and they know you're white. People look at the rest of you and they know you're black. I hate when people ask me stuff like what are you, or what are you mixed with? I'm not mixed, I'm just me. No one ask the rest of you where you belong!"

"I'm sorry." Christen said, "I didn't know it bothered you so much."

"You don't have to live it." Then I looked at Malcolm, "I'm gonna go say hi."

"No don't! He's really mean!" Christen said

"I don't think so."

"Ok it's your funeral!" Christen said taking a bite of her sandwich

Malcolm watched me walk from my end and sit next to him. He didn't smile once, he just watched me. "Your name is Malcolm right?"

"Yep" he said taking a bite of his cafeteria burrito.

"I didn't know eighth graders had lunch with seventh graders." I said

"They don't." He said keeping his eyes on me.

"Oh" I said, "my name is Amber."

"I know," he said taking another bite.

I smiled, "how do you know?"

"I've seen you before. Your Jade's little sister."

"You know my sister?" I couldn't believe he knew her.

"We have all the same classes. She's pretty smart."

"I'm smart too."

"I know!" He said still looking at me.

"How do you know?" I smiled

"You came down here. Your friends are down there too afraid to speak."

I looked back at my group and they were all watching. I laughed, "well you have a reputation for being mean."

"I am mean!" Then he balled up his foil and stood up. "Later!" He walked out of the cafeteria.

I went back to my group they all wanted to know what he said. "He said he's mean!" I shrugged.

I couldn't stop smiling, "do you like him?" Sophia asked

Everyone leaned in for my answer. "I don't know." I said, David looked disappointed.

It was "report season" as Jade called it. We all had at least three reports due in two weeks. Momma dropped us off at the library to do our homework. We needed encyclopedias, etc. to do our reports. My whole group and Jade and her two friends Susan and Jennifer sat at the big circle table. There were a bunch of smaller tables around, Christen's brother sat at a table over to the side with his girlfriend Samantha. Rosalind and Benjamin kept going to look for books together; we knew they were going to kiss. I was deep in thought about my sentence structure when Jade looked up and said, "hey Malcolm you wanna sit down?" She said pointing at the chair next to me. David looked disappointed again, where I was thrilled that he was there.

"Who are you writing your report on in Mrs. Walters' class?" He asked Jade

"Harriet Tubman." She said

"How about you two?" He said pointing Susan and Jennifer.

"Frederick Douglas" Susan said

"Garrett Morgan" Jennifer said

"What about you?" Jade asked

"Malcolm X of course!" He said

Jade sucked her teeth, "a hoodlum!"

"Maybe to the common eye, but there's more to Malcolm than his "by any means necessary quotes." He said

I liked the way he talked, instead of doing my work I found myself listening to him hold his ground talking to my sister. She knew her stuff and she spent more time reading than anybody I knew. In order for him to hold his ground with her he had to be just as smart. That impressed me. After a little while David looked at his watch. "I gotta get home, I'll see you guys tomorrow at school." He didn't wait for us to volunteer to walk him out like we normally did. He grabbed his stuff and hurried out. Cassondra shot me a look then she looked at the clock on the wall. I looked at the time and it was after six. We all needed to get home.

"You wanna walk with us?" Sophia asked Malcolm

"Sure" he said

Christen joined her brother and his girlfriend. Cassondra and Sophia went to find Rosalind and Benjamin who stopped coming back to the table after awhile. They were all giggling when they came back.

"What happened to David?" Ben asked

"He had to go just like we do."

Jade said bye to her friends who were waiting for their ride. "Where do you live?" I asked Malcolm as we started walking.

"In the other direction." He said

"Do you need to hurry home? We could just see you tomorrow."

"I gotta walk you guys home it's not safe in Oakland after dark." Everything he said had the same tone. He wasn't happy or sad he was just serious all the time.

"You won't get in trouble?"

"Nope"

"Malcolm, how come you never smile?" I asked looking at him.

Everyone was trying to eavesdrop on our conversation. He grabbed my jacket to make me stop walking. Then he looked back at my group. They were all waiting for his answer too.

"I don't care! I wanna know too!" Sophia said

Jade wasn't interested in our conversation she moved to the front of our group and picked up her pace. Rosalind and Benjamin joined her.

"You think I don't smile?"

"No"

"Then what's this?" He made the corners of his mouth turn up. It was supposed to be a smile, but it scared all three of us. Then we all laughed. "I'm just not a jokey joke person."

Malcolm was interesting, but I didn't think he liked me even though Cassondra and Sophia swore he did. Sometimes he would stare at me, but he wouldn't say anything.

David stopped hanging around us as much, especially when everyone started teasing me about having a crush on Malcolm. Then Malcolm and Jennifer started going out. I cried on Jade's lap when she told me. I couldn't believe it; deep down inside I thought he liked me too. But I guessed I was wrong. Then I started going out with Percy. He was a pretty boy and a goofy nut. He kept all of us laughing, but when I wouldn't let him feel on me at the library we broke up. He lied and told everyone we made out, and suddenly I had the attention of almost every boy. Sophia wasn't doing bad herself James and Philip fought over her all the time, and she would tell them that she liked them both. Sometimes Malcolm would cut his fourth period to come eat with us or just stare at me, but I stopped paying him attention I had too many options to be worried about him. Cassondra liked one boy Rashaan, but he liked someone else. She said she didn't care, but you could tell it hurt her feelings that he didn't like her. She didn't get jealous about all the attention Sophia and I got either. She would tell us to be careful. I never understood why she wore either big heavy shirts or her coat all the time but she always stayed covered up. She always complimented our clothes, but she never wore any of it.

Momma was in one of her moods this morning. She argued with Daddy last night about her job. Momma worked at Macy's in downtown Oakland. A man was flirting with Momma, which happened a lot. Momma always had men falling all over their selves over her. But she never really paid them any attention. She was in love with Daddy, but a lot of women didn't like her because of it. They would get mad when they found out that she had four kids and a husband. Momma's hair was kind of wavy and poofy; she normally wore it pulled back. She didn't really wear makeup unless Daddy was taking her out. Momma had beautiful brown skin that looked almost red. Her high cheekbones and beautiful big eyes did make you want to almost stare at her face. Her coworker got jealous and told her boss that Momma was being rude to the customer. Momma's boss yelled at her, and Momma came home really upset. Daddy told Momma to quit her job, and that he could take care of us. Momma was just mad cause she got yelled at so no matter what Daddy said she argued with him. They argued a long time, and then they went in their room. After awhile they stopped arguing. Malachi and I were doing the dinner dishes, when we heard the bed. We both frowned at each other. I didn't understand why arguing took them there, but it did a lot. So in the morning Momma was still mad about work, once she was mad every body knew to lay low. But she still got mad at me for not wiping the table off after I left a few crumbs. She yelled that I was gonna bring ants. I made sure not to twist my face or anything but she still slapped me saying that I gave her a look. When Jade came to help me clean up so we could get going she got slapped too and I couldn't even tell you why. Sophia stayed in the living room. Malachi got mad, but he didn't say anything to her. He just told us to hurry and get our things so we could leave for school. In the car he was the only one talking. He was trying to comfort us about this morning, but I was mad.

"My momma has been acting so crazy since she got pregnant. Most times I stay in my room or come to your house." Sophia told me.

"I don't understand why she hates me so much. Sometimes I wonder why I was even born." I told Sophia

"Auntie Annette doesn't hate you Amber. She's just stressed out right now. Daddy says things will get better when the baby comes. Maybe your mom will get better once she stops working."

"Maybe." I said not convinced.

In first period of all days we had a substitute, which meant the class was rowdy. A girl named Tamara snuck in our class. She was one of the main ones being rowdy. Our sub got mad and screamed at the entire class. That just made me madder. In PE Tamara was there again acting ugly, but this time she was in Malcolm's face. He didn't appear to be in the mood for her either. He pushed her by her face and told her to leave him alone. Her feelings were hurt and when she saw me watching she came and got in my face. Everybody was looking! Now this girl was bigger than me in size and solid, and she was in the eighth grade too. I thought about walking away, but before I could get a hold of my temper my fist connected with her jaw. Before she could focus on what just happened I went crazy on her. Tamara never knew what hit her. Every time I hit her I felt better about myself and justified. I didn't go looking for this fight but I had to finish it, my cousin, friends, AND Malcolm were watching. I was trying to mutilate her face when Mr. Turner pulled me off her. I was cursing kicking and screaming. I wasn't done with her and I was mad that he made me stop. I saw fear in Tamara's face as I was being lifted off of her. When Mr. Turner carried me to the office cause I wouldn't calm down the assistant vice principal came and took me to his office. Mr. Tucker had to be at least 6ft 5, and he was solid. The palm of his hand covered my face, and he had the deepest voice I had ever heard. So when he told me to sit down I did.

"What's wrong with you?" He said with a very serious face.

"Mister Tucker she started it. She came and got in my face, I had to defend myself!"

"Ok, but why did Mr. Turner have to carry you in here?"

"Because I wasn't finished!"

Mr. Tucker tried to keep a straight face. "Got you coming in here like some kind of wild animal? Now I'm gonna bring the other girl in here. You better stay in your seat otherwise me and you are going to have problems." He walked out into the office. "Oh my goodness!" He exclaimed as he looked at Tamara. She followed him back into his office. "You did this to this child's face?" He said pointing at Tamara. She had knots, scratches, and bruises that fast. I instantly almost felt bad for her. Mr. Tucker sat at his desk; he put his face on his hand. "Ok, so tell me what happened?" He said unenthusiastically

"She was all up in my business. So I confronted her!" Tamara said still with tons of attitude.

"You confronted her and got your butt kicked! You kids need to learn to respect each other." Then he took out suspension slips. "Amber I hate to have to suspend you. You're supposed to be getting and award tomorrow in the school rally with all the other honor roll students." He shook his head. "You're gonna miss the ice cream party. But I'm sure your sister will tell you all about it. You got some real anger issues girl. You need to get a hold of that."

"Yes sir" I said quietly.

Then he looked at Tamara. "I hope the mirror teaches you to think first and act second." Then he handed us our slips. "Now I don't want to see you two in my office again. Especially you!" He said pointing to me. "You will get a lot further in life when you learn to manage that temper!"

"Yes sir!" I said dreading going home and what momma was gonna do when she found out.

We both went back to the locker room and put our regular clothes on.

"You gonna get in trouble when you get home?" I asked Tamara.

"Yea, this is my fourth one this year. What about you?"

"Yes, my Momma's gonna kill me." I said defeated.

"Good to know somebody can beat you." She said with a smile.

I rolled my eyes. "Shut up!"

I snuck up to the cafeteria to say bye to my group, I was suspended for two days.

"I'll try to tell your momma what happened as soon as I get home." Sophia said

I hugged them then I walked out of the cafeteria. Malcolm was waiting for me when I walked out; he had a smirk on his face. "Are you smiling?" I said happily

He dropped the smirk, "no". Then I started to walk away. "Where are you about to go?"

"Home I got suspended." I said waving my slip.

"You wanna come with me?" He asked.

"Where are you going?"

"Around, you wanna come or not?"

"Will Jennifer be mad?"

"It's not like that, you coming or not?"

"I can't! I'll get in trouble." I said

"You just got suspended aren't you already in trouble?" He did have a good point.

"Go put your backpack in your locker and meet me back here. You got two minutes." Then he walked away.

I had butterflies, I was so excited. Finally I was gonna be alone with Malcolm. I put my backpack in my locker like I was told and I took my purse out. When I got back he was waiting. He started walking and I followed him. David watched us walk away with sad eyes. We walked to the bus stop then he paid my bus fare.

"So why you beat that girl up like that?"

"You saw her."

He smiled, "that was pretty impressive."

"Oh my goodness you really are smiling now." I said excitedly.

"Yea" he said looking out the window still smiling.

"Does Jennifer get to see you smile?"

"Sometimes, it depends." He said still not looking at me.

"On what?"

"If she did something that makes me smile."

"What does she do to make you smile?"

His smile dropped. "Why are you asking me about her. I'm here with you."

"Sorry, I thoughts boys like to talk about their girlfriends."

"Who told you she was my girlfriend?"

"Jade"

He shook his head, "I ain't ever asked her to be my girlfriend."

"She told Jade you guys were going out."

"Nope, we've kicked it from time to time. But I never asked her to be my girlfriend."

"Oh" I said getting excited because that still left hope for me.

"Don't you have a boyfriend?"

"Who told you that?"

"I hear things."

"Not really, I was talking to Chad. But he didn't ask me out yet."

He smirked, "Chad? Really? I would've thought you would've said David."

"David? Why?"

"He likes you."

"No he doesn't, we are just friends."

Then he put his arm around me. "Poor guy likes you and you leave with me."

I was in heaven! I had no idea where we were going or how I was gonna get home, but it all seemed worth it when he put his arm around me. We got off the bus at the Bart station and we caught Bart to Berkeley. A officer stopped us at the Berkeley station.

"Why aren't you at school?"

"We are a part of the better tomorrow program that's touring the college today. She forgot her purse back at the school so they asked me to escort her and meet up with the group." Malcolm said sounding all proper.

"Well you better hurry up!" The officer said with a smile.

Malcolm and I walked towards the college. He took me to a bunch of the different libraries on campus. He told me he loved to come here, pick up a book and just read. He said sometimes he just needed to get away from home, so he would go to the library if he couldn't find something better to do. He barely saw his mom, and he didn't know his father. He lived with his grandmother with a bunch of cousins and a auntie. I asked him if he missed his mom, and he said he used to when he was little. But now he didn't care. He said she wasn't all that concerned when she saw him no how. He said normally when he saw her, she wasn't coming for him. I grabbed his hand; at first he looked like I did something wrong but then he kept talking. I told him having a momma wasn't always great. I told him about my morning and how she always acts like she hates me. I told him how I would never treat my children like she treats us. Then he told me he didn't want to have children ever! He said he had plans for his life than didn't include children. Then I told him about my Daddy and how much I loved him, but he worked so much that sometimes he was too tired to spend time with us. But we all knew he loved us. Then he kissed me, for the first time it didn't feel weird or gross. I loved it. When he held my hand I looked at our skins. His was so dark and beautiful, and mine was so light. I loved the way his hand looked in mine. Then we got back on the bus and Bart. He got me back to school as the last bell rang. He just said bye and walked away. I wanted him to kiss me goodbye. Sophia and Cassondra spotted me. They came running over.

"Where did you guys go?" Sophia asked wide-eyed.

"He took me to the college, showed me around, and then he brought me back." I said glowing

"What about Jennifer?" Cassondra asked

"He said he never asked her to be his girlfriend."

Jade came over, "so I hear you had a pretty exciting day." She looked irritated.

"Jennifer was in tears all day cause you left with her boyfriend."

"He said he never asked her to be his girlfriend."

"Then why would she tell me they were going out?"

"I don't know. I asked him and that's what he said."

Cassondra ran to catch her bus and we waited for Malachi. I had forgotten all about my fight until Sophia started rehashing it. Malachi tried to comfort me and tell me not to be scared, but we all knew I should be. To all of our surprise Momma was home when we got home. It looked like her car never moved. I swallowed hard. She was sitting on the couch with the belt around her neck. We all stopped dead in our tracks when we saw her.

"Malachi, Jade, Sophia go do your homework!" They took off lightening fast. "So I got a call from your school this morning saying you were suspended for fighting. I'm expecting you home by bus an hour later tops. Where did you go?"

I was so scared; I didn't know what to say. Either way I was gonna get a whooping.

"I went to the college to go walk around and clear my head."

"To the college? Which college?"

"Berkeley"

"Who did you go with?"

I couldn't tell her I went with a boy, I was in enough trouble. "I went by myself."

She grabbed me by the arm with one hand and she started swinging the belt with the other. "You are not grown!" She was aiming for my butt, but since I was moving she was hitting me everywhere. My legs, back, sides, occasionally she'd land one on my butt. I moved too quickly on one stroke and she missed me and hit herself. Now she was mad. My whooping started all over. Every time that belt hit me my skin felt like it was on fire. I thought she was gonna kill me.

Malachi had, had enough. He came out his room and grabbed the belt from her. "Momma that's enough!"

Momma's eyes turned small and squinty. "Oh so you think you're gonna use your man strength on me!" She said getting in his face.

"No ma'am. I'm just saying that she's had enough Momma please."

Momma squared off and punched Malachi in the face. He stumbled backwards but he didn't rear up at her. She was waiting for him to stand up so she could keep tagging his face but he didn't. "When I'm disciplining anybody! You don't EVER come and interfere!"

Momma kept screaming, Malachi looked at me and told me to stay down. He didn't stand up, he stayed bent over. If he moved at all she was ready for him, he knew if she saw his face she'd start right back up again. I buried my face in the couch, my body was on fire. Daddy walked in the door after awhile, I was still crying and Malachi was still bent over. The belt was on the floor on the other side of the room. Momma screamed at him telling him everything that happened. Daddy told us to go in our rooms. He got Momma to calm down. Then she calmly told him what happened, I could hear them talking but my body was in so much pain I couldn't focus all that well. Jade and Sophia put alcohol on my open wounds on the back of my legs. It stung like crazy but I knew they would heal faster with alcohol.

"Was it worth it?" Sophia asked

I giggled, "yea".

Jade shook her head and rolled her eyes.

Chapter 4

"Did you hear?" Cassondra burst into my last class with urgency in her eyes. She was lifting me out of my seat. "Jade's getting ready to fight!"

The shock hit me, "where is she?"

"On the PE field!" Cassondra said as she grabbed my things cause she knew I was flying out the door. Mr. Thornton wasn't paying attention as I slipped out or even when Cassondra slipped in for that matter. I ran like the wind. I saw Jade and Jennifer arguing. Jennifer kept saying "she! She!" And Jade kept telling her to shut up. Some other girls I didn't recognize were there. There were fours girls total including Jennifer they had Jade in the middle but Jennifer was the only one talking. Some how I knew this was my fault. Jennifer was really upset about that day when I left school with Malcolm. Instead of discussing it with Malcolm she blamed me. And she was mad at Jade for not making me stay away from Malcolm. Jade tried to stay out of it as much as she could, but she wouldn't let Jennifer talk about me. She would tell Jennifer to talk to Malcolm, but Jennifer only wanted to hear that I would stay away from Malcolm. Malcolm would hold onto his point that he never asked Jennifer to be his girlfriend so he didn't see the problem.

I ran down to the field and I stood next to my sister against all these tall and big girls. "Leave her alone!" I yelled.

Jade pushed me, "move Amber!" but I refused to go. Next thing I know Sophia was standing next to me and Cassondra was standing next to her. I saw Rosalind and Benjamin running over. All this arguing and back and forth was getting on my nerves, but it wasn't my fight. If all Jade was gonna do was argue I wasn't gonna make her fight. But I wasn't letting anybody jump my sister! One of the girls got tired of the back and forth too and she pushed Jade. That started it! Jade fell into Jennifer. Jennifer hit Jade and the most ferocious face came over Jade. I never saw that look before. The girl that pushed Jade grabbed Jade's ponytail braid out of her shirt. I punched that girl in the face. I was coming after her. One girl pushed me trying to stop me and Sophia made short work of her. Jade had Jennifer on the ground. Jennifer's brown hair was swinging every which way her face jerked every time Jade punched her. Cassondra had the other girl pinned on the ground face down with her ponytail wrapped around her hand. I stepped out the circle and the girl squared off. I charged and she popped me good in the face. That made me mad and I really lost it. The girl swung again but missed. I put her in a headlock. I kept hitting her face. Then she started biting my arm. I stomped on her foot when she released me I upper cut her. I felt that punch come from my legs. The girl flew backwards. I was on my way to keep getting her. Suddenly Malachi was there. He grabbed me. Now why every time I'm fighting somebody gotta pick me up. Malachi was so strong he had me in one arm, Jade in the other and he was running to the car. Sophia and Cassondra had our bags and coats. Rosalind and Ben were right behind us. Malachi told everybody to get in the car. And he took off down the street. He dropped Ben at home, and then he parked the car around the corner from our house. "Are you ok?" He asked everyone.

I could feel my lip throbbing. "That heifer busted my lip!" I said touching my face. "Why were you fighting?" Malachi asked Jade with the most surprised voice.

Jade was crying, you could tell she was still mad. "I WILL NOT KEEP DOING THIS!" Jade yelled at me

"I'm sorry," I said feeling really bad. Jade never yells at me. She always protected me, even if it meant losing a friend. I felt worse about her being mad then I ever did about Momma. Jade wasn't a Yeller, and she only cried when she had to.

"What did you do?" Malachi asked

"Her friend likes a boy, but he likes me. Her friend got mad at her." I said through tears.

"Maybe we should wait until dad gets home. Rosalind & Cassondra are you ok? I can take you home."

"Thank you, I do need to get home." Cassondra said

"Me too." Rosalind said

Malachi walked Cassondra to the door. He introduced himself when her father answered the door. He apologized for getting her home late; he explained that she helped his sisters in their time of need. Cassondra's dad was really impressed by Malachi. Cassondra thought her dad was gonna be mad, but he was perfectly ok. When their conversation started to get a little long. Malachi had to excuse himself cause he still had one more friend to drop off, but he promised to come back another day to continue their conversation. The same thing with Rosalind's momma, the look in her eye was weird. Malachi said he had to hurry and get back to the car before she pulled him in. We all laughed, Jade just sat there quiet. She was still upset. On the way home we saw Sonny walking down the street. Malachi picked him up and he sat in the back next to me. Sonny talked Malachi into coming to play basketball with him after they dropped us off.

"How you doing Jade?" Sonny said

"I've had better days!" She said softly.

"Oh really? I'm sorry to hear that. Anything I can do to put a smile on your face?"

"Malachi, can you pull over?" Jade asked.

Malachi did as he was told. Jade got out of the car in the front seat, we all sat there not knowing what she was going to do. She opened the passenger side door and asked Sonny to step out of the car. He did as she asked then she put her arms around him, and she asked him to hug her.

"Aaaaaaa!" Malachi yelled, Sophia and I sat there with our mouths open. "You can cut that out!"

"Thank you Sonny!" She said then she kissed him on the cheek. She got back in the front; seat and she had the biggest smile on her face. Sonny got back in the car with the biggest smile on his face. Malachi had his lip poked out. He looked at Sonny, "not cool man! Not cool!"

Sonny shrugged, "hey man, I asked!"

"Keep it up!" Malachi said not amused at all.

"I didn't know she liked him?" Sophia whispered

"Me neither." I whispered back

When we drove up to the house Daddy's truck was outside. We could hear Momma crying from outside. I readied myself for the worse beating ever. Daddy met us at the door, "your grandmother died," he said as he let us in.

"Your mother?" Jade asked

"No, her mother." He said with sad eyes. We all stood there looking unaffected.

"Just go give her some hugs and let her know you love her."

Momma was in her room in the dark, she was laying in her bed with her pillow over her head.

"Momma? We're sorry to hear about your momma." I said

"Thank you sweetheart." Momma said

We all gave her hugs and kisses then we disappeared into our room.

"What does this mean?" I whispered

"That the coast is clear for now. Just make sure you don't do nothing to get on her bad side." Malachi said then he looked at Sonny. "Man I'm not gonna be able to go."

Sonny was staring at Jade and smiling, "what? Oh yea, cool!" Jade was smiling too.

Malachi stuck out his lip again. "Man! Don't make me not like you!"

Sonny blushed, "I'm cool man!" Then he looked around. "This is a nice room. Which one is your bed?" Sonny said admiring Jade's green and my purple décor. The combination of our favorite colors, Momma added splashes of Gold.

"That's it! Lets go walk Sophia home." Malachi said pushing his friend out of the room.

"Call me tomorrow." Sophia said

When they left I asked Jade if she was still mad at me. She told me she wasn't mad at me she was mad at the situation. She said hugging Sonny made her feel better. For the first time ever she asked me questions about Malcolm and me. She listened just like Sophia does, she laughed, and she giggled. My big sister was back! It wasn't until that moment that I realized how much I missed her. I missed talking to her and sharing everything about me with her. She told me not to fool around with Malcolm anymore until he told me he wasn't messing around with Jennifer anymore. I told her that doing that made me nervous what if he didn't wanna be with me anymore after I told him that. She said if something like that scared him off he wasn't worth my time.

Daddy told us Momma's sister called and told her that their mother died after the funeral. Momma was sad for a long time. She said she was sad that they never made up, and that her mother never apologized for how she treated us. Momma became very attached to Daddy. She quit her job, and now she was at home every day. I had to be very creative with my excuses to be out after school to be with Malcolm.

One time we couldn't think of anywhere to go so we went to his house. His grandmother's house was green and it had a porch full of people. Most of them were as dark as Malcolm and some were a little lighter. When Malcolm walked up to the house with me they all stared.

"Malcolm who dis?" One guy said coming off the porch as we approached.

"None of yo business!" Malcolm said walking past the guy.

I didn't like the way he looked at me. He reminded me of my uncle. Malcolm put his hand on my back and he pushed me ahead of him towards the porch. All of them were looking at me like I was lunch. I walked up the stairs reluctantly. I opened the door and a girl with a baby in only a diaper was sitting in the middle of the floor. She had on a t-shirt that looked like it had been stretched out of shape and shorts with holes on the insides like they had worn out. Her hair was really short; like it had been fried to death from perms, and it was all over her head. She sat up straight when she saw me, then she saw Malcolm.

"Oh hey Malcolm, who's the white girl?" She said not even looking at me.

"You are stupid!" Malcolm said pushing me towards her to walk through the house. There was a room in front of us I pointed at the door, but he turned me to the right. There was a bathroom in front of me. To the left was the kitchen. To the right, right next to the bathroom there was a bedroom. There were a bunch of kids in there. Then there were three stairs and a door. He took keys out of his sock. There were four locks on the door. He unlocked the door.

"Hey Malcolm, who's that?" A little boy said

"Go play!" He barked

He opened the door and pushed me in. His room was full of books neatly organized.

His bed was made, but the room was very dark. He had black sheets up doubling as curtains and decoration. He cracked a window. Then someone knocked on the door.

"Hey Malcolm can you line me up real quick?" The guy said

"You got money?" He said

"I got five," the voice said pleadingly.

"Go away!"

"Please man! I got a J for you too." The voice pleaded. Malcolm opened the door and the guy at the door saw me first. "Whoa! I didn't know you had company. Should I come back?"

Malcolm looked at me, "I'll be right back. Lock the locks behind me." He said

He didn't have to worry about that. I was going to whether he told me to or not I didn't feel safe in that house. I walked around his room looking at all his books. None of them seemed interesting to me. There was a shoebox next to his bed without a lid. I recognized the girl handwriting on them. They were letters from Jennifer. I couldn't see what they said. I imagined her pouring out her heart and Malcolm just letting her. He came back in the room with something white behind his ear and five ones. He locked the door behind him and he walked over to his closet. He had a mini safe that he opened. He put the money in and locked it. I sat on the bed. I asked him about the box and he confirmed that they were letters from Jennifer. He told me I could read them. I asked him if he liked her, he sucked his teeth and looked away. He took the thing from behind his ear, "you want some?" He said pointing it at me.

"What is that?"

"A joint." I shook my head no, and he smiled at me. "You scared?"

"Kind of, but I don't want none."

"Suit yourself!" He took out matches and he lit the joint. He took three long drags on it. Then he put it out in the ashtray next to his bed. He leaned back on his bed. I watched his face change from serious to relaxed.

"Are you my boyfriend?" I asked

He shrugged, "you want me to be?"

"Uh! Yes!"

He smiled, "why?"

"Cause you're so sexy." He laughed at me. "I like you, and I wanna be your girlfriend. So please ask me already."

"Ok! Ok! Amber?"

"Yes Malcolm?"

"Will you be my girlfriend?"

"Yes!" I said then I kissed him. His mouth tasted like he had been smoking. It wasn't a bad taste; I just didn't know what to do with it. "Can you do me a favor?"

"Ok"

"Can you call Jennifer and tell her not to call you any more."

"Right now?"

"Yes!"

"You gotta take your top off first."

"What?"

He put his hands behind his head. "If you want me to call, you gotta strip."

"You said just my top at first." I protested

"It's a limited time offer, take too long and I'll want your pants too. "Then he looked at his wrist and made a tic tock noise.

"Ok, ok! But you can't laugh."

"I would never laugh at you, you're beautiful." Then he realized what he said. He looked embarrassed.

"You think I'm beautiful?"

"Yes" he said blushing.

"Ok"

He sat up. He picked up his brown phone. I took off my jacket and I laid it on the floor. Then I took off my t-shirt. I thought he was gonna laugh at my sorry excuse for breast. But he just stared at my bra. Then he picked up the box. He shifted the papers around until he found her phone number. He dialed her number and then he put the receiver on his ear. He kept staring. "Can I speak to Jennifer... Malcolm...." Then I heard her say a very happy "hello". He exhaled while still staring at my chest. "Jennifer, I don't like you. Don't call me no more." Then he hung up the phone. As he reached out to touch me, his phone rang. He picked up the receiver then he pressed the hang up button. He left the receiver off the hook. He threw the phone on the floor. Then he grabbed my chest. I wondered if he was thinking about how small my chest was. I didn't have breast like Momma and Jade. I always got the short end of the stick. They got the brown skin or in Jade's case browner skin. They got the real breast, but my butt was bigger than Jade's. He started kissing my chest, rubbing on it. Then he unhooked my bra. I put hands up to cover up. He took off his shirt, his stomach was muscular and smooth, and then he moved my hands. He licked all over my chest. He got on top of me and started humping me. I opened my legs wide; I liked the feeling of being chest to chest with him. He kept humping me until I felt tingling down there. Then he collapsed on top of me. He had sweat on his forehead. He kissed me. "Next time you take the pants off." Then he kissed me again.

"My chest isn't too small? I asked

"Your breasts are beautiful!" He said

I liked the way he was talking to me. Then he put his hands under my butt, "next time move this." I looked at him confused. He made me get on top of him. "Now move like this." He said moving my hips. That felt good and the tingles came back right away. "Uh oh! Somebody likes it!" He moved his hands and I kept moving. It felt good unlike anything I ever felt before. I collapsed on him, "like that?" I asked

"Something like that, it'll be better with all our clothes off though."

The next time I went over Malcolm's house I took off my pants, but I left my panties on. He told me I was teasing him. "Next time you gotta take the panties off and you gotta hit this." I laid my head on his chest.

"I'm scared to do that." I said

"Why?"

"Scared it will make me act crazy. Or fry my brain. Or what if it doesn't wear off by the time I go home. Forget my Momma, my Daddy will kill me if he finds out."

"So lets cut school. We can spend the day in here."

"If we get caught, you know what will happen to me."

"You worry too much. That's why you need to hit this."

"You better not hurt me!"

"Trust me, I know what I'm doing."

"You've done it before?" I asked

"Yes" he said nonchalantly

"With who?"

"You don't know all of them."

"All of them? How many?"

"Honestly, I don't know any more. I got started young."

I sat up and waited for him to tell me the story. I thought I would feel uncomfortable sitting almost naked in front of him, but I didn't. He rubbed his eyes as he sat up. He told me about his babysitter when he lived with his mom. He didn't see it as a big deal, he liked it. But his mom gave up on him.

Then I told him about my uncle. He got really mad. He asked me where my uncle was, I told him I only knew he was in San Francisco somewhere. He got up, got a notebook out of his backpack and a pen. He asked me a bunch of questions about my uncle. His face was the most serious I've ever seen it as he wrote down my answers. He asked me questions like how did he wear his hair? Did he have a favorite cereal? What did he like to do for fun? I didn't know the answer to most of his questions. I didn't like thinking about my uncle, and no one in my house mentioned him. It was almost like he didn't even happen, except for Jade started being quiet. I told Malcolm how Jade sometimes still has nightmares. Sometimes she screams so loud that everybody wakes up. She's normally crying and sweating. Sometimes she still pees in the bed, but I didn't tell him that part. Momma always comes in our room, she doesn't wake Jade up. She waits for her to wake up, and when she wakes up Momma hugs her and tells her it's gonna be ok. Now that Momma doesn't go to work, she stays up with Jade. She used to hug her and try to get her to go back to sleep real fast. But now she stays in our room with Jade until she feels better. On some school nights depending on how bad the nightmare was Momma will tell Jade she could stay home from school to rest. But Jade always protests and insist on going to school. One time Momma fell asleep on the bed with Jade. I put my TV blanket on Momma so she wouldn't get cold and wake up. Momma likes it best when she is the one to help Jade. I don't wanna get in trouble so I act like I'm still sleep. Even though Jade talks to me more again, some days she still gets quiet. She still puts her nose in books especially when she has really sad days. I read books when I have to; Jade & Malcolm love to read books. Jade & Malcolm always debate about stuff and it's fun to watch. Jade will say something and Malcolm almost always disagrees, Sophia and I watch them go back and forth like a tennis match. Now that we are boyfriend and girlfriend Malcolm calls Jade his sister-in-law. It spread like wildfire at school that I was Malcolm's girlfriend and a lot of people didn't get it.

Jennifer and Susan didn't speak to Jade anymore. Jennifer especially was scared of Jade now. Jade made new friends who weren't so weird. She still kept her nose in books but now she borrowed my clothes. She couldn't always fit my tops; she dressed so much better now. Momma said it was good so that next year when she went to high school she would be normal. Malachi tried to keep Sonny away from the house as much as possible. He didn't like Sonny talking to Jade, but he liked teasing him about how he acted over a middle school girl. Timothy would call home and talk to Momma a lot. He told Momma that he really likes school. Momma would ask him about girls, she knew he was dating but he always told her it wasn't serious. Then he would ask to speak to all of us. One by one we would come in the living room and talk to him on the phone. He would ask me about school and if I needed help with anything. He would tell me not to worry about boys and focus on school. I always agreed while rolling my eyes as he talked. He would tell me how beautiful the campus was and how he wanted to bring me there so I could get a feel for the campus. Timothy would always tell me I could be anything I wanted to be. All I wanted to be was with my boyfriend, but I would never dare tell him that.

"Love you chipmunk," he would say as we got off the phone.
I told Jade and Sophia what Malcolm and I were gonna do on Monday. I needed them to cover for me. Sophia and I called Cassondra and we told her our plan. I needed Cassondra to put my backpack and jacket on my chairs in my classes. Then when the teachers would look for me she just needed to tell them I was at the nurse's office with cramps or a tummy ache. Cassondra said the same thing that Jade said, she asked me to wait a while. She said if Malcolm loved me he would wait for me. Blah, blah, blah! I let her talk and when she was finished, I asked her if she was gonna help me. She didn't wanna help me but she said ok. Sophia and I met up with Rosalind at the mall. I wanted to get a new bra and panties for Monday. Rosalind asked if she and Benjamin should do it? We told her to wait cause Benjamin wasn't asking for it yet.
I found a pretty Lacey black bra and black panties. We walked around the mall some more. We saw Jennifer and Susan in the shoe store. Jennifer got so mad when she saw me. I smiled at her, daring her to say anything to me. She and Susan stormed away.
Monday morning Jade asked me if I was sure about this. If I got caught I would get in so much trouble. But I wanted to do it and I wanted to do it with Malcolm it was gonna make him love me so much. I put on my new underwear and a cute sundress. When I walked out the room Momma looked at my dress. It's too cold out for that dress, go put on some pants. I fixed my face real fast, the last thing I needed was to make her mad. I went back in my room and put a pillow over my face and screamed. I put on jeans and a top, but I put a skirt in my backpack. We convinced Malachi to drive us to school early so we could talk to a teacher about a paper that was due Friday, and I went straight to the bathroom to change. When I came out the bathroom Malcolm was talking to Jade and Sophia. His face was serious; he seemed normal like today wasn't special. Jade looked concerned like she wanted to tell me not to go. While Sophia was my cheerleader. I gave Sophia my backpack and sweater to give to Cassondra when she got there. Malcolm put his arm around me and led me away. I waved bye to everybody and my heart was beating out of my chest. As we walked to the bus stop, we passed David. The look on his face looked like he knew where we were going. He looked so sad, and Malcolm being the jerk he is made me kiss him in front of him. I felt bad for David, so I returned the sad eyes. I knew he liked me, but Malcolm was the big man on campus. Everybody respects him, David was a nice boy. I didn't want to hurt his feelings. I pulled my face away. Malcolm grabbed my chin and made me kiss him. Satisfied, he let me go and we waited for the bus. I was really quiet on the bus ride, which means we didn't talk because I was the talker in our relationship. Malcolm held my hand, he rang the bell to get off the bus, but it was too soon. He told me to come on; we got off the bus in front of a drug store next to a deli. He reached in his pocket and gave me two twenties.
"Go get us some sandwiches, chips, drinks, and get some cake or cookies. I'm gonna run in to the drug store real quick."
"What kind of sandwich?"
"Whatever, I'm not picky."
The lady behind the counter seemed really happy to see me. She called me all kinds of sugar, honeys, and darlings. She made the sandwiches extra big; she cut really big pieces of cake. She threw some cookies in the bag as well. After I paid for everything I stood there talking to the lady. She was telling me how I should come back to see her. Then Malcolm walked in, he put his hand in my back. Her smile

became frozen as her eyes went back and forth between us.
"You ready?" Malcolm said looking at the lady
"Friend of yours?" She nodded at me
"Girl friend."
"You don't say!" She just looked at us
I didn't know what was going on. She seemed nice enough, and then Malcolm walked in and she got weird. Malcolm said he goes there all the time and the lady was always nice to him. Then he said she had a thing for dark meat. I asked him what that meant, and he said it's all in the past. We walked to his house from the deli. I asked him what he got from the drug store, and he opened a brown paper bag. He showed me the box of condoms. Seeing the box made me nervous again. His house looked different without all the guys hanging out on the porch. There was a Cadillac Seville in the driveway.
Malcolm smiled and started walking faster. Walking up the stairs to the front door I knew there was no turning back now.
"Grandma?" Malcolm said walking in the door. He held my hand.
That girl was sleep on the floor with her baby. There were at least three more babies sleeping around her.
"Malcolm?" A woman's voice said coming from the back of the house. Instead of going right towards the front and Malcolm's room he led me by the hand to the left through the kitchen. There were dishes in the sink and on the table. It looked like all the little kids ate breakfast and then ran off to school. Behind the kitchen was a big bedroom with its own bathroom. There were locks on this door too and you walked down three stairs into this room.
"Grandma! I want you to meet somebody." I squeezed his hand.
"Ok, hold on." She called out from the bathroom. I tugged at my skirt, and tried to straighten out my clothes. Then she emerged from the bathroom. She was a little taller than me. She had a head full of gray hairs. She was full figured and coffee colored. When she saw me she smiled. For once I wished my own grand momma responded to me one time just like that. She put out her hands to hug me. "Hello sweetheart, I'm Momma Shuga." She said taking me in her arms.
"Hi" she smelled like medicine and peppermint.
"Amber right?" She said holding me out far enough to look at me. "Malcolm she's prettier than you said!"
I looked at Malcolm and he was blushing. "You think I'm pretty?" I asked her in complete shock.
"Oh child hush! You're beautiful!" Then she hugged me again, and this time I squeezed her back. She rocked me back and forth. "I can't stay long right now, but make sure you come back and see me."
I didn't want to leave her room, but Malcolm grabbed my hand to lead me out. They said their goodbyes and then we went up to Malcolm's room.
As soon as he locked the door, he turned around and kissed me. Then he walked over to his closet. He hung up his jacket, and he took mine. He set the food on a chair. Then he opened the safe in his closet. He left it open. He asked me if I had change from the food. I reached in my pocket and took out the thirty dollar change and I attempted to hand it to him as I pulled out the coins as well. He told me to keep it. Then he took a plastic bag out I could smell it from across the room. I was nervous about the bag; he looked at me and smiled.
He started talking about his grandma. He told me how she beat his momma up one time. He said his momma came over mad about something. She was talking to

Momma Shuga about something and he came in the room and said hi. He was very happy to see her cause he hadn't seen her in a long time. He said she started screaming at him and then she punched him. He said Momma Shuga put down the dishes she was cleaning and she walked over to his momma and mopped the floor with her. He made me laugh mimicking his momma getting beat up. While he told me the story he broke down the weed and then he rolled a blunt. I asked him why he had so much. He said he sold it. Then he lit the blunt and he took a big draw on it. I was nervous and I didn't want to do it, but Malcolm insisted that it would help me relax. He told me to inhale it and then hold my breath as long as I could. Then I started choking. He rubbed my back and smiled. Then he told me to do it again. My lips started to feel a little numb. Then he took a long drag on the blunt, and then when he kissed me he blew the smoke in my mouth. Then he put the rest of the blunt out in his ashtray. My body felt kind of heavy and my eyes felt heavy. Then he kissed me, his kiss tasted like chocolate. His hands felt soft and warm. He was right, I felt completely relaxed. He stood me up then he took my top and skirt off. He pulled back the covers on his bed. He put a towel down. I asked him what the towel was for, and he said it was just in case I bled. That made me nervous. He changed the subject by telling me he liked my underwear set. Then he took it off. He told me to lay on the bed. He put the box of condoms next to the bed. Then he took his clothes off. He sat on the edge of the bed and put a condom on. I was still a little nervous. He laid in the bed next to me. He sucked on my chest like they were pacifiers. Then he got on top of me. He kissed me and then I felt him press in on me. Even though I was relaxed it felt very real. I opened my eyes to look at him. He was focused on my face. He was trying to be gentle. He moved in a little, I blew air. He humped me only going in that little bit. It started to feel good and then he went deeper. I was saying "ouch! Ouch! Ouch!" He kissed my cheek, and he said, "I know, it will get better." And then he kept going. I thought he was going to rip me in half. When he was only half way in, suddenly he jumped up. The condom broke; there was a little blood on it. He opened another condom, I watched him put it on. This was my first time looking at him completely naked. Although I had nothing else to compare it to he was beautiful. When he came back in he went slow at first, and then with one thrust he was almost all the way in and I thought I was going to pass out. He didn't move right away, but I also clamped my legs around him so tight that he couldn't move. I kept breathing, I didn't want to do this any more it was hurting too much. He slowly pushed my legs down so he could move. It hurt and I wanted to tell him to stop. But then it wasn't so bad. He kept kissing my forehead and cheeks. "You're good! You're good! You're good! You're good!" And with one deep thrust I thought I was gonna die! But he collapsed on me. He laid there for a minute, and then he carefully withdrew. He laid next to me; my stuff was on fire and throbbing. He kissed me and then he started to fall asleep. I started closing my legs. My movement woke him up and he stopped me from closing them. He put his hand between my legs and started rubbing me. That instantly felt good, all the sudden my throbbing didn't exist. He kept rubbing until my body started shaking. Then he sucked on my chest some. Then I felt sleepy too. He put his arm around me and we both dosed off. When I woke up he had relit the blunt, he told me to hit it again. I did it twice. Then he got back in the bed. He opened my legs again and started rubbing again. Right when it got really good he stopped and put on another condom. Scared I tried to hold him back with my legs. He said, "come on baby let me in". Then he leaned on me and started rubbing me, that part felt good. When I relaxed a little, he grabbed my leg and stretched it out so that he slid right in. This time it didn't hurt as bad, and it started to kind of feel good. But I was not a fan of sex. When he was done, he pulled on shorts, and he went to the bathroom. I heard the toilet flush. Then I heard the sink. He came back in the room with a warm washcloth. He cleaned me up, and then told me to take a hot bath when I got home. He said it would help with the soreness.

Then he asked me, "do you love me?"

I quickly replied, "YES!"

He smiled and then he kissed me. He brought the bag of food over to the bed. When he bit into his sandwich he acted like it was the best sandwich ever. I opened my Doritos and I put a chip in my mouth. It was the best chip ever. Then I tasted my sandwich delicious. Everything tasted really good. Malcolm laughed at me, which made me laugh too.

"So, what do you think?" Malcolm asked

"About what?" I asked not knowing what he was talking about.

"You know," he nodded to the bed.

"Hurts!" I said honestly, He laughed again. "I like the sound of your laugh. I love to see you smile! I love when you hold me! I love when you kiss me! I love everything about you!" He started blushing, and then he closed mouth kissed me on account of us eating.

I told him when we grew up I wanted to be his wife. But he told me he didn't want to get married. He told me that he was getting ready to start making moves that would require him not to have too many attachments and liabilities. I didn't understand what he meant but I just nodded like I did. He set the alarm on his alarm clock and then we fell asleep again. I woke to the sound of arguing. It was coming from the porch. All those guys were back. I didn't understand where they came from. Malcolm peeked through the sheets to see who was outside. Since we were up only a few minutes early we got dressed. I put my arms around his neck, and I kissed him. He stuffed something in my pocket. When he told me that I was turning him on I stopped kissing him and I dropped my arms. He laughed again, "virgins" then he shook his head. He told me it wouldn't always hurt and that it would actually get a lot better. I didn't believe him, I pretended like I was ok. As my high wore off I could feel the throbbing more and more between my legs. It felt weird when I sat down I wondered if the pain would ever go away like he said. We got back to school a few minutes before the bell rang. I walked into my last class holding my stomach. I told Mr. Thornton the nurse told me to come get my things. I went straight to the bathroom and took off my skirt and put on my jeans. I was happy to put them on cause it was cold outside and I had been freezing all day. I saw Sophia first; she asked if I did it. I nodded yes and we giggled I told her I was a woman now. Cassondra stopped and gave me a hug as she ran to catch the bus. Rosalind told me to call her later. Jade rubbed my back, but she didn't say anything. Malachi came to pick us up like normal. When we got home Momma was in a good mood. She finished cleaning the house and dinner was in the oven making the house smell wonderful. She told Sophia she was staying for dinner. Her mom and dad were going out to dinner one last time before the baby came. The three of us went in my room. I took my skirt out of my backpack. Something hit the floor as I straightened out my skirt. It rolled under my bed. I retrieved a small pile of money. Jade and Sophia sat wide-eyed as I counted it. There were ten twenties. Jade told me I couldn't keep that kind of money in the house. Momma and daddy would ask too many questions when they found it. In the fifth grade we took a field trip to a nearby bank. We opened savings accounts. I always put the money I got from Nana and Poppa in there. I would simply keep twenty and put the rest of the money in the bank. I didn't know why Malcolm gave it to me.

So I told them how everything happened but I exaggerated how good it was to me. I told them I thought I saw God. After dinner Jade and I washed the dishes, while Malachi walked Sophia home and waited with her until her parents came home. I asked Jade to hurry in the shower so I could take a bath like Malcolm told me to. Everyone was in their rooms, so I snuck in the living room and I called Malcolm.

"Hello"

"I love you!" I whispered trying to sound all sexy.

I could hear him smile in his voice. "Hey you. How do you feel?"

"Sore, but I'm gonna get in the bath like you said as soon as Jade gets out the shower."

"Did you ever check your pocket?"

"Yes! Was that a mistake?"

"No, I wanted you to have it."

That made me smile. "Thank you. I gotta put it in the bank cause Jade said if Momma and Daddy find it, I could get in trouble."

"You have an account?"

"Yep, at Savings of American."

He was quiet, "that's good to know."

Then I heard my parent's room door open. "Ok I love you gotta go!" I whispered real fast. I put the receiver down gently then I laid on the couch in hopes no one would see me. Daddy went in the kitchen; he poured a small glass of brandy with ice. I crawled out the living room and I was almost to my room when Daddy caught me.

"Amber! What are you doing?" Daddy was laughing

I tried to pretend like I was tying my shoes, but I only had on socks. "Oh, um. I don't know." I said nervous

Daddy laughed at me and honked my nose. Then he kissed my forehead. "Ooh! Sweaty head!" He said then he went back in their room.

I was so happy it was Daddy and not Momma. She would've gotten suspicious and questioned me until I told her what I was doing. The bath did help with the soreness. I got in the bed, and imagined how wonderful my life was gonna be with Malcolm as my husband and all our brown babies.

Chapter 5

My chest has gotten HUGE! And oh my GOD! My butt has gotten bigger as if I thought that was possible. Momma keeps looking at me hard. She keeps saying I look different, but when Daddy asks her how she gets quiet. When I look in the mirror I look the same to me. Momma told us to keep our sanitary napkins in our bathroom now instead of our room. Now she asks us who started their period every month when the supply starts to go down. Jade keeps freaking out saying she knows something, SHE KNOWS SOMETHING! I find myself calming her down while I freak out inside.

Malcolm was right, it did get better. I kept avoiding him at first, but then he told me I had to stop running from him, and the worst part was over. It was not good the next time, but I put on a brave face and pretended like it was. He looked me in eyes and he told me I was lying to him. So I came clean, I told him it hurt, and that scared me. Plus I didn't like being high, my body felt too weird. Soooo, then next time he told me to get on top. He told me I would feel better on top. He was right, it did feel better. It felt REALLY REALLY good. When we were done Malcolm had the craziest look on his face. He even acted a little scared when I wanted to go again. Watching his face as he lost it and held on to me was awesome.

At school people were getting suspicious, and asking me if Malcolm and I were doing it. Malcolm told me not to answer any of their questions. He told me not to answer anybody's questions about him. He said it was bad enough that people knew he was my boyfriend, and they didn't need to know anything else. So I didn't say anything.

Malcolm had Momma Shuga take him to the bank and open a savings account too. He also asked for my savings account number. He said he would put money in there for me. But he still gave me money at school too.

David only talks to me in English class now. The other day he told us that he's gonna move to Richmond this summer. Cassondra and I made a big deal about it. I was really gonna miss him though. He was always nice and sweet to me. One time we had an assembly during English class and David sat on the end of the row on the right, I sat next to him and Cassondra sat next to me and the rest of the class filled in. David whispered in my ear he really liked me and he wished he could be my boyfriend instead of Malcolm. Then he told me he loved me. It wasn't until then that I realized Malcolm never told me that he loved me. I always told him, but he didn't tell me. When I told Sophia about it, she told me he might not say it but he shows it. That made me feel a little better. I held David's hand the rest of the assembly in the dark. I didn't tell Sophia I did that, Cassondra saw it, but she didn't say anything. After that David stop giving me sad eyes, but he looked at me like we shared a secret as if we kissed or something. I would've felt bad about it but I saw Malcolm talking to Jennifer in the hallway on our way to the assembly. He didn't look at her like he did me, but it still hurt my feelings. When I asked him about it he just rolled his eyes and wouldn't talk about it. So I didn't mind having a secret.

This morning Momma had a headache so she didn't get up to make us breakfast and see us off to school. I took a bowl of cream of wheat into her and some chamomile tea with honey and lemon. She thanked me and then she asked me to close the blinds. I told her I was taking the flour she bought me to school for our flour baby assignment. For a week everyone had to take care of a flour kid, taking them everywhere with us and caring for them like we would a real baby. In English class Tamiko showed us all the clothes she made for her flour baby. They were fashioned out of paper. She was so creative. I told her I would give her five dollars to make some for my flour baby. She told me she'd have them for me by lunch. In PE we had to run around the track. We had to do four laps. So we put our flour kids in the temp day care, a box to the side, while we did our laps. Once we were finished, we could get our babies and relax the rest of the period. Malcolm and I raced to finish first. He ran next to me like I was no competition for him so I ran faster. I was giving it everything I had and he yawned like it was nothing. At the halfway mark he went in for the kill, he took off and left me in his dust. I never saw anybody run that fast in my life. I told myself second was a good place to finish. Even though Malcolm effortlessly beat me in everything, I wanted to beat him in something just once. When I finished he told me it was about time I finished. Then he told me that watching me run made him want to take me home. I told him I needed to get my flour baby out of day care. He rolled his eyes and refused to go with me to pick it up. when I got my baby and he looked annoyed seeing me hold it like it was a real baby. Then Brenda and her friends started teasing us talking about look at the little family and how cute baby Malcolm looked. Malcolm got mad, he took my flour baby and drop kicked it across the field. I was so mad watching my baby rise in the air and then bounce as it hit the ground. Everybody laughed and I was the only person mad. I screamed at him! I pushed him and he just stood there looking satisfied with his self. "I told you I don't want no babies!" He barked. I ran to get my baby and Mr. Turner came over to talk to him. I cried all the way to my baby. Surprisingly there was only a little tear in the top. Ms. Strickland already had tape out. She said every year when the school did this project flour babies went tumbling around the school all week. Sophia and Cassondra asked me what happened. I told them and they laughed at me, I didn't see what was so funny. First my boyfriend informs me after we do it that he never wants to get married, and then he tries to murder my flour baby. I was so mad all I could do was cry. Sophia and Cassondra took me back to the locker room. I cried my eyes out, and I decided I wasn't talking to Malcolm anymore until he apologized. We put our clothes back on, and when the bell rang we walked to the cafeteria. Malcolm was outside the locker room. I threw my nose in the air and I stormed off carrying my flour baby. Malcolm stood there watching me storm off. Sophia said he rolled his eyes, and then he walked away. When we were at our table I was too upset to eat. People were coming to our table asking me if Malcolm and I broke up. I ignored them. Then Chad came to our table. He seemed too happy to hear about my fight with Malcolm. He was getting on my nerves, so I ignored him. Tamiko brought her designs. I paid her two dollars extra to create a hat to cover the tape patch on my baby's head. Benjamin tried to tell Chad that he needed to leave me alone, but Chad didn't listen. At the end of the day Chad was waiting outside of my class. I told him to leave me alone but he said he just wanted to walk me to Sophia and my sister. I tried to walk fast but he kept up with me. When we walked out the door Jade, Sophia, and Malcolm were waiting for me. Time stood still for a minute. Malcolm's face was serious as usual, he showed no emotion. I walked up to them and instead of being smart and walking away Chad came next to me, and then he put his arm around me and looked at Malcolm like "what you gonna do!" I couldn't believe the guts on this guy. Malcolm's face became evil and he punched Chad in the throat. Chad grabbed his throat and he bent over. Poor Chad didn't stand a chance, Malcolm didn't stop until blood was everywhere and Mr. Tucker had a hold of him. I thought I had anger issues, but Malcolm was crazy. Malachi came running over to the crowd. He said when we weren't waiting for him and he saw the crowd he thought it was us again. I didn't want to leave, but I couldn't think of a reason to stay. So I went home, my stomach was in knots. Momma was up and moving slowly but she said she was feeling better. Jade and I volunteered to make dinner. Malachi was studying for a upcoming test in the family room. We heard Daddy's truck pull up, but a long time passed and he didn't come inside. Jade was taking the meatloaf out of the oven so I went to the front of the house to check on Daddy. I turned on the porch light and then I opened the door. My heart stopped when I saw Daddy sitting on the step talking to Malcolm.

"WHAT ARE YOU DOING HERE???" I yelled!

"Talking to your dad." He said like he was stating the obvious.

"I pulled up to the house and I saw this young man pacing back and forth. We've just been shooting the breeze." Daddy said smiling at me. "Have you eaten?" Daddy asked Malcolm. I thought I was gonna pass out.

"No sir I haven't." Malcolm said

"You're welcome to come eat with us. What's on the menu sweetheart?" Daddy said "Meatloaf, garlic mashed potatoes, and green beans." I said not understanding what universe I was in.

"You can use the phone to call home." Daddy said standing up. He opened the door for Malcolm to come inside.

Malcolm's face was still serious as he walked inside. Malachi came in and introduced himself. They shook hands and then Daddy took Malcolm in the kitchen.

"Sweetheart look who's here!" Daddy said to Jade.

Jade turned around and she screamed when she saw Malcolm. She looked very nervous, "what are you doing here?" She said

"I invited him to dinner." Daddy said with a goofy smile on his face.

I could tell from the way Daddy was acting he thought Malcolm was here for Jade. "Amber set the table for one more person."

Momma's head popped out her room, "who's here?" Oh no! My insides screamed. Momma was gonna know Malcolm wasn't here for Jade. She came out her room still moving a little slow because of her head. She looked Malcolm up and down. "Who are you?"

"Malcolm ma'am, I go to school with your daughters."

"You go to school with them? You look like you should be in high school."

"I will be next year." He said giving my mom direct eye contact the entire time.

"How do you know Jade?"

"We have all the same classes."

"You do? That's impressive." Momma said. I couldn't believe she was impressed by anything.

At the table they had Malcolm sit next to Jade. I tried not to stir in my chair. Jade looked so uncomfortable and like she needed a book real bad. I wished I could slide her one under the table, maybe if she stroked the cover she would calm down. I caught her eye at the table and I mouthed, "just breathe" to her. She rolled her eyes at me. Then Momma looked up and we both straightened up. Malcolm was very quiet but spoke when he was spoken to. He was looking around at my family with an interesting look. He still looked very serious, but not mad. Malachi got him talking about sports, and he came to life. He shared that Mr. Turner approached him today about running track in high school. He said he never thought of his self as an athlete. Malachi told him all about Timothy and how he used sports to get into college. Malcolm was soaking it all in. Daddy liked Malcolm, but Momma kept watching. You could tell she was dissecting him minute by minute. When dinner was over Momma and Daddy said they would do the dishes so that we could ride

with Malachi to take Malcolm home. Momma was even watching to see how we walked out the door; we walked out in single file. I saw her looking out the living room window as we got in the car. Malcolm sat in the front with Malachi while Jade and I sat in the back. Knowing how protective Malachi was the coast was not clear to say anything to Malcolm. Malcolm shared that he got suspended today for beating up Chad. Then Malachi and Malcolm started talking about fighting. They were sharing story after story of how badly they beat people up. They were in their own world bonding while I was sweating bullets in the back seat. All the fools were on Malcolm's porch when we pulled up. A couple even came off the porch trying to see who was in the car. When Malcolm got out they went back to what they were doing. Momma Shuga's car was in the driveway. Malcolm said goodnight in general, then he peeked at me. I knew he wanted to talk to me, but I couldn't get to him. When he got to the porch Malachi drove off. He kept telling Jade that Malcolm seemed cool, but that Sonny was going to be heart broken. He might've even enjoyed that aspect of the whole thing. Jade and I begged Malachi not to tell Sonny. Jade simply said he's not her boyfriend nor did she invite him over. Malachi promised he wouldn't tell Sonny. When we got in the room Jade told me off so badly, that I was speechless. I couldn't say anything I had to sit there and take it. Momma walked into our room, she never knocked first, and someone was getting beat if the door was locked. I quickly wiped my eyes and fixed my face. Momma said that she and Daddy felt it was more than time to have a talk about the birds and the bees. She told me I might as well listen so that she could kill two birds with one stone. Jade shot me a look like she was going to kill me. She told Momma she knew how babies were made. Then Momma said, "so you know Malcolm from school?"
"Yes ma'am"
"Are you guys dating?"
"No ma'am"
"Do you know why he was here?"
"No ma'am I don't"
"I always thought you were sweet on Sonny anyways." We both looked at her in complete surprise. Jade turned red. "That boy may be nice and all, but he's got a real rough side. I can tell, I don't wish that on any of my babies."
"You didn't like him?" I asked
"He seemed nice enough, but there's something cold behind his eyes. Jade be careful of the choices you make while you're young, they can affect the rest of your life." Then she looked at me. "And you better not even think about boys right now."
"Jade can have a boyfriend, but I can't?" Then I braced myself, I thought she was gonna slap me for sure.
"You and Jade are two totally different people. You are too sneaky and idealistic right now. YOU think you know it all, and that you got it all figured out. Jade is a lot more mature, and if she decided to date I feel she would come and discuss it with your father and I before things got out of control and she ends up running away to get married. You don't strike me as being mature enough to handle the emotions that come with dating."
Knowing that I already pressed my luck once I didn't say anything else for fear she'd figure me out or beat me just because. Then she went into her whole spill about the birds and the bees. It was different than the talk she gave us when it was almost time for Jade to start her period. This time she talked about boys and your body. Everything she said was true, about tingles and longings. But she was still telling us to be strong and wait. With her talk I knew I was dead if she ever found

out about Malcolm and I. Jade kept flashing me evil eyes whenever momma looked at me. When momma left I started to whisper something to her, but she put her finger up to her lips and pointed at the shadow under the door. Momma was listening. I broke out in a sweat. Jade got her things to go take a shower. Momma left after a few minutes. Jade hit me three times with her pillow really hard.
The next day at school everybody was talking about how badly Malcolm beat up Chad. They were talking about it so much I got sick of hearing all the different versions. At lunchtime I snuck away to the pay phone around the corner. I called Malcolm but he didn't answer the phone. I waited a few minutes, and then I called again, still no answer. I made it back to school before lunch was over. After school momma left a note for Sophia to stay at our house and that she was going to the hospital with Auntie Lauren to have her baby. I stretched the cord to the phone into my room. Then I called Malcolm, he still didn't answer. I called every thirty minutes. Then after three hours of calling I got a busy signal. I wanted to cry as the busy signal lasted another two hours. My heart skipped a beat when he finally answered.
"Hello?"
"I've been calling you all day!"
"I wasn't home." He said dryly
"I missed you today."
"I bet."
"What happened yesterday?" I asked
"He knew better!"
"You didn't have to beat him that bad."
"Play with fire and you will get burned!"
"But that's not what I'm talking about. Why did you kick my baby?"
He sucked his teeth. "I DON'T WANT NO BABIES! Don't even play with me like that. You hear me?" When I didn't respond right away, he got mad. "You hear me?"
"I heard you! I guess we really won't get married when we grow up, cause I want a family."
He sighed, "I thought I told you I'm not getting married either! I don't want none of that leave it to beaver stuff you guys got going on over there. What I look like sitting at a table like you guys were? It was nice but that ain't me! It will never be me!"
"Then why are we together?" I asked holding back my tears.
"Because you wanted to be with me. I don't need you, you need me."
"What do I need you for?"
"To make you feel good about yourself. Everybody calls you the white girl, except for when you're with me. You need me in order to feel connected to your roots!"
I was so mad I screamed profanity at him and then I slammed the phone down! If he was in front of me I didn't care if it meant he would've beat me up I would've fought him. I curled up in the fetal position on my bed and I cried my eyes out. Sophia and Jade asked me what he said and I couldn't even talk about it. I just kept crying and crying. I wanted my virginity back. I wanted my heart back. In the morning I dried my eyes and I got ready for school. Instead of wearing my hair down, I pulled it up in a ponytail on the top of my head. I let my curls hang free from there. But I needed the high ponytail to give me lift on my eyes and to take away from their puffiness. Malcolm and I were over, I just needed to get through the last part of this school year. Fortunately the school year was almost over. Besides I didn't see how the next school year was gonna work. I wanted it to, but he was gonna be around a

bunch of high school girls. I couldn't even compete with that. There were gonna be more Jennifer's looking for their black Mandingo to lay it down for them. I didn't want to worry about it anymore. I told myself it was gonna be ok, and so what if these little boys at my middle school were all scared of Malcolm, they weren't the only boys in the world.

When I got to school I acted like everything was fine, and like I was so happy. In English class Cassondra took one look at my face and she asked me what was wrong. I kept trying to convince her that I was ok. David watched me; he didn't say anything to me. The next day Malcolm's two-day suspension was up and he was back at school. In PE he didn't even look in my direction once. Brenda and her friends were in Malcolm's face, and he welcomed their attention. I talked to Sophia and Cassondra while my leg was shaking the whole time. I was turning beet red. I told them I was gonna beat the mess out of Brenda as soon as he was gone. Cassondra asked me why I wanted to fight Brenda? She told me not to be like Jennifer. She had a good point, Brenda was just a messy female and beneath me. After a week of acting like Malcolm didn't exist he changed up. While we were running around the track, he ran next to me. He kept trying to entice me to race him, but I ignored him. When I finished running, I was trying to catch my breath. He stood next to me catching his breath but not working as hard as I was to breathe. He stared at me trying to read my eyes. I rolled my eyes and walked away. He stood there watching me walk away. Jade told me later that he asked her how much trouble he was in. She told him she didn't know what he did, and all she could tell him was I was really hurt after I talked to him. She told him she has never seen me like this so she couldn't tell him how to fix it either. The next day he got to school earlier than he normally does. He waited for us to get there then he followed us around all morning. His face stayed serious, but his eyes stayed super serious on me. I still acted like he wasn't there. Whenever daddy and momma fought, as long as momma was yelling daddy would argue too. But if she got quiet, he knew he messed up. So I acted like momma, if he wanted me to forgive him, he was gonna have to try harder.

That night daddy told us that Nana said she would pick Jade, Sophia, and I up one week after school. We were gonna spend at least a month with them this summer like usual. We would get to see all of our cousins. Malachi wasn't gonna be able to go this summer just like last summer on account of his summer job. But he said he would come for the camping trip. One weekend of our stay the grandparents would take us camping. They had a big camper, and all if us kids would pile in. Then the girls would sleep in the camper and the boys would sleep outside in sleeping bags and tents. I couldn't wait to be away from here. No one would be calling me the white girl at least for a month. AND I would have the biggest tan, I loved that part. Up at the lake we would swim, make crafts with Nana, and eat all in the sun. I noticed that this winter I held onto my tan a little, I didn't get all washed out. I was very pleased with that. This past fall Nana and Papa moved to a city called Concord. Daddy has been too busy to take us to see the new house, so we were excited to also be going somewhere new.

I really wanted to get away from Malcolm, his words kept replaying in my mind. I got docked ten percent of my grade because of the tear in the bag. I was so mad! Saturday Sophia, Rosalind, Cassondra, and I decided to go hang out at the mall. We went from store to store looking in the windows at all the clothes we wanted. I told them next time we should plan better, and then I could go to the bank after school, and take a little money out of my savings. But since the bank was closed on

Saturdays there was nothing I could do. Malcolm had given me about four hundred dollars that I put in the bank. Then he gave me money that I kept and spent, but those were smaller amounts. We were looking at shoes when I heard an adult call my name. I looked up and it was Momma Shuga. She looked so happy to see me and I must admit that my heart skipped a beat when I saw her. I ran over to her and gave her the biggest hug. Then I introduced her to everybody. She said hello to everyone then she asked why I hadn't come to see her lately. I pulled her to the side and I told her what Malcolm did. Her face turned very serious just like Malcolm's. She told me that she was very proud of me for standing my ground and that Malcolm was very wrong for treating me like that. Then she said that we were both very young and we had the rest of our lives to figure out such things as marriage and families. Then she took her coin purse out of her bra. She had a roll of money in it. She gave me five twenties and told me to treat my friends and myself to something nice. She gave me another hug and a kiss on the forehead. She told me to still come see her even if her grandson was being a knucklehead. I gave everyone a twenty and that left forty for me. We had pizza, we went to the movies, and I bought a pair of new shoes. Momma Shuga made our day.

I thought about Malcolm all day and especially at night. I missed him so much, and my body was starting to miss him more. I cried myself to sleep. Sunday I went over Sophia's house to hang out and play with her baby brother. Little Jeff was such a cutie. Sophia told me she was going to be an excellent mother when she grew up. She showed me how to change his diapers; we bathed him, and talked to auntie Lauren as she breast-fed him. Watching them care for my little cousin confirmed for me that when I grew up I wanted to have a family. That made me sad too cause I wanted my family to be with Malcolm but he doesn't want one. When I came home there was a big teddy bear in the living room. Momma said they came back from the store and this bear was on the porch with a card. I hadn't taken my jacket or purse off when she handed me the envelope and she watched my face as I opened it. On the front it said "To Amber" the card had a flower in a vase. It looked like a water painting. The inside was blank and it said "I'm sorry" that's it. Momma asked me who it was from and I told her I didn't know. She read the card, turned it over and over like she was a detective. Then she stared at me, sweat started popping up on my forehead. She asked again who it was from, and again I told her I didn't know. Then she slapped me; she hit me so hard I thought I heard ringing. She told me she knew I was lying to her and she didn't appreciate it. Daddy heard the slap and he came charging in the living room to defend me. She yelled at him for interfering. He yelled at her telling her she needed to find another way to deal with me. She told him she knew I was up to something and he needed to back off so that she could get to the bottom of it. She surprised both of us when she punched me in my shoulder because I moved my face just in time. She still knocked me into the wall. Daddy grabbed her and I ran out the door. I didn't know where I was running to, but I just ran as fast as I could. Before I knew it I was at Malcolm's house. I don't even know how I got there. I stood on the corner looking at all the people on the porch, and I debated whether to go over or not, but once I realized Momma Shuga's car was in the driveway I sucked it up and walked over. The guys on the porch watched me walk over. I walked right past them and straight into the house. Momma Shuga was in the living room sweeping the floor. This was the first time that girl wasn't there. Momma Shuga looked at me, she could tell I was upset. She put her arms out and I ran to her to hug her. She hugged me just like Jade would when momma wasn't looking. She took me back to her bedroom, and she had me sit while she made me some tea. I didn't know if Malcolm was there or not, but I wasn't there to see him. She rubbed my back while I drank the tea and cried. Then she told me a story about when she was growing up. My mind kept going in and out of her story. I couldn't focus really. I fell asleep across her lap around eight o'clock. Hearing Malcolm's voice woke me. He was calling out to Momma Shuga like he always did when she was home when he got there. She was watching TV and I was laying next to her. Malcolm was talking as he came towards the room, he stopped mid sentence when he saw me. He rushed over to the bed asking if I was ok. I told him his stupid bear got me in trouble. That was the first time I ever saw him with sad eyes. I told him I wasn't there to see him, I was there to see Momma Shuga. She smiled at him real big when I said it. He sat down on the foot of the bed. He started apologizing for what he said to me. He had really sad eyes the whole time he was talking to me, and he wasn't serious Malcolm at that moment he was truly sorry. Momma Shuga was defending me and telling him you can't just say whatever mean and hurtful thing pops into your mind when you're dealing with someone you love. We both looked at her with funny looks. She blew air and laughed at us. She said we were too young to be trying to act like grown ups. We needed to just be kids. Malcolm apologized again, and then he said he still didn't want no babies or a wife. Momma Shuga shamed him, and then he told her he didn't want to end up like any body in or around that house. I told him it wasn't fair for him to tell me that after we made love. Momma Shuga's eye got big and then she put her fingers in her ears like she didn't want to hear that. All three of us started laughing. Then she told us she couldn't talk to us anymore. Malcolm asked me very politely to come to his room, my mind told me to stay put. But I really wanted him to hold me and tell me how sorry he was. I sat there debating with myself. I looked at the clock and it was after ten. Momma Shuga asked me if I needed to call home. If I spent the night momma would know she was right and nothing would save me. So I told him I needed to go home. He looked disappointed, but he understood. Momma Shuga drove me home, she told my father and the officer she saw me walking down the street, and how she recognized me cause I go to school with her grand baby. Daddy thanked her over and over again for watching over me; he offered her money for her gas. Momma Shuga smiled really big, I could tell she liked my daddy. Most people do because he's a good man. She told him it was her honor to bring me home. Daddy walked her to her car and he opened her door for her. I waited on the porch with the officer. Then daddy thanked the officer for all of his help. He told me they were filing a missing person report and how they were so scared cause they didn't know where I was. He called Uncle Jeff and Auntie Lauren and told them I was home. Momma didn't come out of her room. Daddy and I sat on the couch in the living room. He put his arm around me and he talked to me real calm. He apologized for what momma did. He was trying to explain how much she loved me and how scared she was for me. He said out of all of their children I was the one she worried about the most. He said he didn't understand it completely himself, but he assured me that she loves me very much and that she's just scared for me. Malachi came out of his room to use the bathroom. When he came in the living room he rubbed his knuckles in my head. I guess that was his way of telling me he was glad I was home. Then daddy told me to go wash up and then to go to bed. When I walked in the room Jade had a flashlight and she was reading a book. She told me momma and daddy argued real bad when I left. She said daddy raised his voice and everything. She said daddy looked ten feet tall when he was mad. She said when momma realized how mad daddy was she backed down. Daddy told her to go in the room and calm herself down. Then she said stretching her eyes as big as she could "MOMMA DID IT!" I gasped. All this time we thought momma ran the house, but daddy put his foot down and she did it. The bear was sitting on my bed. After I took my shower I slept with the bear. I loved it!

In the morning momma still didn't come out the room even though daddy left early for work. Sophia came over and Malachi took us to school. Malachi asked me where I went last night. I told him I was just wandering around. He didn't believe me; he just gave me a look. When we got to school Malcolm was there early again. He walked up to me, put his arms around me and he kissed me. Jade gagged and walked away, Sophia stayed and giggled. I was surprised cause he never really touched me in front of people. Outside of kissing me to make David jealous he never kissed me in public. I was so surprised and happy. His face remained serious, but he hugged me tight. He asked me if I forgave him, and I told him I did. Then he asked me when I was gonna come see him. I told him I started my period that morning so we had to wait. He was fine with that. Meanwhile I enjoyed all the affection and attention he gave me. Momma wouldn't say much to me. Her eyes told me she was still mad at me, but she kept her words short and to the point.

I had to stay after school to talk to Mr. Harris about a math test. He said I was having a problem with my test and he needed to talk to me. He called home and talked to momma. He told momma he would bring me home afterwards. So Malachi picked up Jade and Sophia and they went home. Malcolm and I went in the theater room and kissed and rubbed each other for a while. Then he said he'd wait around the school until we left. Mr. Harris saw Malcolm walking me to his class. He looked mad. Then he only let me come in the class. Malcolm's eyes got squinty, but he didn't say anything. Mr. Harris locked the door then he asked me if Malcolm was my boyfriend. I didn't say anything I just looked at him like he was crazy for asking me. I sat in the first desk in front of his desk. I expected him to sit at his desk or go to the board. But he stood in front of my desk. He told me he talked to my momma, and then he smiled and said he sounded black. Again I just looked at him. Suddenly he started reminding me of my uncle and I felt like I was gonna be sick. He started telling me how pretty I was. A lump formed in my throat. I asked what my beauty had to do with my test. He said, "your performance today will determine your final grade, and I know you want an A don't you!" His pants were sticking out and I could feel my heart beat in my toes. I told him I didn't want an A and that I was going home. When I stood up he grabbed my wrist and he twisted it to my back. He told me I wasn't leaving until he was done. I kicked him and I tried to run out the door on the right cause I heard him lock the door on the left side of the room. It was locked and I jerked on the door trying to open it. Mr. Harris started laughing, he chased me around the room and I was screaming for anybody to come help me. I didn't want that thing by me. Then like thunder some one was at the door. They were kicking the door BOOM! BOOM! BOOM! Mr. Harris froze for a minute. Then he said, "Your little boyfriend is strong! I will tell your parents that I saw you with him. And how you made up this whole story to cover up that you were with him." BOOM! BOOM! BOOM! I was screaming at him to let me out. Then a louder BOOM happened and the door opened. My momma walked in. I was in the corner cowering at this man who was closing in. Momma took a running leap and she tackled Mr. Harris. He was so surprised that he just fell backwards. Momma punched his face like she was a boxer. I hit him with my books. You could hear hurried footsteps coming down the hall. Mr. Tucker grabbed momma just like he had done me before. The Principal helped Mr. Harris up. Momma's face was evil, and she was really mad. The Principal asked what was going on. Mr. Harris said momma and I attacked him. He was shaking holding his eye. His lip and nose were busted, he had knots forming on his head, and his cheeks were bruised. I was screaming and I told Mr. Tucker he was lying! I was scared they weren't going to believe me. The secretary had called the police. Mr. Tucker told my momma I was just like her. He couldn't really put her down cause as soon as her feet touched the floor she was trying to get to Mr. Harris again. And now Mr. Harris was scared of momma. Malcolm was in the doorway and he looked really mad. I thought he was mad at me, but if I would've went to him momma would've known. Momma told the police even though she agreed that I could stay something didn't feel right when she talked to "Mista Harris!" She said with hate in her mouth. She said she came to make sure everything was everything. And when she pulled up to the school she saw Malcolm outside. She asked him where the classroom was and she said as soon as they entered the hallway she heard her baby screaming for help and banging on the door. She said they ran to the door and started kicking it when they realized the door was locked. She asked Mr. Tucker why would a grown man need to be locked in a room with a thirteen-year-old girl? She said when they kicked the door together that's when it opened, and she told Malcolm to stay in the hallway. Mr. Harris denied it all, but it was three against one. The police took him into custody and he was fired from our school. Eventually a couple of other girls came forward, but they never said who. Momma didn't let us including Sophia go back to school until she knew for sure Mr. Harris wasn't coming back. We died of boredom at home for three days. Next week was the last week of school and at this point I really really needed to see Malcolm.

Some how I convinced momma to let me go by myself to go look for a job in Berkeley for the summer after we came back from Nana's. She had another headache so I think she would've agreed to anything. I caught the bus early Saturday morning to Malcolm's house he was at the bus stop waiting for me with the brown bag in his hand. When we got to his house the door didn't close good before we were at it. We didn't even make it to the bed. I didn't care if Malcolm never told me he loved me, I knew he did. He wouldn't make love to me if he didn't love me. We made love all day! It was great it was wonderful, it was finally everything I told Jade and Sophia that it was. We used the whole box of six condoms, but two of them broke. He told me he wished I could go on the pill so we wouldn't have to worry about condoms, but there was no way to do that without momma finding out. Then he asked when was the last time I went to the bank. I told him it had been months. He told me he deposited some change in my account. I thanked him not really knowing what change meant. I told him I was going away for a month at least in the summer. He was quiet for a minute then he told me that was a good thing cause he needed to focus on making money this summer and making some moves. He promised we would still see each other, even when the school year started.

Chapter 6

Ugh! Where is he???? I haven't seen or spoken to Malcolm all summer. Every time I tried to call from my grandparents he was never home or the line was busy. I tried not to let it bother me but it did. I would even sneak and call in the middle of the night sometimes, in hopes of just hearing his voice but he never answered. When I was irritated beyond belief Nana asked me if it was a boy. I couldn't believe she knew me like that, I told her about him. Only grandparent appropriate things of course, but my Nana was so tickled by my "middle school romance" as she called it if only she knew... I made her promise not to tell my parents, and she said it was our secret. Then I started noticing she had the same bond with everybody. I even saw Jade confiding in her; I wanted to know what they talked about so bad. Jade is so quiet.

While we were out there Sophia met a boy. He was cute, but she had a problem with him being white though. That tickled Jade and I, we reminded her that she was too. She laughed when she thought about it. But all the cousins agreed race didn't matter, cute was cute.

I had a great time with my family and seeing all my cousins, but I was ready to come home. Momma's headaches were still coming from time to time, and I know Malachi was taking care of her on his off days but I was worried about her. Timothy was home for the summer and I hadn't seen him yet. PLUS!!!!! I needed to see Malcolm.

When we came home the first couple of days we spent them telling our hilarious stories of all the shenanigans all the cousins got into. It was so hot that we had water balloon fights daily. My cousin Gwen's hair poofed just like mine when it got wet. I called her my hair twin.

But now that I've been home I called Malcolm every time I looked at the phone. After two months of nothing from him I started stalking the house. I knew he would never leave his window open unless he was home. That window was always closed, and Momma Shuga's car was always gone too. Then.... I talked to Rosalind and she said she and Benjamin saw him with a girl. He was driving, and this girl was definitely not a relative. They said she was tall and had a woman's body. She was all over him and he let her be. I asked them if he saw them, and she said yes, but he didn't seem to care. He's not old enough to drive! My heart hurt and I didn't know why he was doing this to me when I just wanted to love him. After that I told my heart to just forget about him, cause he clearly had forgotten about me. I went to the bank to deposit the forty dollars my Nana gave me to add to my school shopping money. I gave the teller my account book. She was printing more than just today's deposits in my book. When she gave me my book back I was expecting to see a six or seven hundred-dollar balance. My mouth dropped open when I saw six thousand two hundred and thirty two dollars. I sat in the chair in the lobby and I looked at the dates of all the deposits. Almost everyday he's been putting two and three hundred dollar deposits in my account. My mind spun around, was the hair cutting business going that well? The money he put in my account was for me. He was thinking about me, my heart sang all over again. I walked through the mall thinking I could buy whatever I wanted in this mall, how awesome is that. I decided I would continue saving my money. I didn't want to blow the money on anything stupid.

When I got home Timothy was packing to go back to school. We were talking about our upcoming school years when Sophia came in the door she was really pale and spaced out. Timothy dropped his bag and hurried to her. He was so concerned, Timothy was worse than Malachi in how they watched over us. We kept asking her what was wrong.

"My, my, my momma's gonna have another baby." she said in shock
Timothy and I fell out laughing at her. She snapped out of her trance. "I thought
they would stop doing that after they had Jeff. But they did it again!" Timothy and I
laughed harder. She didn't see what was so funny. We told her parents don't stop
doing it. And she looked like she wanted to throw up. We told her about our parents
and their brass bed, how we were lucky if that was all we heard. She slid on the
floor all dramatic, "I think that's the grosses thing I've ever heard!" She said. When
Jade got home from her job at Raynel's beauty shop, we told her what Sophia said
and how she said it. We were all laughing at her. Eventually she got over the shock
and warmed up to the idea of a baby sister. That's what we're hoping for anyways.
This year like last year we were shopping with Auntie Lauren and Sophia. But this
year Jade was completely into what she was going to wear to school. Momma asked
her if this had anything to do with seeing Sonny this year. Jade blushed but didn't
say anything. Sophia and I were happy with the things our mommas let us get but I
told her we could always come back and get something if we thought it was
something we completely had to have. When we were walking around the mall I
was holding baby Jeff and then right there in my face was Malcolm walking with
the girl Rosalind described to me. She was really pretty and definitely older than
him. I didn't think her body was better than mine especially after my breast came in.
They weren't huge, but I couldn't go out side braless.
It was like watching a horrible movie. I turned my back to them, without seeing my
reaction momma still saw Malcolm anyways. She was genuinely happy to see him.
She called to him, and he came over with his companion. They were holding hands
breaking my heart. Momma introduced him to auntie Lauren. I fell to the back of
the group, my face was stinging and I knew I had turned red. There was no way I
was gonna be able to play this off. He introduced the girl her name was Yvette. I
hated that name! Why would anyone name their daughter Yvette? Momma asked
Yvette what school she went to and she said Oakland
High. Momma introduced her to Jade saying she was going to be starting there in
the fall. I wanted this nightmare to be over. As momma was about to motion
towards me somebody called Malcolm over. He told my momma it was good seeing
her and all of us but he had to go. And just like that they were gone. Jade and
Sophia peeked at me. When we went out to eat I just sat there feeling defeated. I
didn't touch my food and I just felt devastated. They couldn't show signs that they
were comforting me our mommas were watching but they told me not to worry
about him and how the new school year was getting ready to start and there would
be new boys. I was gonna move on with my life. But they didn't understand I had
given him everything, now I had nothing to show for it. I didn't want him to leave
me behind like I was some little kid too little to play his game. I wondered if he
would be so quick to act like I was nobody if I had his baby. Then he'd have to see
me. I got lost in how cute we'd be as a little family. I wasn't paying attention; Jade
had an imaginary phone out. Pretending like she was calling me. I ignored them and
when I went back to my thoughts. Malcolm and I being a family, which would
never happen cause he was never, home to take my calls.
Momma kept looking at us, like she was collecting evidence. I kept trying to keep
my face straight although I was dying inside. When we got home I went to my room
and laid down. Momma asked me why I was laying down. I told her I was tired, she
told me normally I was excited about new clothes. I told her I was excited, but I was
just tired. Then she asked me what was wrong for real, but I stuck to my story. She

left but I knew she was watching me. Fortunately I had nowhere to go, nothing to do. I just waited for school to start. I needed homework to heal my broken heart. I finally understood why Jade put her nose in books. I looked at her stash of books. I didn't want anything too heavy, but I needed an escape. When she came in the room Jade smiled, then she asked me what I was doing. I told her I needed a story to take me away, but something that had a happy ending. She asked if I wanted a love story? Yes! Yes! That's what I wanted. She looked at her bookshelf. Then she selected a solid book. Have you guys reviewed Jane Austen yet? I shook my head no. Then she told me we would cover her this school year. Then she said, "this book contains the infamous Pride & Prejudice, Mansfield Park, Emma, and Sense and Sensibility. The language is difficult to understand but that makes it more of a challenge. Once you understand the language the stories are WONDERFUL! I think you will like it. I suggest you save pride and prejudice for last." Then she told me to read the stories in this order. Mansfield Park, Emma, Sense and Sensibility, and then Pride and Prejudice. She wasn't kidding, I was getting so frustrated I kept reading the opening page over and over. Jade smiled, she helped me find the voice to understand. Once I found it the stories came to life. The next three weeks were nice! I only thought about Malcolm a little. When I had my book open at all hours of the day everyone blamed Jade and she gladly took on the blame. I was so happy for all the heroines in these stories. I especially liked Elizabeth Bennett, she held true to who she was and she did not settle for less. In the end she got the man of her dreams by being herself. That's what I was going to do. I was going to be myself and not worry about having a man in my life. I finished just in time for the first day of school.

It was weird walking into school and not seeing Malcolm or Jade. Momma came to the first day of school. She wanted to make sure they did not bring Mr. Harris back to the school. The Principal explained that Mr. Harris was still in jail, and when he got out he would not be permitted to be a teacher. That made momma relax a lot. Then she gave us permission to go to our homeroom. We were so happy to see Mr. Thornton again, even though he only taught seventh grade classes. He came and chatted with Sophia and I once he passed out class schedules. He even told us a little gossip, not knowing I was the student he told us how "Mr. Harris was arrested for allegedly molesting a student." I took a deep breath he said "when he was released on bail a few other students came forward, but when he failed to show up to court like he was supposed to, the police went to his house. They found him dead! He had been tortured and beaten to death!" Sophia and I covered our mouths; as we didn't expect the story to end that way. He told us the police had no leads on who did this to him. Mr. Thornton was so cool; it felt like we were talking to an old friend and not our old teacher. He said the police told the school to say he was still in jail. They didn't want that type of attention on the school. We talked about our summers, and what we thought this year was gonna be like. I did feel relieved to know that Mr. Harris wasn't just gonna show up somewhere. Momma was surprised too; she said she had mixed emotions about him being gone.

All day I thought about it, at lunch Rosalind and Benjamin were still going strong. I envied them; they have been together since sixth grade, never had sex and are happy together as any couple could be. Her momma knows about them and she's ok with it. I really envied them. Cassondra seemed like she tried to be content with her singleness, but she always liked the boy who didn't like her. The boys that did like her, she always found something wrong with them. Unfortunate for them, but meanwhile since she wasn't distracted by a boyfriend she made and excellent friend.

She comforted me about Malcolm when I told her what happened.
Jade told me she saw him with her own eyes, Malcolm was beyond a shadow of a
doubt dating Yvette. I told myself to be Elizabeth, just be cool.
****
I wanted to get momma and daddy something really nice for their anniversary.
Daddy has been working so hard, and momma has been on best behavior. I thought
about it and they hadn't been on a double date with uncle Jeff and auntie Lauren in a
long time. So Malachi, Timothy, Sophia, Jade, and I collaborated to make the
evening special. I told them I had been saving my pennies. We found a lovely little
restaurant that would be perfect for their night. The restaurant had drippy candles,
live music, and loveliness. Timothy set everything up. When I went to the bank in
three months time I had over ten thousand in my savings. The money confused me,
but I took a thousand dollars out. I gave it to Timothy in stages, I told him I had
been saving all my pennies, I knew he didn't believe me but he accepted the money
anyways. He prepaid the limo, and the meal for the restaurant. Then Auntie Lauren
took us to the store and we bought momma a lovely black dress. We picked out
shoes, and accessories. We even got daddy a new suit from Macy's. Timothy tried
on the suit to make sure it fit. Auntie Lauren was so emotional because of the
pregnancy. The day of their anniversary we surprised momma and daddy with
breakfast in bed. They were so surprised. Timothy even came home for the day, and
we all sacrificed our perfect attendance records to stay home with my parents. He
told them that we planned a special surprise for them in honor of their anniversary.
We washed mommas hair and then we took her in our room. Jade did momma's
hair, Auntie Lauren did mommas makeup, and then Sophia and I got her dressed.
Momma looked beautiful! We told her she looked just like Diahann Carroll. We
weren't exaggerating, she looked beautiful. Auntie Lauren got dressed in our room
too. Daddy and Uncle Jeff got dressed in daddy's room. We covered their eyes so
that they saw each other at the same time. Daddy turned beet red when he saw
momma he told her she was beautiful! He couldn't stop staring at her. His response
to momma was priceless. Then they asked where they were going. We told them
they were going to dinner and to hear music. They got so excited! They hugged us
all and thanked us for their wonderful evening even though they hadn't left yet.
After they left Timothy wanted to talk to me alone. So he and I went in daddy's
truck to pick up a pizza for us. Timothy went on and on about how he left his baby
sister to go to college and he came back to a young lady. I just smiled and said we
all had to grow up at sometime. He looked me in the eyes like momma does when
she's reading me. He told me I was into something and it wasn't gonna end well for
me. Then we went into the pizzeria, we ordered our pizza and then I sat next to my
big brother. He put his arm around me and told me about his school. I pretended to
be interested in the topic. I heard the door open and close, two guys walked in then I
saw that girl Yvette. She was walking behind them. That walk! That stand! It was
Malcolm! I stared at him waiting for him to see Timothy and I. Malcolm turned
around to ask her what she wanted to drink. He stopped talking as soon as he saw
me. His friend finished the order, while Malcolm came to our table. He sat down
and introduced himself. Timothy looked confused, he said a reluctant hello.
Malcolm explained that he went to school with Jade and Malachi and earlier this
year he had dinner with our family. Timothy relaxed, and greeted Malcolm. I didn't
say anything I just sat there. I hadn't spoken to Malcolm in six months and he didn't
appear to be in a hurry to talk to me either. Malcolm introduced his cousin Troy,
and Yvette. I just stared at Malcolm, I missed his mouth, I missed his hands, and I

missed his body. Then he looked at me and just said a nonchalant hi. My blood
boiled! When they called our number Timothy went to get the pizza. Malcolm and I
stared at each other, I was getting so mad! His cousin went outside and Yvette
excused herself to the ladies room. As I stood up Malcolm cracked a smile at me,
before I even realized what I was doing my hand slapped him as HARD as I could!
He didn't even flinch; it was like he expected it and he just smiled. As Timothy
walked back towards us Malcolm made a kissy face at me. How could he act like
my slap didn't affect him? My hand was stinging. If he was light like me my
handprint would've been on his face. He didn't even seem phased, that hurt me
more. I walked out the door with Timothy, when I walked out I looked back as I
held the door open. Malcolm was staring at my butt with a grin. I just kept getting
madder and madder! When we got in the car Timothy was quiet like he was
thinking about something. Then he asked me who was that? I said "Duh! He just
said he goes to school with Jade and Malachi!"
We pulled up to the light and Timothy looked at me. "I know but as soon as he
walked in the door you tensed up. Now you're mad."
"No I'm not!" I said rolling my eyes and looking out the window.
"Is that your boyfriend?" He asked directly staring at the back of my head.
I looked at his reflection in the window. I swallowed hard! "No! If he was my
boyfriend why would he walk in with his girlfriend and bring her to our table?" I
crossed my arms as the words came out of my mouth.
"You like you him then. You can tell me no if you want to, but I can tell." The light
turned green. I changed the subject, Tim followed me but he wasn't fooled. When
we parked in front of the house, I called myself leveling with Tim. "I did like him
last year at school. But as you can see he's not thinking about me. Please don't tell
momma and daddy." He honked my nose and said, "ok chipmunk". I would've died
if he kept pressing the issue. When we got back inside I told Jade and Sophia what
happened. They asked me with horror in their eyes what he did when I slapped him.
Jade looked scared for me. I honestly didn't care, there's nothing he could do that
would hurt me more than how he's hurting me right now. Baby Jeff was such a
good baby, and he did make me smile. When our parents came home they were
giddy and tipsy. Momma described the limo like it was transportation for royalty.
She said she felt so famous riding in that car. They all thanked us over and over
again for their evening. After auntie Lauren, uncle Jeff, Sophia, and the baby left.
Malachi and Jade took Timothy home. I watched momma and daddy slow dance in
the living to one of daddy's jazz records. Tears poured out of my eyes cause there
was nobody to love me. I cried myself to sleep.
****
"Who is that?" I asked
"That's the new boy." Christen said unimpressed. "I think his name is Charles or
something like that."
"He's cute!"
Christen shook her head. "You're always looking at boys!"
"So, what's wrong with that?" I said defensively.
"At some point don't you get tired of them? All these boys are just horn dogs.
They're not thinking about love they're thinking about one thing right now. You
would be silly to think you could get more from any of them."
Although she was talking about the boys at school I knew she was talking about
Malcolm. I didn't know what to say to that, so I just went back to doing my work. In
PE I loved when they had us run laps! I would think about Malcolm the whole time

and how no matter how hard I ran he would beat me. I would race him in my mind and I would be so mad at my heart for still caring.

This school year most people left me alone. No one really challenged me or asked me dumb questions. I got to just be me. Sophia and Cassondra were completely into the Home EC class. Sophia was becoming the master chef supreme! And Cassondra was becoming quite the seamstress. Sometimes she collaborated with Tamiko and they would create the cutest stuff. Mrs. Hernandez the new home EC teacher this year called the three of them her prized pupils. Sometimes after school she would take them to the fabric store to work on new ideas. I always tagged along as part of the package deal. I could cook, but only cause I had to sometimes. Where Sophia was really starting to love it. Since her momma was pregnant and there was a little baby running around, when Sophia got home she did most of the cooking and cleaning. At first she complained but one day she started enjoying it.

Sophia had cooking, Cassondra had sewing, Rosalind had Ben, and I had running. Sometimes I would come back to the school and just run as fast as I could as hard as I could on the track. Most of the time I was crying my eyes out. Momma was in one of her moods today so I came back to the school by myself and I ran. I was so focused on my breathing I didn't realize I had an audience. Charles was standing next to my jacket watching and clapping. When I finished my final lap I walked over to him. My legs were on fire and I was covered in sweat. Charles kept clapping until I was standing in front of him. He introduced himself, and said he had been watching me for a couple months now. I wondered where he was going with this. I wasn't in the mood for the boy girl conversation. My momma was on my nerves and I was trying to take my mind off of it. He was cute though so I talked to him, but I didn't act like I liked him. I didn't know if he liked me.

He started coming to the field on a regular basis. He asked me a bunch of questions about myself, like what classes I had, what did I want to be when I grew up, what kind of grades I got. So I asked him the same questions. We only had two classes together, and neither of them were advanced classes. He wasn't as smart as Malcolm, but he was nice, and he kept smiling at me. Then he told me my eyes were pretty. No one really ever said anything nice about them so it was nice to hear. I started to feel warm and tingly inside. He started sitting with us at lunch. Again Benjamin was so happy to have a guy sit with us.

One day Charles asked me who Malcolm was. I had just finished running and I needed to catch my breath. I told him Malcolm was my boyfriend when I was in the seventh grade. He said everybody keeps telling him to leave me alone because of Malcolm. I told him I hadn't seen Malcolm in over a month and I hadn't talked to him since right after last school year ended. Charles looked nervous but he swallowed hard and then he asked me if he could kiss me. That was different; Malcolm always did it he didn't ask me. I told him he could, and he very sweetly close mouth kissed me. It was sweet, but I thought to myself I'll just have to show him how to do better. He was standing there smiling when I leaned in to kiss him again. I used my tongue to open his mouth. I kept my eyes open and when I put my tongue in his mouth his eyes opened wide. I smiled at him. He looked embarrassed, he said he never tongue kissed before. I told him not to be embarrassed then I showed him how to do it. He had a goofy look plastered on his face after that. He asked me to be his girlfriend and I accepted because Malcolm was nowhere to be found. Sophia was going out with Richard a boy at our school too. It felt good to have a boyfriend again even if Charles was nothing like Malcolm. I had to show him how to do everything. Where to put his hands when he kissed me, how to rub me when we went to the movies. I even had to tell him how to suck my neck. Charles did whatever I told him to do. He was a helpless puppy following me around. Sophia asked me if I was gonna have sex with him, and the thought of it frustrated me. He didn't know how to do anything unless I showed him. I didn't want to have my legs spread open telling him how to do it. Besides he wasn't asking for it. He was square like Benjamin so I was fine with that. But I still missed Malcolm. I went to the bank to get ten dollars, I looked at my balance it was over twelve thousand in my savings now. The teller told me I was quite the little saver. I just smiled, I didn't get it. Charles waited outside the bank for me and we walked hand in hand to Bob's ice cream parlor. We were four blocks from my house. I knew I was risking getting caught by Momma, but I kind of figured as long as it wasn't Malcolm, Momma would find a way to be ok with it. I wasn't in the mood for anything exciting so I just got a scoop of chocolate ice cream, and Charles ordered the same. Charles was declaring his undying love for me when Malcolm walked in the door. I squeezed Charles' hand to tell him to shut up. He looked confused, and then he saw Malcolm walk straight to our table. He was with his cousin Troy. Malcolm looked bigger and meaner, I guess I had gotten used to seeing people smile, so his lack of one was off putting. Charles searched my face for an explanation. I was happy to see Malcolm but I was mad at him for leaving me. Malcolm pulled up a chair next to me and Troy sat down next to Charles. Charles looked scared.

"Who's this?" Malcolm asked me

"Charles" I wanted to say it with an attitude but I didn't want Charles to get beat up. He didn't do anything wrong.

"He goes to your little school?" Malcolm said

"Little?" I said putting my hand on my hip.

"You heard me little girl." Then he looked Charles up and down.

"Why you hanging out with this square, where's David?"

"David moved in the summer. Charles is my boyfriend." I said matter of factly. Malcolm started laughing, but it was a scary laugh. Nobody else laughed. "Ain't you scared your momma gonna get in that butt?"

"No, as long as it ain't you I don't think she'll care."

He stared at me for a minute. "He ain't your boyfriend he's too square." Charles said nothing; Troy was staring at him giving him crazy eyes the whole time. Charles looked scared and I felt bad for him.

"He is my boyfriend and he's just fine." I said rolling my eyes.

Malcolm stood up, "I'll be right back." He said to Troy. Then he grabbed the shoulder of my shirt and pulled me off my chair to the back. Charles sat there looking helpless and scared. He pulled me to the bathroom hallway and he slammed my back against the wall. "What are you doing here with him?" He looked mad

"Malcolm let me go!" I tried to move his hand that he had me pinned to the wall with. His hand didn't even budge. "Let me go!"

"You are my girlfriend! You can't be claiming some other guy! Especially some L7 like that!"

"You are not my boyfriend anymore. This is the first time I've seen you without your girlfriend Yvette. You moved on and so have I."

"That hoe ain't my girlfriend!"

"Every time I see you she's with you!"

"So! That doesn't make her my girlfriend." Then he searched my eyes. I wanted to cry but I wasn't gonna let him see me cry. "I can't call you! I can't come over! What

am I supposed to do?"
"I called you all summer! ALL SUMMER! I even called in the middle of the night!
You never answered! You don't even care about me!" A tear ran down my face.
That made him mad he picked me up slammed my back against the wall again.
"You have no idea all the stuff I did for you this summer, and the stuff I'm still
doing for you! You can't tell me how I feel! If you value your life and his get rid of
him!" Then he put me down.
"I can't do that to him! He's been good to me."
Malcolm reared up like he was gonna slap me like momma does. But he caught his
self. "Amber! Get rid of him! I'm gonna come for you, and if you haven't done it I
will do it for you!"
"You're gonna come for me?" I said surprised.
"Yes, soon. I miss you. The fact that you came here with him means you miss me
too. Don't make me hurt him!" Then he grabbed me by my hair and he kissed me.
He kissed me just right, his tongue was strong and the way I liked it. I didn't want
the kiss to end. "Get rid of him! I don't want to have to hurt him!" Then he let me go
and he walked away. Troy stood up and made two handguns. He pointed them at
Charles as he walked out backwards behind Malcolm. Charles looked really scared,
and then Troy started cracking up laughing. He walked behind Malcolm and then
they were gone. Charles' eyes were big and he looked at me with so many
questions. I sat down I grabbed his hand which was completely clammy and I
apologized.
"So that's Malcolm? He's scarier than everybody said!" He said looking around the
table. "I heard him! Everybody heard him!" I squeezed his hand. "I'm not a loser."
Charles said really hurt.
"I know you're not." Tears ran down my face. "We can still be friends."
Charles exhaled, "yea. Do we have a choice?"
Charles may not have been the smartest guy, but he wasn't the dumbest either.
When we left the ice cream parlor he went to the left and I went to the right. I
waited for Jade to finish sweeping up hair at Raynel's and then we went to Sophia's
house to help her with the baby and cook while her momma laid down. I told them
what happened with Malcolm, they didn't blame Charles for leaving. For once I
agreed with Jade, Malcolm was wrong.

****

A week later I was on my way to second period when I saw Momma Shuga's car
pull-up. I hesitated, and then Malcolm told me to come. If I would've ran he
would've caught me. So I walked over to the car, Troy was in the front seat smiling
at me. "Come on!" Malcolm said. I tried to explain that I had class and he looked at
me like he would throw me in the car if he had to. I huffed and then I got in the car.
I sat in the back seat quietly. Troy looked back at me then he asked Malcolm if I
was always that quiet. Malcolm told him I was only quiet when I was nervous. I
didn't realize he knew that about me. He pulled into the deli parking lot. He turned
around and handed me two twenties, "go get food. I'll meet you in a minute."
Then he opened his door to get out. He walked into the drugstore. Troy looked at
me like you better get moving. I huffed again and then I went into the deli. The
same lady was there, she was happy to see me again. Just like the times before she
made the sandwiches extra big, putting all kinds of extras in the bag. Malcolm came
to get me again, and like she always does she gets weird when he comes in. When
we pulled up to Momma Shuga's house no one was on the porch and there was a
brand new Cadillac in the driveway. The three of us got out the car but Troy stayed

52

on the porch. That girl was still on the floor with her baby and her hair all over her head.

"Grandma!"

"I'm in the kitchen."

I walked in the kitchen holding the bag of food. "Look who's here!"? Malcolm said all proud.

Momma Shuga got so happy when she saw me. I loved her reaction to me, even if I felt like I had no choice in whether I was here or not. "Oh baby!" She said putting her arms out as she came to hug me. "Where have you been? I miss you!"

"I miss you too!" I said

"How have you been?" She said as she took the bag from me and gave it to Malcolm. He took the bag to his room.

"Ok I guess." I was happy to see her. But I wasn't happy with Malcolm. I don't know what he thought was about to happen but I wasn't feeling it. He was gonna have to try harder.

"What did he do now?" She said looking at my face.

"He completely deserted me, then I see him more than once with some girl. Now he comes and takes me out of school like I'm supposed to be happy."

"Yeah she forgot to mention her little boy friend!" He looked mad again

"Do you think you're the only guy who wants me? If you're completely missing in action what do you think is going to happen? I moved on!"

He got in my face, "you broke up with him didn't you?"

I could smell his breath, a smell I had been missing for too long. "Yes! But you threatened him."

"He should've known better. I know they still talk about me at that little school."

"So I'm not supposed to have anybody while you have everybody?"

He looked at Momma Shuga, and then he looked at me. "Yes!" Then he started smiling.

"You're stupider than I thought if you believe that." I said

He smiled at Momma Shuga. "Ooh! She's mad at me isn't she!" Momma Shuga smiled and nodded yes. "Guess I gotta do something to make this better huh."

Momma Shuga chuckled as she went back to washing dishes. Then Malcolm threw me over his shoulder. He spanked my butt, and then he told Momma Shuga he had to go tame me. That girl was smiling when we passed the living room to go up to his room. The baby pointed and said, "hair momma! Hair!" My hair was hanging pretty long since I was basically upside down. He slammed me on the bed. "So lets have it out!" He said locking the door. I looked at him like he was crazy. "You're mad at me for not being home waiting for your call?" He picked up his ashtray. "Right?" I looked at him. "I had work to do! I couldn't be here waiting on you to call." Then he took a drag on the blunt and handed it to me. I refused it. He didn't like me refusing it, but he shrugged and hit it again.

"I called you in the middle of the night too." I said folding my arms.

He shrugged "I was most likely out. It's not like I can call you when I am home. It's not like I could come by your house, or send you a gift. All I can do is put change in your savings account. When was the last time you checked your balance?"

"The other day, it looks like you been putting more than change in my account."

"Nope that's just a little pocket money." He said taking another drag

"You can't be cutting that much hair?"

He smiled at me. "I'm cutting hair, and making a few other moves."

"You don't have a drivers license how are you driving?"

"How you know what I got?"

"You're not old enough to drive."

"I'm driving ain't I!" Then he looked at me, "any more questions?"

"Is Yvette your girlfriend?"

"I told you NO!" He barked

"Then who is she?"

"Just somebody I was passing time with. It sure made your momma happy to see me with her." He smiled

"Where is she now?"

"School I guess, I don't know." Then he exhaled, "why does she even matter? I'm here with you!" Then climbed on the bed behind me. He made me lean back and then he unbuttoned my pants. When I tried to protest he hit my hands away. He pushed the top of my pants down. He made me lift so he could push them down. He pushed my panties down then he started rubbing me. He put his other hand in my bra. I told myself to act like I didn't like it. But I couldn't help it. My body had been craving this for months. He kept kissing my cheek, "you like it! You like it!" I was trying to keep my face straight but it wasn't working. He was doing it perfectly, and I gave in to the feeling. When my body started shaking he took a condom out. As he started to go in, he stopped. "You haven't given daddy's cookies away! Good girl! That's my good girl! I'm the only one who hits this!" Then he withdrew really fast. He was mad the condom broke. He put on another and went back to working me over. My eyes rolled so far in the back of my head I thought I would be blind. When he was ready again this time he made me stand up and bend over the edge of the bed. This was new, and it made him go in deeper, I didn't like that he was deep enough. When I tried to bend my knees he picked me up so that I couldn't move and went to town. I thought he was going to burst through my throat. Then he effortlessly flipped me, he pushed my legs back and went in again! That sealed it he was trying to kill me! But it did feel better this way and I was able to get into it. Again he had to stop when he felt the condom break. He put another one on and went back to work. He was sweating so hard it was like he was pouring water on me. This time when he finished he finished hard! I had mixed emotions, on one hand I loved it and it was worth the pain, but on the other hand he didn't apologize for anything. I laid there wrestling with myself about how to respond.

"How was your summer?" He asked fondling my chest.

"Fine"

"Did you have fun at your grandparent's house?"

"Yes"

"Did you guys go camping?"

"Yes"

"How was it?"

"Fine"

He exhaled, "what's wrong?"

"Seeing you with that girl hurt me, and it was embarrassing. You only cared to see me when you saw me with someone else." I tried to stop them but tears came streaming out of my eyes. "Outside of the money it's like you forgot about me, like you didn't care. I missed you, I needed you!"

I thought he was gonna be mad at me for crying. But he kissed my cheeks, my neck, my tears, and then my lips. "Baby I was thinking about you. I even did something for you. But I don't know if you can handle it." Then he looked me in my eyes.

"Can I trust you?"

"Of course!" Then I sat up.

He still kept fondling my chest, "remember that teacher?"

"That teacher?"

"The one your momma put the Muhammad Ali moves on!"

"Yes"

"Lets just say he won't be bothering anybody anymore." Then he smiled a knowing smile.

"Really? That was you?"

"What was me?"

"Mr. Thornton told Sophia and I how they found him."

Malcolm smiled at me and then he kissed me. "As long as you stay a good girl, you never have to worry."

"What does that mean? Stay a good girl."

"If your pussy didn't still curve to my dick it was gonna suck to be you and that little L7 of yours. These legs will only open for me! You hear me?"

"Ok"

"You belong to me! I claimed you first, and I will be the last!"

"But how can that be? You don't want to get married and you don't want babies. I will have a family when I grow up." He looked at me real serious. "I don't care if you look at me like that, it's the truth."

"Look at these people around this house. All these kids running around here! Dumping them off cause they momma and daddy don't want them. My cousin Renee keeps trying to find a daddy for her baby and then she keeps making more babies. I don't have time for that. Now I might, and I do mean MIGHT rethink the wife thing, if you stay smart and loyal to me. But I can't have no babies, not today, not tomorrow, not ever!"

"I guess that seals it! I will have a family! I'm not scared of you Malcolm; we don't want the same futures. I guess after high school you will go your way, and I will go mine. I will have love in my life, the kind I want!" He stared at me so I stared back. "You don't scare me, do you know who my momma is?"

Then he started laughing. "Your momma is scary! I seen her in action, seeing her made me understand why you're so crazy." Then he laid his head on my lap. "We'll talk about that other stuff when you graduate, ok?"

"Fine!"

Things finally started to feel normal between us. I asked him if he could really tell that a girl has been with someone else. He said since I was a virgin I fit him like a glove, he could tell if someone else came poking around in his glove. I didn't believe him, but I didn't want to find out the hard way that he was telling the truth. He took me back to school in time for my last period. After school Sophia asked where I was all day and I told her that Malcolm picked me up. She asked me if it was good and we both laughed.

Chapter 7

I guess I should be happy that I get to see Malcolm more often now. He says I was spoiled seeing him everyday before. In addition to carrying a heavy class load, he's running track, and thinking about football or basketball. Plus he still cuts hair and whatever he does that keeps him out all hours of the night and away on the weekends sometimes. Jade said she still sees him with Yvette sometimes, or sometimes it's this girl they call Toni. She said they always wanna fight over him and one time they actually did fight. She said he just sat back and watched with a big smile on his face. When I asked him about it he just changes the subject or gets mad. Which means we argue cause I don't care if he gets mad at me. At school Charles still hangs with us, but he makes sure he's not too close to me. He has those same sad eyes like David had, and I just feel bad for him.

****

The school is empty and Malachi hasn't shown up yet. Malachi is never late, and I know Jade has to get to work, so she has to be in his ear about the time. Sophia and I keep looking at each other like what's going on. We went to the office and we called my house, no answer. So we called Auntie Lauren but she didn't answer either. Where is everybody? Sophia and I started walking home. When we were a little ways away from the school we saw Malachi's car coming towards us. The car pulls over and Sophia and I's mouth drop open when we see that it's Jade driving. Daddy had been taking her driving, but now it seems like everybody but Sophia and I are driving illegally. "What is going on?" I screamed.

Jade was crying, "get in!" My heart sank and we got in the car really fast We waited for her to tell us what was going on. She drove a few blocks and then she pulled over again. Her hands were shaking. I grabbed Jade's hand; Sophia and I were in tears already. "Ricky!" Then she started crying again. Ricky was this guy at school that liked Jade. Jade always said she ignored him. A few times he's pressed in too hard and either Malachi or Sonny has got in his face. But I was waiting, what did Ricky have to do with her driving Malachi's car. She took a deep breath. "I was leaving sixth period and Ricky was waiting outside the class. I tried to walk past him but he grabbed my arm telling me to hold on, hold on. I pulled my arm away. He kept pressing up on me, and he wouldn't let me go. Sonny and Malachi came and he started getting up in their faces. Then four guys came out of nowhere. They all started fighting."

"Where were you?" I asked

"I hit Ricky! I hit him a few times. He punched me in the shoulder. He was getting ready to hit me again, but Malcolm and Troy came out of nowhere."

"What did they do?" Sophia asked through tears.

"You guys know, Malcolm is a monster and his cousin is not far from that." She inhaled. "There was blood everywhere, and teachers were coming. Malachi and Sonny went with Malcolm, they told me to come get you guys. Malcolm said to bring you guys to his Grandma's house. How do we get there?"

I screamed! "Now Malachi's gonna know!"

"Seriously? That's what you think about right now? I don't know who's blood was who's and all you can do is worry about your dirty little secret? You are so selfish!"

"Oh come on! I'm not selfish. But there's no bouncing back from this."

Jade got so mad. "Well it's done already. So tell me where to go."

I didn't want to, but I told her which way to go. When we parked in front of the house, the porch was full of people as usual. They looked at the car. I got out the car and Sophia and Jade joined me. They were all looking like they always did. I opened the front door, and that girl Renee was sitting in her usual spot. She looked at us then she went back to watching her baby.

"ALRIGHT! ALRIGHT! 1, 2, 3!" Malachi's voice yelled. Then he yelled profanity. We walked to the kitchen; Malachi was doing the dance of pain, holding his hand. Then he gave his hand to Malcolm, "DO THE LAST ONE!!! 1, 2, 3!!!" Malcolm popped his finger back in the socket. You heard the pop. Malachi screamed again. "What happened?" I asked

"I dislocated a couple fingers." Malachi said shaking his hand. "Thanks man! Thank you for everything."

"Don't even think about it." Malcolm said

"No man, I owe you!" Malachi said, "it was looking pretty bad there for a minute." "Malachi!" Momma Shuga called out from her room.

"Yes ma'am?"

"You got those peas on your eye like I told you?"

Malachi looked around for the bag. It was sitting on the table. "Yes ma'am!" Malachi said putting the bag on his eye.

"Malcolm!" She called out.

"Yes?"

"I'm gonna have to sew your friend up can you bring him something?"

Jade had tears in her eyes. "He's gonna be ok." Malcolm said to Jade as he walked past her. Malcolm came with his ashtray, and a bottle of brandy. I looked at Malachi's eye, it was bruised and it definitely was going to turn black. "Jade in that bathroom right there. In the medicine cabinet there's some witch-hazel." Malcolm said. Jade stumbled around until she found the bathroom. She opened the cabinet and got out the bottle and some cotton balls. She came back in the kitchen. She put the wet cotton balls on his eye. Malcolm came back in the kitchen.

One of the guys from the porch who was a cousin came in the kitchen. He was big and scary looking. "So tell me what he look like again?" Malcolm described Ricky even down to the birthmark on his shoulder, where he hangs out, who he runs with. He told his cousin to go pay him another visit. He told him to make sure Ricky understood if he saw Jade coming down the hallway he better run the other way. He told him all of the Wallace's and their friends were off limits. "Got it!" Then his cousin put his hand out. Malcolm told him he would pay him when it was done. You could tell Malachi was impressed with what he just heard, but it made Jade nervous.

"Can I see Sonny?" Jade asked

"Of course! Come on." We all followed Malcolm. Troy was sitting on the bed. I fell to the back of the group. Troy had a cut over his eye. "Sonny pick your poison! You wanna hit this or take a drink?" Malcolm said holding them both out.

"I'll need one?"

"You could man up and just take it. Or try one of these to take the edge off."

"I can't go home like that either way. I'll just take it." Sonny said

Momma Shuga looked at her audience, "hi". She said with a smile. "I'm Grandma Barb, you can call me Momma Shuga." She said. Malcolm introduced everybody as Malachi's sister and cousin. Momma Shuga looked at Malcolm when he introduced me as Malachi's little sister. "Hi" then she went back to Sonny's eye. She gave Malcolm a threaded needle, she told him to sterilize the needle. Malcolm went to the kitchen and he turned on the burner. I was peeking from the doorway. He swabbed the needle with alcohol then he passed the needle through the fire. Then he swabbed it in the alcohol again. He winked at me as he walked towards me. He

57

gave the needle to Momma Shuga. Then she said, "ok, this might hurt a little". She smiled. Sophia grabbed her mouth as Momma Shuga started sewing the skin above Sonny's eye shut. Sonny gritted his teeth, Jade grabbed his hand. It looked like it hurt but Sonny was doing good.

Malachi, Troy, and Malcolm started talking about the fight. They were really excited and smiling. Malachi was reliving how they were out numbered at one point, and then out of nowhere Troy and Malcolm appeared. Malachi kept saying he owed Malcolm big time. Malcolm looked at me. "You mean that?" I shook my head no. Malachi not knowing what he meant swore it. Troy smiled and he started asking how big. Malachi was trying to think of something big enough.

Momma Shuga said, "there you go baby! And I won't charge you fifty dollars like the hospital." Then she laughed. "You are just as pretty as your sister. Goodness you guys got some good genes." Malachi heard that but it didn't filter. Jade said thank you. Momma Shuga came out the bathroom. "And you look like your daddy!" She said pointing at me.

My heart dropped as I watched Malachi's brain swishing around. "You met my father before?" Malcolm shot his Grandma a look, and she covered her mouth like whoops. "When did you meet my dad?"

Everybody's eyes bounced around the room. The only people who didn't know were Sonny and my brother. I put my hands up, "Ok! Remember that time my friend's mom brought me home?" Malachi nodded. "Momma Shuga brought me. That's when she met dad."

Malachi nodded his head, but he was still thinking about it. "But dad said her grandchild went to your school." I nodded my head yes. "But how would you...." Malcolm was holding my hand. Malachi turned red! "You're kidding right?" Everybody shook their heads no. "In the car now!" Malachi said grabbing my arm. "What's going on?" Sonny asked

Sophia patted his shoulder and followed us.

Malachi rushed me out the door; we were standing in front of the car. "Amber where you going?" One of the guys said

"She just got busted!" Another guy said, they all started laughing.

"Amber this ends now!" Malachi said

"But Mali I love him!" I said pleading with him

"What?" He was pissed. "You don't even know what that means!"

"I do! And I do!"

Malcolm came and sat at the bottom step on the front porch, Troy sat next to him. Jade, Sophia, and Sonny stood to the side watching. Malachi looked at Jade, "you know about this?"

"Ok, Malachi you need to calm down first." Jade said trying to be the voice of reason.

"Calm down?" Malachi started breathing

Malcolm walked over to Malachi. "Walk with me, talk with me." They walked to the corner. Malcolm put his hands in his pockets while he talked and Malachi jumped around like he was stomping the ground. All the people on the porch were laughing at how animated Malachi was. If I wasn't in fear of my life I might've seen the humor in it like Sophia and Sonny did. But my life was flashing before my eyes. Malcolm put his hand on Malachi's shoulder. They were down there for a long time. Eventually they shook on it and then they walked back. We all had question marks on our foreheads.

"Lets go!" Malachi said. We got in the car. Everybody was silent. Malachi drove to the Berkeley marina. He parked the car, and then he looked back at me. "Out!" I looked at Sophia and Jade with pleading eyes. Malachi opened my door, "out!" I reluctantly got out the car. He grabbed my hand and he led me away from the car. "My baby sister!" He was trying to find the words. "Momma and Daddy are gonna be so disappointed!"

"About what?" I didn't understand what everybody else saw that made him so out of the question. I love Malcolm, and being with him made me feel good. How could that be wrong?

"About this! You and Malcolm! You don't see how?"

"No" I really didn't

"He just offered Sonny pot and alcohol in front of his grandmother. It was so normal to them that they didn't even flinch. Malcolm is cool, but not who I want for my little sister. He has girls at school bending over backwards to lick his boots, and you wanna be one of them!"

"No I don't!"

"Do you think that's gonna go away once you're there?"

"I don't know," I said

"Look at Sonny, we all know he likes Jade. We all know Jade likes him. But he's.... He's on a different level. I don't wanna know half the things Malcolm's seen and experienced and he's younger than me. You're not built for the life he lives. But you've already made your choice haven't you?" I shook my head yes. "Momma and Daddy are gonna be so disappointed. Mark my words, this will blow up and when it does. It's gonna blow up big! You're writing a check your butt can't cash." He took a deep breath, "and when Daddy finds out… Ooh! Sucks to be you! You don't even know!"

"Are you gonna tell on me?"

He exhaled, "no, but I won't have to. Like I said its all gonna blow up." Malachi hugged me. "You always gotta do stuff the hard way."

When we got back in the car Sophia said, "so Malachi are you gonna rat her out?"

"Nope I won't have to." Malachi started the car.

We took Sonny home; Malachi went and talked to Sonny's mom and dad. Mrs. Copland came to the car. We all knew it was to get a look at Jade again. "Hello girls!" We all said hi. Then she directed the rest of her conversation to Jade. You could tell she approved of Jade. I was so happy for her. She had the nod from his parents, and our parents. Now it was up to them, and they both were acting gun shy. I would at least do like Rosalind and Benjamin, have a nice and respectable courtship. But who am I kidding? I took Charles beyond the level he was ready for. Maybe I wasn't built for a "respectable" relationship.

****

"Momma Shuga?" I walked in the front door.

"She in da back" the girl on the floor Renee said

I walked towards the back. "Momma Shuga?"

"Who's that?" She replied

"It's me Amber"

"Come on baby!" Momma Shuga was laying down. "How you doing honey?"

"I'm ok, you ok?"

"I got a cold."

"I'll make you some tea." I went to the kitchen before she could protest. I didn't understand why Renee wasn't back here taking care of her grandmother. Oh well that's why I was there.

Carey Anderson

Momma Shuga was the only one who did the dishes. The dishes looked like they had been sitting for days. This was probably why she was sick. I took my jacket off and got to work. I cleaned the kitchen even mopped the floor. She had a whole uncooked chicken in the refrigerator. I took her biggest pot out it was huge! She told me she had fresh herbs in her garden in the back but they had dogs back there. So I convinced little Sterling to be my helper since he knew the dogs. I explained what rosemary looked like and sage. I asked him to pick a twig of rosemary, and a handful of sage leaves. Then he got me some lemons off the tree. I boiled the tea and put lemon and honey in it. Sterling very carefully took the teacup and saucer in to Momma Shuga. I cleaned the chicken then I boiled it with the herbs. When the chicken was done I seasoned the broth, added fresh veggies and noodles. Then Sterling helped me shred the chicken. The soup was full of noodles and vegetables. Everybody was coming inside loving the smell coming from the kitchen. Tiffany and Penny, the two oldest of the little ones, promised to be in charge of storing the leftovers and keeping the kitchen clean. All the kids lined up with bowls. I brought the first bowl to Momma Shuga. I heard Malcolm in the kitchen. "What is going on in here?"

"Amber cleaned the kitchen and she made us soup." A little voice said

He popped his head in the room. He looked really happy to see me. "What are you doing?" But I could see sadness in his eyes.

"I was just helping out. Try my soup."

He disappeared and then he returned with a bowl. "Oh my God girl! This is good." He ate his hot soup really fast.

"Where are you coming from?" I asked

"A funeral."

"Oh I'm sorry!"

"Don't be." Momma Shuga asked him if he was ok. He nodded his head. "How much longer you got?" He asked, I told him I didn't have to be home until way later. He told me to come on. I made Momma Shuga another cup of tea and I brought her another bowl of soup. I noticed that Renee had helped herself to some soup, that annoyed me but I didn't say anything. Everyone was singing my praises. Tiffany and Penny took their assignment serious they enlisted the help of all the kids. They had one-person wash, one person dry, and then two others putting dishes away. One person was in charge of sweeping, and another wiping down the counters. I was impressed they were doing a good job. Everyone on the porch was eating soup too. I asked Malcolm who's funeral he went to, he told me it was a cousin's. When I attempted to ask him another question he kissed me. He was all over me in seconds. He was gentle at first, and then his paced picked up then the condom broke. When he put his last condom on he told me to ride him. With pleasure! He looked sad, so I did my best to make him happy. He flipped us over and he put my legs on his shoulders. He went to town on me, when he finished he finished HARD! When he carefully withdrew, he hopped up and started cursing. I didn't even see right away what the problem was. It looked like the tip exploded and his penis was hanging completely out.

"You didn't feel that?" I asked. He gave me the dumbest look. "It'll be fine, stop worrying." I said

He paced the floor back and forth. Then he told me I needed to leave. I didn't understand what I did wrong. I told him I just wanted to be there for him. He kept cursing and pacing. I got up got dressed. He took a notepad and pencil out. When was your last period? I told him it was just a week ago. He wrote it down, then he

60

kind of shooed me away. This is not the way I envisioned my Saturday ending. I don't know why he's freaking out so badly. It takes more than just one time to get pregnant, right?

****

The phone rang in the middle of the night. I heard voices then I heard Momma and Daddy bumping around. Momma came and said Auntie Lauren was in labor. She told us to go over to be with Sophia and baby Jeff. Jade told Momma she needed to go to school because she needed to take an end of the school year test. My tummy has been upset since yesterday so I was glad to stay home. Momma and Daddy got dressed so fast. I put clothes in a paper bag and I got in the car with them. Momma was so excited, there were mixed reviews on what this baby should be. Daddy, Malachi, Timothy, and uncle Jeff were all hoping for another boy. Auntie Lauren, Momma, Jade, Sophia, and I are hoping for a girl. I got in the bed with Sophia. And like lightening the parents were gone. Sophia and I spent the rest of the morning imagining what it would be like when we were married and had children. Sophia told me that things had gotten pretty serious between her and Richard. She told me they were in love, and that yesterday they went ALL the way. We spent the rest of the morning comparing notes. She told me it didn't really hurt the first time. I looked at her funny when she said that it didn't. We compared notes about size. Sophia said Richard's condom didn't break at all. I told her every time with Malcolm his condom broke. We came to the conclusion that either Malcolm was really big or Richard was really small. I told Sophia that I thought she and Richard were gonna wait like Rosalind and Benjamin. Then she told me Rosalind told her that Benjamin has started asking. I couldn't believe it. I asked her if she thought they were gonna do it. She told me it looked like they were going to.

Malcolm showed up at my school almost everyday last week. He kept asking me if I started my period yet. I hadn't, but I appreciated the attention. Malcolm didn't want me to come with him he just wanted to know. When Friday came and still nothing he got mad. He told me as soon as I started I needed to call him or Momma Shuga, and then he gave me her phone number. I don't know why Malcolm is so worried, I told him it takes more than one time to get pregnant. He got mad at me and called me a little girl. I stopped talking to him and I walked away. Now that it's Wednesday my period is two weeks late. I think Momma is getting nervous just like Malcolm she keeps asking us questions. I don't always understand them, but she keeps looking at me.

Sophia made scrambled eggs, and pancakes for breakfast. I ate my eggs then my tummy got upset. I ran fast to the bathroom. Sophia asked me if I was sick. I didn't know what was going on. My stomach was in knots and my chest was sore. I ate my pancakes slowly. We spent all day listening to records and dancing. I kept getting really thirsty, water never tasted so good. Early afternoon Momma and Daddy came home. They told us that I had a baby boy cousin named Joseph. Disappointed we still cheered for the new baby.

****

Sophia couldn't go to Nana and Poppa's this year cause her momma really needed her help. With each day that passed my heart sank further and further I couldn't think of a reason why I couldn't go. Jade and Malachi got passes cause they had jobs. I had no good excuse. When I called Malcolm in the middle of the night, I told him I wanted to see him. He asked me if I started my period yet. When I told him no he hung up on me. When I tried to call back his line stayed busy.

The last day of school I went with Sophia to say goodbye to all of our teachers. My period still hadn't come, I was three weeks late and my doom was closing in. At first we kept saying it was the stress of Malcolm asking every week for the first three weeks. But now that I'm three weeks late I'm running out of optimism. We told Mr. Thornton how much we were going to miss him and then we went to Mrs. Hernandez's class. She and Sophia were talking about the summer and her new baby brother. Suddenly I felt like I couldn't breathe. Momma was gonna kill me, Daddy was gonna be so hurt. And Malcolm wasn't talking to me. I started crying softly to myself at first and then my cry turned into an enraged scream. How could he just not talk to me? I was scared! Sophia and Mrs. Hernandez came over to comfort me. When Mrs. Hernandez asked me what was wrong I spilled everything. Sophia looked scared for me because after all I was telling and adult who could turn around and call my Momma. I cried so hard! Mrs. Hernandez was very nice about it. She encouraged me to talk to my parents, but Sophia and I knew that wasn't gonna happen. I didn't know what to do. When I finally calmed down Sophia and I walked home. I felt scared and alone. Sophia kept trying to convince me that I could still start my period any day and not to give up. We decided to stop at Bob's for ice cream. I needed something cold and creamy to calm my nerves. As we sat there eating our ice cream the door opened and closed but I couldn't even look up to see who it was. I just didn't have it in me. Malcolm sat at the table, his face was real serious.

"So I take it you haven't started?" He said annoyed. I shook my head no, but I didn't look at him. "Have you told your parents?"

"She's still alive isn't she?" Sophia said annoyed herself and rolling her eyes.

Troy started laughing, Malcolm stared at Sophia for a long time. But she didn't back down, that was her way of protecting me. Malcolm rolled his eyes, "I swear sometimes!" He pretended like he was strangling an invisible person.

Sophia rolled her eyes, "whatever".

"So what you gonna do?" Malcolm asked

"She gonna do? She didn't do this to herself!" Sophia said with more attitude

Troy belly laughed. Malcolm was getting fed up with her. "You know what..." He started to lift up in his seat.

"I don't know Malcolm." I said tugging on his shirt so he'd sit down. "I'm scared! My Momma's gonna be so mad," then the tears came. "And Daddy's gonna be disappointed in me. I don't want to make my Daddy sad!"

"Funny how you wasn't thinking of any of this before." He hissed, and then he leaned back in his chair. "I told you I don't want no babies. You better fall down the stairs or something." He shook his head; "I can't believe you're doing this to me!" I just kept my head down. I felt bad enough and now he was making me feel worse.

"I told you the summer was gonna be busy. I guess I can kiss college goodbye!" Then he exhaled, "how could you do this to me! I trusted you! I shoulda known all your talk about having a family later was just talk." Then he stood up, "I told you I didn't want this. You don't listen. I don't know what to tell you. I hope your Momma don't kill you. If you're smart you'll have an accident. But if you were smart we wouldn't be having this conversation right now would we?" He walked out the door with Troy right besides him.

I put my head down on my arms on the table. I cried so hard, Sophia rubbed my back. I decided I would go to Nana's to buy myself some time away from Momma and Daddy. Jade was so scared for me. I packed my suitcase; I even packed napkins praying for a miracle. I packed more than enough so it would look like I used some for last month too. When Daddy drove me to Nana's house I was really quiet. He said it was unlike me to be so quiet. I told him I was thinking about next year when I would be in high school. When we got off the freeway Daddy pulled over. He wanted to know what was really bothering me. I tried to convince him that it was nothing but he didn't believe me. When Daddy searched my eyes for the truth my heart sped up and then it slowed down too slow. I was so scared I started laughing. He didn't see anything funny; I felt even more horrible cause now I was on his radar too. Daddy hung out for a while he was watching me like momma does. Nana kept asking him what was wrong, and he wouldn't answer. I heard him tell her when he thought I couldn't hear him, "Annette's headaches have been still bothering her. But she won't go to the doctor. She says people get headaches all the time. I think the girls are worried about her. Amber has been acting weird recently." Then they walked into the kitchen I couldn't follow them without getting caught.

That night I snuck into Poppa's office and I called Malcolm, he was sleep. I was crying so hard. I was scared and I couldn't handle him being mad at me. At first he was mean, but then he softened and told me we would talk about it when I came back. Then he warned me, he was gonna be working hard this summer. So he most likely wouldn't be home when I called during the day and sometimes at night he would be out really late. But eventually he would be around. I felt better after he stopped being mean. When I hung up the phone, I sat there breathing. Then Nana walked in the room. My heart stopped. "Isn't it late for a little girl to be on the phone like this." She sat in the chair facing me in front of the desk. "So! You've gotten yourself in some trouble?" Nana looked mad and not nice and sweet like she normally did. I was frozen in fear. I heard stories about Nana and how she was a lot like Momma when Daddy was young. "Who was on the phone Amber?"

My heart was beating out of my chest. "Um!" I swallowed hard.

She slammed her hands on the desk. "Answer me!"

"Malcolm" I said lowly

She sat back in her chair. "Malcolm" she was trying to remember. "Is this the same little boy you were sweet on last summer?"

"Yes ma'am"

She sucked her teeth. "What is happening to the world these days! Are you in trouble?"

I didn't see any point in lying. "Yes ma'am, I think so." I put my head down.

"DANG IT AMBER!!!! You have to be smarter! You have to say no, and you gotta keep your legs crossed! Fortunately for you, there are options for young girls. It became legal just in time for you."

"Ma'am?" I didn't understand what she meant.

"Your momma can take you to the doctor to get this fixed." I didn't say anything. I didn't know what to say to that. What would be worse giving birth or killing my baby? I don't think I could live with myself if I did that. But Nana was so mad I didn't want to argue with her. "Now, I'm not gonna tell your momma as long as you promise to talk to her as soon as you get home. You promise?"

"I promise", I was afraid not to promise.

"Good! Now stay off my tele, Oakland is long distance from here. Come give your Nana a hug and a kiss." I came over and hugged her then she whacked my bottom. "You know your Momma's gonna spank you, don't you?"

"Yes ma'am."

"That might fix you up instead." She laughed but it wasn't funny.

Chapter 8

Even though I jumped off the biggest rock, wrestled with my toughest boy cousin Thomas, my period still did not come. I was out of ideas, I even fell down the stairs at Nana's but I only ended up with rug burn and Nana yelling at me telling me I was gonna break her stairs. I was trembling when it was time to go home. Jade and Momma came to pick me up. Jade was getting ready to take her driver's license test, so she needed all the practice time she can get. Momma and Nana talked for a long time. They laughed at things that weren't funny, at least not to me. Jade noticed how scared I was and she told Momma that we would load my suitcase in the car. Momma didn't understand why it took two people to do that, but Nana distracted her by showing her an herb that may help with her headaches. Jade hugged me and commented on how tanned I got. That did make me happy. She asked when I was gonna tell Momma and Daddy. I told her I was too scared to do it now. Then I told her what Nana said, I asked her if she thought Momma would make me do something like that or give the baby up. She didn't know. Gwen came out and we chatted with her for a while. Then she mentioned that her daddy, Uncle Frank, has been trying to catch Daddy at home for some time. He told her to tell Daddy to call, but since Momma came she asked us to tell him. Uncle Frank was a scary guy. Whenever I saw him I would straighten up like he was my Momma or Daddy. Gwen's mom didn't live with them anymore. I don't know what happened but Gwen has sad eyes when she says her momma's gone. We don't know if that means she died or just went away.

This trip the cousins and I shared stories about the spankings we got. Some of them were really funny, but some of them, we would all get quiet cause we had all been there. Then we talked about fights we had at school. The reasons why may have been different, but we all seemed to be angry about something.

Gwen asked what it was like to be able to go to the mall alone and shop. She always had to have someone with her when she went out. And forget about a boyfriend or a job. She was Jade's age and she envied Jade for being able to be out in the world. It made me sad to know that if I survived the next month I probably wouldn't have any freedom anymore. Once we were feeling really close she told us that one of the guys who works for her daddy is really nice. She has a crush on him, and they kissed before. She made us cross our hearts not to tell. Then Jade shared that she was in love with Malachi's best friend, BUT they both want to go to college before they marry so they were taking things slow. My mouth fell open cause I didn't know they talked. Jade said a lot can happen in a month. I asked her if they've kissed, and she said no. And she seemed perfectly content with that. I couldn't believe it. Then my sharing input just made me feel horrible. I was the youngest of the three of us and I had the worst news to share. I rattled it off so fast that I thought I might be pregnant and I hadn't told my parents yet. Gwen hugged me and told me she wished I would've told her sooner. She had so many questions; she asked me what sex actually felt like. I told her how painful it was at first and how I kept running from him. It took sometime before I really liked it. But I told her I loved Malcolm more than I liked doing it. She asked me if I ever put my mouth on it. And I said Eeewwllll! We all laughed, she said her dad doesn't think they know he always has the housekeeper do that for him. She said her dad and one of his guys talk about it all the time. She asked her housekeeper about it, and she said she was trying to show her on a Popsicle. She said she would teach us as soon as she learned. She said once Daddy and Uncle Frank talked she was gonna come visit us in Oakland. On the car ride home Momma asked how my visit with Nana and Poppa went. I told her it was weird being there without Jade. Then Momma said we're growing up and we won't always be together. Then she told me she missed me. She's never said that before. She said she missed my spunk; everybody's working and resting. I felt horrible about the energy I was about to bring.

The next day I went over Sophia's house. She was so happy to see me. I told her I didn't get my period. She was scared for me. I told her I couldn't figure out how to bring it up. We played with baby Jeff and Joseph for a while and then I went home. I felt like there was a time bomb ticking and my time was almost up. When Momma was out grocery shopping I tried to call Malcolm. Of course he wasn't home. Then I call Momma Shuga. She just happened to be home, as usual she was happy to hear from me. She told me to come over as soon as I could.

****

I told Momma I was gonna go look for a job. So I went to the bank to get ten dollars, my balance was almost at twenty thousand. My brain swirled, I definitely had the money to have the baby. Then I caught the bus to Momma Shuga's. Her car was in the driveway. No one was on the porch so the front door was locked. I knocked on the door and that girl Renee answered. She was annoyed that I woke her up. As I walked through the kitchen I noticed that it was still as clean as I left it. I knocked on Momma Shuga's door. She told me to come in, and she got really excited when she saw it was me. I couldn't even fake a smile. She told me that all the kids have been working really hard to keep the kitchen clean so that when I came back I would make them something else. I smiled but my mind was still troubled. She put her hand on my shoulder and she asked me how late was I. I told her two months, and she sighed. She told me I needed to tell my folks and I told her I just didn't know how, plus I was so scared. Sterling came in the room to tell Momma Shuga something and he got really excited when he saw me. He ran and told the other kids I was there. They all got really excited. They asked me to make them something. We went down the list and everyone agreed on French toast. Momma Shuga took a big roll of money out of her coin purse. She put it in my hand with her car keys. She told me to take her car to the grocery store and get what I needed. I told her I had never driven a car before and I was afraid I would crash. She told me it was only a car and she would just get another one if I crashed. I made all the kids promise to be on best behavior in the store. Tiffany and Penny wrote out the list of things we needed. My hands were sweating as I walked to the car. I unlocked Tiffany's door and she informed the little ones that only the big kids (meaning her and Penny) could sit in the front, and they had to ride in the back as she reached in and pulled up their lock. I moved the chair close to the steering wheel. One of the cousins walked to the car when he saw me warming it up. He laughed when he saw me and ran on the porch he kept saying, "look out world Amber's coming". All the kids had their smiling eyes on me. I wiped my sweating hands on my pants then I put the car in gear. The car started moving and I stood on the breaks. All the kids yelled "whoa!" And then we all started laughing. I did that pretty much the whole way to the store. I was so happy when we made it to the market. We got the things we needed to make French toast, and then we got things to make hamburgers for dinner. I was very proud of myself for making it back to the house in one piece. About six cousins were on the porch when we got back. They saw all the grocery bags and got excited. I made everyone wash their hands and I gave Momma Shuga her keys and change back. Momma Shuga and that girl Renee were arguing about me. Renee said I wasn't even family and she was giving me the keys to her car and money. She was her own granddaughter and she treated her worse than a dog. Momma Shuga told me to go back to the kitchen and not to mind that girl Renee. She was staring me down and that made me mad. But I went in the kitchen with the kids who were all waiting for me to tell them what to do. I put Tiffany in charge of the bacon, Penny was in charge of cracking eggs, and then she was gonna flip the toast once it made it to the pan. Most of the little kids did things like sprinkle the powdered sugar or stir the batter for me in between toast. When the food was ready I brought a plate with syrup in to her. Momma Shuga got really excited and she told me the plate looked beautiful. If she only knew I was copying the stuff Sophia did when she cooked. When the kids sat down to eat all you heard was smacking and slurping. The cousins came and made their selves plates. Fuzzy and Leonard even got in a heated argument talking about one cutting the other one in line for the food. Everybody was singing my praises and that made me feel good. Well everyone except Renee, even though she made a plate that she didn't want to share with her baby she still rolled her eyes at me and mumbled under her breath. I asked Momma Shuga why that girl Renee didn't like me, and she said, "cause she bald-head, black, and miserable!" She said some of her grand kids get jealous of Malcolm and so they were gonna be jealous of me by extension. That made me feel bad, but Momma Shuga said don't pay that girl Renee no never mind. The kids did a wonderful job cleaning up and then they went outside to play. I started feeling tired so Momma Shuga told me to lay on her bed. When I woke up Malcolm was standing over me. Momma Shuga was belly laughing walking back into the room. She was laughing at how I parked her car. She said it was all on the grass.

"So you been driving?" Malcolm said with a smile

I was so happy to see him. I jumped up to hug him and he told me to be careful. Then he showed me the stitches on his side. He was in a fight and the person stabbed him. He said the wound didn't go too deep, but it was sore. The sight of the wound scared me and I started balling my eyes out. Malcolm and Momma Shuga stood there with the same lost expression on their faces. Then Momma Shuga said I was definitely pregnant. Malcolm held me and told me to calm down. I told him I didn't want him getting hurt. Then kids came running when they heard me crying they were all frowning at Malcolm. He asked them what was wrong with them and they were mad cause he made me cry, and Doug said, "yea and she's supposed to make hamburgers later!" He was gonna be mad if he didn't get his burger. We all laughed, Momma Shuga told them to get, and wasn't nobody making nobody cry. Then Malcolm took me to his room. He was so excited! He said this summer had been good, and he was putting in work. Minus getting stabbed it had been a good summer. He asked me if I checked my account lately and I told him I went to the bank earlier. He smiled a knowing smile. Your man has been putting in work he kept saying. I loved seeing his excitement. I sat on the bed longing for him to put his arms around me and just hold me. I didn't want him to be mad at me anymore. In the middle of talking he looked at me. "You are so pretty!" I smiled because I wasn't expecting him to say that. Then he kissed me. I hoped I would see him today, but I really didn't think I would. His kisses even felt better than I remembered. He moaned when he entered me, he said I was so wet, and I was even tighter than before. He didn't put on a condom it was just me and him. He felt like silk and I felt like a willing slave to his rhythm. He never moaned like this before, he always talked to me, which I loved. But this time he couldn't even talk. He could barely keep his eyes open. I was right there with him though, my body started shaking, but the shakes keep coming over me in waves. At the end he squealed a high pitch squeak, that sound like he was trying to hold back or something but my body shakes, throbbing, and ecstasy grabbed him. He collapsed on top of me. He couldn't move, his legs were shaking and his body was still shaking, but so were mine. After a while we looked at each other, "what was that?" He asked me. I told him he was the expert he was supposed to tell me. He asked me if that was even real cause he had never felt anything like that before in his life. The look he had on his face was child like; he stared at my face tracing it with his fingers.

"I still don't want no baby. But I can't leave you hanging." Then he exhaled, "you want me to come with you when you tell them?"

My head popped up, "YES! Please!"

Then the kids started knocking on the door. "Amber can we make hamburgers now?"

Malcolm frowned, "see what I'm talking about!" Then he sat up. "GET AWAY FROM MY DOOR!" You could hear the kids running fast. He told me not to put my clothes back on yet. He said we had to do that one more time to make sure it was real. But first I could go make dinner with the kids. I put his sweat pants and a shirt on. I put his slippers on and I went to the kitchen. Tiffany was on fries; she and Penny peeled and cut the potatoes. Then Penny chopped all the other veggies after the little ones washed them. We had a whole assembly line ready. I made a bunch of patties, and then I told them always serve momma Shuga first cause she was their grandma and cause she paid for it. Momma Shuga said she liked the way I thought. Then I served Malcolm just like my Momma does for my Daddy. Malcolm like everyone else praised me for the food. As I was walking back into the kitchen to put Malcolm's plate in the sink that girl Renee was coming at the same time. "MOVE WHITE GIRL!" She barked at me.

All the kids stopped eating and looked. I kept trying to pull my temper back but I could feel my anger rising. My back was to Malcolm's room so I didn't know if he heard her or not. "What's wrong with you?"

"YOU ARE WHAT'S WRONG WITH ME!" Then she pushed me.

That did it! I knocked her upside the head with the plate and it shattered on her head. I kicked her, and she went flying backwards. I started to charge and Malcolm grabbed me.

"What's going on?" He yelled

All the kids started talking at once. Momma Shuga was standing in the kitchen smiling. "Renee!" She yelled, "you got what you deserve! Leave Amber alone! If you don't, you're gonna have to deal with me!" That girl Renee sat on the floor mad and crying. She had cuts on the side of her face. "Malcolm, I'll talk to you later. You guys go up to your room I'll clean up the mess."

When we got in the room I told him about the argument I heard them having and how she was staring at me. He smiled at me. When I asked him why was he looking at me like that he said, "you look just like your momma!" That was the nicest thing anyone has ever said to me. No one ever told me I looked like my momma, they always told me I looked like my daddy. Daddy was a handsome man, but I think they only saw color when they said stuff like that. Round two was just as good as round one if not better.

When we were done and we both caught our breath. He said we should go talk to my parents tonight. I was scared but I knew it had to be done sooner or later. I put on my clothes and I hugged Momma Shuga real tight. I was scared out of my mind. We got in Malcolm's car and he drove real slow to my house. Malachi was pulling up when we were. He took one look at my face and he already knew. He blew air and he shook his head. Daddy's car was in the driveway and so was Momma's. Malcolm and Malachi stood in the driveway towards the street talking; my mind was spinning so I couldn't tell you what they were talking about. Then a FANCY car was coming down the street. It had everyone's attention. It got to our house and stopped. Daddy got out of the passenger side of the car in the front seat. The driver rolled his window down, it was Uncle Frank and he said, "Malcolm?"

Malcolm's face was very serious then he saw that it was my Uncle Frank. His face was still serious, but it was a nicer serious. He went over and shook Uncle Frank's hand.

"This is my kid brother's place, what are you doing here?" Uncle Frank was studying Malcolm's face.

"I know the family and I came over to discuss something." Malcolm was studying Uncle Frank's face

"I see!"

"Well Tim it looks like I need to head on over to Jeff's. Looks like you got something important to handle." Daddy hadn't said anything he was just looking at Malcolm. "I'll come back around later." Uncle Frank said, and then he snapped his fingers at Daddy. "A!" Then he pointed at Malcolm. "He's a good worker, and very smart! I'm just saying!" Daddy nodded

Then Uncle Frank drove around the corner. Malachi looked at Daddy then he looked at Malcolm. He shook his head and said I told you! Malachi ran up to the house. He convinced Timothy to go with him around the corner to see Uncle Frank. As they were walking out Timothy slowed down as he saw daddy still standing in the street. Malcolm put his hands in his pockets.

Daddy said, "Jade's not home from work yet." And he started walking towards the house.

"Sir! I'm here for Amber!"

Daddy made a wounded sound and he stopped in his tracks. "WHAT?" Timothy yelled becoming enraged. Malachi pulled Timothy away. "We'll go get Jade dad." Malachi said pulling Timothy down the street.

"My baby girl?" Daddy said it with such pain in his voice. Daddy charged to Malcolm's face. "I welcomed you into my home! I genuinely liked you! This is how you repay me!" Daddy yelled

"Sir, by then it was already too late." Malcolm said

Daddy reared up like he wanted to hit Malcolm. Malcolm did not flinch. Momma looked out the window. "Oh no!" I whispered to myself. Then she came to the door. "Tim! Tell him to come inside." Momma's voice was calm, it was too calm. Still standing in Malcolm's face Daddy said, "you heard my wife!"

Malcolm walked inside like a man would, Daddy walked behind him like a bigger man would. I wanted to run away from that woman inside. Then I slowly brought up the rear. Momma's eyes were evil, all she knew was something had her man upset and she was going to get to the bottom of it. She shut the door behind me and I started trembling again.

"Have a seat." Momma said in that calm voice.

Daddy sat in the armchair on the left; Momma sat down in the armchair on his right. They sat there like royalty, waiting to hear from their subjects. Malcolm sat on the couch, Momma looked fine with that. When I sat down next to him you saw her internal light bulb go off. She looked at Daddy, his face showed pain, then she looked at Malcolm who's face was stone, then she looked at me and I was terrified. Momma spoke through clinched teeth, "what is it?"

"Momma" is all I could get out my mouth. I didn't even see her move she moved so fast. All I knew was my face was on fire and I was on the floor. She pulled me up by my hair. "I'm sorry Momma! I'm sorry!"

She punched my face. "Now you're sorry! Now you're sorry!" Then she dropped me. She marched out the room.

"Annette" Daddy said

Momma came back in the room with her belt-swinging wild I stayed on the ground and covered my head. I didn't feel the lashes exactly; my heart was beating too fast. But I knew she was laying into me good. Malcolm had moved out the way. Then I heard Malcolm say, "SIR!"

Then Daddy yelled "ANNETTE! SIT DOWN! IT'S ALREADY DONE! SIT DOWN!"

Momma hit me one more time then she sat down. Malcolm helped me off the floor. He touched my face and his eyes were so sad. Tears were streaming down his face.

"The fact that my brother speaks highly of you mixes in my stomach. That means you're capable of things I never wanted my daughter exposed to. Any of my children. I'm trying to raise well-educated and well-rounded adults. Are you coming to me as a man?"

"Yes sir!"

Daddy stepped in Malcolm's face. "I don't care what you are capable of. In order for you to do this, you clearly don't know who I am!" I looked at my daddy; I guess I didn't know either. Daddy didn't look like Daddy in that moment, and for the first time ever I saw Malcolm lower his head. "Leave my house! But when I call you, you better come!"

"Yes sir!" Malcolm let go of me, and he walked out the door.

"Why Amber? Baby girl why?" Daddy said as tears flooded out his eyes. "I wanted a better life for you than this."

Through my sobs I asked, "than what?"

"You're about to find out." He said

Chapter 9

I feel horrible. Everybody got on momma's case when they saw my face. She blackened my eye, and my nose and lips were busted. Momma said I've been lying to her this whole time sneaking around lying and then smiling in her face like I was an angel. Now I can't recall when have I've ever presented myself as an angel? But she was right, I had been lying and sneaking around the whole time. Jade tended to me as usual. Momma, Timothy, and Daddy argued for a long time in the living room. I was in so much pain that I started to dose off, but suddenly I heard Jade screaming. I forgot about my pain and I ran to the living room. "THERE IS TOO MUCH PAIN IN THIS FAMILY! IF YOU WANNA BLAME ANYONE OR ANYTHING FOR THIS, BLAME THE PAIN. AMBER'S IN PAIN AND NOBODY ACKNOWLEDGES THAT BUT ME! EVERY TIME SHE'S BRUISED OR BLEEDING I CLEAN HER UP! I TELL HER IT'S GONNA BE OK! YOU'RE ALWAYS WORKING, AND YOU'RE ALWAYS BEATING ON SOMEBODY!! YOU WANNA KNOW WHY MALACHI WON'T CHOOSE A PROFESSION? CAUSE HE DOESN'T KNOW WHAT'S GONNA HAPPEN TO US IF HE'S NOT HERE TO PROTECT US FROM OUR PARENTS! THE FATHER WHO'S NEVER HERE AND THE MOTHER WHO HAS HER OWN UNRESOLVED ISSUES!" Her voice started cracking so she tried to calm herself. "This little girl is angry and hurting. She's being sent out like all is well here. What did you think was gonna happen? She met a guy in as much if not more pain as her. What do you think was gonna happen?"

Momma was mad! "How dare you try to blame this on me!"

Jade didn't back down. "The day she met him you were on one of you tirades, and you beat on her and then you sent her outside. How does she catch the attention of one of the most wicked boys at school? Cause she was acting like you jumping on some girl!"

Daddy read Momma's mind and he held her back. "ANNETTE!"

"Look at your daughter's face!" Jade grabbed my shoulder and I whimpered due to the bruise that she grabbed. She moved me closer. "You never look at us after you do this! Look at her! You did this!" Then she looked at Daddy. "And you let her! Where do you think she's gonna run, away from you or to you?"

Everybody was quiet, first of all cause Jade never says anything. And secondly she was right.

Malachi came out his room real slow. "I wanna be an engineer, I wanna design cars."

"That's good son, you will be great at that." Daddy said

"I want to go to the Technology Institute Of Cambridge"

"Why didn't you say anything?" Momma said

"Because I'm needed here."

"No, you need to live your life. Get into the school and we'll handle the rest." Daddy said

Momma looked at me. She started crying so hard. She didn't apologize, but Jade was right, she never liked to look at us after she beat on us. "Now what?" Momma said

"What?" Jade asked

"You're the smarty pants who's been sitting back and judging everybody. So now what?"

"I don't know, but we've got to do better as a family. Amber is still just a little girl, don't let her just hang out there."

Everybody was quiet then Daddy said, "there are ramifications for this choice that I won't protect her from. But she's still my baby girl."

"Ok" Jade said still thinking

"Malcolm is rough, but he's proven to have a heart." Malachi said

"I'm not gonna give him my baby girl, no one is worthy of that!" Daddy said. Then the doorbell rang. We all looked at each other. It had to be Uncle Frank. "Girls, go back to your room. Annette go with them or go back to your room. Everybody give Uncle Frank and I some space to talk."

Daddy went to the door and we went to our rooms. I don't know what they talked about but they spoke for a long time. Jade made a hot bath for me; she put Epsom salt in the water. The hot water felt good. She stayed in the bathroom with me. We talked about the baby, I didn't really know what was getting ready to happen to me or even why. Jade laughed and said if my baby was hanging on through all this I must be having a little soldier. I imagined little Jeff or little Joseph saluting us and we laughed. I told her I wanted a little girl. Maybe if I named her Annette after Momma she wouldn't hate my baby. When I got out the bath I put on my nightgown I was getting in the bed when Momma came. She told us to put our robes on and come in the living room to see Uncle Frank. Uncle Frank was bigger than Daddy in every way, and his presence wasn't soft like Daddy's.

"Looks like you've got yourself in some trouble." He said looking at my face

"Yes sir!" I said putting my head down.

"It's crazy how small this world is, isn't it?" I kept my head down. "Let this be a lesson to you." Then Uncle Frank looked at Daddy. "Are you going to let her keep it?"

I looked at Daddy, he was thinking hard. "How will she ever learn if I don't?"

"So then he lives to see another day. Where does he live?"

I realized he was asking me. "I only know how to get there. I don't know the address."

"Who else knows?"

"Malachi." I said

"Perfect! Go get your boy and lets go have a talk with Malcolm." Daddy got up to go get Malachi. Then Uncle Frank said to me, "Finish school!"

"Yes sir!" I said keeping my head low.

Then Malachi and Timothy came out their room with jackets on. Then the four of them left. I thought about calling Malcolm to tell him that they were coming, but Momma opened her door. So I hurried back to my room.

****

This year's school shopping was so weird. I couldn't get the normal clothes I wanted to wear. I got mostly shoes and under clothes. Auntie Lauren gave me all of her maternity clothes. I had to take them, even though they looked like old lady clothes to me. The doctor told Momma I was about ten weeks pregnant. It took sometime, but Momma started being nice to me again. She told us that she was pregnant with Timothy when she and Daddy got married. Then she told Jade not to get any ideas. Jade shook her head no. Of course Momma wasn't fourteen going on fifteen when she gave birth. I told Momma that I was having a girl and I wanted to name her after her. Momma got so happy about that.

"You really do love me?"

"Yes, you're my momma. The only one I have." I said

She told me to think of a boy's name just in case. But I told her I didn't have to cause I knew I was having a girl.

Carey Anderson

Momma told us that she always loved the name Jade because it was a precious gem. She said that the first time she saw it she fell in love. She said the first time she saw Jade she was precious like the gem. She said they had planned to name her Lucinda if she was a girl. But they changed their mind when they saw her. Thank goodness! Momma said when she was pregnant with me she wanted another gem in case I was a girl. She said she knew I would be just like daddy. She said she liked how Amber started as one thing and then became powerful as something else. She said I've always lived up to my name.

****

Baby Jeff was walking, well running around and baby JoJo wasn't far behind him. I could only go to Sophia's house and home. So I helped her with the babies and her chores. Uncle Jeff taught Sophia to drive so that she could run errands for her momma during the day. Sophia asked when my stomach was gonna start sticking out, I didn't know. My chest had gotten so big, but other that nothing else changed. I asked her if she still saw Richard and she said whenever she could sneak away for a little bit, but never as much as she wanted to. We were in the middle of dancing with the babies when her doorbell rang. She answered the door and started screaming with excitement, I ran to the door it was Gwen. Her driver was standing outside of the car watching us. We brought her in the house. This was Gwen's first time coming to Oakland. Sophia gave her a tour of the house. Auntie Lauren was very happy to see Gwen. Gwen was full of energy she wanted to see everything. We asked Auntie Lauren if we could go for a walk. She wanted to know exactly where we were going and how long we would be. We told her we were going to Bob's for ice cream, and then we'd take Gwen by Raynel's to see Jade at work them we would come home. She thought about it for a minute then she told us we could go, but we had to take the babies. When we started to whine she said or just don't go. So we packed up the kiddies in their stroller and then we started on our walk. Fortunately they fell asleep as soon as we started to walk. I hadn't seen Malcolm since that night, so my wanting to go to Bob's was a little more than wanting to beat the heat with ice cream. We walked real slow down the street. Gwen's driver followed us in the car. I'm sure he was annoyed at our pace, but we had a lot of catching up to do. I told her about the baby. She looked horrified. She asked me if I was gonna put the baby up for adoption. I told her I wasn't gonna go through a beating from my Momma to give my baby away. No way! When we walked into Bob's, Bob was actually there. I introduced him to Gwen. He looked confused. "You're white?"
"No, she is." I said
"But she's your cousin?"
"Yea, Sophia's my cousin too."
"Ok, but I thought you guys were just creole."
"What's that?" Gwen asked
"French black, the creole people look like you two." He said pointing to Sophia and I.
Annoyed with the topic I changed the subject. I ordered a huge sundae, and then I asked them what they wanted. Laughing we decided to share my sundae although I really didn't want to. Bob told us that Malcolm was covering anything I ordered there. Gwen was impressed. Then Bob gave us sugar cookies for the babies when they woke up. We sat at our usual table. We were watching people walk by and laughing. I was really hoping Malcolm would come. Gwen's driver was standing outside in the heat. Bob gave me a double scoop vanilla cone. I took it out to him. The poor guy even had a little sweat trickling down his brow. He was very grateful.

72

Sometimes Love Isn't Enough

Bob asked who the Mafia looking guy outside his shop was. When we told him it was Gwen's driver, he asked if she was royalty. She said sometimes it felt like it. Then my heart sped up with joy! Malcolm walked in, his eyes were serious, but I knew he was happy to see me. I stood up and he gave me the biggest hug. He kissed my neck mid hug and my body instantly started tingling. Gwen's eyes were huge! "This is Malcolm!" I said very proud, "and this is my cousin Gwen."

"Nice to meet you." Malcolm said putting his attention back on me. He was touching my face and kissing my cheeks. "I guess you mean it when you say you love someone! I can't believe you went through all that just for me!"

"I love you! Of course I would!" We hugged again then he sat down.

Gwen was staring at Malcolm like people do me sometimes. I never like it.

"So you're Frank's daughter."

Her mouth dropped, "how do you know?" Malcolm pointed at the driver who was still eating on his cone. She kept staring at Malcolm then she said, "you are beautiful!" Her comment caught us all off guard. "Your skin is so dark and even, your eyes almost match your skin." She was going on and on.

Malcolm looked at me like "what's wrong with your cousin?" I shrugged at him.

Then Sophia said, "Aah! That's just Malcolm!" With a smile.

"Thanks Sophia." Malcolm said now blushing.

Then Troy walked in, "who's the guy in the suit?"

"Gwen's driver." Sophia said

"Who?" Troy said

"That's me." Gwen said giving Troy wanting eyes. Then she asked Sophia if he was hers. Sophia shook her head no as in no way! "And you are?" She said sticking out her hand.

"Troy" he said shooting the same looks back.

Malcolm put his arm around my chair. "Hey Troy watch yourself, that's Frank's daughter."

Troy hopped out of his seat like it burned him. "Really?" He looked disappointed.

"That doesn't mean we can't be friends." She said staring at Troy

"Don't be stupid man, that's asking to die." Malcolm said looking at Gwen annoyed. Then he looked at me. "All my little cousins keep asking when you're coming back. Tiffany and Penny have made French toast so many times we're sick of it."

Then I told Sophia how I taught Tiffany and Penny how to make French toast. "But that's not all she did. She got all them kids working together. They be ready to try and gang up on me, when they think she's not coming back. It took them a long time to talk to Renee again, and she's two of their moms." We laughed.

"Maybe Momma will let Tiffany and Penny come over. Sophia can show them how to make all kinds of stuff."

"Ooh! I like that, my own cooking class." Sophia said rubbing her hands together.

"You cook? I didn't know that." Troy said to Sophia

"Yea and she's really good at it too." I said

Then Gwen said, "I can cook too." The look she gave Troy, made him swallow hard.

Malcolm huffed, "I'm sure Momma Shuga would be ok with that. You should do that soon."

Then Momma and Auntie Lauren walked in the parlor. We all straightened up.

"What did I tell you Lauren?"

"Hello ladies, what can I get you?" Bob said with a huge smile.

"We'll be right there." Auntie Lauren said

"Was this planned?" Momma asked me

"No ma'am." I said trying to reflect honesty in my eyes.

Then Momma looked at him, "Malcolm" she said as she nodded at him.

"Mrs. Wallace" he said nodding back

"Who are you?" She said to Troy

"Troy ma'am." He didn't understand who she was.

Momma walked to the counter, "Malcolm you got this?"

"Yes ma'am, get whatever you like." When Auntie Lauren joined her at the counter Malcolm leaned in and whispered, "should I leave?"

I whispered back, "she kind of seems like she's in a good mood. Stay for now." Plus I really didn't want him to leave yet.

When Momma and Auntie Lauren walked back to the table Malcolm offered his chair then he smacked Troy upside the head and he got up too. Then they grabbed two more chairs. "This is really good ice cream, I see why you guys always come here." Sophia and I gave nervous laughs. "So! What are we talking about?" Everybody was quiet at first. "Don't everybody talk at once."

If no one said anything I knew she would get irritated and then watch out. "We were talking about his little cousins at his grandmother's house. I was teaching them how to make a few dishes before. I was wondering if we could bring the girls over to teach them a few dishes?"

"Who is we?" Momma asked

"Sophia and I"

"Lauren, is that ok with you?"

"I don't see a problem with it. Long as we get to know in advance." Auntie Lauren said

"Who's paying for the groceries?" Momma said looking at Malcolm

"I will" Malcolm said

"Good!" Momma said

"Can we do it tomorrow?" I asked

"I need to check with my husband." Auntie Lauren said

"You work tomorrow?" Momma asked Malcolm

"Yes ma'am I work everyday." He said

"Ok, maybe I'll take you to pick the girls up tomorrow if it's ok with their folks."

"It's just my grandma and it will be fine." Malcolm said. Then he looked at his watch. " I have to get back to work. I can pick the girls up after work if that's ok." Malcolm asked Momma as he handed Bob money. I don't know how much he gave him but Bob was happy.

"That would be lovely." Momma said

I wanted to stand up and kiss him. But Momma would've beat me. So I just waved bye. Momma watched my face as he walked away. She rubbed my arm, and then she changed the subject. Sophia pushed the stroller while I pointed out all the stores on the street. Then we got to Raynel's. Raynel came over and hugged Momma. "Are you coming to see me today?"

"No, my niece is visiting for the day so we wanted to show her where Jade works." Jade was shampooing a customer. You could tell momma was proud to see her baby doing what she said she was, working. "Your daughter is such a wonderful child. She's a hard worker." Raynel told momma. "How about you Lauren, when are you coming to see me?"

"I need to come soon, my roots are starting to show."

Gwen was taking it all in. She was very hot in the pants; every black guy was beautiful to her. Once I realized that I stopped taking offense to her flirting with Malcolm. Then we walked back to Auntie Lauren's house. Sophia took a glass of lemonade to the driver. I asked Gwen why she didn't take the driver things like ice cream or water. She said she never thought of it. I told her, if you rely on these people to protect you I don't know why you wouldn't keep them happy. Gwen was quiet like she was thinking about it. She went home a little after that. Momma and I walked home together. Momma asked me if Malcolm always acts that way with me. Was he always generous? And I told he was, I told her how he always gave me what he called change. She said that was a good sign. She even kind of smiled as she thought about it. She asked me how did he respond to me being pregnant. I told her the truth that he said he didn't want a baby. She asked me why he didn't use anything, and I told her he did but they always broke. I told her that was the first time he realized it too late. She took a deep breath, then she asked me if he and I were gonna get married. I told her we didn't have a chance to get that far yet. She told me I had to finish school at least first. I was fine with that. She told me she could tell that I loved him by the way I looked at him. I blushed. She said he reminded her of Daddy a little bit. I liked talking to Momma like this. She was asking me questions and listening to me. She wasn't staring at me, she was talking to me.

I called Momma Shuga and asked her if Momma and I could come and pick up the girls tomorrow. She agreed.

That night I kept staring at my stomach, wondering when it was going to show a sign of life in there. I jumped around in front of the mirror wondering if I was shaking my baby up. Jade laughed at me when she walked in the room. I gave her a run down of the day. She frowned when I told her what Gwen said to Malcolm, and how she was acting with Troy. She told me to watch out for Gwen, and that it didn't sound like she was up to any good.

****

When we pulled up to the house there were four cousins on the porch. They all stood up straight when they saw Momma. When we walked in the door they started giving each other five's saying Momma was a fox. I smiled at her and she blushed. That girl Renee was just waking up when she saw us come in the door. She rolled her eyes at us. I could feel the heat from Momma. I grabbed Momma's hand.

"Momma Shuga? My Momma's here!" I said all proud.

Momma Shuga came around the corner. She smiled and said hello, but it wasn't the same hello she normally gave me. Momma and Momma Shuga were sizing each other up. I didn't know why though.

"AMBER'S HERE!" Sterling yelled to the rest of the kids in the room. Then he ran as fast as he could to me. I picked him up hugged and kissed him. "We miss you! How come you don't come to see us any more?"

"I have to spend time with my Momma right now. But I'm gonna show Penny and Tiffany how to make something new for everybody, do you like that?"

"Yes!"

"Good!"

Penny and Tiffany came into the kitchen with the biggest smiles on their faces.

"Are you guys ready to go? Get your coats." I said

"Oh, their coats are in the washer. But it's gonna be warm again today. They should be ok." Momma Shuga said

Momma didn't say anything, but her face was not happy. Momma Shuga handed me a stack of bills. Then she went back in her room. She didn't say bye or anything.

"Ok, lets go." The rest of the kids looked sad, but I told them I'd send treats back for them. But they could only have them if they were good and kept the house tidy. The kids scattered and started picking up. As we walked to the door that girl Renee looked at us. "Where are ya'll going?" She asked the girls.

"To Amber's house. "They said together.

She sucked her teeth and got up like she was gonna do something. Momma looked at her, her look told her she didn't want none, and that girl Renee marched to the back of the house huffing and puffing the whole way. Momma looked at me, "what's her problem?"

"I don't know" I shrugged opening the door.

Almost all the cousins were on the porch now. They were all standing at attention with smiles on their faces. Momma stepped out behind me, and you heard somebody gasp. "Amber who dat?" Fuzzy asked

"This is my Momma, Momma these are all Malcolm's cousins."

"All of them?" Momma asked as her eyes bounced from face to face.

"Yep"

"She ain't old enough to be your Momma." Someone volunteered

I just smiled and told the girls to come. They were all in agreement that Momma was beautiful. Momma was blushing when we got in the car. I asked the girls what they wanted to make. They didn't know. We drove to the market and Momma was real quiet. The girls were quiet too. When we got to the store Momma stayed in the car. We walked around the store discussing all the possibilities. I wanted to show them how to make something that would stretch to feed everyone. So this time we agreed on chili and cornbread. I put a big pot and a big pan in the cart. Then I told them to pick out aprons. The girls were so cute, but their hair was wild and uncombed. Their clothes could stand to be freshen up too. I ran out to the car and I asked Momma what to get for their hair. She sucked her teeth then she came in the store. The girls looked a little scared of Momma then she reached out and touched both their faces gently and she smiled, which made them relax. She told me to get the blue hair grease and rubber bands. Then she walked back to the car. I picked out treats for the rest of the kids. We paid for our groceries then we went to the house. I told them we would start with the beans since they took the longest to cook and while they were cooking we would comb their hair. The girls were excited. We washed the beans real good, put them in the huge pot we just bought once the water started to boil we added the spices and turned it down to a simmer. Then I washed both of their hairs. Momma demonstrated on Tiffany's hair how to comb it out, how to put the grease on it and how to brush it. Once I got the hang of it she went in the kitchen to check the food.

Sophia came over with baby Jeff. She told me she had to finish her chores before she came. I did both of the girls' hair, and I was pretty proud of myself. I told the girls to go look in the mirror and tell me what they thought. I heard giggling and they both came back and tackled me with hugs and kisses. They thanked me so much. I told them to take the grease home with them. We showed Sophia what we were making. I told the girls that Sophia taught me everything I knew in the kitchen. Their eyes got big. Sophia gave them more spices to add and she explained why. They soaked it all up like sponges. When the beans and cornbread were ready we covered everything and we let them cool so they wouldn't be too hot in Malcolm's car. We played records and danced. I asked them if they were excited about school, and they shrugged. I gave them the whole speech about how important school is. They listened but they didn't say too much about that. Malachi came through the house really fast, he just got off work and he was gonna go meet Sonny. He said hi to the girls and they blushed. They told me that my big brother was cute. Daddy and Timothy came home. They made the girls blush some more. Malcolm came a little later. We told the girls how high to put the oven on to heat up the cornbread, Malcolm carried the heavy pot. We put the girls and food in the car, Malcolm hugged me. "I need to see you!" He said shaking his leg.

Instantly my body tingled at the memory. "I need to see you too."

"I got my license." He smiled, I hugged him again. "Maybe your dad will let me take you out?"

"Not un-chaperoned," I said disappointed

"I don't want to get you in trouble. I've seen what you're dealing with. I'm just saying that I need to see you." His eyes were real serious.

"Momma asked if we were gonna get married."

He blew air, "did you tell her we're too young?"

"I told her we didn't get to talk about it."

"Whatever. I'd kiss you but your Daddy's watching. I'll just have to see you later." He hugged me. "Thank you for everything."

I reached in my pocket, "wait a minute your change."

"Keep it," he said without looking back.

I walked back to the house feeling frustrated. When I walked in the house Daddy asked me if everything was ok. I said an unenthusiastic yes. Then I went in my room with Sophia. I cried to her telling how I wanted to "see" him I couldn't see how that was gonna happen now.

Then she had the idea, she suggested that he ask Daddy for permission to take me to the movies and that she would chaperone. Then we could pick up Richard and go to the drive in. I scrunched my nose, "you know that means we will be in the same car?" We giggled.

"Maybe Richard could borrow his brothers car. What do you think?"

My body was aching for Malcolm so bad I agreed. That night I called Malcolm and I ran the plan by him. I could hear the smile in his voice. The next day he asked my father and he agreed. I was excited. I was throbbing all day at the idea. I wore jeans so my parents wouldn't question my dress. Sophia wore a dress though. We went to the coliseum drive in not far from the airport. Richard was waiting on the street in his brother's car. We parked next to each other in the drive in lot. Sophia hopped out the car and she got in Richard's car. We climbed in the back seat. "Don't you want to put the speaker in the window so we can hear the movie?"

"Baby I don't even know what movie we're seeing. I don't care." He said coming in for his kiss.

It wasn't all that comfortable in that car. But we found a way to make it work. Malcolm's moans drove me wild; he couldn't get over how different it felt. But for one I was already pregnant so we didn't need a condom, and then all the extras no fear of pregnancy, etc. We stayed at it pretty much the whole movie. He put the box in the window and we watched the last few minutes of the movie. We practiced our summation of the movie in case they asked. We let the car air out as well.

As I put my clothes back on Malcolm stared at my stomach. When I asked him what was wrong. He said he couldn't believe I was pregnant. He never had a father, and he never wanted to be one. But then he said it, "but seeing how much you love me, how could I not love you? Nobody has ever loved me like this. Sometimes I just think, she's a little girl how could she know?"

"Momma Shuga loves you too"

He closed his eyes. "I guess."

I kissed the side of his face. "I love you so much! You are beautiful, and perfect!" I said

He smiled, "I love you too!" Then he took a deep breath. "But you're gonna hate me when school starts."

"Why?"

"Cause a lot of girls wanna be with me at that school. They think if they get me that I'm gonna give them money. You might see me with someone and think its something it's not."

"I will believe you."

"I only love you! And I've never loved anybody before. No matter what anybody tries to tell you! I would never tell any of these hoes I like they shoes!" Then he thought about it. "I don't want you fighting while you're pregnant either. If we have to have a baby I don't want it coming out looking like the elephant man, because you got mad at someone." I laughed, but his face was serious. "All that the other day with Renee could've got bad. I know she's skinny but she can fight. I don't want you to fight her."

"Malcolm I didn't start that. I don't know why she doesn't like me."

"I didn't say you started it, but next time let me finish it."

"Ok, but what if you're not there?"

"Anybody who knows me should know you're off limits. You let me finish it!" Then he kissed me.

Momma and Daddy peeked their heads out of the room when I came home, but they were a little preoccupied so they stayed in their room. The next day Momma was all smiles; she asked me if I had fun. She gave me a knowing look, and then she told me I looked so much more relaxed today. I didn't know what she meant so I kept a straight face. She thought that was funny, I was confused. So I thought I would err on the side of caution.

I told Jade what she said, and she got a confused look too. We couldn't figure it out.

****

The first day of school, I was tired, but excited. I was gonna see Cassondra, Rosalind, and Benjamin. I couldn't keep up with them over the summer like I wanted. Sophia walked over, but she was moving slow. I asked her if she was ok. She was sneezing; she said she felt like she was coming down with something but her Momma told her she had to go to school anyways. Malachi gave us this whole speech about how high school is so much more mature than middle school, and how he would act like he didn't know us if we embarrassed him. I thought my middle school was big, this school was huge. I had six periods just like middle school, but I loved that we could leave campus at lunch. I was looking for Malcolm all morning but I didn't see him. Homeroom was HUGE! That girl Yvette waltzed into the class like she was just the queen bee. Well not really, but that's the way I felt. She knew some girl sitting two rows over from me so she was facing me while she talked to the girl. Yea she was pretty, and her hair was stylish, and her body was nice. But I still didn't like her, and I HATE her name! I talked to Sophia in hopes that she wouldn't see us. Sophia could've cared less; she was dying for some medicine. The morning went so so, I couldn't spot Malcolm anywhere. At lunch I waited in the front of the school for Cassondra and Rosalind and Benjamin of course. Sophia went to lay down in Malachi's car. We walked down the street to the diner to grab burgers. Cassondra told us she didn't really do anything all summer but hang out with her sibs. Then Rosalind swallowed hard, Benjamin grabbed her hand, and she told us they had news. She said that they were engaged. They were really excited, and once again I was envious. He said as soon as he turned sixteen he was gonna get emancipated, they were gonna get married in the summer and then he was gonna join the military. Then she said their baby was due in March. Cassondra and I screamed! "So unfortunately I won't be here the whole school year." She said Then I shared that I was due in February. We all screamed again. Benjamin laughed at us. I asked them if they had seen Malcolm, no one had seen him all day.

Chapter 10

Malcolm said he had something very important to do for work that's why he wasn't at school for the first week of school. I was surprised when Daddy said it was ok for me to ride to school with him. I'm so excited; Momma said it was ok for him to call me too. She just said to tell him not to call too late. She said once the baby comes he's really going to need to be able to call me.

My baby keeps making me sick in the morning. She doesn't like when I eat hash browns or anything cooked in oil. It doesn't matter if it's the morning, middle of the day, or nighttime. If the food is greasy she gets mad and makes me throw up. Timothy gave me a long speech before he left for school. He told me to break up with Malcolm. He said just because he gave me a baby doesn't mean my life is over. I could tell it made him sad when I told him that we were in love. He told me that I may love Malcolm, but Malcolm doesn't love me like I think. I started getting mad so I walked away from him and I refused to talk to him anymore. That made Timothy sad; Momma told him it was no use trying to talk sense into me right now. She told him about when she told me that she didn't like Momma Shuga. That made me mad too. She didn't even know Momma Shuga. Momma Shuga has always been nice to me. She always tells me how pretty I am, and she's always happy to see me. She said Momma Shuga was a sneaky opportunist, and that she was always plotting on somebody. She only met Momma Shuga that one time. Again I got mad when she said that. I think she might've been jealous when I told her that Momma Shuga let me drive her car.

Malcolm pulled up as Malachi started up his car to warm it up. They sat outside chatting. Malachi likes Malcolm I could tell, but he still doesn't want me to date him either. But at least he's nice about it. Sophia wasn't coming to school today on account of her still being sick. I think she caught the flu or something. Momma didn't come out this morning, she had another headache, but she said this morning it wasn't as bad. Jade and I walked outside; Malcolm's eyes were serious as usual. I gave him a hug and he squeezed me tight. When we got in the car he asked me if I went school shopping. I told him Momma said it was a waste to spend money on clothes I wouldn't fit in a minute. Then he said that he hopes I don't get fat. I hadn't thought about that, and I don't know why but when he said it I got sad. It felt like he was saying he wouldn't love me if I got fat. I was quiet the rest of the car ride; suddenly I felt self-conscience about my clothes. When we got to school he introduced me to a bunch of his cousins. Girls and boys, there were so many I couldn't keep up. Some of them seemed nice, and others didn't seem to care who I was, but they all said hi because of Malcolm. Malcolm told me at lunch time he was going to discuss business with some of his people, so to just meet him after school at the parking lot. Suddenly everybody at school was looking at me and whispering. Malcolm told me not to fight so I kept blowing air out my mouth to calm myself. Clearly I had no patience. At lunchtime I waited in front of the school for my friends. Then I heard someone call my name. When I turned around it was Charles. The summer did him well. He was taller and he had a mustache coming in. He gave me a hug, and he looked genuinely happy to see me. It felt like eyes were all over us. Cassondra and Rosalind came over and he hugged them as well. Rosalind said Ben wasn't feeling well so he didn't come to school. Charles offered to take us to lunch so we all accepted. He had his grandfather's car, he asked me to ride in the front. But Cassondra told me not to, her face looked so concerned. So I rode in the back with Rosalind. Without even knowing it he took us to Malcolm's deli. I didn't think the lady Rita was there at first, a man was helping us. But she came from the back and she was so happy to see me as usual. She took over our order, and I introduced her to my friends. She asked if Malcolm was with me today, and I told her no he had business to tend to. She came and sat with us while we ate our lunch. She was telling us about all the places she has traveled to. She made the world seem big and wonderful. I never thought about leaving California before. When we got back to school we thanked Charles for the ride and we all went our separate ways. PE was my last class of the day. Our teacher Ms. Parker had us running laps, I was so happy to do it. When I was finished a girl named Abigail came over to me and started talking. I could tell she wanted something, but she was beating around the bush. Then she asked me how I knew Malcolm. I remembered that Malcolm said not to answer anybody's questions about him. I just shrugged especially because I didn't know where she was going with her question. She waited for me to say more, but when I didn't she got a little annoyed. Then she told me that he is dating her cousin Toni, and she saw me with him that morning. I looked at her, I didn't say anything. Malcolm said they would try this. I asked who Toni was, and then she smiled and said I would find out. Then she walked away. Everybody was looking at me, which was making me mad. I just sat there shaking my leg trying to calm down. After school I met Malcolm in the parking lot. He put his arm around me, which made all my anger melt away. I asked him how was business? And he said it was fine. He asked me how my day went and I told him what Abigail told me. He said, "see I told you this was gonna happen." I told him I wanted to fight her, and he told me to calm down. He reminded me that I couldn't fight anybody right now. I asked what was I supposed to do if she got in my face. He told me not to worry about it. We went to his house and the cousins were on the porch, but Momma Shuga wasn't home. We spent a little time in his room, but everything seemed rushed. He enjoyed it all the same though. Then he took me home. Momma was still laying down. Jade and Malachi were at work. So I did my homework then I made dinner. I called Sophia and she said she was feeling better and would come to school tomorrow. Then Rosalind called me she was in tears. She said she and Benjamin had a fight. She told him about our lunch and all the things the lady at the deli said about all the places she's been. Then he told her that they were going to go to some different places once he was in the military and that she would be able to tell the same kinds of stories. She told him she wanted to stay close to her momma after the baby was born. He got mad and told her she was trying to change their plan. She was crying so hard. She said that they broke up, my mouth fell open. They've been together since the sixth grade. I tried to calm her down, I told her when he calmed down they would get back together. She said they've never argued like that before, and she wasn't so sure he would come back. I told Jade about Rosalind and Benjamin. She told me that's why you're supposed to wait until you're married to start a family. She said anything could happened at the last minute. I asked her how things were going with Sonny. She looked sad, and she said nothing's happening. Nothing at all she said it seems like everyone is having sex except for her, and she doesn't want to. But she won't even hold his hand. I told her there were other things she could do besides having sex. She wasn't interested; she said they all lead to the thing she's not ready for. She said if she loses Sonny because she won't put out then oh well. I told her she needs to at least let him know that she likes him and explain where she was coming from. She said when they kissed she liked it; she said she really really liked it. But she could feel her body betray her by wanting more. So she shut down completely. I told her I felt bad for Sonny cause he probably thinks he did something wrong. She listened to me, but I could tell she was trying to be strong.

In the morning I tried to button my pants and they wouldn't button. I tried laying on the bed and sucking my stomach in, but they would not button! Jade walked in the room and she started laughing really hard when she saw me struggling with my pants. She laughed so hard that Momma came to see what she was laughing at. Momma smiled real big and told me it was time to put those pants away. I cried so hard, I didn't want to wear the old lady clothes that Auntie Lauren gave me. After huffing for a long time. I put on a dress, I told Momma I was gonna go shopping after school. She told me that was fine if I wanted to waste the few pennies I had on clothes that I wouldn't fit in for long. I just smiled cause I had more than a few pennies, and all my savings was gonna pay off today. When I told Malcolm about the pants incident this morning he and Sophia laughed really hard too. I really didn't see what was so funny about me flapping around like a fish out of water trying to get into my pants. But apparently everyone else thought it was hilarious. Again Malcolm told me he was going to be doing something at lunch. Which was fine cause we all piled into Charles' car again and this time we went for pizza. Rosalind was still upset; she said Benjamin is really mad at her still. I hugged her and told her it was going to be ok. Sophia informed us that she and Richard broke up too. She seemed to be ok with it though. Then we all noticed how much attention Charles paid her. It made me feel a little weird, but I told her it was ok if she wanted to go out with him. Can you believe they made plans for a date that Saturday? I shook it off though, or at least I tried my best. I invited Rosalind to come shopping with me after school.

After school Malcolm looked irritated and he told me he wanted to talk to me, but Sophia and Rosalind were riding with us. When we got to my house Sophia left to go home, and Rosalind sat on the porch to wait for me.

Gripping the steering wheel Malcolm said, "why are you having lunch with Charles?"

I had a confused look, "we're just friends."

"I'm not trying to hear that, what is he hanging around for?"

"He's not hanging around me he..."

"Are you cheating on me?"

"NO!"

"Is that even my baby?"

I gasped! I couldn't believe he would ask me something like that. "MALCOLM! How could you? You know you're the only one I've been with!"

He huffed, "I don't know why you're having lunch with him."

"He's not thinking about me. He's going out with Sophia Saturday."

Malcolm was about to say something but my comment stopped him mid breath. He got the biggest grin. "Really? What happened to my man Richard?"

I shrugged, "they broke up."

"Whoa! I didn't know Sophia got down like that!" He said with a big smile

"Like what?"

He was thinking for a minute. "Nothing! We're not breaking up so you don't need to be concerned with it."

"You can't see the future, it's not like we're married."

His eyes turned evil and he looked at me. "Listen to me little girl, I don't care who your Daddy and your Uncle are! When it comes to me and you, I am your first, your last, and your only! You got that?" I didn't say anything I just looked at him. He grabbed me by my hair and brought my face close to his, "YOU HEAR ME?"

"You're screaming! I hear you!"

"They'd have to kill me! And even then that might not help them!" Then he kissed me and put his hand down my shirt. I tried to move his hand, and get my hair free. And he just pulled my hair harder. So I stopped fighting, I didn't feel like having this fight today. He kissed me for a while then he gave me evil eyes and told me to kiss him like I loved him. Then he slightly bit my lip.

"WHY ARE YOU BITING ME?" I yelled touching my lip.

He smiled, "sorry".

I got out of the car and slammed the door. Rosalind looked at me with question marks on her face. I marched in the house, and he pulled off. I looked at my lip in the mirror; it felt worse than it was. I was mad, but I couldn't put my finger on why I was mad. Momma asked me what was wrong, and I told her nothing. Malcolm was just getting on my nerves. Momma was done with the housework and dinner was ready, she asked if she could tag along with us. So she drove us to the bank and then to the mall. When I gave Rosalind a pair of pants to go try on, Momma looked horrified. Rosalind just hung her head low. But Momma was real nice to her; she even rubbed her back when Rosalind started crying. I looked at my Momma like she was a stranger. I know Rosalind needed the affection, but I wish she would've acted like that when she heard my news. I kept blowing air cause I knew I was jealous and it wasn't Rosalind's fault. When we took Rosalind home Momma wanted to talk to Rosalind's momma. They talked for a long time. They actually thought it was funny to ask us if we planned this. Both Rosalind and I just blank stared at them. I just wanted to go home.

I stayed in a bad mood the rest of the night. Everybody was laughing and smiling and I wanted to smash each one of their faces. I went in my room and stayed on my bed. How come my Momma could be comforting to other people, but I get beat up? My feelings were really hurt. I guess my Momma just hates me. Maybe she never wanted to have me in the first place. I rubbed my stomach; my baby would always know how much I love her. She will not have to go through this. I started to calm down then I remembered her stupid daddy bit my lip. WHAT WAS THAT ABOUT?? I was mad all over again. I drank a glass of milk and I went to bed.

****

Sunday morning Sophia called me she wanted to tell me about her date. I wanted to get out of the house, Momma made fish last night, and the smell of it this morning was turning my stomach. I asked her if we could go for a walk. Of course she had to bring the babies, but they were happy to be outside so we took the boys to the nearby park. JoJo was a little wobbly but he followed his big brother everywhere. We put the boys in baby swings and then we pushed them. Sophia was still so pumped up from her date. She said that her momma and her daddy both like Charles. Charles took her skating somewhere kind of far by San Francisco. She said at the end of the night they opened the floor to dancing and they slow danced. She said she was going to come home like a good girl but they ended up kissing when he opened the car door for her. She said they pulled into a random alley and went at it. She said Charles told her he loved her. I tried not to roll my eyes. When she asked me what was wrong, I pointed out the obvious. One date, and no time spent together how could he love her? She said sometimes you just know. She couldn't understand why I was so upset. I told her she just broke up with Richard and now she's sleeping with Charles. I told her she was gonna get a reputation if she didn't slow down. Then she got mad at me and told me I was jealous cause she was free to do whatever she wanted, and I had a psycho boyfriend who knocked me up. She said no matter what from this point onward I was gonna have a reputation no matter

what I did. We were both mad! I told her not to come over my house no more. She yelled after me as I stormed down the street that Charles told her he liked her better, and that he was just using me to get closer to her. I put my fingers in my ears as I ran away. I sat on the porch crying cause everybody was on my nerves! I went inside held my breath, and I grabbed a jacket and my purse. I caught the bus to the Bart station and I caught Bart to the city. I walked around the wharf, I thought about taking a tour of Alcatraz, but changed my mind. I wandered around all day. When I came home it was evening time. Momma was sitting on the porch, she looked mad. She asked me through clinched teeth where I had been all day. She was sitting on her hands with her feet tucked under her. I told her everything that was bothering me. I figured she was gonna beat me anyways I might as well be honest. I told her how it made me feel when she was comforting to Rosalind, but she blackened my eye. I told her about the girls at school who are always
 watching me and whispering about me. And then Sophia was dating my ex who was a good guy. Momma didn't look mad anymore. She put her arms out to hold me and I flinched thinking she was gonna hit me. She laughed told me to stop being silly. But I wasn't playing I really thought she was gonna hit me. She had me sit across her lap like a big ole baby. It felt good too. She rubbed my back and kissed my forehead as she rocked me back and forth. She said everybody was out looking for me. She said when no one knew where I was they assumed I was with Malcolm, but when he called they all flipped out. Sophia told them that we argued about girl stuff. I asked her if I was in trouble? And she smiled and said a little bit. She said she couldn't tell if Daddy was more upset or Malcolm was. I thought about running away again, and as if she read my mind she told me not to even think about running again. We sat there on the porch. Malachi came home first, he gave me a hug and told me next time leave a note or something, and then he went in the house. Daddy came home saying the same thing as Malachi almost verbatim. He kissed my forehead and then Momma, and then Malcolm pulled up. I imagined the baby doing flips in my stomach. Momma stayed seated. Malcolm was visibly upset. As if Momma wasn't there he fired off question after question, where were you? Who were you with? Why didn't I call him? Once he reached the porch he picked me up kissed my lips. Momma looked embarrassed, but I lost all color. I couldn't believe he just did that and in front of my Momma. Jade came home a few minutes later. She had been at work, but she knew they were looking for me. Malcolm asked Momma if he could use the phone. She told him yes, and then when he went inside she smiled at me real big. I was embarrassed, shocked, and rendered speechless. She told me to come inside, and then she invited Malcolm to stay for dinner. Sophia and I made up over the phone. We sat at the table like a real family. Malcolm was even chatting with everybody like he was home. How could this be bad why, did Daddy make it seem like my life was over?
None of my clothes are fitting me anymore. I keep my coat on as much as possible. I try to keep as much attention off me as possible. As soon as the school realizes I'm pregnant I will be sent to a continuation school. I want to stay here as long as I can. But these girls keep getting on my nerves asking me all kinds of questions about Malcolm.
In PE since it was raining we were in the gym. I was faking a pulled hamstring so that I could sit out the game of volleyball. I was talking to a girl named Kelly in my class. She was nice enough. When the PE teacher went into her office Abigail came switching over to me with two other girls.
"Hey Amber, remember when I told you about my cousin Toni? This is Toni." She

said as she pointed to a girl standing with her. The girl really wasn't cute; it was insulting that they even came forward. I said hi in a so what manner. "We noticed you been getting round, you pregnant or something?" Again I just stared at them. "If she supposed to be pregnant, I wanna know by who, cause my man don't do white girls." The girl Toni said matter of factly. Malcolm told me not to fight. I tried to ignore them but they weren't going away. My leg started bouncing. "Malcolm just loves all of this. He can't get enough of me. So I know he ain't messing with this little girl. FRESHMAN!" Then someone across the gym said, "they ride to school together every day!" I couldn't see where the voice was coming from. "Oh so you think you just flash your light eyes, white skin, and curly hair in front of my man and I would just let you have him? Malcolm is my man!" Then she attempted to get in my face and I kicked her as hard as I could I hopped up ready to fight everybody. The gym erupted in thunderous noise. The other girl with Toni stepped back to let her get up to fight me. As she started to charge I looked for something to hit her with. This girl named Bernadette hit her. Toni stumbled it looked like she was going to pass out. Her friends got mad and went to gang up on Bernadette, but her friends jumped in. Bernadette told Toni if she wanted to fight me she was gonna have to come thru her. Bernadette was a big girl, and from the looks of her, if she wanted to lay Toni out she could've. The PE teacher came out her office asking what was going on. The way everyone froze it was like no one had been fighting. My heart was beating so fast. Bernadette nodded at me and walked back to the volleyball court. I couldn't remember if she was a cousin or not. After school I told Malcolm what happened. He got so mad, it was a little scary. Then he told me and Sophia to get in the car. He drove around to the front of the school. Toni was across the street at the bus stop with Abigail and the other girl. He honked his horn at Bernadette, she told her friends to hold on and she walked over to the car on my side as I rolled down my window.

"Hey!" Malcolm said

"Hey Amber, Malcolm."

Malcolm nodded at Toni, "how come she's still standing?"

"I didn't want to get suspended." Bernadette said

His voice got real deep but he didn't yell. "I'm sick of her! Put her down!" Then he reached in his pocket. He handed her a bunch of twenties.

Bernadette's eyes got big and she gladly accepted the money. Then he told her to get in, she called her friends over the four of them squished in the back seat with Sophia. One girl asked Malcolm who I was, and he said I was his girlfriend. The girl said an extended "oooooooohhhhh!" When we got to the Bart station Bernadette and her friends got out the car. He drove across the street and we waited. Malcolm's eyes were evil. When the bus drove away Toni and her friends were bouncing around. Bernadette's friend walked up to them she said something they didn't like. They walked up on her like they were gonna do something. I don't know what she was saying but they were so focused on her that they didn't see Bernadette and her other friends encircle them. Bernadette hit Toni and she went down. Bernadette looked at Malcolm, Malcolm nodded. She made Toni stand up and she hit her in the face again. Then she stood her up again. Anybody who tried to help Toni got beat. Toni was completely unconscious and then they jumped on her. I asked Malcolm to tell them to stop, but he waved me off. It seemed like this was going on forever, a man came yelling and Bernadette and her friends separated none of them running in the same direction. Even though they were pretty banged up their selves her friends went over to try to help Toni who was now laying in blood. I covered my eyes,

Sophia was speechless. Malcolm started clapping his hands and saying, "well done! Well done!" Then he drove up a few blocks to where Bernadette and her friends were catching their breaths. "You know you put that girl in the hospital right!" Bernadette smiled as she caught her breath. Malcolm handed her some more money, then he drove off. He was smiling all the way to my house. Sophia and I looked at him in shock. He completely ignored us. Sophia slowly got out the car. She told me she'd call me later. Then she ran home. I just sat there looking at him. He was still smiling but he didn't look at me. I asked him if he thought that was a bit far. He looked at me real serious, "I told her not to even look at you. Did she look at you?" I looked at him. "She was warned, I guess she thought I was playing." He shrugged. Then he looked at me, "what?"

"Why would you tell her not to look at me?"

"She came asking me questions. I told her it was none of her business!"

"Did you date her?"

"Date her???? Are you kidding??" He blew air

"But you dated that other girl?" He looked at me. "Is this what I can expect when you're done with me? You gonna have your cousins put me in the hospital?"

"Now why would I do that? As long as you stay a good little girl and do as you're told you'll be fine!"

Before I could catch myself I slapped him! "I'm not some hooker you picked up off the corner! You can't control me!"

He smiled at me, "you are so feisty! I love it!" Then he tried to kiss me. I pushed his face away and climbed out the car. I slammed the door shut and I stormed inside. Momma was looking out the window.

The next day everybody was talking about how badly Toni got beat up. No one would say who did it, but everybody knew why it happened. Because she stepped to me. Because I belong to Malcolm, because I'm carrying his child. Now that girl Yvette all the sudden pays me attention. I see her watching me, but she doesn't say anything. At least she's not stupid like Toni, but I do wonder why she doesn't say anything, did I mention I hate her name! Ms. Parker keeps looking at me; I think she's noticing my belly. My days at Oakland High are numbered.

Malcolm has been coming over every day. He and Daddy set up a game of chess in the living room on the coffee table. They come in the house staring at that table long and hard. I don't get what they're doing, but they're both very serious about their strategy. Malcolm moves faster than Daddy, but when Daddy moves Malcolm normally wonders why he didn't think of that maneuver. So I guess Daddy is winning? I can't exactly tell. Even on the weekend when he's not working he's at the house. He and Daddy talk a lot. Daddy stresses the importance of education, he tells him its fine that he works for Uncle Frank now, but he has to have an exit strategy. Malcolm takes it all in. Malcolm was doing a victory dance; I guess he made a good move. Then there was a banging at the door. The sound startled all of us. Daddy looked out the window next to him. He said it was a Cadillac out there. Momma opened the door and Momma Shuga came busting in the door. She was breathing heavy and her eyes were big. She hurried over to Malcolm, "Malcolm honey..."

Malcolm had a question mark on his face, "honey?"

"It's your mother!"

Malcolm was unmoved, "what about her?"

"She's in the hospital!" she said all dramatic

Malcolm didn't seem to care, "why?" He was still studying the board.

"I don't know, but sweetie we need to go!" She said touching his arm to make him stand

"Sweetie?" He said moving his arm not even looking at her. "Why don't you go?"
I was kind of looking at her funny too; she never talked like that before. "What is so important over here that you don't wanna know what's happening with your mother?" She said dramatically again.

He looked at her like you gotta be kidding. "Since when are you so concerned with what happens with her?"

"Oh so, you don't need to come home to screw they daughter no more so I guess you doing that here?"

Momma's face turned evil, I grabbed her hand in hopes that would calm her.

"Grandma! What do you want? We were having a peaceful evening, please don't bring drama over here!" He pleaded

"So now I bring you drama? I'm the only real family you got! You don't even know if that's really your baby!"

Momma started growling. "Barb! I'm gonna have to ask you to leave!" Daddy said standing up.

Momma Shuga sucked her teeth. "Seems like you guys wanna turn my son white too!" That hurt me! I thought Momma Shuga knew how much comments like that hurt me. Momma opened the door; "you must have a guardian angel with you! GET OUT OF MY HOUSE!"

"You guys are trying to take him from me!" She said tears pouring out of her eyes.
I could see the conflict within Malcolm, he was upset she was so upset, but he didn't like the stuff she said. "Grandma! Nobody's trying to do anything. I was just trying to interact with Amber's family like she did mine..."

She shushed him. "Don't discuss our business in front of them! Come home!"
Momma Shuga started walking to the door.

Momma said, "Barb! Don't ever step foot in my house again!"
Momma Shuga looked Momma up and down. "And if I do?"
"I'm not responsible for what happens to you!" Momma said

Chapter 11

It seems like every morning I wake up baby Annette keeps getting bigger and bigger. I can't even see my feet anymore. Sadly I've gotten bigger too. Malcolm thought it was funny to call me a fat girl until I started crying real hard. I was doing fine until I hit six and a half months. Then everything started blowing up. Ms. Parker sent me to the office. My counselor gave me this whole speech about how they didn't want to give other students the wrong impression, and it was for my own protection. When the secretary brought my file in to my counselor. She fell into her chair as she looked at my academic record. "Amber you're an excellent student, I don't understand how something like this could happen to you?" I don't know why that made me cry but it did. She gave me a transfer slip and she told me she hoped to see me again in the fall. But you could tell she didn't think she would.

Rosalind came busting in the office. She showed the counselor her belly and told her to send her too. I smiled cause I didn't want to go to this school alone. Rosalind told me that as soon as they sent me away she was coming too. Benjamin was still mad at her after all this time. I didn't know what was so bad that he could stay mad this long but he was. He even started dating a girl named Roxanne. Rosalind was so hurt.

Once my belly started getting big Malcolm stopped asking to be with me. He still hugs me and kisses me. But there is no passion behind it, no desire burning within him. I knew he wasn't attracted to me like this, which is why he started calling me fat girl, I cried so hard. The baby moves a lot now, but baby Annette is a good baby. She doesn't wake me up like Rosalind's baby does. Rosalind's baby kicks her in her back, her ribs, plays drums on her bladder. Baby Annette is always gentle with me. I rub my belly and I sing to her. She likes when I do that. She likes music too; she tries to dance whenever music plays. At night Jade tells baby Annette how to figure out math equations, mostly things that she's learn that day. She said the book she read says its good to talk to the baby while they're in your stomach. So she has everybody getting belly time. Malcolm talks a little bit, but I can tell it's hard for him. The baby gets happy as soon as she hears him. She starts moving around and kicking. The first time Malcolm felt the baby kick he looked like he was gonna be sick. Momma couldn't stop laughing, but she told him to say hi to the baby every time he comes over after school. He definitely was not into the whole baby situation.

****

Sophia came over in tears. She said her period was late and she didn't know what to do. She and Charles had been dating pretty strong these last few months. I told her to tell her momma and get it over with. She said Charles wants to get married. I wished Malcolm would come to the same conclusion, but he was sticking to his guns about not wanting a wife. So I was really confused as to why Sophia was so upset. She swallowed hard; she told me that she secretly was still seeing Richard too. My mouth fell open cause I had no idea. I asked why would she do that? She shrugged, she said when she and Richard broke up she assumed it was over and started dating Charles right away. Then once Richard found out about her and Charles he came to get her back. But her parents really liked Charles and she cared for him too. She said she kept turning him down, but one day in a moment of weakness she gave in to Richard, that night she had a date with Charles who didn't seem to notice. She said she didn't want to cheat on Charles but sex with Richard had gotten so much better. I asked her why they weren't using condoms, she didn't answer she just looked embarrassed. I asked her who she thought the father was, she said she really didn't know, just to torture her its probably Richard's baby. But she couldn't tell Charles she cheated. I asked her what Richard said about the whole thing and she told me she hadn't told him. I felt bad for Sophia but what could I tell her?

That night Charles came over and they gave her parents the news. Uncle Jeff and Auntie Lauren were upset, but they didn't react like my parents. They agreed to let them get married, but they wanted both of them to finish school. So Charles moved in with them. He got a job for after school and on the weekends. The wedding was very quick and in their backyard. I didn't tell Malcolm about the Richard part although I figured he knew it already and wasn't saying anything. Malcolm came to the wedding and he spent a lot of the time talking with Uncle Frank, Daddy, Poppa, Uncle Jeff, and the rest of my Uncles and cousins. Nana was disappointed when she saw me still big with my belly. I told her what Uncle Frank said, if Momma made me kill my baby they would've killed Malcolm too. Nana rolled her eyes like she didn't care, I was shocked. I didn't realize my family could be so cold. Gwen was still hot in the pants. I didn't like the way she tried to touch Malcolm when she thought I wasn't looking. Malcolm looked annoyed with her, and he kept walking away from her. Whenever she came where he was he went a somewhere else right away. Uncle Frank even noticed it, he grabbed Gwen by the arm and they went in the house. Uncle Frank came out, but Gwen didn't. I went in to check on her and her father's big ole handprint was across her face. She said he told her to cut it out and to never disrespect herself or her family like this again. Part of me wanted to comfort her, but the other part was glad he did it. When the party was over Malcolm stayed and helped everyone load up the tables and chairs. When we walked home he told me that the whole thing was a mess. He said Charles put his whole everything into a lie. I looked at him and he gave me a knowing look. I didn't say anything. We had to walk real slow cause I couldn't walk all that fast. When we got to the house we sat on the porch talking about everything. He told me it wasn't my fault that we weren't married and that it was all him. I just nodded although I wanted to know why he didn't love me enough to marry me. He kept looking at his watch like he had to be somewhere, but I knew it wasn't work so I kept asking him to stay with me. We went inside and the Saturday night movie was coming on. We sat on the couch with Momma and Daddy. I held on to his arm real tight. I fell asleep holding on to him. Momma told him to stay so that I didn't wake up. He held me all night but I could tell he was a little restless. In the middle of the night when I tried to touch him he kept moving my hands away. He was not interested in me like that for now. He kissed my forehead and told me to go back to sleep. In the morning when I woke up he was gone. I fell asleep so hard I didn't even know he left.

The doctor said my baby would be coming any day now. Part of me was scared cause I still didn't understand how the baby was gonna come out. But the other part was ready for baby Annette to come out so I could have my body back. The only nice part about being pregnant was that my breasts were huge, my hair got really long, and my skin was darker. I was almost Jade's color. I hope the tan stays at least. Sophia was due in August, but she started gaining weight right away. Her Momma told her to slow down on all the food and pies she was making but she didn't care. Cassondra would come over after school to visit with us. She and Jade started hanging out and they became good friends as well. She asked me if I was scared and I would tell her how scared I was. Her eyes would get big like she couldn't believe it as I told her how scared I was. She would tell me all the news about school. Who was dating, and who was breaking up. I asked her about

Malcolm and she would get sad eyes and look away. Jade wouldn't tell me either, she said I was pregnant and gonna have a beautiful baby soon. Momma and Malcolm rearranged our room to make space for the baby's crib. Malcolm promised that the crib would be here by the time the baby came home. I wanted to decorate everything in pink, but momma said we should wait until the baby comes or buy neutral colored stuff. I got mad cause I knew I was having a girl; I didn't know why she didn't believe me. Although in that dream I had, my baby was a boy and his skin was just as white as Daddy's. Malcolm got mad at me and screamed at me saying it wasn't his baby. Then Uncle Preston of all people would chase me around the room telling me I was ready like he used to all the time. I woke up screaming, Momma looked surprised when she realized I was having the nightmare. She crawled into bed with me; she rubbed my back and told me it was ok. I was scared to go back to sleep but Momma's rubs relaxed me and I fell back asleep.

****

Malcolm finally came over after not being here or calling the last three days. I screamed at him, I hit him, I told him to never come back! I was so hurt. I know I didn't look sexy to him anymore, and I know he didn't want the baby. But when you love someone you do things because you love them. He didn't pay me any attention, he told me I was over reacting because of the baby. I told him I knew he was running around with Yvette, and he just rolled his eyes. I screamed at him until he left, then I was so hurt that he left. Momma didn't say anything she just rubbed my back. She kept telling me to save my energy for the baby. Malcolm came back with flowers and candy. He was trying to be sweet to me but I was still mad I took the flowers and I started hitting him with them. Then I felt a gush and my pants were wet and the floor was getting really wet. I looked down I saw the water and I got scared. Malcolm's eyes got big and his voice got high pitched, "did you just pee?" Embarrassed I said I don't know. But the water didn't stop when I squeezed my muscles. I called for my Momma, Malcolm backed away from me even though I was still trying to hit him with the flowers. He looked disgusted. Momma came in the kitchen and she got happy, it's time to go to the hospital, she sang. Jade grabbed a few towels. She dropped one on the floor to clean up the water, and gave the other two to Momma. Malcolm was stuck; he just kept looking at my face. Momma popped him upside the head and told him to get ready to drive us. Jade left a note for Daddy and Malachi, and then we hurried out the door. I walked real slow cause the water was still leaking when I walked. Momma put towels down on my seat then she put me real gentle in the car. Then the worst pain I ever felt started at the bottom of my stomach and it traveled all through my body. I screamed cause it hurt so bad. Momma told me not to scream and to save my energy for the pushing. Jade rode in the front with Malcolm and Momma sat in the back with me. Momma told me to breathe like her, and it did help a little. The pain went away and I was happy it was over, but as we pulled up to the hospital the pain hit me again. I cried to my Momma asking her to make the pain stop, she said it was too late. The hospital people brought a wheelchair to the car and I got in it. Momma came with me, and Malcolm and Jade went to park the car. Momma told the lady at the desk my water broke, but my contractions weren't coming on strong yet. I told her if it was only gonna get worse I didn't want to do it anymore. Momma and the nurses laughed because it was too late to back down now. As they wheeled me to my room Jade combed my hair and put it in one long braid to keep it out the way. They gave me a gown, and they told me to get in the bed. As the nurse came to put in my IV a contraction hit me. I grabbed her hand, and she screamed bloody murder until I let go. She told Momma somebody else would have to come do my IV and that one of them had to let me hold their hand. Momma made Malcolm hold my hand although he looked like he wanted to be anywhere but in that room with me. When the next contraction hit me he didn't flinch when I squeezed his hand. But it almost felt like I was squeezing a warm rock. The pain went on for hours. I was crying I wanted it to all stop. None of this was worth it to me. Jade waited in the waiting room with Daddy and Malachi. A little after midnight the doctor came in to check me again, to my surprise he said he could see the baby's head. As they brought in the doctor's tray and got ready. Momma told Malcolm to stay up by my head. He shook his head and listened obediently. Momma stood on the other side of me and they told me to push. It felt like I was straining on the toilet with a really big load to dump. I squeezed Malcolm's hand and I pushed. Momma ran to the doctor's side to look. She got really excited and she started jumping up and down. "She's almost here!" Then she ran back to me. It started to burn, and then I felt pain, I screamed Momma asked what was that. The doctor said he had to cut me. Malcolm looked at Momma, and she calmed him telling him that was normal. Then I pushed and the doctor told me to hold although my body was ready to push again. Then he said "ok push!" And then I felt like I was on fire! The baby started crying and so did Momma. "Congratulations! It's a boy!" The doctor said then they laid the baby on my chest. Malcolm looked confused, "did he just say a boy?" Momma nodded yes with the biggest smile. Malcolm got real excited. Although they kept saying boy my brain kept changing it to girl. The baby stared at me. The doctor sewed me up and then they put ice on me. The ice felt so good. Then the nurse took the baby away to clean it. I was still holding Malcolm's hand. Momma went out to tell everybody. Malcolm kissed my forehead; all I wanted to do was sleep. The nurses cleaned me up, and took my legs out of the stirrups. They brought a wheel chair in; Malcolm picked me up and gently set me down in it. They had him wheel me to my room. Malcolm picked me up and put me in the bed. The nurses took my blood pressure and checked my eyes. Then they told me to get some rest. Malcolm stared at me, and then it dawned on me that they said boy. I asked him if it was true, and he said yes. I started crying. I didn't want a boy. I didn't even have a name for a boy. I was supposed to have a girl. Malcolm said I could name him anything I wanted. I just cried myself to sleep.

In a few hours nurse Bertha came and told me my baby was hungry and it was time to feed him. Momma was sleep on the couch but Malcolm was gone. Momma woke up when she heard the nurse talking. I looked at the baby he was so pretty maybe they made a mistake. The nurse showed me how to get the baby to open wide to latch on. The baby didn't play when it came to feeding time, he opened up and he latched on good. Nurse Bertha told me that he was a good baby, and she could tell he was gonna be special. Momma just smiled real big.

"Do you have a name for this little fella?" Momma asked. I started crying as I shook my head no. "Do you still want to name him after me?" And I shook my head yes. She said what about Andrew?" She told me if I was a boy they were going to name me Andrew, either way I was gonna have my momma's A. I agreed, I didn't really care. After he fed on both sides, I gave the baby to Momma to burp him. I asked Momma why he was so light, and she said most babies come out that way. Then she pointed to his ears and nail bed. She showed me that he would eventually darken to about that color. His ears were coffee brown color. I wanted him to be dark like his daddy no lighter than Momma, but oh well. At least he's healthy. Momma gave him back to me and we stared at each other. He was the most beautiful thing I've ever seen. I couldn't believe he came out of me.

Chapter 12

Malcolm came back to the hospital so excited that it was a boy. He brought so many people with him to see the baby, it was like at school. I couldn't keep them all straight.

The next day Momma Shuga came with a balloon from the gift shop. Momma was standing next to me when Momma Shuga came in the room. Momma Shuga looked nervous as she walked in slowly. She said she came in peace mockingly. Malcolm was holding the baby, and he looked happy to see her. She walked over to Malcolm; Momma's hands gripped my shoulder. Momma Shuga went on and on about how beautiful the baby was. If I hadn't heard her the night she came over I would've believed that she thought my baby was beautiful. I figured if she was saying something that she meant the opposite. Momma and I stayed quiet; Malcolm noticed. He looked at me and then he nudged Momma Shuga. She looked at him with a question mark on her face. Then he gave her serious eyes and nodded at us. She inhaled then she looked at Momma and I. She came over to the bed, "look, I wasn't myself the other night. I was talking out the side of my neck."

"How's your daughter?" Momma asked

"Who?" Momma Shuga asked

"My mother" Malcolm said with a smirk.

"Oh her" Momma Shuga looked down. "She's a junkie, it's just a matter of time." She said looking sad

I felt bad for her. Momma looked at my face. She saw that I was feeling bad for Momma Shuga. Momma got mad. "Bull!" Momma said, Momma Shuga cut her eyes at Momma. "You are so full of it. The only reason you're here is because he's here. You're afraid he's gonna leave, he's your cash cow right now. You've probably been telling him the whole time that the baby isn't his. You've been parading females in front of his face this whole time. You keep those kids around as possible money opportunities. You pump up that poor girl's head in the living room to make her hate my baby. Then you act like you don't know why she acts like she does." Malcolm started laughing. "She read you!"

I guess I was the only one who was in shock. "You don't like me?" Tears poured out of my eyes.

"Amber don't take it personal, she don't like nobody!" Malcolm said

Momma Shuga sucked her teeth. "I didn't come here for all this. I just wanted to see my great grand baby." Momma Shuga slowly walked to the door. Malcolm smirked at her again. I didn't see what was so funny. "Malcolm! You gonna let her talk about your Grandmother like that?"

He took a deep breath, "Grandma it's not like she said something that wasn't true. You just mad cause she called you on your stuff. Stop acting like that. Say you're sorry for busting up in they house like you did and lets just get on with it." Malcolm said

Momma Shuga blew air. She was annoyed, "I apologize for busting in your house like that."

Momma smiled and said thank you. Then Malcolm smiled, I on the other hand was sitting there with my feelings completely hurt for thinking that woman ever cared about me. Daddy, Malachi, Timothy, Nana, Poppa, and Gwen came to the hospital. A little while later Sophia and Charles came. Sophia asked me if it hurt, and I told her there were no words to describe how horrible it was. Her eyes got big but then she whispered that our first times were totally different so maybe our deliveries would be different as well. I told her I hoped so for her sake. Gwen was flirting with

Malcolm again. Nana didn't notice until she saw me frowning, then she saw Gwen's blatant flirting. Nana reached over and grabbed Gwen by her hair. She pulled her away and asked her what was wrong with her. Nana didn't take her out the room she yelled at her right there in front of everybody. She told her that she thought Gwen would've gotten the message when her daddy backhanded her at Sophia's wedding, but she was a stupid somebody! She told her if she didn't want to get slapped again she better shape up and fly right. Gwen turned red matching her hair. She sat in the corner embarrassed. Momma Shuga smiled showing she liked the way Nana handled Gwen. Nana looked Momma Shuga up and down reading her, and then she came over and told me to be careful. Poppa asked how I managed to get a private room in this hospital. Daddy told him he arranged it that way, I was surprised. That night everyone went home leaving Malcolm and I alone with the baby. Malcolm kept saying he couldn't believe it was a boy. The baby seemed like he just stared at his daddy and me. He didn't cry much and all the nurses said he was such a good baby. Malcolm kissed me on the forehead and then he told me he had to go. It was my first night alone with the baby. When Malcolm left we both kind of stared at each other. All the sudden I felt a huge weight on my shoulders. When this little boy grew up he was gonna say, "my momma did this, momma did that, that's why I don't like this or that." I felt horrible, I'm only fifteen years old and now I'm responsible for someone's life. I started crying, a few tears at first, and then I went into a full sob. The baby started crying I think because I was crying. I tried to comfort this tiny person, but it seemed like the more I cried the more he cried. Nurse Bertha came in my room to check on me. When she saw me crying she took the baby from me, which calmed him down and she sat on my bed talking to me. I told her my whole story and she was glad that Malcolm came around. She said a lot of boyfriends don't come around, and they deliver a lot of fatherless babies. She did make me feel better although I still felt horrible. The next day I only had a few visitors, Malcolm didn't come at all. Momma came and sat with me for a while, she talked to my doctor and when my six weeks were up they were putting me on the pill. I told Momma I was afraid of getting pregnant again, and every time I sat down to pee the awful burn from my stitches was reminder of why I wasn't interested. I don't know why she thought that was funny, I told her Malcolm was too big to put him anywhere that had been stitched up. Momma said I was going on the pill anyways. She said just in case I had a moment of weakness. Auntie Lauren and Uncle Jeff came to the hospital to see the baby. They left the boys with Sophia. Everyone told me that Andrew was beautiful; I felt he would've been more beautiful had he been a girl.

Momma and Daddy brought me home from the hospital. Malcolm only came back one more time and it was only for a brief moment. Momma held the baby while Daddy covered my eyes. They led me into my room slowly then they said surprise! There was a crib, a changing table and a dresser all for the baby. Everything was decorated in blue and yellow. Daddy said Malcolm bought all the stuff and he and Malachi put the crib together. The dresser was full of baby socks, burping cloths, T-shirts, and a few clothing items. Momma explained that Malcolm said when I felt up to it I could go shopping for clothes for the baby and he thought that would be fun for me. I guess he didn't understand that with these stitches walking was not fun at all.

Whenever Jade came home she came straight for the baby. She would hold him and sing to him. Momma took lots of pictures. I felt like I was going a little crazy, Malcolm hadn't called or dropped by and it had been a week. Jade said he was at school just like business as usual. He was never home when I called him. Chasing after him with the baby was too much for me. So I stopped calling, I just felt sad and helpless. I was happy to be able to bend over again. I celebrated with a silly dance. Rosalind came over after she got out of school. She brought my missed work to me and volunteered to take it back to school for me. She played with the baby while I did my makeup work. It felt good to think about something other than what Malcolm was doing. Cassondra came by with Jade. She made up this silly song that she sang to the baby. Andrew smiled at her when she sang it; she was very good with him.

Daddy would come and get the baby when he came home. He would be talking about anything and the baby would just look at him like he was taking it all in. I couldn't really say who the baby looked like yet.

****

At my six week checkup the doctor said I was doing well. He gave me a prescription for birth control pills. He told me it would take a few weeks for them to get into my system. If the doctor only knew how unsexy I felt. I was still chubby from having the baby. Malcolm didn't even look at me like he felt anything for me, and that was only when he came around. He said he was working and my bank account showed that he was, but I knew he wasn't working as much as he claimed. I finally got Cassondra to tell me the truth that she saw him with that girl Yvette. I hate her name! I thanked the doctor, but I knew I wasn't going to have sex ever again. I was afraid of the pain, and afraid of getting pregnant. Momma filled the prescription and she told me to take the pills anyways, then we talked to the school. They said I could finish the school year at the continuation school and next year I would be back at Oakland High. Hearing that put butterflies in my stomach. I picked my electives for the next year and I picked dance and Home EC. Momma watched the baby for me while I went to school. By the time I came home my chest would be hurting so much cause of the milk. Fortunately Andy would drink it all and I would feel so much better. Momma would make sure he was good and hungry by the time I came home. I love my little man so much, he's gotten a lot browner, and fortunately for me my skin didn't lighten too much after giving birth. I loved my new permanent tan. But with my tan my eyes seem to stand out more. People would just stare at my eyes sometimes. I stood in the mirror trying to figure out what was so great about my eyes. I didn't see anything honestly, Andrew's eyes were brown but they kind of glowed. I brought him over Sophia's house as much as I could. Andy would smile and laugh at baby Jeff and JoJo. They would be silly around him. Baby Jeff was starting to talk, and JoJo would babble on and on. I asked Sophia how it felt to be a married woman; she plastered a fake smile and said it was great. Of course I got her to talk to me. She said Charles was staying out late some nights, and the sex was awful. She said he had gotten so lazy that she would have to do all the work. She said they both lost interest in it. BUT she still saw Richard from time to time. He told her he liked the weight on her and he made her feel beautiful and young. She said the sex with him was even better with him than before. Then she asked me how the sex was with Malcolm after the baby. I pretended like I was gonna throw up. I told her he didn't even look at me like that anymore, and that I hardly ever saw him. She said I sounded like a old lady.

****

Andy is getting so big. His cheeks are so full and he's fat and sassy. He's a happy baby, and he always makes me smile even though I feel really sad all the time. After school and on the weekends I put on pajamas and I just lay down. Sophia normally gets me to put something on to go walking. I don't even do my hair anymore. It just stays braided in one long braid. But I always brush Andy's head of curls. Momma said you can't cut a boys hair the first year of his life or his hair will be ruined. So I have fun brushing his hair every which way on his head. I even brushed his hair all back into a tiny little ponytail. Momma and I thought he looked so cute, but Malachi hated it and threw a fit about it until I took it out.

Rosalind had her baby; she had a little girl that she named Tanisha. She was so pretty. Benjamin broke down when he saw the baby. He told her he wanted them to be a family. Rosalind agreed to get married and move away with him while he was in the military.

Nana told me to come a couple weeks early before all the cousins come to spend time with her and Poppa. So in a couple weeks on the last day of school Momma's gonna pick me up and we're going straight out to Nana's. Sophia can't come cause she's a married woman and Nana said she needs to tend to her husband. Sophia was so sad she cried. She didn't want to be stuck in the house all summer waiting for Charles to come home. I told her at least he comes home to her. I barely see Malcolm, and when I do it's only for a few minutes. He's bringing me money or something for the baby. He doesn't even hug me hello or bye any more. He doesn't look at me really either. It's like I disgust him or something. I don't know what I did for him not to love me any more. But my savings account continues to grow, especially after having the baby. It's like he put even more money in there now. I don't really touch it except for $10 here and there. I've even taken the baby to Bob's and nothing. He didn't show up at all. Momma doesn't say anything but I know she feels bad for me.

Daddy did his normal routine, he came home studied the board to make sure Malcolm hadn't played his next move yet, then he takes the baby in the family room with him or where ever. Andy gets so happy when he sees Daddy. The way Andy looks at things you'd swear he understood half the stuff Daddy told him. I heard Malcolm pull up so I cracked the door for him. I put on a pretty summer dress and I washed my hair. I tried to look casual, but I was really hoping he noticed my dress. Malcolm walked in said hey and went straight to the board. He studied the board hard then he made a move. He said hi to Momma and he went and said hi to Daddy. He said hey to Andy then he gave me money for the baby. I told him we were gonna go to Nana's for a month and a half. He just said ok and that he'd bring more money before we left. Momma invited him to dinner, but he declined. When he got back to his car Malachi pulled up. They stood outside talking for a while. Tears ran down my face cause he didn't even notice me. I missed when he used to talk to me; I missed when he used to look at me. I felt like I did something wrong. All dressed up and nowhere to go, I put my pajamas back on and I sat on the couch. Momma came and put her arm around me, I needed her hug. She told me I was in a funk and I needed to get out of it. She told me time away would do me some good.

I didn't even want to be there when Malcolm came by. I left the baby with Momma and I went with Sophia and Auntie Lauren to Sophia's doctor appointment. Momma said Malcolm hung around for a while then he left the money with Momma, kissed Andy, and he left. When we got to Nana's house she looked shocked to see me still chubby. She made me sit at the table, Momma was holding the baby, and then she asked me a bunch of questions. She wanted to know why I was sad? What I was eating? How much exercise I was getting? What was happening with Malcolm and I? I was fine until we got to the Malcolm part. I instantly started crying so hard. I told her how much it hurt that he acted like he didn't love me anymore. Nana listened to me cry it all out. Then she popped my cheek, she told me to snap out of it. She said no man loves a woman who doesn't love herself first. She said it doesn't matter what size you are you have to love yourself. Then she asked me if I like myself at this size. I shook my head no. She said I had to find my power and use it to be the woman I wanted to be. She said my power couldn't be dependent on a man's confirmation, because they will always do things to damage my power. She was a great motivational speaker to say the least. In the morning she and I walked to a cafe a mile away. We bundled up Andy and we put him in his stroller and then we walked. We talked about all kinds of things. Nana introduced me to all her friends there. They oohed and awed over the baby. Every morning we made this walk to and from the cafe. Sometimes Poppa came with us if he didn't have business to conduct in his office. I told them how I used to love to run laps at my middle school. Nana took me down to the CVC campus and she told me to run my heart out. It was hard at first. I got so winded, it was hard and I was frustrated. Nana told me we'd come back the next day. I didn't want to but I agreed. The next day there was a guy waiting for us. Nana introduced him as Tag. She said Tag was gonna show me how to run and how to get back to where I was in my running. The next morning Tag was at the house. He took me on a half walk and half run tour of Nana's neighborhood. Tag was really nice; he was a student at the college. He asked me what it was like having a baby in high school. I was honest with him, I told him how I felt and how Nana's pep talk really helped me. Tag said my grandparents seemed like really nice people. After a week I had my breathing down and I was getting stronger in my distance running. When Gwen got to the house Tag and I were just finishing up our run. Gwen instantly started throwing herself at Tag. Nana called her in the house she sounded like she was annoyed. I thanked Tag for the run, and then I ran in the house. Poppa had Andy, and Nana had Gwen in the corner she kept slapping her, and asking her what was wrong with her. Gwen was crying and crying, I almost felt bad for her. But I remembered how she shamelessly flirted with Malcolm hours after I gave birth so I didn't feel too bad for her. After Nana was done with her as if nothing had been happening Nana smiled at me and asked how my run went. That was a little scary how she could turn it off and on like that. Within days the rest of the cousins arrived. Everyone loved Andy; he got so excited to see everyone. Sophia and Charles wanted to come with Jade and Malachi for the camping trip. But Sophia went into labor early, but the baby was fine, they named her Sasha. Malachi said he didn't know how he was gonna go away to school next year, he missed Andrew so much over the past few weeks, Jade told me that I lost a lot of weight. I knew I lost some weight, but I knew I had more to go to be back to my old self. When everyone was getting ready to go home Nana told me to stay. I felt bad when Andrew cried at night, but Nana assured me that it was fine. So when Momma called I told her I was gonna stay. She said she'd tell Malcolm when he came by, and then she'd bring me the money.

****

Momma came as Tag and I were leaving for our run. We waved and then she went inside. When we stopped at our stopping point Tag said he didn't realize that my momma was black. He was staring at me, which annoyed me. So I asked him why he was staring at me rather than going his head like I wanted to. He said he was admiring my features. He said I was very pretty. I wasn't expecting that, so I started blushing. I told him he was seconds away from getting his face bashed in, and he laughed, but I was serious. When we got back to the house, Tag asked me out on a date. I was completely surprised, but I gently turned him down. I told him it was too soon for me. He said he understood and he didn't have a problem with waiting. When I went inside I told Nana that he asked me out. Momma and Nana looked concerned; first they asked me what I said. When I told them I turned him down they felt relieved. Momma said Malcolm expected to see us when he came by. She said he looked very thoughtful when she told him I was staying out here. I stayed in Concord the rest of the summer. When we got back Daddy was going through Andrew withdrawals, so we left them at home while Momma took Jade and I school shopping. Sophia and Auntie Lauren came along as usual. Since the baby came early she was gonna be able to start in the fall with me. Sophia kept telling me how good I looked. I told her how I tried on all my old clothes when I got home. My face looked like me again, I did feel like myself again. Shopping was so much fun, but I think it was more or less my appreciation for my reflection in new clothes. When we came home we passed Malcolm on the street. Daddy said he hung around for a long time, but he had to go. I bought Andy new clothes too. On the first day of school I rode to school with Malachi and Jade. It felt like a real version of going to high school. Only thing is for the first time ever Rosalind wasn't there. At lunchtime I tagged along with Jade and Cassondra eating in the cafeteria, Sophia had lunch with Charles and I didn't want to be a third wheel. I got nervous every time someone walked in. I was avoiding Malcolm cause he hadn't been paying me any attention. Plus I didn't know what his reaction would be to me once he saw how much weight I lost. By the end of the day I wasn't thinking about Malcolm all that much. When I walked past that girl Yvette her friend said, "I thought you said she was fat?" I smiled to myself and I thanked my Nana for that moment. That was the reaction I got from most people all day. Even Charles stared a little harder than a cousin should.

Bernadette said hi and she told me I was looking good. She asked me how much weight I lost and I told her fifty pounds. She asked me how I did it. I told her my Nana put me on a diet and all the running I did. She told me she may need me to help her in the future, but she wasn't ready today. I told her to let me know when she was ready. She asked me about the baby, I took out a picture and she said he was adorable. After school I hurried to Malachi's car. I waited in the car. I saw Malcolm's car pull up and Yvette hopped in. I felt like someone just punched me in my stomach hard. I was so done! I told myself not to cry. I was quiet the whole way home. Momma asked me how my first day back was and I told her it was fine. After a few hours I heard Malcolm's car pull up. I begged Momma to tell him I wasn't there. I ran in her room just in case he thought of a reason to come in my room. But he played his chess move, kissed Andrew, he talked to Momma for a little bit then he left. Momma asked me why I was running from him. I told her what I saw, and she asked me what I was gonna do? I told her nothing. I wasn't ready to have sex again, and I didn't feel strong enough to resist him if he wanted me. Momma didn't say anything she just listened.

****

The next day our dance teacher informed us that we were gonna perform in front of the whole school. I thought I was gonna die! She said we were going to have a full performance in December. She told us that we were going to need to practice at home as much as we could. Once I realized that Malcolm wasn't looking for me I didn't feel the need to rush around the school like a crazy person. I stopped acting like I was under cover. Whenever Malcolm came by the house I would hide. He didn't even look for me. I practiced the dance like my life depends on it. The day of the rally I was a nervous wreck all day. I showed Momma the leotard I had to wear in the rally. She smiled at me. I told her I felt naked; the worse part was that I wasn't worried about the whole school seeing me. I was worried about Malcolm seeing me. She assured me that I was gonna be fine. Malachi and Jade tried to comfort me cause I was so nervous. As I was getting out of the car Malcolm's car pulled up. OF COURSE! Of course I'd see him now. His eyes were serious; he scanned me from my feet to the top of my head. Although I had my coat on, he could still see that I lost weight. I looked at him and then Yvette got out of his car. She froze when she saw me, and I could tell she wanted to see Malcolm's face. I rolled my eyes and I walked away. I didn't know where I was going but I was getting out of there. Then I heard Malcolm call me, but I kept going like I didn't. As soon as I hit the corner I took off top speed to my dance class. Ms. Dubois stared at me. I smiled and said hey. She told me to go warm up. We spent all day practicing for the rally. We showered in the locker room, I was so nervous. We waited in the locker room. I had my leotard, tights, and little skirt on. Kelly and another girl were admiring their selves in the mirror. Kelly called me over to join them. At first I was laughing but then I started checking myself out. Wow! I looked good! If I do say so myself. My legs were defined and sculpted, stomach flat, waist small, arms toned, breast full, skin caramel, hair neatly swept into a bun. I really loved the reflection staring back at me, I said thank you to Nana again. It was show time each of us took our places in the gym. Ms. Dubois addressed the school. She told them that we were there to give them a sneak peek of what was to come in our future performance. I spotted Jade and Cassondra in the bleachers. I decided they were my focal point. When the music started so did we, I could feel Malcolm's eyes on me I just didn't know where he was. The first part of our dance was ballet, and then we finished with modern dance. The school went wild! When we finished everyone was on their feet begging for more. As we walked out of the gym I saw him. He was at the top of the bleachers, and Yvette was trying her hardest to get his attention. Our eyes met, and then I rolled my eyes. We all went back to Ms. Dubois' class. We all cheered and congratulated each other. I grabbed my things, I didn't want to hesitate just in case he was gonna come looking for me. On my way to Malachi's car people were telling me how good I did. When I got to the car Malcolm's car was gone. When we got home at some point I thought Malcolm was gonna show up. I put on my most relaxed outfit so that he would see that I wasn't concerned with him. By the time Daddy came home I realized he wasn't coming. I played with Andrew who was full of words and concentration. Momma and Auntie Lauren took the boys and baby Sasha out in the backyard. Andy was trying to stand to keep up with baby Jeff and JoJo. Momma said he was gonna be walking soon. I cried myself to sleep I was so disappointed. Oh well, I'm done with Malcolm.

****

It was like middle school all over again. No one would come near me on account of Malcolm and he was with that girl again. I didn't have to worry about seeing him, because if I did I would just roll my eyes and go the other way. Every once in awhile he would call after me, but I would act like I didn't hear him. When he came by the house he would ask Momma if I was coming home soon and Momma would tell him I didn't want to see him. He would just exhale and then he would leave. I needed to get away Jade had the Saturday off so we loaded up Sophia and Sasha in Momma's car with us and we went to Hilltop mall for a change of scene. They had a ice-skating rink, a movie theater, and a drive in. The mall was packed. We got donuts from The Donut Place and then we found seats by the fountain in the center of the mall. Then a guy approached us he was cute, but he was interested in Jade.

Jade was nice to him, but she wasn't interested. He walked away rejected and then his friend said, "hold on! I know that girl!" Then out of the sea of guys there was David. He was taller, he had muscles, and oh my goodness he was different. Sophia screamed when she recognized him. It took a minute for my brain to register who I was looking at. He gave me a hug and he smelled great. Then he hugged Jade and Sophia. He asked us what we were doing in hilltop. We told him we needed a change of scenery from Oakland. He looked at the babies, he asked who was who? Sophia reluctantly told him she was married and she introduced him to her daughter. Then I introduced him to Andy. I just knew he was gonna run away and not talk to me. But he said hello to Andrew and then he looked at me, "Malcolm?" I nodded an embarrassed yes. He smiled at Andrew who reached for him. He picked Andrew up and played with him a bit. Then a girl walked up, she was very pretty and she seemed like a nice girl. David introduced us to Patricia; she was his girlfriend, OF COURSE! She was very nice, she even complimented my outfit. I was done with this mall too. We left and I felt so alone and frustrated. After we dropped Sophia off I wanted ice cream, but I refused to go to Bob's. Since Jade still had the car she suggested that we go to Festor's in Piedmont. Excellent idea! In addition to my double scoop sundae, I gave my number to a guy, he seemed nice enough. I just wanted some male attention. When we pulled up to the house Malcolm's car was outside, Yvette was waiting in the car. I screamed when I saw her in the car! I stormed in the door; Malcolm was in the doorway when I came bursting through. I screamed at him, "HOW DARE YOU BRING HER TO MY HOUSE!"
Momma and Daddy looked at me and then at Malcolm. Malcolm's face was serious, "Amber!" He said like I was overreacting.
"Don't Amber me! Don't bring your hookers to my house!" Jade walked in the door with a sleeping Andrew. Malcolm nodded at Jade, and she nodded back taking the baby to the room.
"Can I talk to you outside?" Malcolm said opening the front door. Then he said goodnight to my parents. I was fuming, I stepped on the porch. "Calm down!"
"Calm down? Calm down?"
"Yes! Calm yourself down!" He said trying to keep his voice down.
"Why would you bring her to my house?"
"Amber I haven't seen you in months. Every time I come here you're gone. I call, you're not home. I don't know what game you're playing but I don't have time for games. You should know that the last thing I got time to do is wait around for a female to pay me attention. I guess getting your body back was more important than me."
"So you broke up with me without discussing it with me?"
"No, we got a baby. We'll always be together. But for right now I guess I need more than you're capable of giving me."
"You don't love me!"
"You don't make it easy!"
"What?"
"I gotta go." Malcolm said
"Just like that? You're done with me?" He looked at me. "I HATE YOU! I HATE YOU!" I tried to hit him but he grabbed my wrist.
Then Momma slowly opened the door, "Amber, there's a guy on the phone for you." Malcolm looked at me, he huffed. "Don't worry about my hoe when you got one or two of your own." He let go of my wrist and he walked to the car.

Chapter 13

I guess that guy figured because I had a child I would be easy. After a few conversations with him over the phone I was done. I really didn't have it in me to open my heart anyways. It took everything in me not to go after Yvette. Jade helped me to see and remember that this wasn't about her. Malcolm and I were at fault for this. I didn't understand what Malcolm was doing either. When our paths briefly crossed at school he actually seemed as uncomfortable as me. But he would try to make small talk with me and I would roll my eyes and storm away.

It was time for our dance recital. I had butterflies all day. Daddy came home from work early to make sure he brought Momma and Andy on time. Nana and Poppa came; Uncle Jeff and Auntie Lauren and children came. Charles had to work, so Sophia and Sasha came with her parents. Seeing Andy there clapping for me made me feel wonderful. I didn't tell my family about my solo, or the part of my solo that involved me dancing with a partner. You could see the surprise on their faces. But I couldn't help but notice Malcolm in the far background watching my every move. When the show was over my family all gave me hugs and told me how well I did. Then Malcolm gave me a box with two-dozen long stem roses in it. He kissed my cheek as he laid the box in my arms, and then he was gone. I felt weird about his gift, the roses were beautiful and it was obvious that he spent a lot of money on it. But I didn't understand why? My family took me out to celebrate my performance. I kind of wished Malcolm would've come with us, but I told myself to stop thinking about him.

****

There's a new kid Melvin at our school. He's cute and doesn't seem to scare too easy. He's in my dance class and he's really good. I about died when Ms. Dubois paired him with me. She said she wanted her strongest dancers together. At first I was scared to really talk to him. So I only answered his questions directly and I didn't leave myself open to small talk. But he was so silly and persistent that I eventually gave in to the conversation aspect. I figured it was only a matter of time before someone told him about Malcolm and my son so I waited. At lunchtime he implanted himself with Cassondra, Jade, and sometimes Sophia and I. They all agreed that he was nice and that I should give him a chance, but I was still afraid of rejection. One day our rehearsal after school went exceptionally long. Malachi and Jade had to get to their jobs so they had to leave. I was gonna call Momma or Sophia to come get me but Melvin insisted on taking me home. I was tired and really didn't feel like waiting so I finally accepted his offer to take me home. Melvin used to live in New York amongst other places. He was telling me about all the dance programs he had been in. He said he was gonna study dance in college. When we pulled up to the house he asked me who Malcolm was. I told him he was my ex boyfriend, then I huffed and the father of my child. Then I asked him why he asked, and he said because everybody keeps warning him about him. I asked him who "everybody" was and he continued to vaguely say everybody. When the conversation didn't stop there I was pleasantly surprised. Momma kept looking down out the window. So I invited him in. Momma was very surprised when I brought him inside. Andy came running as soon as I opened the door. When I introduced Andrew to Melvin, he got very shy and laid his head on my shoulder. Momma said he seemed nice enough, but there was something she couldn't put her finger on about him. Malachi didn't really care for him at all. I told him there was no reason for him to have loyalty to Malcolm when Malcolm wouldn't care. After a few times of taking me home eventually he was there when Malcolm dropped by.

We were showing Momma a portion of our up coming dance number. We were in the living room; Momma and Andy were sitting in the recliner watching. Suddenly the room felt cold. I looked at Momma and she said hi to Malcolm who was standing by the wall. His face was serious as usual, but he seemed stunned a little. Andy got down from Momma's lap and ran to his father's leg. Melvin was still catching his breath, but he went over to shake Malcolm's hand. Malcolm looked at his hand and then asked me who he was, kind of like he wasn't even there. Melvin stuck his hand out again. Malcolm tilted his head to the side. He looked Melvin up and down, and then he looked at Momma. Momma told him to be nice. Malcolm folded his arms and nodded, but he refused to shake his hand. Melvin shrugged like he tried then he looked at Momma and asked her what she thought? She went on and on about how good of a dancer he was. Malcolm picked up Andy and they went in the living room to look at the chessboard. Momma asked us to show her again and then she winked at me. I couldn't focus as good on the moves knowing Malcolm was right there probably watching. Malachi came home while we were dancing and he blew air, he was happy to see Malcolm. So he went in the living room with them. Then Melvin asked Momma if he could take me to a party Saturday night, he said there would be a lot of dancing and we could work on making our movements look more natural than rehearsed. She said it was fine with her but she'd need to check with her husband before I got a complete yes. I heard Malcolm suck his teeth, and then Malachi started laughing. Melvin told me he'd call me later. He hugged me and he hugged Momma and then he left. Malcolm and Malachi made fun of him. I stuck my tongue at both of them and told them to shut up. Momma asked Malcolm if he was staying for dinner and to everyone's, well maybe everyone but Momma, surprise he said yes. I sat Andrew in his high chair next to Malcolm. Then I let him go crazy on his spaghetti. Jade came home and sat right down. Momma told Daddy about Melvin. Instantly Malcolm and Malachi poked fun at him cause he was a dancer. Jade and I defended our new friend. Daddy asked Momma what she knew about him etc. then he said I could go. Malcolm did not like that answer but he didn't say anything he shot me a look. I smiled at the satisfaction of being able to put his nose in something. Daddy said he wanted to know where the party was and he said I had to be home by one. Malcolm looked like he wanted to jump out of his chair, but he kept his head down shooting me occasional looks. I was so tickled. Melvin was nice, but I left myself open and he wouldn't get the message. He didn't even mention the party to me. He asked Momma I guess as a way of asking me as well. Saturday morning Momma and I took Andrew to the mall to take pictures and then to find an outfit for tonight. I picked up pants and Momma would say no, no, no. I was getting frustrated. Then she picked up a sexy skirt and off the shoulder top. I gasped when I looked at it. Momma said, "I guarantee you! Malcolm will be there when you leave. And he may show up where you are. You gotta make sure he has a reason to follow." She smiled real big. I couldn't believe this whole thing was about making Malcolm jealous. Momma said of course it was, she said she doesn't think Melvin even likes girls like that. I didn't get why she said that, but now I was curious. I asked her if that was why Daddy said yes so easily having never met Melvin before? And she winked at me. I laughed so hard. I agreed to the sexy outfit. And then we found shoes and accessories. When Jade got home I showed her my outfit and she started blushing but she said she liked it. While we were fixing my hair Malcolm came over. He was trying to be real nonchalant, but you could see him watching everything we did. When she finished my hair, Jade put a little makeup on me. Melvin called to tell me he would be at my house in about an hour. I put my outfit on and Jade and Momma made sure everything was perfect. When I heard Melvin at the door Momma told me to wait until Daddy came to the door and told me my date was here. We were all quiet and straining to hear what was being said but we couldn't hear them that well. After a few minutes Daddy knocked on the door to tell me Melvin was waiting. Momma had to hold me still cause I wanted to run out there. Momma told me when I walked out I had to think Dianna Ross and how would she walk into a room when she knew she was fabulous. She told me to walk slow and to put a sway in my walk. Jade and I took what Momma was saying in like it was being engraved in our memories. She never told either of us anything like this before. Then Momma told me to give Melvin happy approving eyes even if he looked like a clown cause Malcolm was gonna be watching everything I did. Then she told me to be prepared for him to show up tonight. She said when he shows up look happy to see him, but don't forget I was there with Melvin. Then she told me not to break curfew either or else Daddy will never agree again. Momma and Jade walked out first; I took a few minutes to calm myself. Then I put on my performance mindset and I walked out like Momma told me to. Malcolm was the first person I saw when I walked in the room. His eyes turned red instantly, he clinched his jaw. Melvin looked nice, and he told me I looked beautiful. Momma and Jade stood there smiling so big. Malcolm's face was serious but he didn't say anything. Daddy reminded Melvin of my curfew and then we walked out the door. I guess he missed a step cause he fell and slid down the rest of the stairs. He was embarrassed and everyone rushed to the door. "Are you ok?" Jade asked, he said yes dusting off his pants and continuing to walk. You could hear Malcolm's goofy laugh all the way out to the street. We got in the car, and Melvin told me that the party was actually a club. I got excited cause I had never been to a club. He said it was a twenty-one and over club but he knew the bouncers and they would let us in without carding us. I was so excited; I had butterflies in my stomach. Then Melvin asked if Malcolm was always that scary. I told him he doesn't seem so scary all the time once you get to know him. But that was him. Melvin strutted like he was the stuff, he twirled me in front of the bouncers and they gave him five's telling him he was the man. I just smiled; I still went through my ugly duckling phases so it was nice to be looked at as beautiful for a change. We put our coats down at a table and we went right out on the floor. Disco music just made you move even if you thought you could just sit down you couldn't. We would dance and then stand by the door for some fresh air. I was sitting at the table when I saw Troy walk past me. He had drinks in his hands and he was walking to a table. Melvin came to our table with some friends of his. I couldn't hear their names it was too loud. But I shook their hands and said hello anyways. The girl asked if she could dance with Melvin and of course I said yes. The guy took me by the hand and we were off on the floor again. This guy had an "interesting" way of dancing. He moved his hips just like me if not better, he was a great dancer and a lot of fun, but yea he was not interested in me. He told me he loved my outfit and he wished he had my hair. Some of the moves I made he tried to mimic it was like he was taking lessons from me. It was so amusing. When we sat down I asked him his name again and he told me it was Stefan. Stefan was thin and cocoa brown. His clothes were loud and very stylish and he was very dramatic about everything. When Melvin and the girl came back to the table I asked her name again, she said Tammy. She asked me to come to the bathroom with her. Tammy was honey yellow complexion, her hair was jet black and wavy. She had bangs and the rest of her hair was pulled up. Tammy was definitely older than me.

Stefan and Tammy looked old enough to legally be in this club. Tammy was really nice, she kind of confirmed Momma's suspicion. She asked me how I knew Melvin, and she told me that she loved going out with Stefan and Melvin cause she could have a good time and not worry about being felt up. Then she said Melvin sometimes liked girls too. She was giving me a heads up, and I appreciated that. When we came back to the table, I looked back in the direction I saw Troy and sure enough there was Malcolm, MAN! Momma was good! He had gone home and changed he looked nice, but he had Yvette with him. I nodded at him and he nodded back. Then Troy came to our table. "Hey Amber, who's your friends?" So I introduced him to everyone. He was heading to the bar and he wanted to know what we wanted. I had never drunken before so I had no idea of what to order. Tammy told Troy to bring us the house special whatever it may be. Troy came back and a waitress was following him. He pointed to our table. She set a drink in front of each of us. The drink was pink and orange color, with a cherry floating in it. I stirred my drink and then I took a sip. I could taste pineapple and orange juice, it had a little bubble to it like it had ginger ale or something in it, and then there was a alcohol taste to it. But I liked it. Plus it was cold with all the ice in it and I was hot from all the dancing. I drank it like soda; Tammy smiled at me and told me to go slow. But she said that after I had finished my drink. Troy came by the table he took my empty glass and he brought back another fresh drink. Tammy asked Melvin who Troy was and he didn't know. So I told them he was Malcolm's cousin. So then I had to fill Tammy and Stefan in on who Malcolm was. I pointed him out and Stefan said, "oh honey he's so black how could you find him in a dark place like this?" Then he laughed, "who is the FABULOUS vixen sitting next to him?" I huffed, "his girlfriend".

"She may be FABULOUS, but she doesn't compare to you." Tammy said, I thanked her for the compliment. I took a few more sips of my drink and then I told Melvin to dance with me. As we walked to the dance floor my lips felt numb, and I felt tingly. Melvin and I danced song after song. Then I went back to the table to get a few more sips of my drink. Tammy and I went to the bathroom again. Tammy told me that Malcolm was very handsome when she actually saw his face. She said he came over and chatted with her and Stefan while Melvin and I were on the dance floor. She said Stefan was fanning himself after Malcolm left. He kept saying Malcolm was dark and mysterious and how he would have his baby too. We laughed a good laugh. Tammy told me to drink water to start cooling off before I went home and pissed off my parents. She said she liked hanging out with me and hoped I would be able to come out with them again in the future. I told her I liked her too. I drank the rest of my drink then I gulped down water glass after water glass. Malcolm didn't get up to dance once. Troy danced with me to a couple of songs, he wasn't a great dancer like Melvin but he was still a lot of fun. I thanked Troy for the drinks he gave me and my friends and he said that was Malcolm he was just the delivery boy. At 12:30 I told Melvin we had to go, but he could barely stand. I got nervous about him driving. Troy came over and asked if everything was ok. I told him I needed to get home and Melvin couldn't drive. Troy got keys from Malcolm and he told me he'd take me home. Tammy ordered Melvin some coffee cause he was their ride home too. Troy and I got in Malcolm's car. Troy asked me if I had a good time tonight and I told him I did. Then he asked me if I really liked Melvin. I told him that Melvin and I are just friends, and that it was nice to have a gentleman in my life, the alcohol was still affecting me cause my mouth forgot to leave the mystery. Then I asked him why he thought Malcolm broke up with me.

He said it was news to him that Malcolm did break up with me. I told him the only reason he comes around now is for the baby. Troy said he couldn't answer any of that, and that I'd have to talk to Malcolm. Then Troy asked about Gwen. I told him she was fine, and still hot in the pants. He smiled. I made it in the door with five minutes to spare. Andrew was sleep in his crib. I gave him a kiss, threw my clothes on the floor and crawled into bed. Momma peeked her head in the door as soon as I laid down, she asked if I had fun and I said a happy yes. She said she wanted details in the morning. When she left I whispered everything to Jade. She was surprised, Melvin likes boys and girls. I told her that's what Tammy told me. I told her I couldn't wait for her to meet everyone. She sounded shy about the whole idea. I told her that her next Saturday night off we were gonna have to go out again.

In the morning Melvin called apologizing because he didn't take me home. I told him it was ok, and I was glad we had a backup. He told me he really had a good time with me and he was glad that I didn't make his friends feel awkward or ashamed of who they are. I told him I was the teenage single mom, and they didn't treat me like a dumb kid, so I appreciated that as well.

****

Malcolm's staring at me again. At school he finds his way to wherever I am and then he stares. I don't know why he does this, am I supposed to be scared when he does that? I don't know what it means. There's a rumor going around school that Yvette is trying to flunk the twelfth grade just so she could be at Oakland High one more year with Malcolm. I blew air, she better not be that stupid, and I wondered why it was ok for her to be stupid and he told me to be smart.

Now that we have only three months left in the school year Sonny has finally got the guts to come sit with Jade, but that was after she finally listened to me about showing him some encouragement. They are so square they smile at each other and get all blushy about everything. But I'm happy for her all the same. I can tell she really loves him, but she's just scared. She's probably scared of ending up like me. And I can't say I blame her for that. Sonny is going to Morehouse college, he keeps asking Jade to consider Spellman so that they could be together while they're in school. I don't want Jade to go so far away, but I know she has to make the best decision for her life. Malachi got into The Technology Institute Of Cambridge I cried tears of joy for him, tears of sadness for me. Malachi was going to leave his car for Jade. I was gonna miss him badly when he went away in the Fall but we still had the summer to all be together when Timothy comes home.

****

Sophia asked me to be honest with her. Did I think Sasha looked like Richard or Charles? I asked why she even did this to herself. Sasha was not premature when she was born, but she was born early. It doesn't take a scientist to figure that one out. She said the more Sasha's face changes the more she sees Richard. She's so scared to tell Charles because she thinks it might open a can of worms. It's one thing if they were together before and she didn't know, but since they hadn't stopped she was afraid of being found out. I told her I didn't know how she lived with that guilt, I would die. Sasha was so pretty though. She was browner than me and she was only a baby. Sasha reminded me of Jade. I asked Sophia if she was gonna have any more babies after all she was married and could have more if she wanted to. She said once they graduate their focus is gonna be on getting a place of their own. I asked her about school and she just didn't know how she would manage that.

We heard from Rosalind the other day. She said things were still a little strained between her and Benjamin. She said she didn't doubt that he loved her, but he knew

105

her heart wasn't into being so far away. She said she tries to make the best of it though.

****

"Can I take you home?" Malcolm asked me after my dance rehearsal, "I need to talk to you."

His words put fear into my heart, but I told him I needed to let Melvin know. When I told Melvin he wasn't happy but its not like he could tell me I couldn't go. Melvin and I were just friends and once I found out that he sometimes batted for the other team, the attraction disappeared. We were like best friends, we talked about almost everything. He knows how much I love Malcolm and he doesn't want me to get sucked in.

"How have you been?" Malcolm said in a gentle tone that only made me more nervous.

"What do you mean?" I asked

"I'm just asking you about you. We haven't talked since the baby was born."

"Are we about to fight?" I asked getting in the car

He laughed, then he got in the drivers side of the car. He put his key in the ignition, but he didn't start the car. "I wanna ask you something, but I need you to be honest with me." I nodded, but I thought he better not ask me if Andrew is really his baby. If he does I'm punching him in the mouth! I waited! "Do you still love me?" I blew air and rolled my eyes. "What does that mean? I speak English."

"WHY? Why in the world does that matter? You've got Yvette why care about me?"

"It's a yes or no answer, it's not that hard to answer."

"I don't want to answer that cause its none of your business whether I do or not. All that matters is your son. What I'm feeling doesn't. You made that clear."

"How did I make that clear?"

"You stop talking to me, touching me, or even acknowledging me after Andy was born. You come and do for him like you should, but you forgot about me."

"You were never home, what was I supposed to do track you down?"

"That was after you forgot about me." I tried to breathe to fight back the tears. "You wouldn't even look at me, like I was disgusting to you or something. I wasn't even liking myself; you were the one person who was supposed to love me because you wanted to. You shut me out, but I was wrong for shutting down! Now I'm sixteen years old with a son and barely any dignity and what do you do? You kick me! With the same girl! Go! Be with her! Be happy with her! Don't worry about how much I hate you! Don't worry about my regrets! Just go be happy! Spreading your seed all over the planet!"

"Yes or no answer Amber!"

"I hate you! How about that!"

"Yes or no!"

"I hate you!" Then I opened the door, and ran out the car.

He sat there looking at me. My legs felt like spaghetti, I had been dancing for three hours straight. The thought of walking to the Bart station was more than I could bare. Who knows when the next bus was coming and everyone at the school was pretty much gone. Malcolm got out of the car and he walked to me with both hands open. "Yes or no?"

"I'M NOT ANSWERING YOUR QUESTION! IF THAT'S ALL YOU HAVE TO SAY TO ME WE HAVE NOTHING TO TALK ABOUT!" I screamed while tears poured out my eyes.

"Amber" I wanted to run but I couldn't. He hugged me, "Amber I still love you. I just wanted to know if you still loved me." I started screaming into his chest, and trying to hit him. But he wouldn't let go. "Things are getting heavy on my end. It's getting hard to know who I can trust. I just need to know if you still love me." I didn't answer, I kept crying. These tears felt good coming out cause I had been holding them in for so long. "Your Uncle has given me more responsibility and there's some people who don't like it. Something's brewing I can feel it." He said. This is the first time in over a year that he's touched me on purpose.

"You don't love me! If you loved me you would do right by me. You don't love me."

"How am I not?"

"You keep leaving me. I didn't get pregnant on purpose! But you act like I did this to you. My life is messed up not yours."

His breathing got heavy and he squeezed me tighter. "I make sure you have everything that you need, that you don't want for anything! I'm paying all your bills, and I'm leaving you?"

"I do want for something, I want a real family. A man that's gonna love me and ONLY me. I want a husband!"

"I already told you, I don't want a wife, and I didn't want no baby. You had the baby anyways."

"Then what does it matter how I feel? If you can't be what I need move out the way!"

"Why do we have to talk about this now?" He said

"Because you keep asking me dumb questions! You don't want a wife, so why does it matter what I think of you. It's only gonna make you mad."

"Amber, I'm trying to tell you something. You're not listening!"

I stood up straight and made him let me go. I wiped all the stupid tears off of my face. "What are you saying?"

"Things are getting hot. I don't know what's gonna happen tomorrow. If something happens to me, I want you to know I love you! I love our son, even though I didn't want a baby you did good. I know I messed up! I keep messing up with you. You keep taking so much for me. Your parents, having that baby, raising him. All because of me, and then I keep hurting you. All those books I've read, all these classes I take, nothing tells me how to handle having someone like you in my life. If I knew how to be a husband, I would do it in a heartbeat. I'm not husband material."

"Are you trying to tell me you're gonna die soon?"

"I don't know what's gonna happen. But if I do, I wanna die knowing you love me."

"Yvette is your girlfriend take her love to your grave!"

He smiled at me; he held the car door open. "Get in" he said. I looked at him like he was crazy! "Please get in!" I didn't want to but I knew I wasn't gonna walk home. I reluctantly got in the car. When we pulled up to my house he told me to stay in the car. He came back with Andrew and his diaper bag. Momma looked out the window and she waved at me. I waved back. He gave me the baby and then he took us to a restaurant. It was a newly opened place called Gonzalez's! He ordered a cheese quesadilla for the baby to gnaw and chew on. I had a couple of steak tacos. We ate dinner and it was nice, but I didn't understand what we were doing. Then he pulled up to Momma Shuga's house. My heart started pounding out of my chest. "Why are we here?"

"We won't stay long but I got to get something for you and the baby. Come on." He got out the car and then he opened my door. I didn't want to get out but all his

cousins were looking. I held on to Andrew and he grabbed the diaper bag.
"Girl, where you been? We haven't eaten good in a minute." Fuzzy said
I smiled but I didn't say anything. He opened the door and I stepped in. That girl
Renee was in her usual spot, but this time she was pregnant again. She sucked her
teeth when she saw me. I felt bad for her, I couldn't be mad anymore.
I heard a big gasp, and then all the children erupted screaming my name. The
sudden noise startled Andrew. He didn't cry but he gave all the kids the evil eye just
like his daddy does. "You had a baby?" They asked in amazement. I shook my head
yes, then I put Andrew down so they could say hi to him. They all circled around
him saying hi. He was happy to see other little kids so he erupted in excited
laughter. The kids were happy and making a bunch of noise. Momma Shuga came
around the corner yelling, "didn't I tell you kids to SHUT UP!" Then she saw
Andrew, her steps hurried and she picked him up. Andrew started crying he didn't
like her. Malcolm took the baby from her, and she just looked at me. She didn't
frown but she definitely did not smile. Malcolm told me to come on and I followed
him to his room. He gave the baby to me as he opened the door. Momma Shuga
yelled at the kids and told them to get back in their room. When we walked in
Malcolm locked the door behind us. He told me to sit on the bed, and then he
opened his closet. He opened his safe and took out papers. He showed me his plans
to open a barbershop. He said he's been saving to do this. He said he's been working
on his exit plan like my father told him. He gave me a safe deposit key. He told me
to put it in a safe place. He said he had money and documents in there that name
Andrew and I as his sole beneficiaries of the money he has spread over a few
accounts, CDs, bonds, etc. I asked him with tears in my eyes what this all meant. He
told me it was time to prepare for the what ifs. Then he kissed me, "I love you!" He
said. I cried, Andrew looked at my tears and then he started crying. Then Malcolm
took a ton of money out of his safe, he took everything out the diaper bag, he put
the money in the bottom and then he put everything back in the bag. Then he told
me to come on. When we came out the room Momma Shuga was standing in the
kitchen. She looked anxious but I knew she wouldn't say in front of me. She asked
Malcolm if he was coming back tonight, and he said maybe. When we pulled up to
my house Andrew was sleep in my arms. I asked him where he was going if he
wasn't gonna go home tonight. He said he's been staying in a motel laying low. I
told him he was scaring me. He asked me to tell him I loved him, but I told him I
couldn't say yes or no because he had a girlfriend, and her love was the only love he
needed confirmation of.

Chapter 14

After that night when he gave me the key to his safe deposit box. I didn't see him around for a couple weeks. I asked daddy if Malcolm was really in danger, daddy confirmed that things had gotten a little stressful. After school I had Malachi take me by the bank. I opened the huge safe deposit box, and just like he said there was a ton of cash in there, bank statements with account numbers highlighted and circled. The balances were circled and as of dates were on them. Real Estate papers, etc. he needed to be eighteen to purchase the spot he had his eyes on. Legal documents naming Momma and me as his power of attorney. I knew he liked my momma, but I didn't know he trusted her so much. Momma Shuga wasn't mentioned anywhere. I was a nervous wreck I didn't know what to expect every time Daddy came home. When my nerves were at their peak and I thought my heart was gonna pound right out of my chest Daddy came home, he was smiling. He said there was something on the porch for me. When I opened the door Malcolm was there. I was so excited I jumped on him wrapping my legs around him. He looked like he had been through a lot. He didn't want to talk about it, but he came to me first. His leg was hurt so he limped for a little bit, he had scrapes and bruises. He slept on our couch for the next week. We talked every night for hours, I started to feel my resolve to stay away weakening. But after that week, he got a new car and I saw him with Yvette again. Hurt my wall went back up. She has been looking at me again. She looks like she wants to say something to me, but she doesn't say anything.

****

Since Malachi's going with us Daddy said as long as we stayed with him, they'd watch the baby for me. We were going out with Melvin again. When Jade came with me last time we had so much fun. We danced the night away, and Stefan kept us in stitches. Troy delivered the drinks Malcolm watched from the corner again. This time we're going to some club in the city. Stefan said he could get us into Club Luxurious in San Francisco, which made the old hang out in Oakland look like the hole in the wall it is. There were way more people, the decor was nicer, and the music, it pumped right through you. We found a table over to the side kind of along the wall. Melvin and Jade danced right away. Malachi asked Tammy to dance, and then Stefan went into drool mode over Malachi. I told him he was a mess. Then Stefan said that sexy darkness has come over us. I looked up and Malcolm and Troy were approaching our table. Besides the fact that Malcolm's hat made him look super delicious, how in the world did they find us? They came and sat down at our table. Then Troy hopped up, "drinks, we need drinks!" Then he told Stefan to come with him to bring them back. Malcolm sat back in his chair and smiled at me. He slowly scanned me from my feet to the top of my head. Then he smiled at me. I smiled, but then I looked for my people on the dance floor. Troy and Stefan came back with drinks for everyone. They set them on the table. I asked Troy what the drink was; he shrugged and said it was the house special. It tasted like spicy sweet cola with a kick. It was so good. Malcolm was drinking some kind of cognac. He kept looking at me and smiling, well his version of public smiling. Malachi and Tammy had come back to the seat and gone back out on the floor. Tired of sitting I asked Malcolm how come he never dances, he said he likes to watch. I asked him if he could dance and he said he could. I stood up, put my hand out, and I told him to prove it. He huffed but then he got up. I saw Stefan get excited. I really didn't know what to expect when we got on the dance floor. Malcolm just stood there at first. My drink had kicked in and I was already feeling myself. So I danced around Malcolm thinking he needed my decoration on the dance floor. Malcolm grabbed me and positioned me to dance with him. My baby could dance; he didn't dance like Melvin, which only relieved me. But I was having so much fun with him. Then they put on a slow song and I hurried back to the table. Troy was dancing with a girl, and everyone else was back at the table. I had a fresh drink; I drank it like it was soda. Jade told me to slow down, but I told her I was having fun. Then Malcolm asked why he didn't get to slow dance with me? I told him it was too intimate and I'd rather not go there with him when he has a girlfriend. He told me I was his only girlfriend and I laughed like yea right.

After a few songs and another drink, Malcolm took me back on the dance floor we danced some more. This time when a slow song came on he grabbed me before I could run. I forgot how strong his hands were. When I started to run he effortlessly picked me up. He told me I was going to dance with him. My body was tingling and having his hands on me wasn't helping me. The tingles were outweighing my fear of sex, but I was trying not to let it show. While we danced Malcolm kept looking me in my eyes. When I tried to look away he made me look at him. In the middle of our dance Troy came and handed Malcolm keys. When I asked Malcolm what they were for he smiled at me. My heart was pounding. When we went to sit, Melvin asked me to dance. He told me that Troy told them he got a suite in a hotel a couple blocks away and that they invited us to come. He said he wanted to say no but he didn't think that by the time we left Luxurious he would be able to drive home. He asked me if I was ok with it. Trying my hardest to hold onto my clarity I told him it was ok. He looked at me and told me I was still in control and I didn't have to do anything I didn't want to. I shook my head in agreement, but there was a part of me that wanted my man back. I knew my lack of intimacy was what kept us apart. Then Melvin pointed out Tammy and Malachi on the dance floor. They looked drunk and like they were having a good time. At the last call we all got a drink for the road. I couldn't feel my lips so I was slurring my words. Malcolm was tipsy himself, when it was time to leave Melvin came over. He told us he had a hook up and he wanted to know if we would mind taking Tammy with us and he would come get her in the morning. Tammy was fine with it, Malachi was over joyed. Troy had some girl he just met on his arm. Jade and Stefan were holding each other up. Troy led the way as we walked out of the club. The cold San Francisco air was almost sobering. When we got to the hotel we quietly and all very giggly walked through the lobby to the elevator. Malcolm held my hand the whole way. When we reached our floor Troy explained that there were two rooms each had a bedroom and a pullout couch. The rooms were next to each other and really nice. Jade pulled out the couch and climbed in shoes on and everything. Stefan laid on top of the covers next to her. I didn't worry about her cause I knew she didn't have the right equipment for him. Tammy told Malachi they should take the room. Troy and Malcolm gave Malachi fives, then Troy handed Malachi a box of condoms and told him to have fun. Malachi was all smiles, but I could tell he was beyond tipsy. We closed their door and then we went to our room. The girl with Troy wanted the bedroom, Malcolm told him to get his girl. When we went in the bedroom I told Malcolm that I had power and I wasn't gonna sleep with him. He smiled at me. I told him I was serious, and he just kept smiling. Then I told him I had to pee, so I excused myself. Troy and that girl were kissing and rolling around on the bed. I wondered how they weren't dizzy rolling around like that. I went in the bathroom and washed the salt from my sweat off. I did my best to try and wipe myself down. I tried to calm myself and think clearly cause I was still very tipsy. When I came out the bathroom they were still rolling around, they didn't notice me passing through both times.

Sometimes Love Isn't Enough

When I walked in the room Malcolm was naked all except the hat. When I asked him why he was naked, he shrugged and said that's how he always slept. I stood by the door not knowing what to do. He was folding his clothes. His body looked like a statue, like Michelangelo's David but covered in black clay and definitely more endowed. He told me to put my jacket on the dresser. I hesitated for a minute then I told myself to suck it up. I could do this. I took off my jacket. Then I decided to take my dress off. I figured as long as I had my underwear on I was protected. When I took my dress off Malcolm looked at me with a surprised look, but then he instantly started looking over my body. He touched my stretch marks on my hips. He said, "I did that" I didn't know if he meant that in a positive or negative way. I climbed on the bed and got under the covers. I asked him to turn off the lights. He turned off the wall switch but he turned on the lamp next to the bed, and he got in the bed next to me. I told him I was going to sleep and he smiled at me and raised the covers to look at my body. He kept looking at me. Then he kissed me; I had been dying for this kiss all night long. He took his hat off and put it on the nightstand. That's when I noticed the two condoms on the nightstand. I told him I was scared it might hurt more than when I was a virgin. He told me we could go slow. When I was too nerved up to get into the kiss, he started rubbing me and telling me he remembered what I liked. After awhile I gave into the feeling and I relaxed some. For the first time I watched him put the condom on. Part of me wanted to tell him I was on the pill, but for some reason I didn't. There was the feeling again, I loved the feeling of first contact. He did go slow, he kissed my cheek. "You waited for me. You're such a good girl!" He said as he slowly entered. I was definitely tight, but it wasn't painful like my first time. As soon as he was in good the condom broke. Malcolm cursed! He grabbed his last condom and a little bit to eager it tore while he was putting it on. I thought he was gonna lose it. He was up pacing cursing, and fighting an invisible person. I told him to come back to bed, he looked like he was gonna cry. I kissed him, but he was reluctant to give in to my kiss. I put his hands on my body, he was right back at attention. I straddled him, his eyes got big. I told him it was ok, he sat there motionless staring at me. When I moved my hips his eyes rolled, but he tried to stay focused. I kissed him and then I told him that Momma put me on the pill. He sighed a sigh of relief, and then he took control of the situation again. We'd finish and nap and then it was on again. When I woke up in the morning he was staring at me. He kissed me morning breath and all. Then he held me and told me how much he loved me. I felt like I was on top of the world. It seemed like forever that I had been waiting for him to openly express his love for me, without the threat of death hanging in the background. He told Troy to look at the wall as he walked me out with a blanket covering me to the bathroom. We showered and I put my clothes back on. Although starving I felt loved and relaxed. Troy and that girl were doing it when we walked out. Troy looked at us and smiled while the girl covered her face. How embarrassing especially when he didn't stop like she asked him to. We went to the room next door. Stefan and Jade were watching TV and the room door was closed. Jade said they were a little busy at the moment. I turned so red hearing my brother and Tammy. Jade covered her ears pretending like she passed out, and Stefan acted like Malachi was cheating on him. Malcolm said we should all be starving by the time they were done. Melvin came up to the room; the question that no one wanted to ask was did he hook up with a woman or a man. Melvin never discussed his preference with me, and he only talked about women with me but then sometimes he would just be quiet. Like now, he wasn't saying anything he just looked satisfied.

Malachi came out the room with no shirt. Stefan screamed and acted like he passed out, Jade bumped him and asked him what was wrong. He told her he couldn't handle it, Malachi was too beautiful! We all laughed, Malachi blushed and went to the bathroom. He washed up and then he sat on the couch next to me. Malcolm went to get Troy. Tammy came out the room, she looked embarrassed. She rubbed Malachi's head then she sat next to Melvin. Melvin kept looking at me with a funny look on his face. Then Malcolm told us to meet them in the lobby, they were going to checkout. Malachi called home, Momma answered. He told her we spent the night with friends and that we would be home after breakfast. In the lobby Troy sent the girl on her way. He was kind of cold blooded by the way he did it. But she didn't look surprised or confused by it. Melvin asked him why he didn't at least invite her to breakfast; Troy blew air like the thought of it was against nature or something. We drove a little ways and then we went to a local diner looking spot. We sat in a huge booth by the window. Melvin was quiet, but everyone else was laughing and having a good time. Troy and Stefan were sitting on either sides of the ends of our booth. I was sitting between Malcolm and Jade. I was talking to Malcolm when all the sudden Jade's leg started shaking. I looked at her hand and it was trembling. Her eyes were locked forward, and I followed her eyes that's when I saw him staring at us. He made a kissy face at me when I looked at him. He was smiling extra big. I grabbed Jade's hand as tears poured out of my eyes. Malcolm looked at us and then he sat forward. He saw him, but he didn't know who he was looking at. Malcolm bumped Malachi to ask who the guy was. Malachi's smiled dropped instantly. Then he walked over to our table.
"Now girls where's your smiles for your Uncle Preston? You miss me?" He reached out to touch Jade, and in one swift move Malachi slid across the table and his fist connected with Uncle Preston's jaw. I guess uncle didn't see Malachi cause you could tell he wasn't expecting that. Uncle staggered backwards and Malachi kept coming for him. He picked up a chair and knocked him in the head with it. The waitress was on the phone while Malachi was going crazy. Troy grabbed Malachi, Malcolm told them to go. Malcolm told Tammy to move as he slid out the booth her way. Uncle was trying to get his bearings about himself. Malcolm walked over to uncle, "who are you? What happened to the white boy?" Malcolm told him not to worry about who he was. Malcolm put his hands in uncle's pocket and pulled out his wallet. He took his drivers license and read the address to him. Uncle stood up still dazed and grabbed his wallet. He grabbed a chair and sat down. Malcolm told us to come on. He dropped five one hundred dollars bills on the table, he told the waitress it was for our meal and the mess. Then he took Jade by the hand and helped her out the booth and out the door. I wanted Malachi to finish him. Jade and I walked down the street to the car crying and holding each other. Malachi and Troy were in Malachi's car. Malachi pulled over and came and hugged us, we were all crying. Malcolm told Melvin and them to leave. They didn't understand what just happened but they did as they were told. They rounded the corner, then I saw Melvin's car leave. Troy scooted to the drivers seat in Malachi's car. He told us we needed to go cause the police would be coming soon. Malcolm was showing Troy uncle's drivers license when Uncle came around the corner. He had a knife in his hand he cut Malachi's arm when he missed stabbing him because Jade screamed when she saw him. He was focused on trying to stab Malachi so I kicked him as hard as I could in the back. When he swung around he cut my leg. My heart was beating so hard all I felt was warmth running down my leg. Malachi lost it when he saw that uncle cut me. Uncle kept swinging the knife at me and Malachi, Jade was

motionless. Malcolm walked straight up to uncle, uncle sliced his arm too but Malcolm took the knife from him. Malcolm hit him and he flew backwards. Malcolm picked up the knife, he stabbed him a few times then I closed my eyes I reached for Jade and I made her look away. The police came around the corner. They grabbed Malcolm and threw him up against the car. The other officer told us to put our hands up. Uncle was screaming talking about we attacked him. The restaurant owner and the waitress came running around the corner. They screamed to the officers to let us go. They told the officer that uncle had been harassing the waitress all morning then he started messing with us. Uncle went crazy ran in the kitchen and stormed out the door with their knife. They told the officers we acted in self-defense. One of the officers picked up Uncle's license off the ground. He read his name out loud, then sighed he knew him. An ambulance came and took him to the hospital. I know it's not right, but I was disappointed that they got there so fast. The police took statements from everyone, and then they took pictures of our cuts and the restaurant. They told us to go to the hospital Malachi's arm and my leg were gonna need stitches. Momma and Daddy came to the hospital. Momma looked so worried, all they told her over the phone was that we had been injured. She came in the room as they were numbing my leg to stitch it. Daddy was in the waiting room talking to Malcolm and Troy. I was worried about Jade. I hoped this whole thing didn't make her stop talking again. She was sitting on the edge of her chair just staring at the floor. I couldn't stop crying as I looked at her. Momma wanted to know what happened. All I said was Uncle, and she gasped and hugged Jade real tight. I told her we were having breakfast and then Jade saw him. I stopped talking when the nurse came back in. The nurse poked me to make sure I was numb, and then she started sewing me up. It only took twelve stitches to close me up. The nurse put a gauze over the stitches and then she told me how to clean it. I asked Momma where Andy was and she said he was with Sophia. As we walked to the waiting room, Momma was holding Jade, while I told her what happened. When we walked in the waiting room Malcolm and Troy's face were stone. Malachi was still angry and Daddy was talking. Daddy looked at Momma, "Do I have to say anything?" He asked her. Momma squeezed Jade a little tighter. "No Tim, I know." Then Daddy looked at Malcolm, and he and Troy left. I asked Daddy where they were going and he said to handle business. Daddy was angry and really quiet. Jade rode with Momma and Daddy. When I got in the car with Malachi he was still mad. He put the key in the ignition but he didn't turn it on. He said he got so angry when he saw Uncle that he couldn't think straight. I told him it was the same for me, and then he had that knife. Then Malachi started beating the steering wheel. He said he didn't know why Momma and Daddy let him stay after that first night. He said he knew something was wrong he just didn't know what. He blamed Uncle for the things happening in Jade and I's lives. I told him we were ok though. I told him that he's always done a good job protecting us, and he did good today. My brother started crying. I told him that because of him it didn't get worse. I thanked him for being an awesome big brother, and I told him I didn't know who I'd be if it weren't for him. He cried harder, he said Uncle took from all us something that could never be given back. I told him we are stronger for it. I begged him to stop blaming himself for not knowing. How could he have known? We thought he understood what family meant, it's not our fault that he didn't. I rubbed his back and told him it was gonna be ok. Malachi calmed down slowly, then he said the only redeeming factor was that he wasn't gonna be able to hurt anyone else ever again. I asked him what that meant and Malachi looked at me. We both cried again.

When we got home Jade was laying down. She was fast asleep; Momma was in the family room with a box. She was crying looking at the pictures. I laid Andy on the couch and then I sat next to her. She showed me a picture of her father, of her mother, of her sister, and her brothers. Then she said they were all dead, I didn't know if she meant literally or figuratively like she told grand momma on the phone that time. She told me if I thought she was bad, I would've hated her mother. She said Barb reminded her a lot of her mother. I told her about that night that Malcolm took me over there how she looked at me, and how Andrew didn't even like her. She said she wasn't surprised. Then I asked Momma why she was looking at these pictures. She said sometimes you need to remember where you came from to remember why you're moving ahead. She said a lot of bad things happened when she was growing up. She couldn't believe that Daddy loved her so much. She said it took her a long time to accept it. She said that when Daddy would get upset about her family it was hard for her because his family wasn't full of saints either. But at least his family didn't try to hurt us. Not like her family at least. I hugged Momma and I told her it wasn't her fault. She cried hard, I had never seen Momma cry like this. Daddy came out, his face was still mad. But he softened when he saw how much Momma was hurting. He got down on the floor with us and he took over hugging Momma. He kissed her forehead like Malcolm kisses mine. There was a knock at the door Malachi opened the door. Malcolm and Troy were wearing different clothes. Malcolm nodded at Daddy and Momma started crying harder. Daddy tried to quiet Momma. He told Malcolm and Troy to go to the bathroom. Troy waited in the hallway, when Malcolm came out Troy went in. Malcolm threw the clothes he was wearing in the fireplace. When Troy came out he did the same. Malachi brought wood inside and they built a fire. Daddy made the fire real big. Troy and Malcolm went in Malachi's room. They shut the door and talked for a while. Daddy held on to Momma, when Andrew woke up he pounded on Malachi's door. They let him in. I went in the kitchen to make dinner. My mind was all over the place, I couldn't really focus. I kept touching hot pots and pans. My poor fingers were burnt up. When the beef stroganoff was ready I stood at the sink wiping the same plate over and over. Malcolm put his arms around me and he squeezed me. When I turned around to face him he wiped my tears and told me that Uncle would never hurt us again. I laid my head on his chest; there was no safer feeling than being in his arms. When we sat down to eat at first everybody was quiet. Then Malachi started rattling off knock knock jokes that were so corny they had to be funny. The mood at the dinner table shifted, even Jade laughed. I felt a little better when I saw her laugh, but I was still worried about her.

****

Things were back to normal. Jade didn't stop talking. I think a lot of that had to do with Sonny being able to be there for her. She told him she wanted to be wherever he was gonna be. She told him she would apply to Spellman. He was so happy. Daddy told Jade like he told Malachi get into the school and the rest would be taken care of. Timothy was completing his fourth year in his five-year bachelor's degree program. He already had his internship set up upon graduation and then he'd take his architect registration exam. If he didn't get hired at the firm he interned at he had his eye on another one, but that one was in New York. I didn't want him to move that far away, but he said we'd cross that road when we came to it. I still didn't know what I wanted to do yet. My siblings had all these prestigious ambitions, was I gonna be the black sheep of the family? The one who didn't amount to much? Jade talked to her counselor the other week about Spellman and they talked in detail about the psychology program. Jade didn't know what aspect of that field she wanted to go in, but she told us all that she was going to major in psychology. With one-week left of school I felt like I needed to know which direction to go in. Malcolm suggested that I talk to Ms. Dubois about dance and the options that could be available to me.

I told Ms. Dubois that I wanted to talk to her after class. Melvin had been acting funny since the morning after Luxurious. He got annoyed with me the next day when he called and Malcolm was there. He's been distant and sometimes just rude. When he heard me say that he huffed. When I asked him what was wrong he stared at me like I was supposed to know. Then he complained about having to wait for me. I told him I could call my momma if it was too much of a hassle. Then he backed down and said no. After class I talked to Ms. Dubois about my future. I told her I didn't know what I wanted to do. She suggested the dance program at the University of Berkeley. I hadn't thought of it. She said I could be a teacher easily. I liked the sound of that. On the way home Melvin said he had to speak on the elephant in the room. I had no idea what he was talking about. He asked me point blank if I slept with Malcolm that night. When I said I did he looked disappointed. I didn't understand why he was reacting this way. He asked me what about him? I didn't understand what he meant. Then he said, "I like you, you didn't know?" I was surprised. I told him I thought he might have at first, but as we became friends he didn't seem interested in me in that way. I told him I thought he knew I was still in love with Malcolm. And he said he did but that's also why he didn't push me to choose him. He knew I needed time, but he wasn't giving me time to go lay back under him. I apologized for not understanding his intentions. He was mad that Malcolm didn't even consider that he liked me. But I told him honestly I didn't think he would've cared if he realized it. But then I remembered Charles and I took it back. He asked me why I would give myself to someone who had a girlfriend. I hadn't thought about Yvette. I hadn't even considered whether they were officially broken up. My stomach started to hurt. Then he said, "here I am in love with you. And you're playing second string to a whack job who would actually try to flunk high school to hang on to a guy!"

I was quiet the rest of the way home. When Melvin pulled up to the house he told me I deserved better, and he couldn't just sit back and watch this happen. Then he sighed it was the end of the school year. He told me last day of school he was cutting me loose cause I was messing with his self-esteem. I felt horrible but he kept going on and on. Like if he would've stopped there I would've let it go and took all the blame. But since he didn't I asked him who did he hook up with at the club. He got quiet, so I asked him again. Still he said nothing. Then I said, "and you wonder why I didn't know you were looking at me?" He sat there looking busted. I told him even Stefan would've shared, but no he's always so secretive like no one could tell. I told him to pick a team and play for it. And don't use me as an excuse for why he hates women. He couldn't even look at me after that. I told him I enjoy out friendship, and whenever he had it figured out he should call me. But I told him that friendship is all I was offering him. Then I got out the car and slammed the door. Momma looked out the window as usual. When I came in the door she asked what was wrong so I told her, and she was surprised. She said she really didn't think he liked girls too. I looked at Andrew walking around the living room talking to himself. I started wondering what type of man he was gonna be. Would he be a good man or would he walk around blaming the world for his problems. All the sudden I felt that pressure again.

When Malcolm came over two hours later he asked me why Melvin was sitting outside. I looked out the window and he hadn't move since earlier. As I approached the car I could see he was upset. I tapped on the window, and he rolled it down. I asked him if he was ok. He shook his head no. I asked him if he wanted to come in, he looked at Malcolm standing on the porch and he said no. I asked him if he needed to talk, and he shook his head yes. His eyes were really red from crying. I started to walk to the passenger side and Malcolm called me. I put one finger up to Melvin as I hurried back to Malcolm. He asked me what was wrong and I told him I would tell him later, but I was gonna go talk to him. Malcolm looked at the car, and then he grabbed my arm. He told me something didn't feel right and not to get in the car. I looked at Malcolm and I tried to convince him that Melvin was my friend and he needed me right now. Malcolm told me not to go. Melvin saw us arguing and growled at us! He screamed out, "I HATE YOU!" And then he sped off. I stood there in shock and Malcolm stood there waiting for and explanation. Momma came to the door and asked if she just heard someone screaming? I told her Melvin screamed at me and then he sped away. I told Malcolm the story. He was thinking about it the rest of the evening. At about two o'clock Melvin's grandmother called asking if I had seen him. I told her the last time I saw him he was really upset with me and he was speeding down the street, but I didn't know where he was going. She told me she was going to file a missing person's report if he didn't come home in the morning. And she did, the police found his car at Fort Point under the Golden Gate Bridge. There was a note with all his things, but they never found him. Tammy said he wasn't just mad about me; there was a lot of pain in his life. His grandmother wouldn't let any of us read the note or tell us what it said. She said he was gone, and then she slammed her door in our faces.

Chapter 15

I was so hurt by Melvin's grandmother's reaction. Momma told me to give her some time and maybe she'll be willing to talk then. Malcolm asked a ton of questions about Melvin right after that. I tried my best to explain things in a manner that would help him to understand, but I could tell there were things he didn't understand. Like when Melvin and I danced it wasn't the same as when he and I danced. Dancing with Malcolm always led somewhere. If he and I danced pelvis to pelvis it turned me on. But when Melvin and I danced it was about the music, the expression, and the whole artistry of the dance. Any passion expressed in our dance was about the love of dance and maybe and outlet for whatever. I didn't want to be Melvin's girlfriend even if he thought my dancing said so. Our final performance at school was AMAZING! We danced so well if I do say so myself. Ms. Dubois was in tears when we finished. She led the standing ovation.

Now I dance at home with Andy. He's really good for a one year old. The way he rocks in place to the beat is amazing (proud mother sigh). He really likes when I play The Jackson's records. No matter what he's doing he stops and rocks.

******

Malachi's graduation party is huge! He invited a few people from school, there's a ton of family, and he even invited Tammy and Stefan. Malachi and Tammy have gone out a few times but they never got serious. Tammy said he's a good kid, and she didn't want to hold him back. I really like hanging out with Tammy and Stefan. Stefan is hilarious and his relentless crush on Malachi and Malcolm keeps all of us in stitches. Stefan is the one who pointed out that Malcolm was built like a horse as he called it. I have nothing else to compare him to, but when we were talking about how I ended up pregnant I told them the condom broke and that they ALWAYS break with him. Stefan in the most dramatic way told me that my baby was hung, and that he had a gift that must be shared with the world. It was funny but I wonder if Malcolm really thought that.

Charles actually came to the party. He still wasn't too comfortable around Malcolm, and Malcolm didn't want me around Charles anymore than I had to be. So Charles would move to whatever side Malcolm and Troy weren't on. Sophia thought it was childish and that Charles needed to let it go. But Charles would stare at me a lot when no one was looking. His stare wasn't like Malcolm's or even Momma's; Charles' stare was like can I please have my clothes back. It gave me the creeps. When Uncle Frank and Gwen arrived I immediately looked for Malcolm. It was like she was instantly turned on by the sight of Malcolm, but she'd settle for Troy. Malcolm said anyone crazy enough to mess with her is asking for a death wish. Troy on the other hand liked playing with fire. He'd flirt a little with her, but at least he was somewhat discreet about it. I was talking to Malcolm when Uncle Frank came over and threw his arm around me. He gave me a big kiss on my cheek and then he called me his sweet little niece. He asked me how school was coming along, and I told him I was still excelling in all my classes. That made him happy, and then he asked where his great nephew was. I pointed to Andrew who was playing with Sasha, Lil Jeff, and JoJo. Uncle Frank said he was a good and strong little boy. Then he told Malcolm to excuse us and he walked away with me under his arm.

"So, how are things?" He asked

"Good" I said

"Did you know you're one of my favorite nieces?"

I smiled really big, "no, I didn't."

He smiled, "oh yea! When you were born Gwen would always give me dirty looks

117

cause I always had to hold you. Jade too, I love my little girls!" Then he kissed my forehead, and I put my arm around him. "I keep telling myself to stay out of it, but I have to know. How are things?"

"At school? Good!"

"Well yes, school. But I mean with the father. Is he taking care of you?"

"Yes! He's been taking care of me even before the baby."

"Oh yea, how so?"

"Since the beginning he's been putting money in my savings. He told me that money is for me. So he still brings money for the baby, and it's always more than we need."

"You have your license yet?"

"No"

"Why not? Aren't you sixteen?"

"Yes, but I hadn't focused on driving yet."

"Get your license. You need a car."

"Ok"

"What's your plan for after school?"

"It's not set in stone, but I think I want to teach dance."

"A teacher huh?" Uncle Frank was quiet for a minute. You could see his brain ticking. "Hhmmmm, now that could work. But I need you to think bigger."

"In what way?"

"This is just off the top of my head. But why not open a school? You could teach there as well, or you can have your own set up. You're going to school aren't you?" That was more of a requirement than a question.

"Yes of course."

"Good, major in dance minor in business. You get your degrees, I'll finance the endeavor."

"Really?"

"Yes! Of course! You always have to think bigger. Especially since you have your little man. You can't be dependent on someone else to live. Don't ever let someone make you feel like your life is over or less because you have him."

"Ok"

"When are you gonna come spend time with your Uncle Frank?"

"Whenever you like."

"What's your plan this summer?"

"We're going to Nana's for a month. Then my teacher told me about this center in Richmond that I want to check out."

"Oh really what's it called?"

"The Center for Performing Arts of The East Bay. I wanna take a class or two for the summer. And I want to see how young the classes start for Andrew."

"That baby is barely walking." Uncle Frank said

"I know but he dances. Watch what happens when they put on a Jackson's record. If not this summer, definitely next summer."

"Richmond is a little ways from Oakland. You're gonna need a car Baby-girl. Get your license."

"I will."

"If I could trust Gwen not to give it away to the first person who says hi to her, I'd let her get hers." I turned red, I was embarrassed for Gwen. "That girl acts just like her mother!" Then Uncle Frank got quiet.

Malcolm sat over to the side watching us. I knew he wanted to know what Uncle

Frank was talking to me about. Then I saw Gwen watching too. But she was watching us trying to figure out if she had time to talk to Malcolm. Uncle Frank said he would call me and we could plan a day.

The music came on and Jade and Sonny were first on the dance floor. Timothy was shocked; he came over and asked what was going on. So we had to fill him in on all that he missed. How they promised their selves to each other and how they have a whole plan. He frowned at first then he went and talked to Malachi about it. Whatever Malachi said put him at ease. Malachi danced a little with Tammy, but Momma shot him a look so then he danced with Gwen. Cassondra came to the party and she was telling me about all the money she made last year designing and making dresses for the junior and senior prom. I asked her if she would make mine and of course she agreed. Cassondra danced with Malachi and Stefan. The party was a lot of fun, but for some odd reason I felt like I was being watched. If it wasn't Gwen, then it was Malcolm, if it wasn't Malcolm it was Momma, if it wasn't Momma it was Daddy, if it wasn't Daddy then it was Poppa and Nana, if it wasn't Poppa and Nana, it was Uncle Frank, if it wasn't Uncle Frank... See! Somebody was always watching. So I just put on my performance face and tried not to let all the eyes bother me. Normally I would've sulked in the corner just because but I couldn't do that. When Andrew started getting tired I started carrying him around. We danced with Malachi and I for a while. When I started dancing with Timothy, Malcolm told me to put Andrew down and to stop babying him. I didn't like the way he said that, and I didn't think showing my son love was babying him. So I gave Andrew to Momma cause I knew he wouldn't say anything to her, or at least that's what I thought. As I was dancing with Timothy I saw Malcolm talking to Momma and then he put Andrew on the ground to stand. He took Andrew by the hand and had him say goodnight to everyone then they went inside the house. After awhile Malcolm emerged from the house, but he didn't have Andrew with him. Sophia took Sasha inside and then she came out childless too. I asked Cassondra to check on Andrew because Malcolm was now watching me with even more serious eyes than his everyday serious. Cassondra gave me a thumbs up and then she went back in the house. When Timothy and I finished dancing Malcolm came over. He said he wanted to dance. While we were dancing he told me never to undermine him like that again. He told me if I keep babying Andrew like I do he's gonna be soft and a sissy. I told him there was nothing wrong with a mother showing her son love. He told me I knew nothing about men, and if I keep babying him he was just gonna end up as a good for nothing wimpy bum. Malcolm's face is always serious so no one would know by his face that we were arguing. I plastered a smile on my face to try to mask what I was feeling inside. I was angry and maybe he was right, but I was not going to stop loving my son just so he could grow up hard and hardhearted like his father. I stopped talking and then Malcolm said he wanted to drop the topic, he didn't want to spend our last few minutes together arguing. Momma came out the house. She told Malcolm that Daddy forgot to get the ice cream for the cake, she asked him to grab some real quick. He asked me to come with him. I didn't want to, but I agreed. When we walked into the house I peeked my head in my room. Andrew and Sasha were both standing up in his crib laughing and clapping while Cassondra sang her silly song to both of them. She asked if they could come out the crib since the excitement of the house was keeping them up. I told her to wait until we left then she could take them out. I walked with Malcolm down the street to Bob's. It was just before closing and Bob was sweeping up. Bob got really excited when Malcolm told him he needed a whole tub of vanilla. Bob said he would deliver it personally so that we didn't have to carry it down the street. Malcolm held my hand as we walked back to the party. He told me he was gonna miss me the whole month I was gone with my Grandparents, and I told him I always felt the same. I told him the summer time is always when we fell apart, he agreed. He told me next school year was gonna be different. I couldn't help but know a large part of that was because Yvette had to graduate. But hey out of sight out of mind right.

Malcolm put our bags in Nana's car. There was almost a sadness in his eyes like he wanted to tell me not to go or something, but he kept talking and staring. I hugged him and he tried to act like he didn't like it, whatever. Then he gave me a huge bear hug. He kissed my neck and told me he missed me already. I kissed his cheek, and then he started walking away. I told him to wait to say bye to Andrew and he just waved and kept walking.

Poppa and Nana kept raving over my last performance that they came to. They said I had a very good technique especially for someone who's had no formal training. I thanked them for the compliments, but they made me think of Melvin. I wanted to know what he said. His grandmother seemed to always like me before but maybe that was because she thought he and I were more than just friends.

Andrew passed out on the car ride over. I didn't understand why Malcolm wouldn't want to say bye to him. He wouldn't see Andrew the same length of time. That night my dream was so crazy. Malcolm and Melvin were playing tug of war. Instead of having a flag or something in the middle of the rope I was. Neither one of them were winning which was interesting cause I doubt Melvin would ever be a match for Malcolm. Then a third strand was added and my baby was on the end crying for his momma. I couldn't believe I was being pulled in three different directions. No one was gonna win so I had to choose. Of course I chose my baby. But choosing my baby made us fall. When I woke up Andy was sitting up looking at me. He looked like he had just woken up and he was smiling at me. My hair was all over my head. I could smell fresh coffee in the air. I picked up Andy and we walked down the hallway into the kitchen. Nana and Tag were sitting at the table. Tag's face lit up when he saw me. I gasped and used Andrew as a shield. I asked Nana what he was doing there. He said he was here for our morning run. She didn't even warn me that he was coming. They had a good laugh at my expense. Nana took Andrew from me, she told me to go get ready for my run and to hurry up because Tag had been waiting long enough. Tag kept smiling at me during the first stretch of our run. He said I looked so much more mature. Then he told me he missed running with me all year long, and that summer couldn't come fast enough. I laughed and asked why a guy in college would think about a little girl in high school. He got quiet when I said it. I didn't know if I insulted him or not, but I felt stupid for thinking to apologize. He changed the subject by asking about my plans for the summer. I told him the same thing I told Uncle Frank. Then he asked if he could come to my next performance. I told him he could and that he could probably ride with my grandparents since they always come. That seemed to make him smile, and he was happy again. He told me that he was still at CVC and that he'll probably have enough saved in two more years to afford to transfer to a university.

Tag came every morning to run with me. He was really sweet, a nice guy. That's when I realized that Tag was actually cute. I guess I really didn't pay attention last summer. I couldn't believe I didn't pay attention before. Tag had jet-black slightly wavy hair. His eyes were a deep blue; they made him look so dreamy. Once everyone started coming more cousins came on our runs. Tag was very good at teaching them how to breathe and how to work through the pain. I used the stuff he taught me to help with my breathing while dancing as well. Gwen of course came on our runs. She would come almost naked it seemed like. Tag didn't seem to notice her though. It was like the stuff she did went over his head.

Nana and Poppa invited Tag on our camping trip. Tag is closer to Timothy's age so they were talking about life on a level the rest of us couldn't relate to. Sophia and I were playing with the babies in the water with Jade. Tag came over and introduced himself. Jade and Sophia shot me looks, I shrugged.

Later I was taking Sasha and Andrew for a walk when Tag caught up to us. He grabbed Andrew's hand. When he asked my permission to ask me a question I knew it was bad. "Where's his father?"

"He's around?" I said not knowing how to answer.

"So he's involved in his life?"

"Yes"

"Is he involved in your life?"

I didn't really want to answer but I did. "It's a difficult situation. I love him otherwise he wouldn't be Andy's father. But...." Tag didn't say anything he waited for me to find the words. "I honestly don't know with him sometimes. He's very smart, a hard worker, and he tells me he loves me from time to time. I.... I just don't have the words to explain it." Tag was quiet for a while; it looked like he was thinking about it. "You know Tag I value our friendship, but my male/female relationships have been sucking lately. I can't afford to lose yet another friend."

"What do you mean?"

"I love Andy's father very much. If he asked me to marry him right now I would say yes!"

"Ok" Tag turned a little red, and he was quiet for a while. Then he changed the subject for a while. He said he really values our friendship too. Then he asked me to go for a walk tonight just he and I after the little ones were down for the night. I agreed but didn't know how I would manage that. We walked those poor babies forever. On our way back the babies couldn't hang so I carried Sasha and he carried Andy. We fed them and they just about passed out. We were all sitting out by the fire talking and being silly. One by one and sometimes two's everyone started getting sleepy. They either went to the camper or one of the tents. I think everyone forgot to pay attention especially my brothers. I think they both assumed that the other was still out with us. Tag told me to come on and he handed me a flask. He told me he brought a few on our trip. It tasted like straight vodka. He smiled big when I knew what I was tasting. I took a can of cream soda out of the cooler. I went back and forth taking a drink of both. Then he told me to walk with him. We walked a little further than the circle we walked the babies in earlier. Tag was talking up a storm. Suddenly I felt the throbbing that I normally only felt when I was with Malcolm. It confused me that I was feeling them now. Tag grabbed my hand and he led me a little further out. The only light came from the moon and our campfire that was now so far away; there was no one around but he and I. We came up on a picnic area. He sat me on the table. He started telling me how much he liked me, but he understood that I was in love with someone else. He told me about the girlfriend he had before the summer he met me. He said she was older than him and she taught him a lot of things. He said she got a job in another state and she had to move away. He said he missed her terribly until he met me. He said spending the summer with me last year was just what the doctor ordered. He said he understands that I have a boyfriend and the timing isn't right for he and I, in this moment it was just the two of us and he didn't think we would ever have it again. A little tipsier than I wanted to be I didn't move when Tag stepped into my personal space. My throbbing started to get faster. He kissed me and he tasted like cream soda. I had never thought of kissing Tag, but I was happy to note that kissing him wasn't bad. His hands were warm and the air out had a nice crispness about it. His hands felt good on my body. But when he pulled at my pants the reality of where this was leading snapped me back to reality. I slapped his hands away and I looked at him like he was crazy. He smiled at me. Then he asked me to let him give me something. And I told him I did not want his sausage. We both laughed. He promised that he would keep his pants on and I could keep my panties on, but he wanted to give me something. He said since I didn't know what he was alluding to, I probably never had it. Everything was kind of spinning, I made him promise me that his dick was staying zipped up in his pants and his belt would not loosen. He promised on his scouts honor. Then he took my shorts off and his jacket. He spread them out on the table then he set me on the table again and told me to lay down. I hesitated so he kissed me again. Then he moved to my neck, then my chest, then to my stomach, then he laid me back and he kissed the top of my panties. When he started messing with them I told him to leave them on. Using his finger he moved them aside and he put his warm mouth on me. WHOA! I asked him what he was doing but he didn't respond. It was like he was kissing me. My eyes rolled backwards, this was a new feeling and I couldn't believe how good it felt. He started sucking the source of my throbbing; I couldn't breathe it felt so good. This went on for what seemed like forever, then my body started shaking and I felt a wonderful release. The throbbing was deep and the shakes were out of this world. I looked up and the stars in the sky were beautiful! Tag stood up with the biggest smile on his face. He pulled me up. And then he asked how did he do on his oral exam? It looked like he was pitching his own tent in his pants. He sat down next to me and undid his pants. He started massaging his self while looking at me. I had never seen one outside of Malcolm's, and Malcolm's was way bigger. I wondered if that made him small or Malcolm huge. I didn't know what he was doing so I watched. He didn't mind me watching, and my watching seemed to turn him on. I put my shorts back on and then I continued to watch. Then he asked me to kiss him. I hesitated cause I didn't wanna taste myself, but I felt kind of obligated so I did. I didn't taste bad and I could still taste the cream soda. His breathing got heavy; he took my hand and put it on him. I released him and told him I didn't know how. He took my hand and he told me to think of it as a joystick. He moved my hand up and down, and then he told me to move my thumb over the top every once in awhile. His breathing got heavy, and then he said I was doing it right. It was kind of fun to hold him in my hand like that. My throbbing was coming back, but I wanted to get out of these woods. I started moving faster and he turned red. He licked all over my neck then his body stiffened and I could feel him throbbing in my hand. He erupted like a volcano. I had never seen it happen so I was fascinated. I wondered if Malcolm's looked... OH MY GOD MALCOM! My insides screamed! Did this count as cheating on him? If he found out would he still call me his good girl? I instantly felt guilty and like I wanted to cry. All throbbing instantly stopped. Tag put his jacket back on, he tried to kiss me and I moved away. Although I was still tipsy, I felt horrible. I felt like I just let Malcolm down. Tag asked me what was wrong, and I said I had a boyfriend and I should've never come out here with him. He tried to assure me that I didn't do anything wrong, but I didn't feel that way. I asked him not to tell ANYONE, and he agreed but only if I kissed him goodnight. I kissed him, but now I felt worried. I wanted to walk faster back to the campsite, but Tag strolled along at a slow pace. He knew the way back I didn't. Then he told me one day he hopes that I would be willing to make love to him. But as for tonight he was gonna cherish the memory, and feel good in his heart knowing he was my first. He held my hand and strolled back while I died ten thousand deaths with every slow step. When we got to the campsite Sophia was getting a soda from the cooler. She did a double take when she saw me. My eyes were red and I was upset. She grabbed me by the hand and pulled me in the opposite direction of the camper. She waved goodnight to Tag, who stood there looking at first. She asked me what was wrong, I tried to convince her that nothing was wrong, and she threatened to tell my brothers. I made her PROMISE not to tell a soul. Then I told her what happened. She smiled real big. Then she gave me a huge hug and told me to snap out of it. She asked me why I was worried about being faithful to Malcolm when we all knew that he at least was with Yvette and more than likely others. She said she wasn't encouraging me to play the field, but Tag was probably the only person he wouldn't find out about. She said she and Richard do everything together. She said they try things, experiment the whole nine. Then she got sad, she said sometimes she thinks Charles knows something but doesn't say anything. She said she loved Charles she just doesn't wanna break his heart by telling him the truth. She said they got together too soon after she and Richard broke up, and they have a lot of unresolved issues. When I asked her like what, she swallowed real hard then she said she really thinks he still has feelings for me. A single tear fell out my eye, which made me feel horrible. She said the more she thinks back on how everything happened and him asking her out in front of all of us, the more she realized that wasn't even about her. She should've never dated my ex even if it was just a mostly innocent junior high thing. She cried, she said she feels so stuck. She said Charles isn't happy but he tries to make the most of it. She said she keeps telling herself it will get better after graduation and they have their own place. Then she said I had no reason to feel guilty, Malcolm isn't exclusive to me, and he hasn't ever promised to be. Then she pointed out that for all he knew Melvin and I could've been dating, and somehow every time we went out he was there watching and blocking. She asked me if I stopped to think that when Melvin yelled out "I hate you" if he was talking to Malcolm and not me? I always assumed that he was talking to me, but he didn't say Amber I hate you. I guess he could've been talking to Malcolm. But she said she thinks Malcolm stopping me from getting in the car was a good thing. Clearly he was unstable and something could've happened to me that night as well. I sat there thinking about everything she said and she was right. Malcolm and I never officially said we were back together, so I shouldn't feel guilty. I still didn't want to sleep with Tag, but my convo with Sophia did put me at ease. When we stepped on the camper Nana and Gwen were up. Nana asked where we had been, and we told her we were talking. Tag and I snuck off one more time before the trip was over. I wanted to feel that feeling again, it was a wonderful feeling. Then he told me that my hands felt great on him, the second time I paid attention to the technique, and how he showed me to massage him. I got him there a lot faster the second time. He told me I was a quick learner, I smiled.

Tag asked if he could call me from time to time. I gave him my number, but I told him not to call after eight. Andrew and I rode home with Jade, Timothy, and Malachi. It was the four of us plus Andrew just like it used to be. Well before my baby of course. We stopped along the way to have dinner. I suggested it in the car and I offered to pay for it. As we were in the restaurant Timothy asked me how I could afford to pay for dinner when I was the only one who didn't have a job. I told him that Malcolm gives me money, so of course he asks where Malcolm works. When I told him he works for Uncle Frank, he stared at me for a minute. Then he asked how in the world that happened. I told him how we met in school, and how I didn't find out about him working for Uncle Frank or him finding out that I was his niece until after I was pregnant. Timothy said it was definitely a small world. He said he would've thought Uncle Frank would've made him disappear. I changed the subject by telling them what Uncle Frank told me. They all said he made similar offers to them as well. Timothy said that Poppa wants his whole family taken care of. So all the grandchildren are strongly encouraged to go to school. Timothy said Poppa and Nana gave Daddy such a hard time for letting me keep the baby because they were afraid it would ruin me. Daddy had to assure them that I would keep moving forward. Then we all looked at Andrew who was just beaming with happiness and love. I silently thanked Daddy for allowing me to keep my beautiful baby.

****

Monday Cassondra and I caught Bart to Richmond. We walked from the Bart station a couple blocks over to the EBC. I liked The Center as soon as we walked through the doors. There were multiple shades of people all over the place. They offered ballet, modern, jazz, tap, etc. dance classes. They also taught musical instruments and voice, and acting. The problem was that I wanted to take everything, but I needed to figure out what I could take and what I couldn't. They said as soon as Andrew was two I could sign him up for ballet which would give him fundamentals for any type of dance I wanted him to take next. I talked Cassondra into filling out the paperwork to take a few classes with me. Since we were out there one of the students told us about a park we could take Andrew to. It was up the street, but she told us to take the bus, as the walk could get a little long. She said the park was called Nichol Park and I couldn't miss it on the right side of the street. Along the way we passed a Hot Dog place, and couple blocks away there was the park. We walked back and had lunch. We all had cheese dogs. We loved them! Andrew ate an entire hot dog. Well the hot-dog minus the bun, but he really liked it. Then we walked back to the park. There was a little petting zoo, and a little train ride around the park. Andrew played his heart out. We put him on the swings; I think we had just as much fun as he did. We rode Bart home happy but exhausted from our day. We went over Cassondra's house and we shot around ideas for our prom dresses. She kept sketching ideas, while I kept throwing them out. When it got late I called a cab, then I went home. When we pulled around the corner Malcolm's car was parked in front of my house. I took a deep breath. When I walked in the door Momma and Malcolm were sitting at the table talking. Momma smiled and asked how it went. I pulled the catalog out of my diaper bag. I excitedly showed Momma the classes they offered. She asked which ones I wanted to take. I jokingly said all of them, but I hadn't decided. I told her Andy was too small to take a class just yet but next year he could start ballet. Malcolm sucked his teeth, Momma looked at him. He didn't like the idea of Andrew dancing for a living. I told him just because he takes a dance class doesn't mean that's what he'd want to be. I told him dance would help him with whatever sport he wanted to take up in the future. Malcolm sat there thinking, but I could tell he didn't like the idea. Malcolm kept looking at me, but I could tell he was trying to read me. That made me nervous. Momma was hugging Andrew up; Malcolm asked how my visit was with my grandparents. I told him it was good. Then I got quiet. When I got quiet he looked at me, he was still trying to read me. I looked at Momma, my eyes were pleading for a subject change. She asked Malcolm if he was going to Uncle Frank's party in a couple of weeks. He said he was, but he kept his eyes on me. I put Andrew in his high chair. I fed him some of the dinner Momma made while they talked. Poor Andrew was exhausted, and he could barely keep his eyes open to finish dinner. I bathed him really fast then I laid him down in his crib. He was sleep before his head hit his pillow. Jade was on the phone talking to Sonny when I came in the room. Malcolm said he wanted to talk to me. My heart sank, I peeked my head into Momma's room. I asked if it was ok for me to step out with Malcolm, she said yes. I grabbed my jacket and purse and I followed Malcolm out the door. In the car we didn't talk much. He pulled into a motel parking lot. He told me to stay in the car. He went to the counter; I gave myself a pep. When he came back, he drove the car to a parking space in front of room number eleven. We went inside the room. He sat on the bed, and I sat at the table in a chair. Then he asked me how things went at my grandparent's again. I made myself continue to talk although I wanted to crawl under a rock and hide. I kind of rambled but I figured it was better than being quiet. I asked him why we were there at the motel. He told me he hadn't seen me in a month, I knew why we were there. I looked at him like he had to be kidding. He asked why I was acting funny. I told him this whole scene wasn't romantic; he looked at me like he didn't understand. Then I asked him if he was still seeing Yvette. His whole body flinched, and then he looked away. I asked him why he had to see her still? He was with me first, but he kept leaving me hanging for her. He made an exhausted wounded sound, and then he told me he didn't bring me there to argue. I told him I didn't come with him to be treated like a whore. I told him it was bad enough that he felt like he needed more than one girlfriend, but then he kept acting like she was more important than me. He kept asking me if I was joking cause he wasn't laughing. I told him I was so serious! I told him whenever someone else started paying me attention that's when all the sudden he was paying me attention again. He eyed me, and then he asked me if something happened while I was away. I said I talked to a few people who told me they saw him with Yvette and how I was sick of hearing about him and her. Then I asked him if he loved her? He said no. I told him it made no sense to me why he had to see her if he didn't love her. He didn't have a response. I started crying asking him why couldn't it be just he and I. He looked annoyed, and then he asked me what else could he do to show me how much he loved me. He asked when the last time I went to the bank was. I told him I hadn't needed to go since he gave me all that cash which I barely touched cause he still brought money over regularly. He said he shares everything he has with me. He told me that I have his son. He said he doesn't really give her anything. To which I said he gave her my time, my attention, she still got to have a piece of him and I didn't want to share. He didn't say anything to that. Then I told him it wasn't fair that every time I went out with Melvin he was there. Then he gritted his teeth and asked me if this was about Melvin. I said it was kind of. He got mad, "he's not even here and you wanna argue about him!" I told him I didn't want to share anymore. He looked at me but he didn't say anything right away. Then he asked what did sharing have to do with Melvin. I told him he broke up with me, but as soon as someone else came around here he came. I told him that was the second time he's done that to me. He didn't seem to care. I told him I was tired of it. Then he stood up; he asked me if this was about another guy. When I said no, he told me to prove it. I didn't ask him what he meant. I went and stood by the door, I told him I wanted to go home. He said he wasn't gonna take me home without making love first. I told him I didn't want him to touch me. I put my jacket on and I grabbed my purse. He leaned back on the bed with a pissed off look on his face. I told him I was ready to go, he blew air and looked at the bathroom. I opened the door and walked out. When Malcolm came after me I tried to run. But of course he caught me like I was Andrew running from him. He carried me while I tried to escape, I did everything but scream. When he brought me back in the room he locked the door, put the chain on it, and put a chair under the knob, then he put me down. He told me we weren't leaving without making love. He said even if it took me days to come around so be it, but we weren't leaving. I tried to lie and say I was on my period. He laughed and told me my period was a week and a half ago. When I looked surprised he told me he knew me better than I knew myself. I stood there looking stuck. He kicked off his shoes, and then he told me to take my jacket off and put my purse on the table. I did it reluctantly, and then I stood there. He told me he didn't understand why I was being so difficult. I gave him a dumb look, and then he asked if I stopped loving him? I told him I hadn't. He said he missed me while I was gone and he couldn't wait for me to get back. He said the couple of conversations we had while I was gone made him miss me more. He said he's dying inside and it's taking everything in him not to rip my clothes off. He said he needed to be with me in the worse way. I told him he wasn't showing it. I told him just because I had his son didn't mean I was beyond needing romantic gestures. He asked how he could fix that right at that moment. I told him I hated that cheesy room. I told him nothing about that room felt romantic. His brain was ticking; you could see him thinking hard. He grabbed the blanket off the bed, and then he told me to grab my stuff. He un-barricaded the door. Then we got in the car. We drove through the tunnel and then we were in Alameda. I wondered what he was thinking of but I didn't say anything. He drove along the beach until we were on a secluded end. We got out the car, he told me to leave my things in the car. Then he held my hand as we walked in further away from the street. The moon was out and it was huge and beautiful! Still shoeless he walked on the sand, I took my shoes off and I put my socks in them. Then he found a spot and he put the blanket down, he sat down and he asked me to join him, I was throbbing at this point but I was waiting for his move. He told me to sit in his lap. When I sat down he pointed up, with one hand he pointed out constellations, the other hand went up my shirt. Ok, this I liked. He kissed my neck and rubbed my chest while telling me stories about the constellations he pointed out. When I responded positively to him, he kept going. He loosened and pulled his pants down then he did the same to me. He started rubbing me and he whispered, "there's my good girl, you had daddy worried you didn't love me anymore." Then he kissed me strong and deeply. That's when I knew there would never be a touch like Malcolm's. He knew me so well; I didn't have to tell him what I liked. Most times he knew it before I did. He stared me in my eyes as he went in, my body responded with small shivers when he was half way in. Then his eyes rolled, "you're still my good girl. Don't give daddy's cookies to no one else." I didn't know what made him say that, but I was too lost in the moment to ask. We made love on the beach, under the stars, next to the water. As we were leaving the beach my legs felt like jelly. He kissed me long and hard, and then he looked me in my eyes. He told me he knows something happened this summer that I'm not telling him. He told me he would know if I gave my cookies away. He told me he didn't know what he'd do if that ever happened. He warned me to never be that dumb.

****

The past two weeks Momma, Jade, Sophia, Auntie Lauren and I have been all over

Sometimes Love Isn't Enough

East Mont and Hilltop mall putting together outfits for Uncle Frank's party. Cassondra agreed to watch all the little ones that night. When the day finally came we spent all day getting ready. Jade straightened Momma's hair then I asked her to do the same to mine. My hair was ridiculously long and I was so excited. Even after she trimmed my ends. Momma looked fantastic, Daddy smiled really big when he saw her dressed and ready to go. He whispered in her ear and she blushed as she playfully hit him. Jade-pinned Auntie Lauren's hair up in a up do that made her look ten years younger. For Sophia's hair she put big beautiful bouncy curls in her hair. For her own hair she swept it to the side, and then she put a big flower in. I told her she looked beautiful because she did. When Sonny arrived his eyes were huge, he kept telling Jade how beautiful she looked. Malcolm couldn't take his eyes off me once he saw me. He didn't have to say anything it was all in his eyes. When Uncle Jeff and Charles were outside we came out the house. I gave Cassondra the number to Uncle Frank's just in case she needed us; the babies were all down for the night so we told her there shouldn't be any problems. Malachi, Timothy, Sonny, and Jade rode in Malachi's car. Auntie Lauren and Sophia rode with Uncle Jeff and Charles of course. And Momma and Daddy rode with us in Malcolm's car. When we got to Uncle Frank's we were one of the first persons there. His house was huge, and his yard was even bigger. All of the furniture was very modern and nicely decorated. He had a pool table in the house in his game room. Off the kitchen there was a room that had glass walls, he called it his sunroom. It had a beautiful view of the city below and a lot of greenery. There was a set up bar in the back and lots of tables and chairs. The pool even had a few floating flowers in it. Uncle Frank said we could've brought suits if we wanted to swim. Uncle Frank told us to make ourselves comfortable and more people would arrive shortly. Poppa and Nana arrived next, and slowly but surely other people started to arrive. A lot of family came, and a lot of people who worked for Uncle Frank. So it didn't seem odd when suddenly there was Troy. He was telling Malcolm about some of the women there. Malcolm nodded, but he didn't seem amused by that. Malcolm introduced me as his girlfriend to a few of his peers. One guy told him I was prettier than Malcolm led him to believe. I blushed and thanked the guy for the compliment. Out the corner of my eyes I noticed a woman walk up to Daddy and put her arm around his neck. Daddy immediately took her arm off him and walked away. My blood started boiling, and Malcolm tried to distract me. I introduced Malcolm to the cousins he hadn't met yet. I kept an eye on this woman. Clearly she had the hots for daddy, but I didn't know who she was. Did she know Daddy or did she decide that he was her prey for the night. She kept following him around, Daddy looked annoyed. I saw him talking to Uncle Frank, Daddy pointed her out. Uncle Frank went over to her; his face was stern as he said whatever he said to her. Then she went inside the house. I excused myself I told Malcolm I was running to the restroom. I could tell he didn't believe me, but he nodded anyways. On the way in the house I saw Malachi and Timothy talking to girls, or I should say women. In the house the woman was talking to another lady. She was telling her that Uncle Frank told her to leave Daddy alone and that he was there with his wife and children. The lady asked her which brother she was talking about. So the woman pointed out Daddy. Then the lady said, "oh that's Tim" then she pointed out Momma, she said, "there's his wife". The woman gasped, "she's black!" The lady said "yes, and she's beautiful!" That made me smile, but that woman flipped her blonde hair and she told her friend she wasn't concerned with Momma. I saw Malcolm coming up the stairs so I ran to the bathroom. I shut the door and pretended like I was just coming out. Malcolm smiled wide, and then

Carey Anderson

he said he saw me run, we both laughed. I told him about the conversation I over heard; he shook his head and said that woman would be a fool to start something tonight. When we went back outside that woman was dancing with some guy. I figured her friend had talked some sense into her. I asked the bartender for a rum and coke, Jade and Sophia had the same. I was on my third drink when I noticed when the woman walked past Momma she bumped into Momma making her spill her drink. She gave Momma the fakest apology and then she kept walking. I was on my way to get her right then but Malcolm caught me. He held on to me and told me to stay cool. I still took the bobby pins out of my purse and pinned my hair up in a low bun. When Jade and Gwen saw me put my hair up they asked me what was wrong. I pointed out the woman and I told them what she did. Gwen said she had never seen her before. I pointed out her friend who was talking on the other side of the party. Gwen knew who she was; she said that was the interior decorator that worked for her daddy. She said that lady always decorated her daddy's offices and she even decorated their house. She said she was really nice, and we assumed that woman came with her.

Then it happened, Daddy was sitting on a chair drink in hand talking to someone when that woman walked over and sat on his lap. I couldn't believe the nerve of that woman. Nana looked horrified, and she started looking for Momma who was on her way over. Daddy was caught off guard by all of this, he was telling the woman to get up when Momma came over and picked the woman up by her neck. Momma picked her up and tossed her aside like the cheap garbage she was. The woman started yelling at Momma and calling her names. Before anyone could stop her Momma had upper cut that woman and she had her on the ground. Momma stayed on her face, the woman's arms were flying every which way, but she couldn't land a punch to save her life. Her friends came running, and before Malcolm could grab me I took off. One woman was coming to hit Momma with a chair and I kicked her as hard as I could and she flew to the side. I ran after the woman as I passed Jade and Auntie Lauren who were running towards Momma. The woman stumbled back and when she looked at me she smiled. I guess she thought I would be easy to beat. She punched me in my face and I heard it but I couldn't feel it. I kicked her again and then I followed with a right hook and then a left. As the woman raised her leg to kick me I kicked the other leg, which snapped backwards, and she went down. She hit me in the face again but nothing could keep me off her, she tried to hurt my Momma she was gonna bleed. I pinned the woman by her shoulders and then I stayed on her face. Malcolm picked me up, I was still trying to get to the woman and he held me in the air. He said that was enough. I wasn't finished and I was mad he stopped me. Uncle Jeff had Momma, Uncle Frank had Jade, Timothy had Auntie Lauren, and Daddy had Sophia. The music had stopped and there were women laid out sporadically on the ground. Uncle Frank's voice boomed, "GET THIS TRASH OUT OF HERE!" Then Uncle Frank apologized to Momma and Nana. Uncle Frank's workers collected the trashy women and escorted them out of the party. They had to carry the woman I was fighting out on account of her leg being broken. Malcolm wouldn't put me down, because he knew if he did I was going after that woman again. None of them let any of us down actually. Momma's breathing was heavy Uncle Jeff was saying something to Momma as she tried to calm down. Daddy carried Sophia over and they carefully swapped women. Daddy hugged Momma; he had the biggest smile on his face. Seeing Momma smile made us kind of relax. Then the music came back on. Malcolm put me down slowly, he was smiling at me. Then he asked me if this meant that no matter what I would always be feisty like Momma. I smiled at him and I went to check on Momma. She didn't have a scratch on her. My cheek was bruised and I had a knot on my head, but I didn't care. Each one of us came and hugged Momma. She thanked us for having her back. Then the lady came over and tearfully apologized for her disrespectful friends. Momma accepted her apology, but Nana was not satisfied. I saw her say something to Uncle Frank who was still fuming. He motioned for the lady to follow him. I was curious to know what he was going to say to her. So I told Malcolm I was going inside to get some ice for my head. He eyed me as I walked into the house. I didn't see them in the kitchen so I walked towards the bathroom. Uncle Frank's office was right next to the bathroom. I heard a loud smack then he closed his office door. I went in the bathroom and put my ear to the wall. Uncle Frank was yelling at her for bringing such trashy women around his family. The lady was crying and apologizing. He smacked her again and she lightly screamed. He told her to tell her friends that they better never step a foot in the same mall as any member of his family or he would have them sleeping with the fish. Then he told her to fix her face and then she needed to go make things right with his mother if she could, and that he said she better or else.

Chapter 16

Dance classes at the center have been amazing! Ballet had Cassondra and I so sore the first two weeks. Muscles I hadn't ever used before were on fire. Jazz dance was a lot like modern to me. There was a lot of interpretation in that dance, but I loved it all the same. Now it got interesting in the modern dance class. Our teacher was a young guy, he was teaching us muscle isolations. He was playing the kind of music you really only heard at clubs. The dancing was as soulful as modern but a little more free formed. I looked forward to this class most. At home I would practice to the Jackson 5 Dancing Machine. It was the cutest thing watching Andrew copy me. Malcolm didn't like the idea of Cassondra and I taking Bart so he would take us to and from the center. I think that was his excuse to come to the center and check it out. He watched the people who were coming in and out of the center. I talked to Daddy, I told him I was going to sign up for driver's Ed and training in the fall. Then he asked Jade if she wanted a new car and I would get Malachi's car. Jade agreed, Malachi sat there helplessly as the fate of his car was decided.

Malcolm told me he had an idea. Since there wasn't an age limit on the classes, he wanted me to get Tiffany and Penny enrolled at the center. He wasn't really asking, he was telling me. I got so angry I hung up the phone. He's been acting weird ever since I came back from Nana's. But then again so have I, but all I've been doing is asking for more than the honor to hump him. When he wants me, he comes and gets me, and then just like that. I say I'm not gonna do it even though I know and he knows I want to. I'm just tired of doing everything on his schedule. The last couple of times I've gone with him I almost got away without putting out. He acts like he doesn't like me challenging him, but then he keeps breaking his neck to see me more. I like that aspect of our cat and mouse game. But this thinly veiled jealousy is getting old. When he called back I told Jade to tell him I was in the bathroom. Five minutes later I was on my bed reading Andrew a book. I heard the front door then I heard footsteps, I thought it was Jade. I looked up and it was Malcolm. He was mad! Momma and Daddy were out with Uncle Jeff and Auntie Lauren. Timothy and Malachi were out with friends. I jumped when I saw him. "WHY DID YOU HANG UP ON ME?"

"Cause" I said

"CAUSE?" Andrew looked at my face, and then he looked at Malcolm. He started crying. Malcolm looked at Andrew then he looked at me. Jade came and got Andrew although he acted like he didn't want to leave me.

I stood up and I put my hands on my hips. "Cause!"

Malcolm rushed me and grabbed my chin. I tried to pull my face away, but he had a firm grip on my face. "You are gonna be a good little girl, and do like I told you aren't you!"

I tried to pull my chin away, but he wouldn't let me go. "No!"

He gave me crazy eyes, "what do you mean no?"

"You heard me! The center is my place away from here. I love the girls but I want a place of my own. You just want them there to keep and eye on me." I said pushing on him so that he released my face. I tried to walk around him and he grabbed me by my arm and threw me on the bed. Then he kicked the door closed.

"If I tell you to get them enrolled you do what I tell you!"

"You are not the boss of me Malcolm! I don't have to do what you tell me. I'll just go to another school if you enroll them there without me."

"Are you hiding something?"

I sucked my teeth. "You don't trust me?"

"You're hiding something, I feel it!"
"Tell me what I'm hiding so we can get this over with." I said with attitude.
"Are you cheating on me?"
I huffed. "Are you cheating on me?" I shot back. Malcolm looked like he wanted to backhand me. He stood there not knowing how to reply. He looked like he kept going over reply after reply in his brain, but he couldn't come up with a good response. I stood up again and I put my hands on my hips. I smiled at him waiting for a response. Then I closed mouth kissed him. "The center is my space, leave it alone." Then I kissed him again. He gave me a defeated look, but I knew this wasn't over just yet. But I was still gonna enjoy my short-lived victory. I threw my arms around his neck and I kissed him. He looked down at me squinting his eyes and smirking at me.
Then he kissed me back. "You win this time." Then he kissed me deeply. "You and your mom are probably the only females who don't back down to me."
I smiled, "that turns you on doesn't it?"
"Only when you do it, I don't think anybody could get away with this." I kissed him again, and then I took him out of my room. My parents would be home soon and the last thing I needed was for them to tell me he couldn't come around when they weren't there. Jade had Andrew in her lap, while she was on the phone. She was rubbing his curls. He wanted me the moment he laid eyes on me. I started to go to him, but Malcolm grabbed me and looked at Andrew. "This is my woman!" He said to Andrew. Andrew looked confused. I rolled my eyes and picked up my baby. Andrew frowned at Malcolm, and Malcolm stared him down. I told him to stop doing that to Andrew. Malcolm got irritated all over again. He told me I was gonna make Andrew soft. I just rolled my eyes. Jade got up with the phone on her ear and moved to the next room. Malcolm sat down at the chess table. He smiled when he saw Daddy's last move. He sat there thinking for a long time. Andrew didn't take his eyes off of Malcolm or the frown off his face. Malcolm raised his hand to make his move, but then he took his hand back. He did this for about thirty minutes. Then I took Andrew back to the room and we finished our story. I heard Momma and Daddy come. Daddy and Malcolm spent the next hour or so talking. I bathed Andrew and I put him down for the night. Then I went in Momma's room and chatted with her about their night. Eventually Malachi came home and all three of them were in the living room talking about something that had them all pumped up. Malcolm was acting weird so I didn't go see him off.

****

I hugged everyone goodbye. It was my last class of the summer. The center director really wants me to enroll in Fall classes. I really wanted to, but without a car and a evening sitter it was gonna be pretty close to impossible to do. The director told me to come by as soon as Andrew turned two. He said normally the child had to be two almost three but they would make an exception for Andrew. That made me feel really special and wanted. It was time to prepare for my junior year and to focus on my plan. I pretty much put all my eggs into one basket; I hadn't done much research outside of Berkeley. I had to go there! Besides, that was the first place Malcolm ever took me. Every time I think about that my heart gets weepy. That seems like such a long time ago.
I told all my dancing buddies I would be back, next summer at the latest. Cassondra and I waited a whole hour for Malcolm to show up. Then we decided to walk towards the Bart station in hopes that we would see him along the way. A car was passing by and it honked at us and stopped. When neither of us went back it drove

131

off turning right at the next corner. We saw the car loop around, but we couldn't see the driver. The car parked across the street in front of a Chinese food restaurant on the corner. The driver got out and then he crossed the street illegally and started jogging towards us. Cassandra's eyes got big, and I didn't know whether to prepare to fight or not. The guy was tall and solid, and then suddenly Cassondra screamed "David!" And she took off running to meet him on the curb. I instantly felt embarrassed even though Andrew wasn't with me. So I maintained my pace until I met up with them. Cassondra and David hugged and when I got close enough David hugged me too, he smelled good. I was nervous thinking Malcolm could pull up at any moment and with the way he's been acting lately this would be the last thing I needed. Oh LORD! How did little old David turn out to be this fine? I tried not to look at him too much cause like I said Malcolm could pull up at any moment. David and Cassondra went over the what are you doing out here questions and answers and I stood over to the side quietly. David said he just got off work, and he was trying to think of somewhere to grab a bite to eat. Then he asked if we wanted to come along. Cassondra was ready to say yes, but she looked at me. I asked him where he wanted to go. He asked if we wanted Chinese food, he said there was a spot up the street. I looked at Cassondra; she was ready to go so I agreed. I made her ride in the front and I climbed in the back. We drove past that park that we took Andrew to, and then he parked behind a small building. The restaurant "The Palace Golden" didn't have any open windows, I was so thankful and it was kind of dimly lit. We sat in a booth. I wasn't saying much, I just felt embarrassed. I couldn't even explain why, but I did. David kept looking at me, but Cassondra was doing all the talking. She kept looking at me too, but I could tell she was wondering if I was ok. "How's your little man?" David asked me

I was trying to stay even, but when I felt heat flash over my face I knew I turned red. "He's good."

"How old is he now?"

"He'll be two in February."

Then he looked me in my eyes, "how's Malcolm?"

I really turned red. "He's fine."

David sort of smiled then he turned his attention back to Cassondra. I died ten thousand deaths. When the food came I kind of pushed it around my plate. I didn't really touch it. I had the waitress wrap it up for me. David wanted to take us home, but the fear of Malcolm made me say no. But he insisted, so we had him take us close to Cassondra's house. When we got out the car, he stuck a piece of paper in my hand. "Call me when you can, we need to catch up." I turned red again. I got out the car and Cassondra was smiling at me. She saw him slip me his number. She said it was always obvious to the world that he liked me way back when. Somehow Malcolm swooped in and took over. We laughed. I called home when we got to Cassondra's. Jade was going to the store for Momma so she was gonna come pick me up. Cassondra and I drooled over how much David had matured. I asked Cassondra if she liked him? And she shrugged; she said he never looked in her direction so it didn't really matter. She said her mother keeps telling her to hang in there and that eventually there would be someone for her. Plus she's had the hugest crush on some guy who's a friend of her family for years now. She and Jade talk about waiting, and saving their selves for something beautiful. I admire that; sometimes I wish I would've done the same. But I'm always happy when I see Andrew. I don't ever regret him. When Jade came I hopped in the backseat with Andrew who was always excited to see me. Jade said Malcolm was on the phone with Momma as she walked out the door. He's never left me hanging before, I wondered what kept him. I put David's number in my bag inside one of my dance shoes so I wouldn't lose it, and it wouldn't slip out at some perfectly timed weird moment. When we got to the house Malcolm's car was outside. He helped us bring in the groceries. Then he told me to come on. I begged him to let me shower first. He sucked his teeth, cause Momma told him to let me shower or else I might funk out his car. Plus I wanted to put my dance bag away. Andrew and I walked into the living room where he was studying the board. He looked at Andrew then at me. I could tell he wanted me to leave Andrew but I had been away from him all day. I wanted him with me. I strapped Andrew into the backseat, and then I got in the front. He drove out to East fourteenth, and a couple of blocks later he stopped. He pointed at a building. "Drew's!" He said still pointing.

I looked at the building, "Drew's?" I asked

He parked the car, and opened my door. I got Andrew out the back. "My barber shop!" He said with the biggest smile. He took out keys to open the gate. When he opened the door it was just empty space. Concrete floors, bare walls, completely empty. He was so excited. He ran from wall to wall explaining how he wanted it all set up. He said he was working on the deal all day. I asked him how he was gonna do this, he wasn't eighteen yet. He told me he worked out the deal with Uncle Frank. His friend Moses had his barbering license. He said he was going to go to cosmetology school to get his Barber's license. He had a whole plan; eventually he was going to buy Uncle Frank out. He was so excited about all the details he kept jumping around completely animated. He told me he got the fictitious business license today, and it was official that the shop would be called Drew's! We both looked at Andrew who was spinning in the space. I told him that was really sweet of him and that I was really happy for him. Then he told me to be happy for us. I told him I was happy for us, I was just a little tired. He was so excited that I couldn't steal his thunder. He said he had so much to do. I asked him how he was gonna manage everything? School, Track, Business, my Uncle, and us. He told me he had a plan, and then he smiled.

****

School started with a bang. Jade and Cassondra rode to school together. Malcolm picked me up, it was nice pulling up to school together. Sophia and Charles pulled up just before we did. I waved good morning to Sophia, and then I grabbed my bag out the car. When I stood up Malcolm was eyeing Charles and Charles was walking very hurried towards the school. Then Malcolm looked at me with the craziest look on his face. When I asked him what was wrong he looked mad and he shook his head. He was mumbling something under his breath, but I couldn't make it out. I told Sophia I would catch up with her at lunch. Then Malcolm asked me why we never had lunch together. I told him he always has "Business" to take care of. Then he grabbed my hand and told me he wanted to have lunch with me. Now I don't know what just happened between him and Charles, but it was working to my advantage.

I'm so happy I got my bid in early, on the first day of school four girls approached Cassondra about their prom and junior prom dresses. I helped her schedule out the time and figure out exactly how many dresses she could make before prom. I came up with the discount for early orders. She would start delivering dresses in November. The earlier the delivery date the bigger the discount. The closer to the prom the more expensive the dresses would be. Then with the help of her Home EC teacher Ms. Bradshaw she came up with a few designs and then a few customizations that could be added to make the dresses individuals. Ms. Bradshaw even got her discounts on fabrics. Jade and I managed her books. We felt so official.

Ms. Dubois and I cried together when she asked me what happened to Melvin. I told her I really didn't understand what happened. She told me time explains everything and to hang in there. I told her about my classes at the center. She applauded me for continuing my education over the summer. I told her about my current direction to open a school slash center of my own. Her eyes got really big, and she said she'd help me in anyway she could.

After school Malcolm and I walked to his car. I told him I was going to take the drivers Ed class in the morning next week. He looked like he wanted to tell me not to, but that would've been a waste of breath. Then Sophia and Charles came out the school. They were arguing really badly about something. Charles kept looking over towards us as he argued with Sophia. I got in the car while Malcolm stood outside ear hustling. Charles drove away you could tell they were still arguing in the car. When Malcolm got in the car he asked me if Charles came on our camping trip. When I told him no he searched my face so I bucked my eyes at him. Then he started asking a ton of questions about Charles. I told him I barely see Charles. Then he asked me why Charles was always looking at me. I told him I had no idea and that I don't really pay him any attention. Malcolm sat there staring at me. I got irritated. I asked what he was searching for. He said I'm hiding something from him. I frowned at him; I asked him if this was reverse psychology to hide something he was doing. He just looked at me, and then I asked how Yvette was doing. He sucked his teeth and started the car. When I got home Malcolm didn't come in, he had "work" to do. Momma was laying on the couch. She had a headache, and she was very thankful I made it home when I did. Andrew was building something with his blocks. Then he stood up and kicked it down. He would laugh so hard when the blocks fell then he would gather them and build again. That boy is so silly. After watching him for a minute I went in the kitchen to start dinner. Momma had steaks defrosted in the sink, potatoes on the counter, and there were a couple of bunches of broccoli in the refrigerator. As I was peeling potatoes the phone rang. My heart sped up as I realized it was Tag. He said he was happy to finally catch me at home. He asked about my summer, and how my first day of school was. He asked me if they mentioned when our first performance was going to be. I told him I didn't know yet, but I'd let him know as soon as I knew. I told him I needed to focus on dinner, he gave me his number and then we got off the phone. My hands got sweaty as I went into my room. I took David's number out of my shoe. My heart fluttered when I looked at it. I sat there debating with myself. I needed a just cause to call him. I kept wrestling with myself. I couldn't come up with anything. I put the number in my shirt drawer in the back left corner. Feeling defeated I went back to finishing dinner.

At lunch over the next few weeks, I was reintroduced to a lot of Malcolm's cousins. Jade and Cassondra had lunch with us too. Jade and Malcolm were going back and forth about some book they read junior year. Everyone myself included got lost in the symbolism that they referenced in the book. The book sounded like a real doozy. Jade asked Malcolm a question about a part of the book that stumped him. We all sat there in disbelief. Bernadette laughed real loud and then she gave Jade a high five. She was impressed that anyone could stump Malcolm. Malcolm sat there thinking for a while. Then he stood up, as unattached as he could he said, " I guess when it comes down to it, no matter who it is. Business is business, and you always have to do what comes next. No exceptions!" Everybody was quiet; Malcolm's face was stone. No one asked him if he meant it, it was obviously a stupid question. Saved by the bell we all disbursed to our classes.

****

Finishing driver's Ed was a piece of cake. Driver's training was great as well. Momma took me to the Oakland hills and made me practice parallel parking between two cars, talk about pressure. She gave me one of her looks and told me I better not bump either of the cars. Sure enough I got it, I was so proud of myself. Malcolm has been so busy lately. In the morning he goes by the shop to check the progress daily. Then he comes to get me for school. Sometimes he has lunch with us and other times he has "business" to tend to. People have been telling me that they've seen him talking to this freshman. When I asked him about it, he got mad and told me not to believe everything I hear. That girl Yvette comes around still looking for Malcolm. Sometimes it seems like she comes looking for me, she looks at me. She doesn't challenge me or anything, it's weird but she watches me as if she wants to talk to me. But after seeing what happened to Toni I don't blame her for staying away. After school Malcolm is gone, Sophia picks me up from practice. My driving test is in two weeks. As soon as I have my license I'll be able to drive myself to school, I don't know when I'll see Malcolm at that point, but I can't stop progress just to hold on to him, right?

There's this new sophomore Sammy something. People say he was a pretty big deal at his old school. He got expelled from his last school so now he's at our school. Bernadette said he's been watching Malcolm trying to figure out how to get at him. I thought to myself nobody has to be that stupid. Bernadette said he's been watching everybody trying to figure out who is who. He stares at Jade and me. Malcolm says he's not worried about him, he said if he's smart he'll stand down.

I GOT MY LICENSE!!!!!!! I ran screaming through the DMV. I hugged Momma so tight! I was so excited! Andrew got so excited even though he didn't know what he was cheering for. I tried to have the sexiest smile for my license photo, Momma laughed and said I was gonna hate that picture. Then Momma let me take her car. I moved Andrew's seat to the front. Then I asked him where he wanted to go. He just smiled; I told him lets go see what daddy's doing. We drove by the shop and it was dark inside of there. I swallowed hard, and then I drove to Momma Shuga's house. Malcolm's car was parked across the driveway. I parked in front of the house. When I got out of the car with Andrew some of the cousins started oohing. When I opened the door that girl Renee was on the floor holding a baby. She cracked a evil smile at me, my stomach flipped. I could tell I was walking into something but it was too late to go backwards. Momma Shuga was yelling at Penny about something, she stopped mid-sentence when she saw me. She stood up straight and smiled big. Penny shot me the saddest eyes when Momma Shuga said Malcolm was in his room. I looked at the door at the end of the hallway. If I knocked on it he wasn't gonna answer. So I stood there. Penny came over to say hi to Andrew. She asked me if she could hold him, Andrew was leaping for her. So I gave him to her as I debated on what to do. So I pulled a chair from the table and set it directly in the hallway. Momma Shuga pulled out a chair and she sat down next to me. She asked me what was new and we cordially chatted for a while. Andrew was having a ball with Penny; she had him laughing really hard. Tiffany came home and she got so excited when she saw me. She gave me a huge hug and then she proceeded to play with Penny and Andrew. Momma Shuga kept trying to draw me out, she was getting a kick out of seeing me squirm. When the door opened I saw manicured feet. She had on one of Malcolm's t-shirts ONLY! I expected to see Yvette come down the stairs. But I don't even know who this girl is. She paused when she saw me, and she turned around to go back in the room and I charged. My feet didn't even touch the stairs. I tackled her as she entered the room. Malcolm was laying in the bed. At the sound of us hitting the floor, Malcolm popped up and hopped into shorts lightening fast. I hopped up to get to him and the girl grabbed my leg which made me stumble. Malcolm's face was so shocked; I turned over and booted the girl in the head. She let go of my ankle. Screaming every profanity I charged at Malcolm. I swung at him and he grabbed my wrist and spun my body around, he wrapped both arms around me. The girl jumped up like she was gonna do something. Malcolm told her to stand still. But she came charging at me. Malcolm let me go, I popped her face as she came at me. She stumbled by the door. Holding her face she came at me again. This girl was stupid, I wasn't gonna make this about her. I was coming for him, but she call herself trying to protect my man from me. He told her to stand down she didn't listen so now... She started wind milling at me while she was screaming. I stopped and looked at Malcolm, and I gestured at him like is she serious. Then he told her to stop. Then he asked me what I was doing there, I told him it didn't matter. He didn't have to worry about me ever coming over there again. He asked me to calm down.

"Calm down! Calm down! You've been riding me about cheating on you. Why? Cause look what you do! You run around with all these hookers!"

"Who are you calling a hooker?"

"Shameka shut up!" He said

"Malcolm you just gonna let her sit over there and call me names?"

"She ain't lying, you need to just shut up!"

The girl got mad and started yelling and screaming. Malcolm picked up her clothes and her shoes; he threw them in the hallway. He told her to get out, and that she wasn't worth the headache. She tried to tell him she wasn't leaving. He pushed her by her face out the room and then he shut the door. You heard everyone erupt into laughter as the girl tumbled down the stairs. He turned to me with sad eyes. He walked to me slowly and as soon as he stepped in my circle I slapped him as hard as I could. He kept coming. He kept saying he was sorry. I told him he was only sorry cause he got caught. He put his arms around me to hold me and I kept punching, elbowing, and scratching him. He kissed my forehead. I reached up and popped him in his mouth. I told him to let me go. I told him I hated him! I told him he ruined my life! He let me go and then he touched his lip. I busted his lip. He looked at his hand and frowned and then he smiled at me. I prepared for him to hit me, but he bear hugged me and then slammed me on the bed. He told me to calm down. I stood up on the bed and screamed at him. I told him he's ruined my life, I refused to calm down. He snatched my feet from underneath me and I fell on the bed. I started kicking and punching the air. Then I heard Andrew crying. I proceeded to curse him out with everything in my soul. Then I snatched the door open. Penny was trying to calm Andrew down. I tried to calm myself as much as I could then I went to Penny to get my baby. Andrew almost leaped into my arms; he was crying my tears for me. Momma Shuga stood over to the side. As I started towards the door, I heard glass shattering. My heart stopped at the thought of my Momma's car getting busted up. Momma would kill me. That girl Renee was sitting on the floor laughing. I held on to Andrew and I ran out the door. That girl was looking for another rock to throw through Malcolm's car windows. His windows were all busted up. All the cousins were inside; they all came rushing out the house. They started laughing and oohing. Then she turned to Momma Shuga's car. She started throwing rock after rock through her windows. I got in Momma's car. I put Andrew in his seat as Malcolm came running out the door. I saw his hand go up in the air towards that girl, and I pulled away. I drove away and finally tears poured out of my eyes. I looked at the clock and it was only seven forty-five. I got on the freeway and I drove. The next thing I knew I was pulling up to Nana's house. I sat in the car for a minute wiping my face. I waited until my eyes lost most of their redness. I put on a smile then I took Andrew out of his seat. Poppa saw us coming up the walkway, he opened the door. He was really happy to see us. He gave us a hug and asked to what did he owe the honor of our presence. I told him I got my license and I was just out for a stroll. He said Nana was out with some of her friends, but he was happy I stopped by. I asked him if I could call my Momma so she wouldn't be worried. When I called Momma picked up on the first ring. I told Momma to pretend like I was someone else.

"Hey Lauren what's going on?" Momma said

"Is Malcolm there?" I asked

"Yes girl!"

"Did he tell you what happened?" I asked

"Not really, but you should of seen it. It was so sad."

"I'm at Poppa's, I don't wanna see him. What should I do?" I asked

"I guess I could call you back later. Let me go look in my closet." She said, "I'll call you back."

Then we hung up. Poppa had Andrew's jacket off and he was feeding him mashed potatoes. I felt horrible I forgot to feed my baby. The phone rang and I told Poppa it was my Momma. Momma said he showed up in a jacket with no shirt, no socks or shoes on, he had on shorts, and a busted lip. She said he had a few tears. She said he looks all unglued. I told her I don't want to see him. Momma asked what happened, I told her to look at his car and that her name was Shamrock or something. Momma just said, "oh I see".

Chapter 17

That little girl Shamrock, I mean Shameka has turned out to be a real headache. Turns out she is the freshman that everybody was telling me about. When I went to school on Monday her little friends call themselves confronting me as soon as I stepped foot on campus. It was four of them and I was seemingly by myself. Before my bag hit the ground Bernadette and her friends came out of nowhere having my back. I didn't have to fight anybody. They swooped in like locust. They laid them girls out grabbed my stuff and me. We were gone before teachers made their way over there. Sammy somehow seemed to be sitting back and watching all of this taking it in.

Malcolm tried real hard for a while to talk to me, but every time I would see him my heart would hurt. At first I was trying to be strong and just tell him to leave me alone. But then he kept pushing. When I finally broke down crying, and he knew it was because of him, it seemed to repel him. He would back away and give me space.

At school I would focus on my classes, in dance class I would dance like I never danced before. Which was actually good for my form and technique. At home I would mope around, and cry in my room a lot. Jade or Sophia would come and make me go out. We'd take the kids to the park or just go for a walk. I know Momma told Daddy cause they both look at me with sad eyes but they don't say anything. It's like I can hear them saying in my head, "see we told you!" Daddy put the chess game away. Momma restricts Malcolm to the porch now. Sometimes she'll go out there to talk to him. She said he's a mess, but I don't care. He's broken my heart for the last time. I don't want to see him. I even stopped taking my pill. Momma and I got into a huge argument about it too. She told me to never stop taking them cause I never knew if tomorrow he and I would make up and then I would be stuck. She said it's hard to go back to condoms when you're used to being skin to skin with someone. I told her there was no risk of that cause I didn't want to see him or be alone with him. I don't know why she doesn't believe me. But Momma started getting that all too familiar look in her eyes and I grabbed my baby and we got out of that house. Momma's patience has been real short with me ever since then. So now I try to stay out of the house as much as I can.

Malachi's car cut out on me a couple of times. So Daddy said he would buy me a car. He said it wouldn't be brand new like Jade's car, but it would be good enough to get me around. We put a cover over Malachi's car and put it in the garage. So Daddy bought me a little bug, I call him Herb 2. I liked my little car so much better than the huge boat that is Malachi's car. I was happy that Jade had the brand new car too. She gets straight A's, did I mention her SAT scores were off the charts, she does what she's told, and she hasn't brought Momma and Daddy half the drama that I have. She deserves every big fuss they could make over her. Where I on the other hand brought this whole thug element into our lives.

I try to focus really hard during the week and get all my homework done. And then on the weekend I load up Andy and we get away. Lately we've been landing on Tammy's porch. She told me I could come over whenever. She has an apartment in Albany that she shares with Stefan. Jade goes over with me sometimes when she's not working or she'll come after work. Depending on Momma's mood sometimes I can spend the night or I have to come home. On the nights that I can spend the night, if Cassondra can swing it. I pick her up and she stays with Andrew and we go out dancing. I normally try to stick to dancing with Tammy and Stefan. Every once in a blue moon I'd dance with a guy at the club. But most of them want to talk and they try so hard to hook up. I go to dance and to drink. I have no interest in going home with anyone. When I told Tammy and Stefan that they laughed at me. They said half the fun of going out is hooking up with someone. More than twice I was going back to their apartment alone or with Jade by my side. In the morning when they came home hung over or whatever I'd have breakfast and the coffee ready for them. The club clothes I bought would stay at Tammy's house. Momma knew about us going to clubs when I was with Malcolm, but suddenly they weren't ok now that we weren't together. Once she realized who Tag was she started giving me evil eyes when I would get home and she'd tell me he called. Normally when I got home it was too late to call him back or I just wouldn't feel like it. I just didn't feel up to being deeply involved with him. He was dang near about to tell me he loved me the last time I talked to him. And I'm sorry I just don't feel like believing him. I feel like he's too old to be so love struck over a little high school girl like me. Malcolm was always quick to remind me that I was a little girl to him and he's only a year older than me. Tag isn't quite Timothy's age, but I'm supposed to believe he has loving feelings for me. He's not ugly, I'm sure girls like him, I don't understand why it has to be all this.

Sometimes I look at David's number, but I feel so embarrassed every time I even think about calling him. Finally to end my misery I tore up his number and I threw the paper in the fireplace. When I told Cassondra what I did, she gasped like she couldn't believe it. I told her his number was hanging over my head like a cloud. I couldn't stand to face him. She didn't understand but she rubbed my back anyways when I started crying. I just wanted a fresh slate. I needed to start over.

"How you doing Ms. Amber?" Sammy said, I looked at him like he had to be joking. "Can I talk to you for a minute."

"I gotta get home, and I'm tired." I said as I kept walking. I just finished rehearsing; my winter performance was in two weeks.

"I was wondering why I don't see Malcolm around all that much any more."

"You waited two hours after school to ask me about gossip?" I said rolling my eyes and still walking.

"Well it's not gossip if it comes directly from you." Then he tugged on my jacket. "Slow down, I'm trying to talk to you."

"I told you I gotta get home. I don't have time for this."

Then he grabbed my arm. "You ain't going nowhere until you answer my question!" I shot him a look like he had to have lost his mind. "Don't you EVER put your hands on me!" I yelled yanking my arm away. He grabbed my arm again and tighter. "I don't know what your problem is but you better take your hands off me!" I said yanking my arm again.

"Or else what? You think your ex boyfriend will care that I grab you?"

"I care! I don't want your hands on me. You need to back off!" I said snatching my arm away and running to my car. He didn't chase me, but I got in my car as fast as I could. I didn't know what his problem was, but whatever was between him and Malcolm was between them. When I got home Momma asked me what was wrong. I told her about Sammy grabbing my arm. She told me that I needed to tell Malcolm. I refused, I told her I wasn't talking to him and I meant it. When Daddy came home Momma told him what happened at school. Daddy's eyes got real serious; he asked me if Sammy did anything to me. I told him the story just like I told Momma. Daddy put on his jacket and he left. Sophia called a few minutes later asking what happened. She said Daddy came and got Uncle Jeff and they took off. I told her about Sammy, and she got quiet. Then she said she wondered where they went I did too. I asked her why she and Charles were arguing so much lately. She said she didn't know, but lately he has no patience for anything. And that it just seemed like she couldn't do anything right. She got quiet for a minute then she changed the subject. She told me she talked to Rosalind; they were going to come out for a visit this summer. We chatted a little longer and then we got off the phone.

The next day at school Malcolm was there bright and early. He asked me what happened with Sammy. I told him as quickly as possible. Malcolm stood there with a serious face thinking as I walked away. I didn't want to talk to him, but I also didn't want to be harassed everyday behind someone trying to get at him. At lunchtime I moved my car to the teacher parking lot. After school I told Ms. Dubois what happened the day before. Her eyes got big; she asked if I thought he was targeting me to get to Malcolm. I gave her a look that said duh! When I walked out of the class Troy was waiting in the hallway. "COUSIN!" He yelled when he saw me, Ms. Dubois and I jumped when he did that. He started cracking up laughing. I told him he plays too much! He came and gave me a huge hug. He told me everybody misses me, and he asked how long was I gonna keep Malcolm in the doghouse. I shot him a look and he put his hands up. He walked Ms. Dubois and I to our cars. She waved as she drove off. Then he asked me how long again. I blank stared at him. "I'm just saying though. Amber you know he over there hurting and you over here acting like you don't care." He said

"He only feels bad cause he got caught! That fool has been acting insecure all summer. I guess because he was up to no good. He wanna be with other females, now he got the space to do it. He has ruined my life!"

"How did he ruin your life?"

"Seriously???"

"Yea, he's been hooking you up from where I'm standing."

"He's been running this show from the beginning to now. I got a baby; he wanted to have me on lock down waiting for him on everything. All I wanted was for him to give me what he demanded from me exclusivity."

"Who the what?" He had a confused look.

"Exclusivity?"

"Yea"

"He wanted me to ONLY have eyes for him."

"Oh, but that's not his fault though. He be on good behavior most of the time."

"I want a husband who's on good behavior all the time!"

"Husband?" He acted like I fed him something nasty.

"Yes, husband! Andrew needs a daddy."

"Andrew has a daddy."

"Malcolm's not concerned with Andrew. He never wants me to bring Andrew with us. He always trying to leave him behind. He doesn't try to be about his son. Malcolm and I are over. He never wanted Andrew so it's fine. My son needs a daddy, I need a husband."

Troy put his hands up like he couldn't say yes or no to what I was saying. I told him I had to go. Then he said the shop was gonna be opening in a week and that I should come by when it does. I shrugged and then I got in the car.

****

As promised, I looked out into the crowd and there was Tag sitting next to Nana and Poppa. My family was all there as usual. Malcolm was posted in his usual spot. He was sitting with a bunch of his cousins; I noticed that he had Andrew in his lap.

I knew Troy was gonna run back and tell him everything I said. As I peeked through the curtain I couldn't help but notice how Malcolm didn't look natural with Andrew, but at least he was trying, right. I told myself not to think about them. My new partner Scott was good, but he was no Melvin. We still performed very well. Standing ovation, then Ms. Dubois had a special surprise for me. One of her friends from Berkeley came to see her class perform, but really to check me out. His name was Al Campbell. Mr. Campbell said he was very impressed with my movement and expression. He said he could tell that I didn't have formal training, but that aspect really gave me an artistic edge. Then Ms. Dubois took him out to introduce him to my family. When I came from the back Tag was right there by the curtain as the first person I saw. He gave me a bouquet of daisies and other wild flowers. He kissed my cheek and told me that I danced beautifully. I thanked him for the flowers. I told him I was glad he enjoyed the show. I hugged Sophia, Cassondra, and Jade. Then Malcolm walked up, he looked Tag up and down. He gave me the box of two dozen long stem roses, and then he kissed my cheek and told me I danced phenomenally. Then he looked Tag up and down again. Andrew grabbed my legs and kept saying "yay mommy!" Then Penny and Tiffany came and congratulated me as well. I was so happy to see them. Sophia asked them if they had made anything good lately. They started going down the list of things they've tried to make. Sophia said she would make them a personalized cookbook of recipes she really liked. She said she wanted to hear from them to know how they liked them. The girls got so excited. Malcolm stared at me the whole time. Tag watched the interaction between Malcolm and I but he didn't say anything. Malcolm eventually asked, "who are you?"
"Tag, and you are?" He said sticking out his hand.
Malcolm looked at his hand, "are you a relative?"
"Friend of the family." Tag said
Malcolm looked at Tag and then he looked at me. I tried my best to keep my face even. He didn't say anything he just took it in. I could tell his mind was working fast. Poppa came over as an angel of mercy and he told Malcolm to come talk to him. Tag looked at me when they walked away. I asked him to walk with me. Penny and Tiffany looked Tag up and down like they were about to attack. I thanked him for coming out to see me perform. Then I told him my life was a little complicated right now and I didn't want to hurt him or see him get hurt. He tried to argue with me, but I insisted that we could only be friends, and that even that had to be done at a distance. He wasn't happy, but what could he say? Malcolm watched us from across the room even though he was talking to Poppa. I could tell Tag didn't understand but eventually he just let it go. When it was time to go out to eat Poppa invited Malcolm to come with us. Malcolm declined, so I asked if the girls could come and I told him I would drop them off. They got so excited, he agreed. The girls, Jade, and Andrew rode with me. We rode to Emeryville to Murphy's Carlos. I loved their shredded beef nachos. Plus this restaurant had a beautiful view of the Bay. Charles came straight from work to the restaurant. Penny and Tiffany were all smiles cause they had never been to this restaurant before. I sat in the middle of Tag and Andrew. Our table was long and we had a blast. I went over the menu with the girls; I told them they could order whatever they wanted. Their eyes got really big. But they still stuck to cheaper meals on the menu. I asked them if they ever had Shirley Temples, and the looks on their faces as they shook their heads no. We all had them and they were in love you could tell. As if this dining experience wasn't already a system overload, they were delighted when we told them to order dessert. Tag was

quiet all dinner, but I didn't press him about that. We were all talking and at one point as my hand rested on the table Tag put his hand over mine. His touch startled me and Tiffany shot me a look like she didn't understand. I quickly moved my hand and without looking at him I shook my head. That was his last attempt. Then all night I caught Charles looking at me longer than he should've been, but when momma caught him she looked like she wanted to kick him. Uncle Jeff noticed it too, that made the butterflies in my stomach flutter. Sophia was busy tending to Sasha, so she didn't notice. When our meal was over I thanked everyone for coming out to support me. I told them all that their continued love and support meant the world to me. Our same five loaded up in my bug and then we took the girls home. Tiffany asked me if Tag was my boyfriend. When I told them no, they wanted to know if I was going to get back together with Malcolm. I told them I didn't see that happening. I told them that Malcolm and I's time had come and gone. They looked sad and disappointed. Penny asked me not to forget about them just because of what happened with Malcolm. I told her that I loved them both dearly, and they could call me whenever. As we pulled up to Momma Shuga's house the cousins were on the porch, they were surprised when they saw me step out of the car to let the girls out of the back seat. Malcolm came down to the car, he had been drinking. He asked the girls if they had fun, and they both shook their heads yes, then they hurried in the house. Malcolm got in my face, he smiled, "so you dating the white boy now?" I told him no, then he said I was a liar. He said the white boy is why all the sudden nothing he did was good enough anymore. I asked him what he was talking about. He said all the sudden he had to move heaven and earth to please me. It was because I was cheating on him with the white boy. I told him it wasn't true. Although I knew it was. He just kept calling me a liar. Then he asked why it had to be like this and that he loved me, but all I wanted to do was take his money and mess with his head. I told him that wasn't true, but I knew it was pointless to argue with him. He got in my face like he wanted to kiss me, but then he backed up and said he wasn't good enough to kiss me. He said I was the only person who never made him feel like he was too black or that the color of his skin wasn't an issue until today. I started crying when he said that. His skin has always been beautiful to me. I started to explain to him why that wasn't true, but Jade told me to get in the car. She told me it was pointless to argue with a drunk person. So I told him the reason we're not together has nothing to do with his skin, but has everything to do with how he made me feel. No matter what I did, I wasn't enough for him, I told him I can't continue to be the best me on that kind of negativity and disappointment. I kissed his cheek then I got in the car. Jade grabbed my hand as I drove away.

****

Since we're out on winter break I decided to roll by the center. Cassondra needed a break from her dress making so she agreed to go with us. When we got to the center it was really empty, the center was on winter break as well. I talked to the director and I told him part one of my issue was solved now that I have a car. As if everything was perfectly lining up he told me to have Andrew start the first Monday in February. I felt so grown up signing the enrollment forms for Andrew as his parent. I signed him up for Beginners ballet, and myself for Modern dance. Both classes started at the same time in the evening on Wednesdays. Cassondra said she would have to wait until summer cause her load was a little heavy at the moment. Cassondra said she needed to get something from the grocery store. As we drove down MacDonald Ave we passed a Montgomery Ward's department store. We said we would go back around after we left the store. There was a Lucky's on one side of the street and a Safeway on the other. As I asked her which one she said she wanted to go to, she chose Safe house. When I realized we were at David's store I felt like I couldn't breathe. Cassondra asked me to come in and all I could do was shake my head no. She asked me if Andy could go. I shook my head yes, but I wanted to cry. Then she told me to relax, for all we know he's probably not working today. They went in the store and my heart felt like it was gonna jump out of my chest. Then I wondered if he would even want to see me. Maybe, he could feel rejected cause I didn't call. Cassondra came out with a huge smile on her face. She didn't have Andrew. I asked in a panicked tone where was Andrew. She said David had him. Then she said that he gets off work in two hours. He wants us to hang out and then he'll take us to get something to eat if that's ok with me. I got out the car to go get my baby. I told Cassondra that was fine and that I was going to curse her out as soon as we left the store. David emerged from the store with Andrew in his arms. Andrew was smiling from ear to ear, he's never responded to Malcolm that way. David was smiling and he gave me a hug. He told me that Andrew was a cool little guy. Then he asked if we could hang out until he got off work. His eyes kind of pleaded with me to say yes. I said yes as I took Andrew from him. I told him we were gonna go to the Montgomery Ward's we just passed. He smiled and said he would find us in the store. He walked us to my car and then he got a burst of energy. He hugged me, and then he squeezed the life out of Cassondra. Then he told Andrew he was gonna see him in a minute. He did a very energized jump and fist pump in the air as he walked back inside. I smiled at Cassondra and I told her I didn't like her. She got so excited, and she started filling my head with a ton of what ifs. I drove across the street to the Savings of American bank. I forgot to bring money with me so I filled out a withdrawal slip for sixty dollars. I almost passed out when I saw the balance; I had almost eighty-five thousand in there. Tears filled my eyes and instantly I felt conflicted. How could I deny what he's done for me? My book said the last deposit was yesterday. That made my heart sink as well. I came out the bank in tears. Cassondra was shocked by my total 360; she asked me what was wrong. I had never shared with her about the money. I didn't tell her how much. I told her he's still putting change in my account. She got quiet, and then she rubbed my back. We went inside the store; since we had time to kill we browsed from section to section. When we got to the toy section Andrew fell in love with a basketball. He gave me pleading eyes as he asked for it. I got him the ball and it was almost the same size as him. But it kept him occupied as we bought him some new clothes and shoes. We were in the mattress section; Andrew and I were sitting on a mattress saying ooh! And Aah! Cassondra had found heaven in a rocking chair slash recliner. David dove on the mattress next to Andrew. Andrew erupted in excited laughter. Andrew was responding to David like he responded to Malachi and Timothy. It stung me all over like a thousand bee stings when I thought about the fact that Andrew doesn't respond to Malcolm like that. Andrew showed David his ball; David said we need to go break the ball in. He took Andrew by the hand and asked us if we were ready. He parked his car next to mine so he told us to get in. He put our bags in his trunk and then he asked what we had a taste for. Then he mentioned National's hamburgers. We agreed, so he drove there. Cassondra rode in the front again after I made her. I rode in the back with Andrew. David pointed out San Pablo Dam Rd, he said that road takes you up to Tilden park and over to Orinda. I asked what Tilden park was. He smiled real big, he said little man would love it and that he would take us some day. Cassondra smiled at me. When we got to National's we placed our orders then he told us to pick a table. I didn't want to sit by open windows so we sat in the area to the left in a booth that was just around the corner. Andrew wanted to sit next to David and I had Cassondra sit on the other side of him. I sat on the edge of the booth. The whole time I felt a little edgy, David kept looking at me but he didn't mention my demeanor. Then he told Andrew they had to break in his new ball. We climbed in his car again. He went up San Pablo Dam Rd over the freeway and turned right on the first corner. We drove about a block on the frontage road, and then he turned left into the school parking lot. He took Andrew by the hand and basketball in the other, he looked at us. "Y'all coming?" We got out the car and followed them to the basketball courts. Andrew had an absolute blast with David, he had him dribbling the ball and trying to pass the ball under his leg, which was hilarious cause he didn't raise his leg high enough he couldn't. We laughed so hard watching them play and have a good time. Andrew pulled Cassondra up and he had her trying to do what he just saw David do. David smiled at me, and then he said that Andrew was a great kid. My heart felt heavy, I said "thank you" and then I got quiet. He looked at me, "since when you ever been this quiet?"

I blushed, "I'm just trying to be cool. There's a lot going on right now, and I don't want to be confused anymore than I already am."

"Talk to me, what's going on?"

"Just like that? You expect me to just tell you all my business?"

"Amber we go way back. We should be able to just dive right in. I asked you to call me, but you never did."

"You know, I took your number out a few times. I wanted to call you, you know catch up. But you know how Malcolm is. I don't wanna get nobody hurt."

"Are you guys still together?"

"No, but it gets complicated. He seems to think once his always his. I don't want you to get caught up in nothing like that. You're better than that."

"I'm not asking for your hand in marriage. I just wanna be friends, I thought we were friends."

"Yea, we are. But I remember a certain someone declaring love for me in the little theater in middle school."

We both laughed, "I'm kind of in the middle of something myself. I'm in no position to press you for a relationship. A lot can happen in two and a half years. I just wanna be friends."

"I can handle being friends." I said

"Good! Me too!" He said

Then I gave him my number.

Chapter 18

Momma gets really irritated whenever David calls. Sometimes it feels like my breakup with Malcolm has cost me more than just my relationship with him. Momma acts like she's ready to swing on me at any irritation all over again. She hasn't actually hit me yet, but I can see it coming. Especially when Malcolm stops by and she goes out to talk to him on the porch. Sometimes she's out there so long Daddy goes out there too. Sometimes they come in right away other times the three of them sit out talking forever, as it seems. Daddy took me for a walk one afternoon and he asked me what type of life did I want to have? I told him I just wanted to be happy. He told me, I have a funny way of trying to find the easy way out. He told me that instead of holding on to my virtue, I gave in at the first temptation. I wondered what Malcolm was telling them that would make them turn on me like this. Or maybe they were never on my side. I didn't know.

At school Malcolm would stare at me, but again it was a different look. How many serious looks does this guy have? It wasn't like before when he was trying to act like I didn't exist, or when he was trying to get with me. He would just look at me like he was watching me to see what I'm doing.

People thought he did something to Sammy for grabbing my arm that day, it turns out Sammy was suspended for breaking a kid's nose that he bullied. Sammy keeps trying to "talk" to me and I haven't the slightest idea what for. I avoid him like the plague though.

Although Troy graduated a year before Malachi he seems to always be there when I leave rehearsal. He still calls me "COUSIN" and seems happy to see me. He walks me to my car, and he puts a plug in for Malcolm. I've driven by Drew's a few times and the place is always packed. A lot of the guys from our school have started going there to get their haircut. Business appears to be doing well. Troy tells me that Malcolm is floating through Barber school, and that he'll be licensed in no time. I just smile and say that's good or something like that.

****

Momma told me I couldn't go anywhere this morning. She was in a mood; she kept making me clean room after room. Tammy called and asked if I was gonna be able to come out and play. I told her it didn't look like it, but I'd let her know if Momma suddenly had a change of heart. Andrew was full of energy and he was running all over the house with his basketball, his best friend. Momma started getting a headache, and that ball bouncing up against the wall wasn't working for her. No matter how much I got on her nerves, she is always as sweet as pie to Andrew. But she told me to take Andrew out and to be home by twelve. That meant no club for me, I was disappointed but what could I do? I decided to swing by Tammy's for a little bit, and at least see them off to the club. When I parked behind Stefan's car I saw a car that looked a lot like Troy's car. When Stefan opened the door he looked drunk. It was only four o'clock, so I didn't think he was getting a jump on drinking this early. He said they weren't expecting me, and then I heard Troy's voice. I came in the door and he was sitting on the couch. He looked a little surprised to see me. But he said a loud "COUSIN" when he saw me. Then he asked me what I was doing all the way out there. I told him they were my friends, he frowned a little then he said he would suggest that I found new friends. Stefan told him to mind his own business and Andrew and I were always welcome at their home. Then Troy stood up, he told Stefan he had to go. Stefan rushed to his room and he came back with money. He handed it to Troy. Troy looked at me and he said, "you better never!" His eyes were serious then he looked at Andrew and then at me. He told me I needed new friends. Stefan told him to stop trying to pump my head with negativity. Troy walked out as Tammy walked in the door, Troy mumbled something to Tammy and she looked at me with a very busted look on her face. She said she thought I wasn't coming. I picked up Andrew I asked them what was going on, and since when was it a big deal for me to drop by unannounced. Tammy looked at Stefan, and he blew air. He said he didn't know what the big deal was. He said it had been a long week and they needed a little pick me up. Tammy went in her room and put her purse down. She rubbed her hands together as she walked out of her room. They both excused their selves then they went in Stefan's room. When they came out Tammy was more relaxed. It was like she forgot I was standing there. She looked busted all over again. I asked her since when did they have Troy over. She rubbed her nose and said that they see Troy from time to time. Then I asked Tammy if Malcolm ever came over there. She made a disgusted face and said no. I told her I didn't see why they were acting so weird about being friends with Troy. There was a weird vibe so I only hung out for a few minutes. I called David from their house but a girl said he was at work. So then I called Sophia, her parents went out and she had all the kids. So I went over her house. She was finishing up dinner, and the kids were playing in the boy's room. I told Sophia about how weird Tammy and Stefan were acting. She said maybe they were just embarrassed that someone knew they were friends with Troy. I told her it didn't seem like that, they never acted weird like that before. That night I couldn't figure out what was wrong with them. I fell asleep trying to figure it out.

In the morning David called me just after eight am. I was up feeding Andrew who was always an early riser. He asked me if I had plans for the day and I told him I didn't. He told me he wanted to take Andrew and I to the San Francisco zoo. I got a lump in my throat; I hadn't gone back to the city since everything happened with Uncle. I caught myself freaking out a little. Then he said we could go to the Oakland zoo if I liked that idea better. Being in Oakland was too close to home for my comfort. Although David and I were just friends, I knew Malcolm wouldn't see it that way. I didn't want anything bad to happen to him. So despite my fear of the city I agreed to go to the zoo out there. I didn't want David to come to the house so I told him we'd pick him up. He reluctantly agreed, as he wanted to pick us up. When I pulled in front of his house he came right out. He didn't give me a chance to get out the car or anything. Andrew got so excited when he saw David. They gave each other skin, and then David directed me. He sat there for a minute taking me in, and then he asked me what was wrong. I asked him why he thought something was wrong? He said my shoulders were hunched and I kept gritting my teeth. I had to make a quick decision, which story I was gonna share. My Momma's family? No way too heavy. Tammy and Stefan? Nope, I wanted to think about that some more. So I told him about how my parents have been acting since I broke up with Malcolm. He listened to me as I talked; he put his hand on my shoulder. He told me he understood what I meant. He said his Aunt really likes his ex-girlfriend, and although we are just friends he didn't want me to meet his aunt until his uncle was there. As we hit the bay bridge my hands started sweating. I asked why he and his ex broke up. He kind of shrugged. He said she wanted more than he could give her. He said he doesn't have an endless supply of money. He said she wanted things that were beyond his means a lot of the time. I told him being with someone who has money isn't all that it cracked up to be. We talked about the reasons we love our Ex's. I really appreciated being able to be so honest with him and open. But David is just an amazing person like that. Andrew had dozed off before we got there, but as soon as Herb 2 stopped purring his little head popped up. David carried Andrew at first, but when Andrew wanted to get down he put him down and he encouraged Andrew to be curious about everything. Every time Andrew touched something or pointed at something he explained it as simply as he could and when it came to the animals they would mimic the sounds. I told David that he was great with Andrew. I asked him if he planned to have children. He said, yes and that he wanted a huge family. He said he wanted to have as many kids as his wife wanted to have. That was the COMPLETE opposite of Malcolm. Malcolm only ever wanted me, not a family, and even in that space it wasn't like he wanted to marry me. If he wanted to marry me he could've. With the way Momma and Daddy were acting about our breakup I'm sure they would've allowed us to get married if he wanted me. But looking at how good David was with Andrew it just made me feel bad for ever choosing Malcolm. The sad part was that I could still feel in my heart how much I loved Malcolm. It surprised me when David didn't act weird when he asked me about Malcolm, and then he was ok with me telling him as Frankly as possible how I truly felt. Even Melvin would fidget when I expressed loving feelings for Malcolm. At the time I didn't notice it, but talking to David shines light on all the clues I missed with Melvin. We had such a good time at the zoo. Then David drove my car as he showed us around Golden Gate park. Since it was Sunday there were a lot of families there. He parked at the beach and he and Andrew took off in the sand. It wasn't all that warm out especially by the water, but all the running they were doing it was like they didn't notice. I didn't want sand in my shoes so I watched from the top of the stairs. I kind of felt guilty cause as I stood there I wondered what Malcolm was doing. I wondered if he felt like this with Yvette? She clearly knew who I was, but she seemed fine with being number two. But who knows what Malcolm tells her.

We stopped at a little cafe and had dinner since junk food kept us satisfied around lunchtime. Andrew was deliriously tired, but he was fighting to stay awake. David picked him up and then Andrew fell asleep on his shoulder. I asked him why he was so good with babies. He shrugged and said it wasn't hard to be good to Andrew, he said Andrew was a good kid. I tried not to, but tears welled up in my eyes and forced their way out. He asked me why I was crying and I told him about how Malcolm never wanted him. I said that Malcolm tries to be good to Andrew, but children weren't his strong suit. He said everyone is not meant to be a parent. He carried Andrew to the car and I strapped him in. Then I drove David home. The whole way home we talked about relationships. Him and his ex, me and Malcolm. I appreciated that he didn't make her sound awful, and I could tell he really cared about her. He gave me a hug and thanked me for hanging out with him. He didn't linger or act like he was waiting for a kiss. He got out the car and walked inside his house. I had a smile the whole way home; I even went the long way so that I could drive past the shop. Sure enough it was still packed in there. When I got home Momma asked me where I had been. I told her I went to the zoo with David. Momma's breathing instantly got heavy. She told me I better not come home with no more babies. That hurt me; I guess she thought I just slept around with everybody. I tried to tell her it wasn't like that, but it's like she didn't believe me. I called Cassondra and I told her about my day. She talked to me while she was working. I told her she should come hang out with us one of these times. She said that sounded good but she was already getting preorders for next year's prom. Cassondra was going to design school after graduation in San Francisco. Then I told her about Tammy and Stefan, she said they have been acting funny lately. We couldn't figure out what Troy meant by "I better never". We just chopped it up to him being weird.

****

I was so excited! After school I hurried home, got Andrew dressed and then we hurried off to the center. We were super early so I got him a snack and then we watched the other ballet class finish. Andrew sat and observed the dancing. Then his teacher entered the room as the other class exited. She made a beeline over to Andrew. She said he must be the new student she just found out about. She turned on music "lets have our own jam session" as soon as the music started Andrew was off his chair. He started dancing and the teacher was surprised. I guess she thought he would just rock in place. He was all over the floor mimicking moves he's seen me do, but as a little boy would do them. Other students for this class started to come in. One by one the kids joined the dance party. Little kids made friends so easy, I wish it was always that easy. The teacher waved me on she said Andrew was going to be fine. I think my class seemed more thrilling because I didn't have to worry about Andrew.

Our classes were fulfilling and I signed up for all day classes in the summer. Sometimes we'd meet up with David after classes for dinner. Every once in awhile I'd catch David checking me out, but for now he never made a move. We truly were just friends.

****

Tammy asked me to go out with her and Stefan. It had been a few months since I had gone over their house just because they were so weird last time. I asked her what that was about. She said it had been a rough week, and they just needed to relax she said it was just bad timing. I told her I would check with Momma and then I'd call her back. I actually saw Daddy first. I asked him if it was ok if I spent the night at Tammy's. He was fine with it; excited I called Cassondra and asked if she could come. She was happy cause she said she needed a break from sewing. Sophia called me as I packed Andrew and I's overnight bag. I told her that I was going to Tammy's. She asked if she and Sasha could come. She said Charles was out of town with some cousins and she could use a getaway. I asked Tammy if Sophia could come. Tammy hesitated but then she said ok. I didn't know why it would've been anything to think about. But she knew if she said no, I wasn't gonna go. Andrew was excited when he saw Sasha, then he asked about Jeff and JoJo. We told him they couldn't come this time. Sophia climbed in the back when Cassondra came we were all excited about the idea of being away from home. When we got to Tammy's she and Stefan were so happy we were there. They said tonight was going to be amazing. Tammy needed to talk to Stefan about something real quick in his room. They both went in there and shut the door. Suddenly I had an off feeling. I looked at Sophia and Cassondra we all exchanged looks. We waited a few minutes then I started pacing. Sophia told me to sit down cause I was making them nervous. I gave Cassondra the keys to my car, I told her to take the kids to my house if anything weird happened while we were gone. I told her something just didn't feel right. Finally Stefan came out and he was excited and ready to go. He was extremely animated and ready for the fun to begin. Tammy came out of his room sneezing and running to her room. She said she needed a jacket and then she'd be ready. Sophia and I looked at each other, I mouthed to her that I was so happy she was there. In the car Stefan was talking so fast, it was funny at first. We went to a club in Emeryville that I never heard of. At the door we walked right in past the line. They said tonight they had VIP status, normally we were in line just like everyone else at new clubs. The music was pumping and they walked to the VIP section. Stefan said something to the bouncer guarding the section and he pointed to the second booth. I was behind Sophia and she stopped dead in her tracks when she saw who was in the booth. My heart dropped I already knew who she was looking at before I rounded the corner. I looked at Tammy and Stefan who were already making their selves comfortable in the booth. They looked like two loyal puppies eager to please their master. It just hurt that their loyalty wasn't to me. Sophia looked at me with a what do you want to do look on her face. I walked around the corner and Malcolm and Troy were sitting there. I sucked my teeth then I looked at Tammy and Stefan. Neither one of them looked at me. Malcolm looked at Sophia and I, and he asked us to sit. I made Sophia sit on the side closest to Malcolm. Malcolm looked good, but I didn't care, I didn't want to see him. I stared at Tammy and Stefan who did everything but look at me. Then Stefan told me to come dance. My body was stiff on the dance floor and I was beyond pissed. Stefan asked me not to look at him like that. He said he felt horrible, but he didn't have a choice. I told him I didn't understand why he didn't have a choice. He dropped his eyes and he said just cause. Sophia was dancing with Troy; they were having a good time. I told Stefan I couldn't understand why he would betray me like this. He asked me to be nice and to try and enjoy the night, he begged me. When I came back to the table Tammy was working on a drink and Malcolm's eyes were glued to me. There were drinks all around the table. Sophia's was half gone. Tammy pointed to my drink, but she wouldn't look at me. I huffed and I sucked down my drink lightning fast. When I put my drink down Malcolm waved his hand and the waiter came over a few minutes later with a fresh drink and he removed my empty glass. I rolled my eyes at Malcolm as I started on my second drink. Malcolm looked at Tammy when I hit the bottom of my second drink. The waiter came over with another drink. Tammy took Stefan over to the dance floor. Malcolm scooted close to me; he put his face by my neck. He inhaled deeply, and then he told me he missed my smell. I told him I didn't care! Then he moved my hair and softly kissed the back of my neck. I closed my eyes and forbid my body to respond to his kiss. I slapped his face, I told him, "DON'T YOU TOUCH ME! DON'T YOU EVER TOUCH ME!"

He grabbed my wrist and he got in my face. "I'm trying to be patient with you. But this has gone on long enough."

"It's not your place to decide when I get over anything!"

"I told you I was sorry what else do you want from me?"

"You don't even mean that!"

"How you gonna tell me what I mean? You don't know!"

"I know you will just do it again. I don't want to spend the rest of my life going through this. You won't stop; you'll just get better about hiding it. Then one day someone's gonna get pregnant. I want a husband of my own."

Malcolm sat back and exhaled. "You ain't even old enough to get married but you constantly talking about it."

"Cause that's what I want."

"So then you get married then what?"

"Then I live happily ever after!" I said rolling my eyes.

"See you don't even know. Marriage is a death sentence. You don't need to be married to be with someone. And when it doesn't work out, you can both go your own separate ways. You don't need a piece of paper to say you're dedicated to them."

"That's because you will never be dedicated to anyone but yourself! I don't expect you to understand. I'm not gonna keep playing your little game. You keep breaking my heart!"

"Like you don't break mine?"

I sucked my teeth "Malcolm! Please! What have I done besides take your crap like some love sick puppy?"

"You stopped coming to see me. The only time I saw you is at your parent's house. Then you avoid me completely, I don't see you or talk to you for months! Then you start going out with some little Richard looking fool. Then you come back from your grandparent's house and then you're uninterested in the things happening in my life. Suddenly you got all these plans and ambition, that part was cool, but you don't include me in any of it. Everything I do is for you, or it benefits you. You're all the sudden out for yourself. How do you think that makes me feel? Then that white boy? Really?" I sat there feeling horrible. I didn't think anything I did affected him. "Did you sleep with him?"

"NO! NEVER!" I said, "and I didn't go out with him. He was just a friend I made while I was out visiting my grandparents. I told him about my recitals and he said he wanted to come."

"But you knew he liked you."

"What difference does it make? You were with Yvette the whole time, which was bad enough, and then you had so many others. Even while you're sitting there doing whatever you call this, you've got two or three other females hanging on waiting for your call."

"Maybe, but I'd leave them all alone to be back with you."

"You would?" I smiled

"Of course! I love you! That will never change."

I could feel my drink taking affect. "Until miss new booty shows up! You may love me, but you got a messed up way of showing it. One wrong spoils a thousand rights. I can't trust you with my heart Malcolm. All I ever wanted was you. I'd give you every last single dime back if it meant that you could be as faithful to me as you demand me to be to you. Otherwise it's not even worth it."

He sat there thinking but he didn't say anything. Sophia and Troy came back to the table laughing and out of breath. Sophia asked me if I was ok. I shook my head yes and then I tossed back my third drink. Then I pulled Troy to the dance floor. I wanted to dance and not think about what Malcolm was saying to me. I only came back to the table to drink my next drink and then I went back on the dance floor. I didn't care that Sophia was dancing with Troy I went out there with them. I was grooving with them when Malcolm came and spun me around. He put his hands on either side of my face and kissed me LONG, DEEP, and STRONG! My mind said run, but my body melted to his touch. Everybody on the dance floor paid us no attention. That kiss lasted for what seemed like forever! I forbid my arms to move from my sides, but my lips and tongue didn't get the memo. He picked me up and held me tight. "I miss you! I need you!"

"Leave me alone Malcolm!" I said unconvincingly.

"I want you Amber! Please! I need to be with you!"

I put my finger up to his lips. "Stop it! You will just go home to some other female when I deny you. I refuse to play this game with you." My lips were numb and everything was getting fuzzy. I walked best I could back to the table. Tammy was sitting there with a drink, there was also a fresh drink waiting for me. Tears started pouring out of my eyes. Tammy looked so sad and guilty as she pushed my drink in front of me. "Sorry" she said as she watched me take a sip.

"I thought you were my friend." I said drinking some more.
Sophia came back to the table she was wasted too. Then I heard Malcolm tell Troy to take them back to the house and that he would catch up to them in the morning. I tried very hard to focus, but as the waves hit me I kept feeling more and more powerless. Malcolm told me I was coming with him. I told him I was not! I told him I hated him, and I was going with my cousin. Then I hugged Sophia's neck and thought I was holding on. He grabbed me by the hand and told me to come on. He told Troy they needed to leave too. I thought I was fighting him off when he sat me in the front seat of a car I didn't recognize. He closed the door, and then I saw Sophia get in the car with Troy, Stefan, and Tammy. I asked Malcolm where he was taking them, and he said they were going to Tammy's. I asked him where we were going, and he said he needed me. My body started throbbing. I fussed at him the whole way to the hotel. I asked him why he hasn't come to see his son, or taken him anywhere. I told him it was a shame that he has a whole barbershop and he's never even cut his own son's hair ONCE. Then he said, "I know you're mad at me, I'm sorry! But I need you!"
When he opened the car door I stood up and the cold air hit me in the face. My mouth started watering. I pushed past him and I threw up in the bushes, he held my hair while my stomach emptied everything it had. He put his jacket around my shoulders, and then he held me as I walked very wobbly under his arm. He kissed my forehead as we walked. When he opened the door to the room, I found the clarity to tell him I wasn't on the pill anymore. He paused smiled, and then he exhaled, then he said, "I don't care! I need you!" He brought me in the door and the room spun. I was so gone that I kept coming in and out of reality. I remember Malcolm kissing me tenderly as he unzipped my dress. I remember the first contact and hearing relief and excitement as he said I was still his good girl. I remember my legs going all the way backwards as he went to town on me. I woke up in the middle of the night, he was still on top of me dead weight, and still inside of me, but he was knocked out. When I moved my leg he woke up and started pumping me again. I started throbbing instantly, which let me know my body, had responded positively to the betrayal of my heart. He kissed my neck and went right back to what he was doing. He raised my leg, which made him go deeper and I gasped. He was too into it, my body was shaking but I still wanted him to back up. I told him he was trying to kill me. He smiled and growled at me. Then his breathing doubled and each stroke was deeper than the one before. I kind of screamed in a mixture of severe discomfort and ecstasy as my shaking doubled. I could tell he was nutting and when he wasn't backing up, I started trying to push him back. But he locked in on me and pushed down deeper. He kissed my cheek, I tried to push him off but his grip remained tight on me. Still drunk I fell asleep again. When I woke up my head was pounding, and my mouth was dry. Malcolm was sleep but he had me tight in a bear hug. My legs hurt, and I was throbbing but not in a good way. I moved my hand and Malcolm woke up, he kept kissing my head. I pushed him a way. He had his legs and arms intertwined in mine. I broke free and moved to the edge of the bed. My head was pounding and my stomach was upset. I stood up and my legs felt like Jell-O. Malcolm hopped up and helped me walk to the bathroom. He set me down on the toilet and then he put the coffee pot on. He brought me a big cup of water and two Aspirin. He told me to take them for my head. As he helped me walk out the bathroom I noticed he wasn't even the slightest bit hung over. I asked him if he drank anything last night, and he shook his head no. He helped me back to the bed. I laid down, then I remembered and I asked him why did he turn my friends

against me? He told me they weren't my friends anymore, they were slaves to nose candy. I looked at him, so you used their addiction against me? He said he needed to be with me last night. I asked him why, what was so urgent about last night? He said he's been planning last night for a while. I asked him why? And he said he feels like he's dying without me. He said he can't live without me. His face was intense and serious. I told him I did not want to get back with him and I did not want to see him. I told him I should've caught a cab as soon as I saw he was there. He sat there listening to me but not responding. His eyes looked so sad. I told him as soon as I walked out the door I didn't ever wanna talk to him again. He looked at me, then he said that may be what I want but I was gonna have to talk to him when my period doesn't come. I swung at him and he hopped up. I hopped up screaming every curse word in the book. I couldn't move like I wanted to but I chased him around the room. He told me I didn't leave him a choice. I couldn't believe he did this to me. He told me was moving into an apartment at the first of the month. He told me he'll have keys for me as soon as he gets them. My head hurt too much to cry and the room started spinning from my brief rant. I closed my eyes waiting for the Aspirin to kick in. When I felt calm my eyes popped open. Malcolm was on the phone with someone. I wished I could hit him with something like in the movies and he would collapse and then a cab would be waiting for me in the lobby. He turned around and saw my eyes open. He told the person on the phone he had to go. I sat up on the bed my clothes were neatly laid out on the other side of the bed. I moved slowly towards them and I put on my things. Malcolm sat in the chair looking at me. Once I was dressed I walked to the door and I waited for him to follow me. I opened the door and I walked slowly to the elevator. I got in his car, and he drove in silence to Tammy's house. Sophia came running out when she saw me get out of the car. She asked me if I was ok. I didn't say anything and she proceeded to cuss Malcolm out so bad, even I was surprised with where her mouth went. She threw her arms around me and took me inside, Malcolm had no reaction. Troy was on the floor drawing with Andrew and Sasha. Tammy and Stefan peeked out of Stefan's room like prisoners. Cassondra was sitting on the couch behind the kids. Andrew screamed Mommy and he ran to me. Sasha followed Andrew's lead and ran to me too. Malcolm stood in the doorway looking. Cassondra looked at me and she asked me if I was ok. I didn't know how to answer that. I knew that my body responded positively to last night, and I knew the only part of me that didn't want last night was my brain. If I truly didn't want it then I wouldn't have drank like I did, I would've left when I could've. Malcolm didn't force me to do anything; he just waited for the alcohol to do its magic. As the night came back to me I remembered initiating the kiss. The kiss that started everything, but I was mad that he didn't even try to not get me pregnant. I told Cassondra I was ok. Malcolm asked Troy if he paid the minions. Troy looked at Tammy and Stefan peeking out the door. He chuckled and shook his head no; he said he gave them enough to keep them at bay. Then he told everybody to get their stuff. Sophia asked me about the clothes I had in Tammy's closet. I told her I didn't want it. Sophia went in Tammy's room; I could hear her going through the closet. She grabbed a garbage bag and she put a few things in it. Then she said she was done. We grabbed all our things then Troy dropped a small bag on the coffee table. Tammy and Stefan hurried out of the room. Troy shut the door behind him.

Chapter 19

I feel like everything is moving in fast motion around me, but I'm moving in slow motion. I keep looking at everyone and sometimes I don't understand what they're saying.

On the first of the month just as he promised Malcolm came over to pick Andrew and I up after school. Momma looked at us like we jumped off script when Malcolm came over. I didn't look happy about going with Malcolm, but I felt so defeated. If my period didn't come, I was gonna have to run away. Momma would kill me. Malcolm was being so gentle with me, which was unlike him, I wasn't saying much riding in the car with him. Malcolm pulled up to a building next to the lake. He parked in front of a garage. Then he opened the car door for me. As I got out he got Andrew out the back. He held Andrew's hand as we walked up to the door. He pressed numbers on the intercom and the door unlocked. We got in the elevator and he pressed the fourth floor. Out the elevator I followed as he walked to the right as we stood in front of the door he put keys in my hand. He showed me which one opened the door. I opened the door and the smell of fresh paint hit my nose. The windows were huge and all faced the lake. The carpet was brand new. Malcolm watched my face for a reaction, but I didn't have one. The apartment was beautiful, two bedrooms with two bathrooms. The living room was the biggest room in the whole place. The kitchen was a good size and all modern in green and cream. There was a balcony that stretched across the front of the apartment. I told Malcolm his apartment was beautiful. He said it was our apartment, and I looked away without saying anything. Andrew looked around but he stayed by my side. Malcolm asked if I was ok, and I told him waiting to know how the rest of my life was going to turn out wasn't a good feeling. Then I told him he didn't even want children so I didn't understand why he did this to me. He looked me in my eyes and said desperate times call for desperate measures. I rolled my eyes and walked away from him. He told me Troy was going to take me to pick out furniture. I didn't say anything I walked out on the balcony holding Andrew. I felt so trapped and like I didn't have a choice but to accept what Malcolm was putting in front of me. Malcolm was standing inside watching us.

****

Malcolm and Jade graduated a couple weeks later. My parents were planning for Jade's graduation party. Momma asked me if Malcolm could come to the party, I told her I didn't care. Jade got into Spellman on a full scholarship, she cried so hard when she got her acceptance letter. Then she called Sonny. She said they were so excited that everything was going to plan. That night she asked me a ton of questions about sex. I turned on the light to look at her. She was sitting up and looking nervous. I asked her if she planned on going all the way with Sonny. She shrugged and said she didn't know but she wanted to be prepared if she did. She said the only things she knew about sex were the things that Uncle did to her, and she wanted all of that out of her brain. I hugged her and I told her I understood. I told her that she should do it because she's ready and nothing more, if she needed to wait that was fine too. She said she thinks she would be ready. She said Daddy told her he would pay for her to have an apartment off campus, and she wanted Sonny to live with her. I told her that she should ask Momma to take her to get birth control pills. Then she asked me if my period came yet. I told her no but it was only a couple days late. I changed the subject back to her. I told her to make sure they had time to take their time the first few times cause she would need time to get comfortable. Jade looked like she was taking mental notes. I told her she should start taking the pill a month before she planned to go through with it. She said she would talk to Momma on the plane when they flew to Georgia to find her apartment. I told her not to tell them about Sonny living with her, but she wanted the BC's just in case.

****

Malachi was so happy to be at home, he kept hugging Jade and I. He said his first year away was challenging and exciting. The night his flight got in I picked him up from the airport. Andrew had dosed off in the back, then he heard Malachi's voice and he woke up. As soon as we pulled up to the house they were all over each other. I didn't realize how much he missed Malachi until he was in his presence. I left them to their male bonding. Malachi asked me what was wrong; he said I wasn't my normal self. I told him I had a lot on my mind. Malachi swallowed and then he told me to talk to him. We went for a ride in his car, and I told him everything. About my plans for school, about Malcolm and I's breakup, how Momma and Daddy have been acting, about Sammy, about David, about Tammy and Stefan. I told him everything. Malachi took it all in. He looked sad when I told him that Tammy was strung out. He asked me what I was gonna do. I told him I couldn't do anything, but accept what was happening to me. I was more than likely gonna have another baby, but I was gonna have to get away from Momma before she realized it. I told him I was gonna have to forget about school for now. I could probably graduate from continuation school. And I would have to wait to go to school. My dreams of a dance school would have to wait. Malachi sat there looking like he felt guilty for leaving. I told him this was my life based on my choices. I told him I would be fine, I needed a minute to adjust and accept it. Malachi asked me if I considered the alternative. I told him I couldn't look at Andrew and do that in good conscience. He understood, his brain was turning over trying to figure out the answer to my riddle. I kissed his cheek, and I told him I loved him. I asked him to just be my brother and to let me go through this. I asked him not to try to fix this for me. He tried to ignore me, I begged him to promise me he would just let this be. I told him it was all my fault; I made my bed now I had to lay in it. Malachi cried for me, and I assured him that I was gonna be ok.

****

At Jade's graduation party I did my best to be as normal as possible. Before the party I went by Momma Shuga's house and I picked up Penny and Tiffany, Sterling asked why he couldn't come with us. I told him I would have to plan something with him. Momma Shuga wasn't there but that girl Renee was. She was too busy stressing out to worry about me. She was on the phone begging some guy for money to get formula, diapers, and most importantly cough medicine for the baby who was laying on the sofa cause she couldn't move. Renee was in tears pleading with the person on the phone to help her. She didn't know what she was gonna do. I wondered why none of the cousins on the porch would help her. Renee hung up the phone in defeat; she was sitting in the chair next to the phone sobbing deeply. I took Penny and Tiffany to the store. I bought a bunch of boxes of diapers. I got two cases of formula, and I got two big bottles of baby cough medicine. I put a thermometer in the cart, and anything else that I thought would help the baby. Penny and Tiffany asked me why I was buying all this stuff for Renee when I knew she didn't like me. I told them that didn't matter, the baby needed help. And I couldn't in good conscience do nothing if I was in a position to help. I asked Fuzzy to help us take all the stuff in the house. When we walked in the door Renee was sitting on the floor holding her baby crying her eyes out. We put the bags down around her. Her eyes were bloodshot red, I handed her the medicine in her hand. She was in complete shock. She couldn't move fast enough to open the medicine for the baby. Fuzzy said Momma Shuga was gonna take her stuff and sell it. She wouldn't be able to keep it all. I asked Penny and Tiffany if they would hide Renee's stuff until she needed it in their room. Both of the girls huffed. They said they didn't like her and she was always mean to them. I begged them to do it for me. They agreed to do it for me to Renee's surprise, and Fuzzy helped them hide everything in their room. Renee was sitting there crying with the medicine, one package of diapers, and one canister of formula with her. She was giving the baby the medicine as we walked out the door. Everyone promised they wouldn't say anything, I told them I'd send food. When we got in the car I cried a little bit. Penny and Tiffany told me that Momma Shuga was mean to everybody. I ordered six extra large pizzas paid for them and then Tiffany gave the delivery address.

Malcolm and Troy came a little later to the party. I worried about how Malachi would respond to them. When he saw Malcolm he took a deep breath and then he kept his promise. He went over and talked with them like he normally would. Sonny and his parents came a few minutes later. Momma was eyeing me all night, so I kept my distance from Malcolm. But honestly I didn't want to be up under him no how. I still hadn't warmed up to him. I picked out the furniture for his apartment, I bought all the necessities. I turned his apartment into a home. Malcolm really liked what I did with the apartment, but I couldn't bring myself to feel all warm and fuzzy about him. He kept trying to get me to talk to him, but I couldn't. I told Nana I couldn't come until the camping trip. She looked disappointed, but she agreed.

Sophia left for a minute and then she returned with Cassondra, Rosalind, Tanisha, and Benjamin. I got so excited I ran screaming! When Jade saw them she started screaming too. I jumped on Rosalind and I kissed her so hard! I hugged Benjamin too, and then I snatched up Tanisha. She was such a pretty little girl. I took her over to the kids and they all instantly hit it off. Benjamin and Charles exchanged excited hellos. When Benjamin saw Malcolm he got so excited. They hugged and they started catching up. I was so happy to see Rosalind, she was smiling but I knew she felt the same way I did on the inside. I grabbed her hand I squeezed, and then I introduced her to Penny and Tiffany, and anyone else at the party she didn't know. Momma asked Malcolm to get ice cream from Bob's again. He asked me to come with him, I exhaled to myself. Momma watched us walk down the street. He grabbed my hand, "I know you're still mad at me. But I'm trying over here."

"Malcolm, you..."

He interrupted me, "how long you gonna stay mad at me? I know I hurt you, I'm not trying to let things stay that way between us."

I didn't have the energy to yell or throw attitude. "Did you ever stop to think that maybe I didn't want you back in my life? Did you ever think I don't want to spend the rest of my life like this? You're not gonna change, you will be good for a little while, but eventually there will be someone else. If it's not Yvette it'll be someone else. What you gonna do, keep me pregnant the rest of my life? I had plans that are all coming apart in front of my eyes. I'm flattered that you're finally where I was. But it's only a matter of time."

"Matter of time for what?"

"Before whoever you're seeing rises to the surface."

"Amber I don't want to hurt you anymore."

I exhaled, "I don't trust you Malcolm. Even how you did this, I don't trust you."

"I was desperate!"

"I guess that makes it ok."
We walked into Bob's; Malcolm told him he needed a repeat of last summer's order. Bob happily complied with Malcolm's request. When we stepped out the shop Malcolm stopped me, "I love you! I will make this up to you. We're gonna be happy again."
"Ok, sure." I said not interested in discussing it further.
I forgot to tell Timothy to tell David that I wasn't home. When I answered the phone David hit me rapid fire with question after question. When I didn't answer, he told me he needed to see me and if I stood him up he was gonna come to my house. He knew that wasn't gonna work for me. I was trying to think of a safe place to meet. I told him to meet me at that Chinese food restaurant he took us to. He told me to meet him at the Palace Golden at one o'clock. Malachi and the guys were planning a boy's day. Malachi had Andrew dressed and ready to go. I kissed Andrew and then I told Jade where I was going just in case there was a reason I needed her to know it. I hopped in my car and flew down the freeway. I got to the restaurant at twelve forty-five, David was already there. He was sitting in a booth in the back. He looked good! When he hugged me he smelled so good! I wanted to cry as soon as I sat down. He asked where Andrew was and I told him about my brothers, father, uncles, and cousins spending the day in the park together. He looked a little disappointed, but then he regrouped. He asked me how long Malcolm and I have been back together. I sat there like a deer caught in headlights. He laughed at me, he said anyone else would understand we were just friends, it had to be Malcolm. I told him how everything happened and his smile disappeared. He got up and scooted next to me. He put his arm around me and I rested my head on his shoulder while I cried. He said he felt sorry for me being so caught up. I cried harder, I told him my life kept tumbling and tumbling before my eyes. He rubbed my head and he told me it was gonna be ok. I felt more relaxed in his arms than I felt in a long time. He told me that it looked like he was gonna be getting back with Patricia. It made me feel a little sad when he said that. I asked if we would still see each other? He said of course we will, he couldn't afford to be away from Andrew any more than he had to be. I sucked my teeth; I poked fun and said he didn't have to see me to see Andrew. He smiled at me, then he told me he was gonna miss me too. I looked at him; I forgot we were so close. Both of us sat there waiting for the other to lean in. We both turned our heads in the opposite directions at the same time. I shifted in my seat and he got up and moved back to the other side of the booth. I felt so disappointed, but he got respect from me for moving. Then he swallowed, "so lets have the talk".
"Ok" I didn't know what he was about to say.
"Why didn't you like me in Middle school?"
Blushing I said, "I did like you. But you were so nice and sweet. I was the angriest at that time. I thought you were too good for me." Then I mumbled, "I still do".
He looked so surprised. "You think I'm too good for you? Why?"
"You've always been nice, sweet, respectable, the whole nine. I'm always mad about something, fighting, short fuse like you wouldn't believe. I didn't call you because I felt embarrassed about how my life has turned out."
"I'm not a saint. And I can't believe you put me up on a pedestal like that." He sat back in his seat. "I thought you didn't like me because Malcolm was the big man on campus. I know he had that whole scary mystery thing going on. And I was just an ordinary guy!"
"You're not ordinary," I said tapping my foot under the table.

"I'm not?" He said not making eye contact with me.

"No, you're sweet, very kind hearted, and very forgiving. Those are all winners in my book." He blushed, "did you like me?" I asked

"From the first time I saw you." He completely blushed

I blushed, "really?"

"Oh yea, and then you were smart too! I looked forward to going to school everyday just to talk to you or hang out with you."

"I guess the whole Malcolm thing was a major turn off."

"Disappointing, but not a turn off."

"So what was?" I asked

"What was what?"

"What was the turn off?" I asked

"Who says I was ever turned off?"

I squirmed in my seat. "You said you only wanted to be friends."

"Yea! You didn't call me until there was no pressure. I'd have said anything to get back in your life."

We both laughed. Then I squirmed, "but Malcolm is not one to be mocked. I couldn't live with myself if something happened to you. You deserve so much better." I said feeling depressed as the words came out my mouth.

"I only agree with the mocking. The rest is not true!" He said staring at me.

"Ok, so are we saying goodbye?" I asked

"Is that what you want?" He asked

"No, but I think we've just compromised our friendship."

"How about we check in once a quarter?" He said

"That sounds good to me."

"Who knows one day we might catch each other truly free."

"Free with two kids, yea that's hot!" I scoffed

"That doesn't change who you are." I squirmed in my seat again. "So when do you go to the doctors?"

I told him I had an appointment this coming up Thursday. He told me to call him after my appointment.

We sat in that restaurant for hours. A part of me wished that he would come back next to me, but I knew that was a bad idea. It started to get late and he had to get ready for his date. So we hugged as usual and then we went our separate ways. I stopped by Cassondra's on my way home. Rosalind and Tanisha were over. So I hung out for a couple hours. I told them about my lunch with David. Rosalind was a little lost, but I told her Cassondra would get her up to speed. When I drove home I noticed a car kind of following me. When I pulled up to the house all the men were getting out of their cars. The car kept going and I didn't see who was in it.

****

Thursday morning I got sick eating breakfast. Thank goodness Momma was gone. Jade rubbed my back as I hugged the toilet. It was official in my mind; I just needed the doctor to confirm it for me. I left Andrew with Jade. Malcolm came and picked me up. I told him I threw up this morning. He had serious eyes as he looked at me and apologized. The doctor said I was about eight weeks pregnant, another February baby. Malcolm kissed my forehead; he said he hoped it was a girl. It was weird seeing him excited about the baby. My heart lightened seeing him excited. He made sure we went and got my prenatal vitamins right away and then we went to Gonzalez's for lunch. I could really see that he was trying and I appreciated the effort he put forward to try to win me over. I could feel my resolve to hate him forever lighten. Then he took me to the shop. It was packed full of customers, they all sat up straight when they saw me. Malcolm introduced me to Moses. Moses was an older man with a round belly. I guess when he was younger ladies used to go crazy for him. Cause the way he presented himself you could tell he thought a lot of himself. I never did like that slick talking type of guy. He kissed my hand and I looked at him like he had to be kidding. One of the customers told him his game was tired. And they all erupted into laughter. Malcolm didn't laugh though his face remained serious the entire time. He took me to the back to his office. He showed me the safe, and gave me the combination. He told me only I had that combination. He broke down to me the daily routine at the shop. He had each customer sign in as they showed up. He told Moses it was a way to keep track of the order, but he also said it helped him keep track of their daily take. He said only he or Troy handled the actual bank deposits. I asked him if he trusted Moses, and he said not enough to be blind to who he is. This was my first time meeting him and I didn't care for him all that much.

He told me once he had the revenue together he was going to look into opening another shop. Meanwhile he was going to take business classes in the fall at Laney College. I felt that sinking feeling cause I wasn't gonna be able to graduate with my class or finish the school year with Ms. Dubois. Then Malcolm changed the subject, he asked when Andrew and I were moving in. I told him I didn't know, Malcolm wanted me to pack my things today. He didn't want a repeat of what happened with Andrew. And he said with me getting sick, it was only a matter of time before Momma figured it out. He was right but part of me was afraid to move in. I called home; Jade was getting ready to go to the mall with Sonny and Malachi. I told her to hang on for just a minute and Malcolm and I would come and get Andrew. As we stood up Malcolm's phone rang, his eyes got real serious. I could tell it was business, I asked him for his keys and then I'd come right back. He put his caller on hold by putting his hand over the mouthpiece. He said we should hang out at the apartment just the three of us tonight. I had been avoiding him for so long, but he was as sweet as pie all day. I told myself I wouldn't be weak if I gave in today, besides he never came to one of Andrew's doctor appointments. As I put the car in gear I saw Troy pull up. He waved at me when he saw me. As I drove up east fourteenth I saw a car following me in my rear view mirror. It was that same car that followed me in Herb 2. I stopped at the light in front of Bob's. Instead of stopping the car behind me sped up and slammed into me full speed. My car projected into on coming traffic and a car coming from on coming traffic plowed into me at full speed on the driver's side. The impact knocked my whole body into the passenger's side. When I opened my eyes I saw Sammy, he was cursing when he saw it was me. Then he stood there looking at me, he told someone I might not make it then he smiled. I heard footsteps running away, then eventually sirens. The paramedics asked me my name, I held on to my purse strap. When they moved me out of the car everything hurt, my whole body felt like it was on fire. The doctors shined lights in my eyes, they kept asking me questions. A nurse wrote down my phone number then she hurried out the room. The doctors were checking everything. I kept coming in and out of consciousness. I was trying my hardest to stay awake. I was afraid that Sammy was right. I couldn't leave Andrew! I told myself to stay awake. Even though the doctors and nurses kept talking so fast around me. I told the doctor I was pregnant and I just saw my doctor earlier today. They told me I had a broken leg, it was the same leg uncle cut. As they were focusing on my leg a nurse said I was still bleeding. She was focused on my leg until she noticed the blood when they elevated my leg. Then I heard a doctor tell someone he thought I was losing the baby. I fell asleep right at that moment. When I woke up it was dark in the room except the light just above my bed, my broken leg was elevated and my left arm was extremely sore. I moved my right arm and I saw a head pop up. It was Jade; her eyes were puffy from crying. She kissed me on my forehead, and then she grabbed my hand. She said Andrew was with Momma and Daddy at home. She said Malcolm stepped out but he'd be right back. She asked me if I remembered the car accident, and I told her I did. Then Malcolm walked in the room, his eyes were puffy too. He kissed my lips, he told me Andrew was with my parents. Then he asked Jade if she told me, she shook her head no. Malcolm held my hand while Jade touched my shoulder. His voice kept cracking as he told me I lost the baby. Tears started pouring out of my eyes. Malcolm had sad eyes. Then I said, "Sammy" just above a whisper. They both froze and then Malcolm asked me what did I say? I told him Sammy thought I was him in his car, he was mad when he saw it was me, but he smiled when he said I might not make it. I was afraid I was gonna die. Malcolm's face turned to stone. He kissed my forehead then he left.

Chapter 20

Jade told me that Daddy was completely shocked when they told him they couldn't save the baby. Momma on the other hand didn't seem as shocked but she was upset all the same. She said that Momma had some choice words for Malcolm. As she was talking my room door opened, Uncle Frank walked in slowly. His face was very serious, Daddy was right behind him. They both kissed my forehead. Uncle Frank's eyes were serious as he sat down. Then he told me he heard I was in trouble. I didn't say anything at first, cause I couldn't tell where he was going. Daddy asked where Malcolm went. I told them what happened at the crash site. Both of their eyes got big, they asked where Malcolm went I told them I didn't know. I told them that he left as soon as I told him about Sammy. Uncle Frank told Daddy they had to go, sometimes Malcolm could be impulsive and this could get ugly. My heart rate sped up. Jade and I looked scared. Later on my doctor came in the room, she asked if I knew when Momma was coming back to the hospital. Jade called home, Momma told her she would be back in a hour or so. Jade told me they heard sirens when they were at the house waiting for me, but they didn't think anything of it. After awhile she called Drew's and talked to Malcolm. He told her he was getting ready to call her cause I should've been back to the shop by then. She said they got in Malachi's car and they saw Malcolm's car all crumpled up and police were on the scene collecting evidence for their report. She got out of the car and as she was talking to the officer Malcolm pulled up in Troy's car. She said Malcolm got out the car and he looked like he was gonna lose it. She said when they got to the hospital Momma and Daddy had already been called and had only got there minutes before they did. Jade said everyone was trying to be strong for Andrew. She said the tears and dramatics didn't start until Andrew dosed off. Once they knew I was definitely gonna be ok Daddy took Momma and Andrew home. Momma looked mad when she walked in the room. She didn't say anything right away she sat in the chair and looked at me for a minute. Jade said she would be back and she left the room. Momma sat there staring at me, and then when she finally spoke she asked me how I felt. I told her I was really scared. She said the guy who hit me from the left side was really shook up. She said he kept apologizing even though the police said he wasn't at fault. He told them he was a father as well. She said he told them about the guys who ran away. Then I told Momma what I told Daddy and Uncle Frank. She closed her eyes like she was sleeping for a few minutes. Then she asked if Sammy was that guy from school. Then she asked me about the baby, she asked me why I didn't tell them. I cried as I told her she already warned me not to come home with any more babies. I told her I just went to the doctor that morning. Malcolm and I were discussing our next step. I told her he wanted Andrew and I to move in with him. She asked me if that's what I wanted. I told her I didn't know. Then Momma proceeded to go off on me. She said I wanted to get pregnant otherwise I would've stayed on the pill like she told me to. She accused me of playing games and writing checks my butt couldn't cash. I just held my breath and braced myself for her to hit me every time her rant came close. She looked like she wanted to hit me and if it weren't for this hospital she would've hit me. She said she didn't understand why I would sneak and do this when she and Daddy were trying their best to be relaxed with me. She said she didn't choke me out when I went out to a twenty one and older club, spent the night with my boyfriend doing God only knows what and she gets a phone call the next day that two of her children were injured in a knife fight ALL THE WAY IN THE CITY! She said that amongst me coming home hung-over at times. They were trying to be patient with me. All they asked is that I didn't bring any more babies home, and I couldn't even do that. Momma said my rebelliousness is getting too out of hand, and it was time I had to grow up. Momma said I could come home to recover, but I was gonna have to move out. I felt like she just shot me. I didn't say anything tears rolled down my face. I didn't try to explain how Malcolm set me up, cause in the end I shouldn't have been there in the first place. I cried and cried, Momma stood there strong and unyielding. I didn't want to live with Malcolm if I didn't have to, but I didn't have anywhere else to go. I wasn't eighteen so it didn't matter if I had the money or not, no one would rent to me. What was I going to do with Andrew while I was in school? I found myself hating Malcolm again. Then Momma left, when Jade came in the room I told her that Momma kicked me out. Jade couldn't believe it. Momma said I could come home to recover, but I didn't see the point. I asked her if she would help me pack up my things as soon as I was released, I didn't want to cause Momma any more pain. I couldn't even process how I felt about any of this. The doctors told us everything looked good considering everything I went through and I could go home Saturday afternoon as long as nothing came up. Malcolm came back to the hospital Friday night. I told him what Momma said, he was surprised as well. But he tried to play down his excitement about having Andrew and I with him. Malcolm told me that Uncle Frank and Daddy found him before he could carry out his thoughts. He took a deep breath and said he wasn't thinking the whole thing through. He said Sammy will be dealt with. Malcolm said between the three of them you couldn't tell who was more upset. He said he thought he was until Daddy came, and then once Uncle started talking, whoa! Malcolm turned to stone, and then mumbled something. I asked him what he said, and then he sat down and stared off for a minute. I'd never seen him like this so I didn't know how to respond. He was lightweight talking to his self trying to figure something's out. Malachi and Andrew came in the room and Andrew ran to me. He was smiling until he saw my cast and the bruises on my left side. He didn't cry but he was definitely taking me in. Then he had a thoughtful face just like his daddy. He hugged me and put his head on my chest. His little heart was beating so fast. I smiled at him and I tried to be upbeat. Malachi sat next to Malcolm they were having a very low but serious conversation. I tried to get Andrew to lighten up, but I could see his little mind running a mile a minute. So I snapped my fingers at the men. "Hey! Hey! The vibe in this room is too dark. We need to lighten the mood for Andy's sake."

"NO AMBER! Life is not always happy times and he needs to know that. He's not gonna be happy all the time. And sometimes he's gonna have to do what comes next! There's no song and dance about that!"

"Malcolm, he's only two."

"Doesn't matter! This is serious! That fool tried to kill my baby." He slumped back, "while he killed my baby". Malcolm's hands went up to his head while he turn his face to the floor.

Andrew watched Malcolm, even though he's only two it's like he understood everything Malcolm said. He sat up straight on my lap and didn't say anything. Malachi sat there looking four times bigger than his normal self. I guess I was the only one who wasn't getting it so I just shut up.

Malachi took Andrew home with him, and Malcolm spent the night. In the morning the doctor came in and explained how my at home care should be. How to care for my cast, what to expect with my bruised ribs, and lastly the part that was music to my ears NO SEX FOR THREE WEEKS!!! I asked the doctor to refill my birth

control pill prescription along with my pain medicines. As they were preparing my papers for discharge Nana and Poppa walked in the room. Both of their faces were very serious. I swallowed hard when they took their places in front of the bed. Poppa had his hands in his pockets jingling change as if that was the only sound to keep him calm. They asked me what happened. I told them how the accident happened. Poppa looked at Malcolm and asked again what happened. Malcolm told Poppa he underestimated a kids promises as idle threats. Poppa asked him what he was going to do about it. "It's gonna be handled sir."
Poppa gestured towards me, "you don't ever let them take your queen! EVER!"
"Yes sir!" Malcolm said
"Lets not have this conversation again!" Poppa said
Then Nana hugged me gently and she asked when do I go home. I told her they were releasing me shortly. She said that was good and that they would meet us at the house. I swallowed again, but I only said ok. When they walked out the room I wished I could run and hide. I looked at Malcolm and he looked like he was running the numbers in his mind. He was quiet for a long time. Cassondra called the hospital, Malcolm had just walked out. I begged her to get a pen and paper. I rattled off David's number. I asked her to call him for me and tell him that I was ok, but that my world had just turned upside down, and that I didn't know if I could honor the quarterly agreement, but I would try to catch him when I could. She asked me if he would understand all that? I assured her he would. I told her I would go back to my parent's house to get my stuff, but she could visit me at Malcolm's tomorrow. I told her I would call her.
Troy picked us up to take us to my house. We stopped at the grocery store to get discarded boxes to put my things in. When we got to my house there were a ton of cars outside. I used my crutches to walk which were weird and it was annoying cause I wanted to move faster than I actually could. Malcolm held the door open for me. The sliding back door off the kitchen was open and I could hear all the child laughter coming from the back yard. There were a bunch of people all throughout the house. Nana told me to sit on the couch and put my leg up. Then she looked at the broken down boxes in Malcolm's arms. He took them to the room and set them down. Jade came out the room and hugged me as she started crying. Nana looked at Jade and then she looked at me. Suddenly she yelled, "TIM!" Everybody FROZE! Daddy hurried in the living room brandy in his hand. When he saw Jade and I he had sad eyes. Nana asked him what was going on? Why was Malcolm carrying boxes, and Jade in tears like she was losing her best friend? He sighed and told Nana I needed some tough love. She told him she didn't understand what he meant. Now Daddy might've been the man, but even he couldn't stand the glare of Nana. He downed his glass and then he put his arm under Nana's and asked her to step outside. They had an unwanted audience; Uncle Frank followed them out the door and Nana yelled at him to get back inside. Watching him come inside pouting like a little kid made everyone laugh. I didn't know where Momma was, but I could feel her eyes on me while Jade and I continued to hug each other and cry. We could all hear Nana going off on Daddy. Poppa went out there to be the peacemaker, and quickly came back in completely red. Daddy came inside looking flustered he told Poppa Nana wanted him. Poppa went outside and you could hear her going off some more. Poppa came inside and he picked up Nana's sweater and her purse. Nana came inside and she kissed my forehead, she told me she didn't agree. She told me to call her if I needed anything and she'd see to it that I got it. I thanked her, and then Nana and Poppa left. You could still hear Nana going off outside, until

they got in the car. Sophia slowly walked in the living room. She asked what was going on. I told her that my parents said I had to go. Sophia's eyes got big, and she looked at Malcolm, "I BET YOU JUST LOVE THIS DON'T YOU!" Malcolm looked at her with no emotion. "MY COUSIN WILL ALWAYS HAVE SOMEWHERE TO GO AS LONG AS I HAVE BREATH IN MY BODY!!!" Malcolm sarcastically clapped his hands at her. Sophia joined our tear fest. Sasha came inside for some water. She saw all of us crying and she started crying too. Malcolm threw up his hands and said, "REALLY?" Troy laughed at him. Then Uncle Frank put his hand on Malcolm's shoulder and told him to step outside, and then he invited Troy too. Jade told me to give her the number over there as soon as I got in the door. We went in the room and Sophia and Jade packed my clothes. I told them I didn't want to take more than clothes. My heart was heavy once my clothes and shoes were all packed. Andrew had a big boy bed at Malcolm's already so there was no point in taking the crib. As it got late my heart started pounding cause I was gonna have to leave. Malcolm came in the room to collect the boxes then he asked about the crib, and I told him we could leave it for now. He shot me a look, but he didn't say anything. I didn't know what the look meant, so I just kept talking. When he left Jade whispered and asked me if he thought I was going to get pregnant again. I hadn't thought of it, and we hadn't discussed it. But mister I don't want no babies was definitely confusing me. He didn't ask me to marry him, so I wasn't gonna consider another baby before then. He set me up last time; since I don't know how this is gonna go I gotta be on guard. Momma didn't say anything to me all afternoon or evening. Daddy even came and hugged me. He told me he loved me and that he was gonna miss me. Momma acted like I didn't exist. I didn't know that my actions hurt her that much. She never said anything, if I thought apologizing would save me, I'd throw myself on her ankles and plead with her not to make me go.

Malcolm drove my car, and Troy followed us to Malcolm's. Andrew looked around he, was trying to understand our things were coming into his daddy's house. I hung his clothes in the closet. As I put his clothes in the dresser he saw his basketball. He got so excited when he saw it. He picked it up and kept saying "Mommy look! Mommy look!" I knew what he was saying. He missed David, but I couldn't say any thing about that either.

****

I'm so happy to get that stupid cast off! Trying to dance in that thing was close to impossible! My leg is a little weak but I don't let that stop me. I do as much as I can on it, which normally means its on ice when I get home. Home. Home. I come here; I know I call it that. But without Momma and Daddy it doesn't feel like it. I spent as much time as I could with Jade and Malachi this summer. Jade brought back pictures of her apartment, she was so excited. She said Momma offered the Birth Control before they left, Momma told her she better not bring home any babies. We made plans for Andrew and I, and maybe Malcolm to go out for our winter break to visit Jade.

Because he couldn't get a location on Sammy he said it wasn't safe for Andrew and I to be out by ourselves. He normally had his cousins Fuzzy and Leonard follow me to the center and then they were there before it was time to go. He got them walkie-talkies and they would give him play by plays of everything happening. I thought it was stupid, but it made him feel better to carry those big ole bulky things around. David would come by the Center during our lunch breaks on his off days. Andrew would get so excited when he saw David. The first time David saw me with my cast and bruises, he stopped in his tracks. He was so happy for me when I got my cast off. He told me he missed hanging out with me and talking to me on the phone. I asked him about his girlfriend. He exhaled, and just nodded his head yes.

****

I found a daycare for Andrew close to school. When I took him to the daycare he looked around at the kids. The place didn't seem as happy as it did the day I signed up. Andrew told me he wanted Grand Momma! I didn't blame him for not wanting to stay; the vibe at that place wasn't a happy one. I was too afraid to call her, so I called Auntie Lauren instead. I asked her if I could pay her to keep Andrew for me. She said she was relieved that I called her cause she didn't want to interfere, but she said my money was no good there. I hurried to her house and Andrew was so happy to see all of his cousins. I was thankful that I left early that morning. I rushed to school; a lot of people heard about my accident so a lot of them asked me about it. Malcolm's cousins were everywhere and all of them were clearly watching me. If that girl Shamrock, I mean Shameka even twisted her eyes at me somebody was in her face. Bernadette said Malcolm keeps giving her a ton of money to make sure I stay safe. I think my accident turned up his paranoia a notch. At lunch I ate with Cassondra and Sophia.

When Andrew and I came home, we were greeted to the smell of dinner. Malcolm ordered dinner and had it in the oven for us when we came home. He was being extra sweet and nice. I knew what he wanted. The doctor told me to wait three weeks somehow I stretched it out to six weeks. When we walked in the door I knew he had waited long enough. We ate dinner at the table as a family; I silently sat pumping myself up to what was about to happen. I told myself Malcolm had been more than patient with me. He came home every night, he always was exactly where he said he was gonna be. He wasn't acting like his old self at all. He was very attentive to me, and I don't think he could've stressed to me any deeper how much he loved me. So why was I sitting at this table feeling like doing anything but making love. This would be the first time it didn't feel like I was sneaking. I had to do it tonight, and I had to be into it. Malcolm's eyes were full of love and desire for me. Realizing that helped me melt a lot of the ice around my heart. I played the memory game with a deck of cards with Andrew while Malcolm attended to business over the phone. When Malcolm got off the phone he sat there watching us. He didn't say anything but I knew he was ready for our game to be over. I bathed Andrew then I put him to bed. Malcolm turned on a record in the living room. He had a glass of brandy waiting for me when I came out. I drank it fast and poured another. As I started to pour the third he took the bottle from me, he gave me a tiny bit more and then he put the bottle away. He took me in his arms and slow danced with me. He kept his face on my neck and he kept kissing me. I was nervous and I didn't know why. I kept bracing myself for anything. After the entire record played Malcolm took me in the bedroom. He undressed me then he laid me on the bed. As he started to enter me I was dry as the desert. He backed up and looked at me. He kissed me, my cheek, my neck, my chest, and my stomach I wondered where he was going with this and when he moved down and kissed me I was completely surprised. Malcolm had never done this before, at first I laid there in shock but the feeling took over. As soon as the feeling took over and I began to shake Malcolm mounted me. My eyes rolled into my head. I didn't even think sex with Malcolm would be this good. I found myself surrendering to every feeling that night. When we were finished I wanted to ask him where he learned how to do that? And how come he never did it before? But I knew better than to ask, I had a feeling I wouldn't like the answer. I felt my heart rip open that night. After that night it didn't take much, I was all over Malcolm. Sometimes he didn't make it in the door good, and I was all over him. This good feeling lasted for maybe two months.

****

It was Saturday morning; we switched cars so that he could take my car to get tires. I took Andrew out to breakfast and then we did a little shopping. Andrew needed new shoes. Andrew spilled a little bit of his water in the car and I didn't want to hear Malcolm's mouth about us trashing his new car. I reached in the glove compartment and there were condoms. I sat at that light suspended in time. He couldn't tell me they were old or from before, this car was new. I told myself it was too good to be true. I started crying and Andrew stared at me. His faced looked sad, like he understood my pain. I pulled up to the apartment; Leonard was waiting outside with his walkie-talkie. I sat there looking at him; he opened my driver's side door. I didn't want to stay there, all my hatred for Malcolm came bubbling to the top. Leonard was startled when he saw me crying. He picked up his walkie-talkie, and said, "she's crying". Malcolm responded quickly asking why. I reached in the glove compartment and I threw a condom at Leonard. I closed my door and I pulled out of the driveway. Andrew didn't make a peep. I drove by Momma and Daddy's house and Daddy's car wasn't there. I drove around the corner to Sophia's house. Her car wasn't there. I went by Cassondra's house but she wasn't home. I found myself on the freeway to Poppa and Nana's house. Nana was getting out of her car when I parked on the street. She didn't recognize the car so she kept walking. When Andrew got out the car he yelled "Nana!" Nana turned around and she put out her arms for Andrew to come to her. I don't know who was more excited. I couldn't even pretend like I wasn't upset. Nana looked at me, then she looked at the car. She smiled at Andrew and she told him she'd take him to Poppa. When we walked in the door she told me to stay in the doorway. She called out to Poppa; she told him she had a special visitor for him. Poppa came around the corner and he and Andrew got excited when they saw each other. Then she told Poppa that she and I were gonna go for a ride. He said ok, but he focused on Andrew. Andrew was full of chatter and excitement I knew he was gonna talk Poppa's ears off. Nana said the car was nice and she wanted me to take her for a ride. I asked her where she wanted me to take her. Then she said she wanted to show me something. So we got back in the car. Before I could start the car she asked me what was wrong. I opened the glove compartment and I showed her. Tears came streaming down my face. She sucked her teeth in irritation. She asked me what I was gonna do. I told her I couldn't do anything, Momma still hates me. I'm not eighteen so I couldn't rent an apartment. I was stuck. She asked me if I wanted to go back, and I told her no. I told her I didn't want to go, but I didn't have a choice. Then she told me to drive. She told me to go to Oakland. She directed me a few blocks up from my parents to a small apartment building. There were men outside working on it. She said there were three units in this building. She pointed to the one in the back, and she said that one was mine. This building wasn't as fancy as Malcolm's, not in the least bit. It was very modest in appearance, but to me it looked like a Grand Palace. She said she bought it as an investment property. And then when she found out about what my parents did, she started moving faster with the renovations. She said she was very disappointed in my parents for making such a ridiculous decision. Then she exhaled, she said my unit would be ready in two weeks. I squeezed her and I cried. We got out the car and we walked inside. The kitchen was small, but there was space for a small table and chairs, the living room was small. There was a half bathroom under the stairs.

Up the stairs there was a bedroom on one side. The bathroom in the middle and a slightly bigger bedroom on the other side. There was a backyard area where Andrew could play out back, and a garage. My heart leaped for joy. I never had my own room before. I kept hugging Nana and crying. She told me the only reason you should ever be with a man is because you love him. Never out of obligation! I asked her what she would charge me for rent. She said she'd think about it. She told me there were a few things that still needed to be done, but she gave me the keys to the front door. She told me she'd let me know as soon as it was ready. As we drove back to her house, my world seemed so much bigger. I didn't feel trapped anymore there was a light at the end of the tunnel.

Chapter 21

I didn't go back to Malcolm's until two am. Then I got in the bed with Andrew. In the morning Malcolm was standing in the doorway staring at us sleeping. When I saw him I rolled my eyes and laid back down. He came and sat at the foot of the bed. He touched my foot and I jerked it away. He exhaled and then he walked out the room. A few minutes later he left. Andrew sat up and said good morning, but he didn't look happy. I laid out his clothes and I told him to get dressed. I took a shower, got dressed, I took money out the jewelry box and then I went downstairs. Fuzzy was leaning against the building. I told him we were going to Merritt bakery for breakfast. I told him he could join us if he didn't call it in. Fuzzy looked torn, he knew he needed to tell Malcolm. But Fuzzy hated to pass up a meal. He pleaded with me to understand, I stood there uncompromising. Andrew stared up at us, he was watching our interaction. Fuzzy pleaded with me to think about all the what ifs and how it was not a good idea. When I still didn't budge he picked up his walkie-talkie and told Malcolm we were on our way to Merritt Bakery. Fuzzy walked behind us looking sad. I thought about it along the way, he was right to call it in. The bigger picture was that we weren't safe, AND Malcolm was paying him quite handsomely to protect us. When we got to the bakery I apologized, and I told him I'm really emotional right now. He looked so relieved when I invited him in. As our waitress set Andrew's chocolate milk on the table Malcolm and Troy sat at our table. Malcolm looked at Fuzzy who was sitting next to Andrew in our booth. "Well doesn't this look cozy!" He gave Fuzzy a mean glare. "What are you doing?"

"We're about to eat breakfast." Fuzzy said

"No you're not! How are you protecting anybody sitting right there!" Malcolm said sternly. Fuzzy looked confused. "You didn't even see me coming until I was up on you. Sitting right there, you got Drew covered, but what about my queen? She's sitting out here vulnerable, assailable, unguarded, and naked! That's not gonna work!" It looked like Fuzzy was trying to figure out the words instead of focusing on the point. "GET UP! GO BACK OUTSIDE! YOU EAT ON YOUR TIME!" Fuzzy sucked his teeth, "man! But I already ordered!" From the sound of this conversation you would think Fuzzy was some little kid. But Fuzzy was a husky man, who only let Malcolm, me, and Momma Shuga talk to him like this. I've seen him make short work of others for less.

Malcolm looked at him and Fuzzy got up. He reluctantly walked out to the front of the restaurant. We could see him fighting the air. We all chuckled, and then Troy asked Andrew to come help him pick out a song on the jukebox. Malcolm sat next to me, I looked at my hands. "He needs to eat Malcolm." I said

"Have the waitress take his plate out there. He shouldn't be in here." He said

"What if he stays out there and whoever is already in here? Does me no good for him to be out there then. "I said

He thought about it for a minute. "Good point, I'll make sure there's two." I sucked my teeth. "Changing the subject, cause there's no point to argue there." He looked at me. "You sleeping in Drew's room now?"

"Yep" I said still looking at my hands.

"For how long?"

"Until I turn eighteen or I can move out whichever comes first."

"That's a little extreme don't you think."

"HOW IS THAT EXTREME???"

He looked at me for a minute. "I could kiss you right now!" I gagged. He laughed at my reaction. "I don't even know why." He sighed. "I love you! It's you and me until one of us dies first. But I don't know what it is, or even why. How do you want to make this work?" He said leaning back in his seat and putting his arms up.

"What do you mean?" I was lost.

"I'll marry you, I actually want a daughter. A little girl who looks just like you." He smiled at the thought of it.

I looked around the booth. "Am I on Candid camera?"

"You're funny."

"What was that? I hope you don't think that flies as a marriage proposal for one!" He blew air. "Now you're gonna start numbering everything." He rolled his eyes.

"Two! I don't want a husband that I have to share! If I have to be faithful so do you! Three! I don't even like you, why would I marry you?"

He rolled his eyes, "you love me. Maybe if I gave you a chance to experience these broke, little dick fools you'd understand why it doesn't get any better than me."

"Maybe you should!"

He looked at me seriously, and then he smiled. "You know better! You're mine, but I want you to have your wedding so your parents can stop losing it. Then we can have another baby. You can have your little school eventually."

"Malcolm, I don't want to be with you."

He kept smiling like he didn't hear me. "I should look into buying a house huh. So Drew and little Amber can have a yard to play in. Maybe a little Malcolm and a Amber junior junior." He made himself laugh.

"Are you sniffing your own powder? Malcolm, I don't want to marry you, I don't even want to be your girlfriend."

He sat up and looked at me. "Amber, what am I supposed to do? I love you! I try to forget you and it's like I get sick or something. From the moment I saw you beat that little girl down I knew you had to be in my life. I changed my whole life plan just to have you in it. Since I can't live without you..."

"I don't know what you're supposed to do Malcolm. But I can't live like this."

"Like what? Everything you could ever want for is provided for you. You've never had to work, and you never will. You could go buy a house right now. There's nothing you can't have." The waitress brought our food. I asked her to take Fuzzy's plate to him outside. Malcolm handed her a twenty and asked her to seat Troy and Andrew on the other side of the restaurant. Andrew was happy to sit with Troy but he gave me sad eyes about being so far away.

Malcolm picked up a piece of my bacon. "All the money in the world won't change the fact that I don't have what I want. A man who loves me."

"I do love you." He said rolling his eyes.

"But only me!" He sighed. "You keep breaking my heart Malcolm. I can't even trust you with my heart anymore."

"I'm sorry. I don't even know why. But I'll stop, I won't do it no more."

"You don't mean that." I said

"I do! I do mean it. You can't tell me." He said

"I can't believe you. Actions speak louder than words."

****

Nana called me Friday and told me the apartment was ready. Monday I went down to the phone company and the electric company on my lunch break. They promised to have everything on by tomorrow. I got excited, my freedom was close. That night I was so excited that I had a celebratory drink after I put Andrew down. Malcolm came home and he started reading me. He asked me how much I had drunken. When I said just a little, he stood in my face. He stood there and when I smiled at him he told me I had more than just a little. I smiled and disagreed. He kissed me and I didn't reject his kiss. He told me I was drunk. I smiled and said maybe just a tad bit. He walked away, and I went back to straightening up. He stood there thinking and then he went away. When he came back in the living room he was naked. He kissed me again; he asked me if I loved him. I told him I loved him so much it hurt. He apologized as he took my clothes off. He told me to stop taking the pill; he needed me to replace the baby we lost. He was making me sad, he said no one was ever gonna hurt me again. He kept telling me he was blessed with a good girl.

In the morning I put almost all of Andrew's clothes in his hamper as if they were dirty. I did the same with mine. I took them to my car, and if the guys asked I was taking them to the laundry mat. I put Andrew's basketball at the bottom of the hamper. The guys didn't ask, nothing even seemed alarming about it to them. At lunchtime I went to the apartment and as promised there was electricity and a working phone line. I could smell the freedom. I did the same thing Wednesday morning. That only left a few things to grab. But since they were used to me going to the center on Wednesdays no one would be at Malcolm's apartment right away. I went straight there after school and I got the last few things I needed from his apartment. I put a note in the middle of the bed, and then I ran out. I went over to Auntie Lauren's and I grabbed Andrew. We went to the grocery store; I filled the cart up with groceries. We had bags everywhere in the car. I told Andrew we were going home. When we pulled up to the apartment he looked at me with a funny look. I told him this was our new house. He smiled and then we took all the groceries, pots, pans, and dishes that I bought inside. I opened the garage door, and then I locked Herb 2 away in it. Andrew helped me put away the groceries while he told me all about the games he's played with Jeff, JoJo, and Sasha. I looked at my watch as time passed my heart kept speeding up as I imagined Malcolm coming home, Leonard telling him I hadn't come yet. Malcolm going up to the apartment and losing it. He'd call everybody and pop up everywhere, but Nana is the only one who knows where I am. I didn't want anyone to lie and more importantly for him to know they were lying. I gave Nana my number. Then Andrew and I played go fish.

****

Nana called me in the morning. Her voice sounded a little panicked. She told me to go to my parent's house, and that Uncle Frank was already there. Uncle Jeff, Daddy, and a lot of the guys that work for and with them were all at my parent's house. When Andrew and I walked in the door Auntie Lauren took Andrew to go play with the rest of the kids. Everyone was talking and looking serious. Uncle Frank came and sat next to me on the couch. "So young lady, where were you last night?" His voice wasn't angry but he was serious. Daddy and Uncle Jeff came close to hear.

I shifted in my seat, "in my apartment".

"Apartment?" He asked

"Yea, I just got it. Last night was my first night there." Everyone's faces were serious. "What's going on?" I asked

"Malcolm's in jail." Uncle Frank said they all watched my face for a reaction. I felt like the room was spinning, "What do you mean?"

Uncle Frank told me that Sammy and his little hoodlum friends lashed out last night. Leonard was at the apartment they thought he was guarding me. "He's dead!" Uncle Frank said matter of factly. "They broke in the apartment and vandalized the whole place. Malcolm came home; he thought they took you guys. Uncle Frank said

169

he couldn't get here fast enough. Malcolm and his cousins found Sammy and his friends. As Sammy pleaded for his life he told Malcolm he didn't touch you. Fuzzy found your note on the floor; he read it over the walkie-talkie. It was still too late for Sammy. The police got there just as Sammy was dying. The police raided the apartment, but Malcolm kept that place clean. They found something in his car though. We're trying to find out what the charges are so we'll know which lawyer to send in. But it doesn't look like he'll escape without serving anytime." Daddy's eyes were sad as he watched me. Uncle Frank continued to tell me how things were gonna run. Once they knew the charges, they'd send the lawyer. The good news was that Sammy and his gang were no longer a threat to business etc. The Shop would continue, Malcolm told them I had access to all of his finances. So all his money would run through Momma and me. Momma looked at me but she didn't say anything. A little while later Poppa and Nana came through the door. Uncle Frank reported everything to Poppa while he sat in the chair listening. He asked where they were holding Malcolm. Uncle Frank told him, and then Poppa told me to come along with him and Nana. Poppa seemed ten feet tall when we walked into the Police station. Suddenly I felt like I was two years old again. Poppa knew the Captain there. They talked for a while. Then Poppa told Nana and I to come. We went in a office, the captain brought Malcolm in. Malcolm looked so relieved when he saw me. He threw his arms around me so tight, and then he cried a hard felt sob on my neck. He said he thought they had me. The captain shut the door to give us some space. Malcolm wouldn't stop kissing me or let me go. Tears kept streaming out of his eyes even though he was trying to calm himself. He took a deep breath, and then he told Poppa he could focus now. Poppa rattled off information, Malcolm shook his head taking it all in. Then Malcolm gave Poppa information but it was like they were speaking another language literally. Poppa told him to gird his loins cause it was about to get bumpy. Poppa told him to remain calm and to know he would be covered when he got out. Then he released me and put his hands on my face. "We're gonna talk." I did my best to smile, then he told me Troy was gonna find me. Malcolm and Poppa talked some more, Poppa told him Uncle Frank would come.

When we got back to the house Daddy was stomping some guy into the ground. Everybody was standing around watching no one was saying or doing anything to stop it. Daddy reminded me of Malcolm right in that moment. I didn't know what was going on, but by the look of everyone I knew better than to interfere. Uncle Frank grabbed Daddy and he pointed at us. Daddy told one of the guys to get the guy off his property. A couple of guys came to remove the guy. I looked at Daddy, he was so big, and I had never seen him like that. Uncle Jeff was laughing while Uncle Frank talked Daddy down. Momma was standing on the porch watching, her breathing was heavy and Auntie Lauren was standing with her. Poppa put his hands in his pockets as he approached the men. Nana and I went in the house. Nana asked me about Malcolm's financial information. I took the papers that I had in my things at my parent's house out of my old diaper bag. Momma and Auntie Lauren came inside. Momma stopped in her tracks when she heard me read off her name to Nana. Nana asked what was going on outside. Auntie Lauren said that guy assumed Momma was single for whatever reason. He took things too far. Momma looked embarrassed.

Troy walked in the door, he said hi to everyone. He told me he was looking for me all night. I told him I left a note. He said we were going to have to go see Malcolm together so we'd know exactly how everything was gonna be carried out. Troy asked me to come outside, then he told me a lot of things were gonna change. He said he knew things weren't right between Malcolm and I when all of this went down, but Malcolm and I had been through too much together for me to turn my back on him now. I didn't say anything to Troy cause this day was turning out to be one trauma after another.

Nana and I went to the apartment. She said I was gonna need furniture, I told her I was gonna get that this weekend. She asked me if I had money. I told her about my savings account. She asked me how much I had. When I told her the balance last time I checked, she told me I needed to spread that money out and I couldn't leave it sitting like that. She said it would raise too many questions. She took me to the bank and she requested to speak to a personal banker. When we sat down with the lady, Nana told her I needed to diversify my assets. The lady's eyes got really big when she pulled up my account information, she was almost sweating. Nana told her that she deposits money into all her grand children's accounts, but I was the only one who didn't spend it. You could still see the question mark on the lady's face as Nana continued to talk. Nana told her that we were going to need cashier checks to shop around different interest rates at different banks. The lady seemed a little hesitant. Then Nana mentioned that she had a checking and savings at this bank as well, and that she'd need a few cashier checks of her own while we moved my money around. The lady relaxed when she pulled up Nana's accounts. Then the lady went into her whole sales pitch about why I should stick with Savings of American bank for all my investments. Nana instructed her to leave ten thousand in my savings. To put five thousand in a interest bearing checking account. She told me I could allow thirty five thousand to stay with this bank spread out over CD's and Bonds, but I should really spread the other hundred thousand out at other banks to earn better interest on my money. Then she instructed the lady to give us cashier's checks in ten thousand dollar increments for my money. Then Nana told the lady to give her five ten thousand dollar cashier checks as well for her own money. The lady jokingly asked if Nana would adopt her. Nana gave her a courtesy chuckle. The Bank Manager had to approve the cashier's checks since we were moving so much money. Nana looked at me and smiled. The manager came over and introduced himself, and basically started kissing Nana's butt. He told her he was very honored that she banked with them and to personally notify him directly if she ever needed assistance in the future. Nana took his card and she thanked him. The lady handed us envelopes containing our checks. And a checkbook for my new checking account. Then I told the lady I needed to enter a Safe Deposit box. I took Nana in the room with me once we pulled the box out of the vault. I showed Nana all of Malcolm's documents, and the huge stash of cash. She looked at the statements and documents. She asked me why I didn't move my money around before it got so big if I knew Malcolm was moving his. I told her I wasn't paying attention and that I barely came to the bank since he still gave me cash. She told me I was going to need to pay better attention. Then she said the strong and the smart survive, the rest get messed over. I didn't know if she was calling me stupid so I put my head down. I guess she realized how she sounded and then she told me that she was really proud of me for being frugal with my money and living simply. She said people who had to have the biggest and the best draw too much attention, and because of our lifestyle we all need to fly under the radar. Then she explained each of the statements to me. She told me that Momma was gonna need to see the stuff that he named her on as well. The thought of being alone with Momma made me nervous. As we went from bank to bank, all banks that Nana banked with as well, we opened checking and savings accounts, CD's, etc. but for those accounts I asked that the banks hold those statements in their branches as Nana advised. I asked Nana if I should feel guilty for wanting to wait for Malcolm? She told me that Malcolm and I were a family, and she thinks that in the end he and I will end up together. But if last night hadn't happened we wouldn't be together at this exact moment. So it was ok for me to move on. Then she cautioned me about who I brought around Andrew. She told me not to bring men in and out of his life cause that wasn't healthy for anyone to see their mother in that light.

Chapter 22

So much has happened in the past month that sometimes I don't know if I'm coming or going. They moved Malcolm from the local jail to the county jail. They're trying to charge him with first-degree murder and possession with the intent to sale. Uncle Frank has a whole Legal team working on the case. They're working to prove self defense and to have the possession charge thrown out, because they did not have a warrant to search Malcolm's car, and if they could, they were going to say that the drugs found in his car were planted. Since Malcolm had no priors, didn't own the Shop and was only listed as an employee, had completed Barber's school. They could paint the picture that he was a model citizen.

Right before I received my subpoena from the prosecution to appear in court, Troy said there was a problem. He knew that Yvette had been served with a subpoena, but now she was hiding. Then I got mine. The lawyers were drilling me all day and night on my responses and preparing me with answers. They dug into every aspect of my life, when did I meet Malcolm, how long were we together, what was the nature of our relationship, everything. Dancing and drinking were my only escapes. I'd dance as much as I could at school. Attend the center on Wednesday nights and then have a nightcap so that I could sleep.

"I know I don't know all the things going on in your life right now. Just go out there and do your best!" Ms. Dubois said then she kissed my cheek. Tonight was my final winter performance and I felt like I was going to bust. I was in tears the entire time before my performance. People around the school knew what was going on, but they didn't know the details. When it was time, I composed myself best I could and then I went out to perform. Tears continuously streamed out of my eyes, but every leap made me feel taller. It was so quiet in that auditorium you could hear cotton hit the floor. I forgot about my audience and my dance was my scream to anyone who would hear me! I could see the surprise on Scott's face when he realized I was crying. But in the end we nailed it. The audience erupted in thunderous applause; I could feel the vibration in the floor as I bowed. When Ms. Dubois came to me, she saw I was still crying and she had been moved to tears. She said it was crazy cause she'd seen us practice this routine for months and tonight it was like she was seeing the whole thing for the first time. I couldn't stop crying though, I just didn't know how everything was gonna pan out and I was really nervous. When I came out Ms. Dubois' friend Mr. Campbell was there again and he sang my praises. He spoke to my parents and grand parents. It was a force of habit to look for Malcolm, but the reality that he wasn't there hit me like a ton of bricks. Troy brought Penny and Tiffany, and I squeezed the life out of both of them when I saw them. I kissed them both and I told them I loved them so much. I thanked them for coming. I invited them to come out to dinner with us again, and they cheerfully accepted. I asked Troy if he wanted to come but he declined. I told him I would bring them home after dinner. When I approached my grandparents that's when I saw Tag. He had another wild flower bouquet, and he complimented my performance. I completely missed that he was in the audience. I thanked him for the flowers and then I hugged Nana and Poppa. Momma was watching Tag, I know she probably thinks I invited him, but I didn't. Penny and Tiffany were watching Tag with the same look as Momma. Sophia asked the girls how they were coming along with the cookbook she made them. They got so excited, they told her about all the dishes they made and the mistakes they made.

At the restaurant I sat between Tag and Andrew again. Penny and Tiffany tried to keep me engaged in conversation with them so that there was no time to talk to Tag.

But once Sophia got them talking about the cookbook they were distracted. Tag asked me where my boyfriend was tonight, and I shrugged. I tried to change the subject by asking him about school, but he looped back around to the boyfriend topic. I told him that right now wasn't a good time to discuss it. Daddy noticed my demeanor and he started watching us. Tag was more persistent tonight, and with everything going on in my life right now, it was just bad timing. I was trying to keep my cool, but it was clear as day that I wasn't interested. Suddenly Daddy had, had enough and he told Tag to step outside. Uncle Jeff jumped up knowing his brother and he followed them outside. Nana asked me what happened, and I told her that Tag wanted to talk about more than I could handle tonight and I guess daddy noticed. Nana shook her head and then she told Poppa to go save Tag before Daddy rips his head off. Twenty minutes later when they came back in they made JoJo switch seats with Tag. That made Tag sit next to Uncle Jeff. Tag looked like he had been scolded, and Daddy gave him evil eyes the rest of the night. Tonight all of us girls had Virgin Strawberry daiquiris, I found myself really wishing there was alcohol in these drinks, but I told myself to hold on until I got home then I could relax with a glass of anything. I didn't mention my apartment to the girls, I don't know why, but I just didn't. When it was time to go, Tag walked out to Poppa's car he didn't say goodbye to anyone. Daddy walked the girls, Andrew, and I to the car. Then he told me to call him when I got home. As I drove the girls home they told me that that girl Renee asked why I had to convince them to help her. So they told her she's always mean to them, and she never tries to help them even when it's her kids that they're dealing with etc. They said she's been trying to be nicer to them. But then Momma Shuga always puts them up against each other especially when they finally get everybody to cooperate. They said its like she don't want them to get along. When I pulled up to the house I got up so Penny could get out the backseat. Momma Shuga was in her car it looked like she was getting ready to leave when I pulled up. She got out her car and came over to the car. All the cousins on the porch watched.

"How's the baby?" She said

"Andy's good" I said

"Listen" she said walking to me. "Has Malcolm said anything about money for the house?"

"I haven't discussed money with him. Right now we've only discussed the charges."

"Right. Right. Where is he again?"

"He's in county right now."

She started wringing her hands together. "I'm a little stressed about money right now. I need to make my mortgage payment, and I haven't heard from him." I felt bad for the girls. "Did he leave you holding anything? Can you help me out?" She asked.

"We weren't on good terms when he went in." I said, feeling uncomfortable about her asking me for money. I never asked Malcolm about his support for her, but thus far anything he left open was for a reason. If I was supposed to give Momma Shuga money he would've mentioned it at some point.

"I know, I know but you guys were living together. I figured he left something at the apartment."

"No, I moved out before all this happened. I took my clothes and Andy's. Outside of maybe sixty dollars I didn't take money away from there."

"That doesn't mean you're not holding something. I'm desperate over here." She said

"I really don't have anything, especially on me right now. Let me talk to Malcolm,

I'm sure he has a plan for you."
She blew air, " I don't need you to talk to Malcolm for me. I can talk to him myself.
Never mind Amber! Forget it!" Then she stormed off. She wasn't even in her car all
the way when she started the car and put it in gear to speed off. That's when I
realized she was driving a new car. Maybe she bought the car over a month ago.
Fuzzy came off the porch and he asked me if I was ok. I told him I was fine. Then
he asked me what Momma Shuga wanted. I asked him why he didn't help her make
her mortgage payment. He gave me a funny look. Then he said, "what mortgage?
She inherited this house from her husband when he died. He said the property taxes
are paid out of his trust account. He asked me if I gave her money. And I told him I
didn't because I didn't have any money on me. He told me to be careful because
people were gonna start coming to me with sob stories, he said tell all of them I
don't have no money. Then he said, "I still got your back cousin, call me if you need
me".
When I got home I told Daddy what happened with Momma Shuga when I took the
girls home. He said it was a good idea for me to stay away from there for now. He
said, "Barb is not right in the head she pimps her own grandchildren." I lost my air
when he said that. He said that's why Renee's always pregnant and has so many
babies. He said once she loses Renee she'll move on to Penny and Tiffany. I started
crying, I told Daddy I couldn't let that happen to them. Daddy said we can't save the
world, and he hopes that they get out of there before that happens, but he doubted
that they would. He said there were a lot of things that happened over there that
would be beyond my comprehension because I was raised differently.

****

I couldn't go to Jade's for winter break because of everything that was happening
with Malcolm. I told Jade that I would come as soon as everything was everything.
I asked her how college life was treating her. She said she was still adjusting. I
asked how things were going with Sonny, and she said ok. Then she told me to hold
on. She took the phone into her bedroom. She said they hadn't had sex yet. She said
she starts freaking out when she realizes what's coming next. I asked how Sonny
was holding up. She said he was patient and loving, which only made her feel
worse. She said at this point she'd feel better if he broke up with her or cheated so
she could break up with him. I told her she didn't mean that, she exhaled and
agreed. She said she doesn't know how to get out of her own head to let it happen. I
told her she was over thinking the whole thing. I told her, "One, you need to relax.
Two, try turning on soft music. Three relax with some wine. Four look at Sonny.
Five, talk to him the whole time if you need to. Have him reassure you that he loves
you the whole time if that's what you need. Six take your time. And seven, which
was the most important! Call me immediately afterwards!" We laughed, she said
she'd try that. She sent him to the store to get some wine while we were on the
phone.
The next morning she called me crying, but they were happy tears. She told me that
they made love last night and all morning. She thanked me for helping her through
it. Then she said right before she called me Sonny proposed. I screamed into the
phone! Apparently he asked Daddy for permission at her graduation party. We
giggled and chatted for a long time. She said that was why Momma was adamant
about her getting her birth control before she left. Then she asked how Momma was
acting with me. Out of nowhere the tears came, I told her that Momma hated me.
She assured me that Momma didn't hate me. I told her Momma only talks to me
when she has to. Otherwise she just ignores me. Then Andrew came in my room.

175

He was still rubbing the sleep out of his eyes. He got excited when I told him Auntie Jade was on the phone. That boy could talk; he was rolling with the conversation like he was and adult or something. I could hear Jade cracking up through the phone at some of the things Andrew said to her. She said he sounds so big. I told Jade that Sophia and Charles were moving into the apartment next door this weekend. Sophia was hoping that the space would do them all some good. She said that they fight so much now and it was taking its toll on their relationship.

****

I just realized why I've been in such a funk. It's February and I'm mourning the loss of my baby. The closer my due date gets the more depressed I get. I didn't realize I was so attached to that pregnancy. I know I was very upset with Malcolm about it, I hated him for trapping me like that, but I wanted my baby. I look at Andrew and I wonder who did I lose. It hurts so much! Malcolm's not even here for me to be mean to him about it. I'm tired of being sad, but I don't know what to do. Cassondra said she's worried about me, so she's been coming over and spending as much time as she can with me. I thank her every chance I get for hanging with me or allowing me to help her with her dresses. Anything to help me get out of my head. I wished my Momma didn't hate me so much; I could really use a hug from her right now! Oh well as soon as I put Andrew down I'm gonna drink until all I can think about is how drunk I am.

"Ugh!" The phone was ringing and it was loud. I answered and I spoke slowly. It was David! If I wasn't so hung over I would've popped up. He told me I called him last night crying, I gave him my number just before I hung up on him. I had no recollection of any conversation with him. He asked me for directions to my house so he could come take care of me. I snapped at him and told him I didn't need him to take care of me. He waited a minute and then said in a little bit I was going to have a three year old bouncing off the walls and it didn't sound like I was in any shape to deal with that. He said he was just trying to be a good friend, but if I wanted him to back off he would. I laid there thinking about it. Andrew was gonna be talking and singing, and it was taking too much energy to have this conversation. So I gave him directions to my house. I got up and put a bra and pajama pants on under my gown. When I heard his knock I drug my body out the bed, when I cracked the door the sunlight outside hurt my eyes. He had a couple bags in his arms. I hugged him and asked what was in the bags. He said he was making breakfast. I waved him towards the kitchen then I went back to my bed. Andrew came in my room rubbing his eyes. He sniffed the air; he asked me what I was cooking. I told him I wasn't but there was a special guest downstairs for him. Andrew slowly walked down the stairs. Then I heard him gasp and then they erupted in laughter and excitement. If my head wasn't killing me I would've been tickled. A couple seconds later I heard both of their feet coming up the stairs. Andrew whispered, "Mommy we got medicine for you". I opened the eye that wasn't smashed into the pillow. I shot both of them daggers with my eye. Andrew had the aspirin and David had a drink in his hand. I asked him what it was, he told me not to ask and not to smell it, just drink it and I would feel better in a few minutes. I took the aspirin and then I swallowed that horrid drink. Andrew laughed watching me display how horrible that drink tasted. The only thing that was good about that drink was that it was cold. He said I should feel better shortly, and then they went back downstairs. Literally I could feel my headache lifting. I could hear Andrew down there talking David's ear off while they watched Saturday morning cartoons. I stopped taking the pill again once Malcolm was locked up, so now my

176

period came when it felt like it which was annoying. It used to come like clockwork, but now it's all over the calendar. I went to the bathroom expecting to see that I started, but I was dry as a bone. Didn't matter I was just happy I wasn't waiting for confirmation of pregnancy, cause this would've drove me crazy. I looked in the mirror and my hair was all over my head. I tried to fix it as much as I could without looking like I fixed my hair. I hadn't talked to David in months. I didn't want his girlfriend getting the wrong impression.

When I went downstairs they were both laying on the floor watching cartoons. Both of them smiled at me when they saw me. David asked me if I was ready to eat. I told him not just yet but it smelled great. I glanced in the kitchen expecting to see a mess like whenever Malachi or Timothy cooked it looked like a tornado hit the kitchen. But to my surprise everything was clean. Andrew said breakfast was yummy. There was a little knock at the door. Andrew sat up excited, I opened the door and Sasha was at the door with a big smile on her face. She obviously dressed herself. She had on her brown Mary Jane shoes, light turquoise pants, and a dark red shirt. Her hair was all over her head.

"Good morning sweetheart!" I said looking down at her looking adorable.

"Good morning Ambur!" Her little voice said then she invited herself in. She put her hands on her little hips and asked Andrew why he wasn't dressed, because it was time to go outside and play. Andrew laughed then he explained that he was watching cartoons. She shifted her weight from one leg to the other. Then she told him to hurry up. Andrew put his foot down and told her he would get dressed as soon as his cartoon went off. When they came back from commercial the credits were rolling. David belly laughed as Andrew sighed in defeat. Andrew told Sasha to wait right there and he would be right back. Then he took off running up the stairs. Sasha turned on her toes, and then she looked David up and down. Like she was grown she asked him who he was. He chuckled and said David. She put her finger to her chin and she thought about it. She agreed to his name like she could make him change it if she didn't like it. David shook her hand. She asked David why he was there. He said he was visiting us. She asked him if he knew her Momma. He looked at me to say who her mother was. I mouthed Sophia, and he told her he did. She asked him if he was her uncle like her uncle Richard. David looked confused. Then Andrew came downstairs, he told Sasha to come on and they went out in my backyard to play. David brought me a glass of water. I told him that Sophia and Charles lived next door. We sat there for a minute looking at each other. It was an uncomfortable silence.

"SO........." David said, I smiled at him not knowing what he was going to say. "So you and Malcolm broke up?"

"How do you know that?"

David smiled, "you told me. You don't remember calling me last night?"

"No, what did I say? I didn't even know how you got my number."

"You called me, you were crying because he left you to deal with everything on your own. You were really sad about the baby, you told me you really loved him and he keeps breaking your heart."

"Geesh! I really said all that?"

"You said a lot more, that I always smell good. Thank you for noticing by the way. You said Andrew really likes me and that's good because I like him too. But you wanna know what you said that robbed me of my sleep?"

I swallowed hard, I was already embarrassed. "What did I say?"

He sat on the couch and he leaned forward. "You said I was cute." Then he put his

hand over his mouth.
I could've died. "I didn't say that?"
"Yea, and other stuff. But I'm not telling you about that."
"Other stuff like what?"
"Oh I'm not telling, but my head was pumped up pretty big."
I rolled my eyes, "whatever".
I went in the kitchen and turned on the stove to heat up the food. Then I heard an adult knock at the door. I called out that it was open. "Hey-low!" Charles said coming in the door. "Whoa!" I knew that response was in regards to David. So I called out who each person was. I came in the living room with my plate as I told David that Charles came right after he left our middle school. David jokingly said that Charles was the replacement David. David and I laughed, but Charles didn't. He seemed annoyed, I told him Sasha was in the back with Andrew. Charles turned on his heels and walked out. David asked me what was wrong with him. I shrugged, as I tasted David's potatoes. They were really good. There was a heavy knock on the door as Sophia opened the door. She had the biggest grin, and then she screamed when she saw David. She ran in the door and hugged David so big. Charles returned kind of sulking he plopped down on the love seat. Sophia, David, and I sat reminiscing about our seventh grade year. Charles mumbled that we never acted like that about our eighth grade year. We all stopped and looked at him sulking. Then Charles blurted out that nothing explained why David was there today. David just looked at him then he looked at Sophia. He asked Sophia what was wrong with her man. She looked so annoyed and embarrassed. She told him it was none of his business why David was there. Then she asked him why he even came over in the first place. He started stuttering, and then Sophia started mimicking him. Then she told him to take it all in because she better never catch him over my house again without her being there first. David looked at me like he was missing something. Charles started to argue back, but he couldn't come up with a decent argument to save his life. Clearly Sophia had no respect for Charles. They argued all the way back to their apartment. Then I heard whimpering at the door Sasha was crying and Andrew was trying to comfort her. I picked her up and comforted her. Then David asked what the kids were doing outside. He went in the backyard and Andrew explained that they were playing store. David pretended like he was the crazy butcher. The kids started having fun again. So I straightened up the apartment while they played out back. Sophia came back over, she was so irritated, she apologized for the scene. I told her it was ok, I told her about Sasha's reaction. When David and the kids came in for some water, Sophia asked David if she was gonna see him around more often. He looked at me and he said he hoped so.
****
Daddy asked me to come over. He said the family was coming over and we needed to discuss something's. I told Sophia to come with us. As we loaded the kids and pulled out of the driveway, Charles was pulling up. He saw Sophia in the front seat, so I guess he figured that meant he could follow us. When we pulled up to the house Daddy was outside talking to Uncle Jeff. Daddy was fine when he saw Sophia and I pull up. When he saw Charles pull up behind us he almost lost it. "No! No! No!" Daddy told Sophia she could stay but Charles could not. Now I thought Sophia would do the right thing and leave with her husband but Sophia told Charles he had to go home, and she'd be there later. Charles drove away but I knew he had to be hurt. Uncle Jeff pulled Sophia to the side. While they were talking Troy pulled up. He came straight to me; he told me Malcolm wants to see me. I exhaled and just

shook my head ok. Daddy told us to come inside. Daddy asked Troy how things were going at the shop. Troy said he's having a little miscommunication with Moses right now, but he'll get it resolved. I told him I didn't trust Moses. Troy nodded his head like he understood what I meant. Uncle Frank and Gwen came in carrying pizza boxes. It seemed like they ordered two of every kind of pizza. Momma didn't say anything directly to me, but she sat next to me when Uncle Frank started talking. Then the front door opened, I guess Momma Shuga didn't expect the house to be full of people. She hesitated but it was too late to back down. When she laid eyes on me she asked me if she could talk to me. Troy stood up and asked Momma Shuga if it could wait cause we were kind of in the middle of something. Momma Shuga cursed him out for saying anything. Daddy told Momma Shuga to get out! She wrinkled her lips like she was gonna say something to Daddy, I didn't even feel Momma leave my side. Momma kicked her out the door. She was yelling that she told her not to come back to her house. I flew off the couch so fast cause I knew Momma Shuga wasn't stupid enough to come to my house by herself. That girl Renee, Bernadette, and Bernadette's friends were waiting at the bottom of the stairs. I saw the surprised look on Renee's face when she saw Momma. Momma Shuga backed down the stairs with the evilest grin on her face. Momma followed her down the stairs all the time ready to swing. Renee put her arm in front of Bernadette and shook her head no. I asked that girl Renee what was going on as I was tying my hair backwards. She opened her mouth to speak, but Momma Shuga said, "it turns out that you were messing around with that boy. You stole all Malcolm's money and double crossed both of them!" The girls looked at Momma Shuga like they were confused. You could tell that wasn't the story that brought them there. "Tell your family how you were just using him for the money. That's why you got pregnant, and using food to try and turn my family against me! Where's the money Amber!" I walked down the stairs and I put hands out. "So you bring your grand daughters to my house to fight me? How is that supposed to get you your money?" Momma Shuga glared at me. "Why did she tell you, you were coming here?" All of them dropped their eyes. "What is it Momma Shuga? You want money? How much you want? I'll ask Malcolm for you, but don't bring drama to my house! This is so unnecessary!"
Momma Shuga looked at the girls and she got mad when they all had their eyes to the ground. "YOU GONNA LET HER TALK TO ME LIKE THAT?"
"Renee why she always trying to make us fight? I don't know what she said or did to make it seem like I had something against you, but I never even got a chance to know you."
Momma Shuga saw Renee swaying with her eyes to the ground. She got mad, and swung to hit me. I backed up even though my natural reaction was to duck and come back with a upper cut from my legs. But Momma came over my shoulder and clocked her in the face, while she pushed me out the way. The girls looked shocked, Bernadette came forward to defend her grand mother. Momma kept Tagging Momma Shuga's face, Momma Shuga was stunned and fell backwards. Bernadette came swinging and she hit Momma in the jaw, you heard the contact. As Bernadette was moving forward I clothes lined her in the throat. I remember what she did to Toni. Momma stumbled backwards. Bernadette couldn't believe I knocked her down. As she attempted to get up I kicked her in her chest. And when she bounced back I hit her with a right and a left. I couldn't let her stand up. Renee made Bernadette's friends stand down. Momma Shuga slowly got up and she was trying to egg Momma on. Then we heard three gunshots in the air. Nana had her gun out,

which I didn't know she carried one. "ENOUGH!" Nana yelled! "If you value your life and that of your grandchildren, which I highly doubt! You will get off my son's property IMMEDIATELY!!"

I put my hand out to help Bernadette. I told her, "you better go!"

Bernadette looked at me like I was crazy. Renee tried to help Momma Shuga, and Momma Shuga started cursing her. As Renee turned to walk away I saw a glimpse of her pregnant belly. I got a lump in my throat.

Chapter 23

"Thank you for coming." Malcolm said while he read my face. I nodded my head. I didn't want to be there. I didn't want to hear anything he could say to me to mess up my head anymore than it already was. "You've been drinking a lot." He said as his eyes rolled over my face.

I sucked my teeth, "so now you're judging me?"

"No judgment, I'm just telling you what I see. Your skin is all dried out." He said

"What do you expect!" I know I was defensive, and over reacting a bit. But I didn't want to be there. "Momma Shuga brought Renee, Bernadette and them to my house looking for a fight. She keeps coming at me about money. First she said she needed it for her house. But Fuzzy told me that wasn't true. Then when she comes to my parent's house, with some story about how I played you and Sammy against each other, and I was trying to take your money and run."

Malcolm smiled, "what did your momma do?"

I smiled, "she kicked her out the door and beat her in her face. But Bernadette hit her in the jaw. It was swollen for a minute, but she's ok."

He looked me in my eyes, "what did you do?"

"I knocked Bernadette down, and I wouldn't let her get up until Nana fired her gun and told them to leave."

Malcolm chuckled, "I love your family!"

"Did you leave money for her?"

Malcolm sat back in his chair, "no". He said nonchalantly.

"Were you giving her money before?"

"From time to time, but just because she's my grandmother." Then he sat forward. "Look Momma Shuga will do anything for money. Even if it means conspiring against her grandson. Have you seen her new car?" His eyes were on fire. I nodded yes. "I didn't buy it for her, so how she get it?" He turned in his chair. "She better hope they try to keep me in here for a long time." I could see him turning inside. "She got her own grandson killed! She doesn't even care. No burial for him or anything! All she cares about is the money. Stay away from her!"

"But what about the girls? Sterling? I can't see them anymore?"

"If you show her a weakness she's gonna use it against you! You can't go over there to see them no more. If she hurts you again!" Malcolm exhaled to calm himself. "How are you doing on money?"

"I'm fine. But a few of your CD's are maturing what do you want to do with them?"

"Roll them over. Get the longest term you can at the best interest rates. I'm gonna need you to have more of a presence at the shop, especially when the summer hits." I sucked my teeth. "I don't want to be around Moses."

"I think he's shorting me. I need you to keep a tally for me for a month. Then I can forecast a better monthly projection. I know business slows down in the winter after the holidays. But the back end deposits aren't syncing up and I got Troy on other business for me. There's only so many places I can have him be at one time." I rolled my eyes, cause he wasn't really asking he was telling me basically. "Hey!" He said wanting me to look at him. "You still my good girl?"

"Maybe that's the problem Malcolm! You're only a year older than me, I'm not a girl."

"I know you're mad at me. But as soon as I get out of here, we're getting married and everything will be fine."

I gasped. "Malcolm! I'm not gonna marry you! You're not offering me anything. If you think I look dried out now, what would I look like in five years after dealing

with you're heartache. You're not even sorry about it anymore. Now it's just something I need to accept about you." I shook my head. "Did you forget the reason why I wasn't home when Sammy came for me was because I left you?"
Malcolm let those words dance around for a minute. "So what are you saying?"
"I'm not your girlfriend. I'm Andrew's mother."
He licked his lips, and then he ran his hand over his mouth and chin. "Amber, I need you to hear me on this." He exhaled like he was trying to explain something basic to a child. He opened his mouth then he closed it. "Your mom and dad, uncle Jeff and auntie Lauren, heck your Nana and Poppa. You're my Bonnie and I'm Clyde. You can be mad at me if you want, but we ride out together."
"No Malcolm! I'm Amber and you're you. All those couples you mentioned only sight one woman. It's not Bonnie, Clyde, and Toni and Yvette and Shameka and whoever else. One man, one woman! I can't give someone what they're not giving me. I CAN'T!"
Malcolm inhaled slowly then he exhaled slowly. Then he slammed his hands on the table! "SO WHAT ARE YOU SAYING TO ME AMBER? You wanna go put yourself out on the hoe stroll? Become like all the hookers out there?"
"I'm not a hoe and you know it. But I refuse to accept what you're offering me. Why don't you marry Yvette? She seems to be fine with being second string."
"IF IT'S NOT YOU! IT'S NOBODY!!" He yelled everybody looked at him, but he didn't care.
"I guess it's nobody then." Then I exhaled. "Lets talk business, tell me what you need and I'll get it done."

****

My stomach was in knots. I didn't know what to expect. I took Andrew to Auntie Lauren in the morning. She gave me the motherly hug I needed. I cried a little bit, and she assured me that it was gonna be fine. Momma and Daddy were waiting in the car for me. I got in the car quietly; Daddy had the Isley Brothers playing while he sang a long. Momma didn't say anything the whole car ride. Daddy parked in a parking garage two blocks away. Daddy told me to keep my eyes forward no matter what once we entered the courtroom. There were a lot of people in the courthouse. We found Malcolm's name on a list and the courtroom assigned. There were a lot of people waiting outside the courtroom. I noticed Yvette, Toni, and Shameka immediately. Toni had a eye patch and if you looked closely she would shake every so often. I inhaled deeply, this didn't look good. The bailiff called the number assigned to Malcolm's case. A ton of people stood up. As we entered this room it reminded me more of an office than a courtroom. Since Sammy and his friends were still minors at the time of their demise it was not an open courtroom. If you were not specifically involved with the case you could not enter. The jury was made up of women and men, black and white, and a variety of ages.
They brought Malcolm in, and then four men all in suits joined him at the table. There were three people at the other table. The judge sat at a big desk looking table where the stenographer sat close by ready to record.
I sat in a seat second in on the row next to Daddy. I didn't know what happened to Momma, but Daddy told me to keep my eyes forward so that's what I did. The judge and legal teams went back and forth about things I didn't understand. Then the prosecution said that it was their goal to provide evidence that Malcolm was a very dangerous man capable of committing cold-blooded murder in the first degree. They called their first witness to the stand Camille Caruthers. A very gorgeous and voluptuous woman sashayed to the chair next to the judge's desk. Her dress was

short and a little tight. The bailiff swore her in. Then she sat down and crossed her legs. She smiled at Malcolm, I couldn't see his face. But I wished I could see it. They asked her to state for the record what her relationship was to the defendant. When she said she was his girlfriend it seemed like the entire audience started whispering and turning in their chairs. I wasn't surprised, as soon as I saw her I thought of sex. But I wondered why this was such a surprise to everyone. They asked her questions about their relationship, and she sat up there declaring her undying love for him. When she slipped in that she met him at the mall, and she always paid for everything whenever they went out. Outside of breaking the loyalty of the rest of the females in the audience I didn't see the point of having her up there. Then the defense asked Camille when was the last time she had spoken to Malcolm. She couldn't remember exactly. Then they asked her where she currently lived. She said lowly that that she lived with her husband. The defense asked how long she has been married. She said lowly again five years.

Then they called Toni to the stand. They asked her about the nature of her relationship with Malcolm. She said he was the big man on campus. She said she threw herself at him. Then she heard rumors about him and Yvette going out. She said that she and Yvette were friends before that. She said it broke her heart when he didn't defend her or choose her over Yvette. But she was determined to win. He warned her not to even look at Amber regardless of what she heard about her. She said that when she tried to confront her his cousin defended me. Later that day she was beaten unconscious. She woke up in the hospital; she had broken ribs, arms, and severe head trauma. She lost her eye and now she suffers from seizures. The prosecution asked if Malcolm reached out to her after the fight, she said no.

The defense asked if she knew for a fact that the attack she suffered was as a result from her confrontation with Amber Wallace. She said she was pretty sure. The defense asked her if she only had confrontations with Yvette and Amber. She said no, they asked if she was a widely liked person at Oakland High? She said a lowly no. But she knew for a fact she was beaten because she disobeyed Malcolm. The defense asked how she knew. She couldn't offer any facts, she just knew. The defense asked why a court of law should trust her hunch. She sat there quietly.

The prosecution called up Scarlett Shipp. I was completely surprised when Melvin's grandmother walked past me. The prosecution asked how Mrs. Shipp knew Malcolm. She said she did not know Malcolm personally. But her grandson knows Malcolm. She proceeded to read Melvin's letter. His letter stated that Malcolm was threatened by his relationship with Amber Wallace. Malcolm had threatened his safety on numerous occasions. One night everything came to a climactic end. Melvin and Amber argued. Melvin wanted to resolve the matter but he saw Malcolm approaching the Wallace home. Amber came out of the home to talk to Melvin, but Malcolm wouldn't allow Amber to speak with him. Melvin said he left in fear of his life. Mrs. Shipp said she felt Amber led Melvin on to make Malcolm jealous. A tear rolled down my face. Mrs. Shipp said Melvin has been retained in a mental facility ever since, and even in attempting to writing this letter Melvin has experienced several emotional setbacks.

The defense tore into that letter so badly. In the end you wondered if Melvin really wrote that letter or if the letter was Mrs. Shipp's interpretation of what happened. The defense had the letter and Mrs. Shipp's testimony stricken from the record. My head spun because I didn't know how much of that was true.

The judge called for a thirty-minute lunch break. I followed Daddy out of the courtroom. I didn't know where Momma was but Daddy and I went down to the cafeteria. Daddy put his arm around me while we waited to pay for our lunch. When we sat down Daddy asked me how I was holding up. I just shook my head. Daddy rubbed my hand; he said Malcolm is still very young. I didn't say anything I just kept my head down.

When the jury re-entered the prosecution called Yvette Bates to the stand. I sat up in my chair; I tried not to seem as interested in her testimony as I was. The prosecution asked Yvette where she met Malcolm and she told them at school. They asked her why she and Toni fought. She said because she and Malcolm started dating even though he was dating Toni. The prosecution asked why she would do something like that. She said there was something about Malcolm that draws you in. He's very intelligent, very smooth, and he was very charming. The prosecution asked what her current relationship to Malcolm was and she said fiancée. My heart dropped! People stirred in the courtroom. The prosecution asked if Malcolm was a good provider, and then she told them that she worked she didn't need him to provide for her. They asked if he was a good protector. She told them that he once had a fight with her brother and her brother was a big guy, and Malcolm beat him up easily so she believes he would be a good protector. The prosecution focused on the fight with Yvette's brother heavily. I didn't know how the defense was going to deflect that. I felt my body temp rise, and I told myself they're trying to manipulate me. They had all these FEMALES declaring their love etc. for Malcolm in hopes that it would upset me. It's all a game, even though I would be lying if I said I didn't care. The prosecution asked Yvette how Malcolm explained his relationship with me. "He told me she was this little girl who followed him around." He always calls me "little girl", that one wounded me. She explained that she always knew that I liked him; she wasn't concerned about what a little girl did. One of the prosecutor's looked at me, as I turned red. Daddy grabbed my hand to tell me to calm down. She said Malcolm told her that my son wasn't his, and that he didn't want children period. So he would never allow anyone to get pregnant. The prosecution held up a picture of Andrew. I squeezed Daddy's hand; I hated seeing my baby's picture being used as a prop in this courtroom. So you're saying this little boy is not Malcolm's son? Yvette looked at the picture. She studied it long and hard. Then she said, "No! This is definitely Amber's son, but the features that could be mistaken as Malcolm could be anyone's." I wished I could see Malcolm's face. I needed to know how much of what she was saying was true. Yvette went on and on about how she and Malcolm were in love, how she was the one for him. I didn't understand where the prosecution was going with having Yvette up there all love struck and gushing. The defense asked Yvette how long she and Malcolm have been engaged. Yvette shifted in her seat, she said since the summer. The defense asked if that was before or after I miscarried after getting into a car accident while driving Malcolm's car. Yvette looked surprised, she shifted in her seat. She looked at Malcolm with a deeply hurt look. She asked when was the accident. They looked at the paperwork Thursday July 17th. Yvette said she wasn't sure, but she thinks it was before. One of the defense lawyers asked to see Yvette's engagement ring. She said they hadn't picked out any yet. Then a defense lawyer asked her if they were in love like she claims why were we in court today? If Malcolm responded so passionately in defense of a woman he saw on the side wouldn't that make him a monster? Yvette sat quietly looking at Malcolm, tears perfectly falling out of her eyes. "Oh, Yvette I have a question for you. Can you tell me who this gentleman is?" It was a picture of Leonard. Yvette shook her head no. "Oh really? This was Malcolm's cousin Leonard. He and Malcolm were actually pretty close. Did you ever know any of

Malcolm's relatives?" Even when she cried she was beautiful. Yvette shook her head no. "Oh see this guy died trying to protect Amber and the son you just knew wasn't Malcolm's. He was keeping an eye out when Sammy, you know the guy who's death brought us all here attacked and killed him in front of the apartment that Malcolm and Amber shared." He paused for dramatic affect. "Sammy was coming for Amber and Malcolm's son. How could we explain Sammy's death if Amber meant nothing to Malcolm?" Then the lawyer asked how Malcolm proposed. I tried not to lean in. Yvette started shifting in her seat.
"We discussed it." The lawyer mocked her and asked how did they discuss it? Yvette tried to speak above her tears as she relayed the conversation. Where basically she brought it up, Malcolm never really agreed to marry her. She mistook his avoidance of the topic as an agreement to marry. She assumed that they were engaged.
The judge looked at the time. Because the prosecution and defense had spent so much time on Toni and Yvette they decided to dismiss and reconvene in the morning. I hated this; I didn't want to come back. Daddy held my hand as we stood to leave. I could feel Malcolm's eyes on me as he was removed from the courtroom but I didn't want him to read me, so I focused on Daddy. Out in the hallway Yvette gave way to a heartfelt sob. I knew that cry; I had done it too many times myself. All the women watched me as Daddy and I exited the courtroom. Their stares made me angry; Daddy tightened his grip as he led me through the people and towards the exit. About a block away Momma came out of nowhere and she silently walked with us. They both kept looking at me, but neither said anything. They had looks of "I told you so!" On their faces. When we got to their house Daddy told me to come inside. The defense team called and they said today went well. They said the female charade was basically just a tactic to make it appear that Malcolm didn't care about anyone, and to break any loyalty I may have had to him. Poppa called and Uncle Jeff came by. They all wanted updates.
While they talked Momma sat on the couch, she looked tired and a little sad. But ever since she kicked me out, she only spoke to me when she had to. Even after the fight with Momma Shuga, Momma still stuck to her guns. I got her some ice for her jaw. She thanked me for it, but she still wasn't talking to me. Nana was the one who comforted me and checked to see if I was okay. Nana told me she was proud of me for standing up to Bernadette cause she was a BIG girl. Nana checked on me later to make sure everything was ok at school the next day. I told her Bernadette came out of nowhere and hugged me so tight. She apologized for coming to my house. She told me she didn't know they were coming to my house. All Momma Shuga told them is that some girl stole from her and they were going to teach her a lesson. She even apologized for hitting my Momma. She said it was a reflex reaction. Then she poked fun at me, because she said that Malcolm was so adamant about not letting me fight, that she thought I couldn't fight. Bernadette said after Momma Shuga beat up Renee for not doing anything, Renee shared how she and I never got a long, and then how I helped when her baby was really sick. Bernadette put her arm around me and called me cousin like she always did. That was relief especially when I didn't see her coming that could've ended badly. Nana said that's why she always told us to be good to people cause you never know what could happen. I wanted to tell Momma about all of it, but she never showed any interest in talking to me.
When Daddy got off the phone he told me it was best that I spent the night. He told me he'd take me to get a change of clothes, and that Uncle Jeff said it was ok to leave Andrew at his house. They were going to make a big fuss over Andrew

sleeping over and that he should be distracted enough that it would be ok. Daddy took me to my apartment to get a change of clothes. I gave Daddy the quick tour of my modest home. He said he liked it, and that he was so thankful Nana did this for Sophia and me. As we were talking there was a knock at the door. I asked Daddy to get it as I went to the kitchen to get foil to wrap around my toothbrush. Charles was at the door and Daddy was glaring at him. He had a busted look on his face. He was stammering when I saw him. Daddy moved to the side so he could come in. When Daddy shut the door behind him, you could tell Charles was uncomfortable. I asked him what was up, and he said Sophia wasn't home, and he saw my light on and assumed she was at my house. Then he shrugged and said oh well as he backed away to the door. Daddy put his hand up to the door to stop it from opening. He asked Charles if he saw Sophia's car outside. Charles said sometimes Sophia rides with me so he wasn't sure. Daddy said even if she rode with me her car would be outside. Daddy got in Charles' face and he told him he didn't like him. He told him that he was weak and devious! Daddy told him not to come next door ever cause if he did he would be sorry. Charles was visibly shaken, and then Daddy told him to get out. In that moment I wondered why everyone reacted to Charles that way. Malcolm completely disregarded him, Sophia definitely does, and even David shakes his head at him. Daddy made fun of Charles and said he probably went home and cried. I didn't say anything, as Daddy was still calming himself.
Back at my parent's house it was so weird being there without Jade. I wanted to call her, but daddy told me to get some rest cause tomorrow it was gonna be my turn. We sat in the same seat order in the audience. The defense and prosecution started with their legal jargon, then the prosecution called my name. My heart was racing as I stood up. It felt like everybody was looking at me, and I didn't like it. After they swore me in and made me state my name for the record the female prosecutor asked how old I was. When I said I was eighteen, she said I was the baby of Malcolm's long list of women. I just looked at her cause I didn't know how to respond to that. She asked how I met Malcolm; I kept all my answers as short as I could. I told her in middle school. She said we came from such different backgrounds and we even looked so different in appearance, she asked where was the attraction. I told her I couldn't speak for him. She asked about my attraction to Malcolm. I told her we shared a common bond and it was in regards to ignorant people's responses to our complexions. Then she asked me "what" I was. I played dumb like I didn't understand the question. She asked me if I was mulatto or something like that. The question sent FIRE through my body. I told myself to calm down cause I was already mad. I told her I was just me and I didn't need to define myself, and the need for such a ignorant description was other people's problem. Then she asked me if being mulatto made me "special" and more important than other black people. Ugh! I could feel the fire in my stomach get bigger; I wanted to beat this lady up. I told her I wouldn't know because I wasn't mulatto. She asked me if Malcolm liked me because I was mulatto. I didn't say anything, it was a dumb question and I couldn't speak for Malcolm. When the judge told me to answer the question I gave him an irritated look. I stated again that I was not mulatto and I couldn't speak for Malcolm. Malcolm sat there motionless, and he would not take his eyes off me. The lady said that I was really young when my relationship with Malcolm began. She asked if my parents were happy about it. I told her they didn't know about it until they found out I was pregnant. She asked me how old was I when I found out I was pregnant. I told her I was fourteen but I was fifteen when my son was born. The lady was dramatic saying how young that was and how my parents must've been

upset about it. I told her they were very disappointed. She asked me how Andrew has been supported thus far. I told her that Malcolm has provided for Andrew. She asked how a sixteen year old provided for a child. I told her that ever since I've known him he has cut hair. She mocked me and said the hair cutting business must be really good to support a child by it, I shrugged. The lady asked me what the nature of Malcolm and I's relationship is. I didn't understand the question. She said it was obvious why Malcolm was attracted to me. I rolled my eyes at that comment cause it was stupid. But she asked why did I like Malcolm? I told her she's just listened to female after female state why they were in love with him, I told her I couldn't say anything that hadn't already been said. She asked me if those women spoke for me. I rolled my eyes. I told her he was the first person to acknowledge me as a person and not ask me dumb questions like what am I or attribute beauty to light skin. The audience laughed. The lady went on to ask me more annoying and dumb questions. The defense lawyers all smiled at me Malcolm's face was completely serious the entire time. Then the lady asked what was the status of Malcolm and I's relationship today. I told her we weren't together. She pretended to be surprised. I couldn't stop rolling my eyes. She asked why we broke up. I told her it was the same reason every time we broke up. Malcolm had too many women. The lady asked why he needed other women if I was so special to him, I shrugged. The lady kept trying to provoke me but I stayed cool as ice except for her comments about my complexion.

The defense asked questions about Malcolm and I's relationship. Thinking about all the things that happened between us made me feel like I was making a mistake, like I was throwing it all away for nothing. But as I walked back to my seat all those females glaring at me reminded me why I couldn't do it. I spotted Momma in the far corner, she looked straight ahead.

The prosecution called lastly the officers on the scene at the time of the crime. The officers both testified that they were responding to calls reporting gunshots. They said they heard yelling and screaming then they heard two more shots. When they found Sammy in the house he was dying. Malcolm was angry and had the weapon in his hand. He didn't resist arrest. When the defense questioned the officers they both testified that Malcolm seemed like he was hanging on by a thread.

The defense began calling their witnesses. They called Rita Mosby to the stand the lady from the deli. She testified that Malcolm was a hard worker and very smart. They called Uncle Frank who gave the same testimony. Uncle Frank said he got the idea to open the shop from Malcolm, and Malcolm's clientele is what has made the shop what it is today. The defense called character witness after witness. The prosecution tried their best to tear holes in the defense, it just wasn't working. The possession charge was thrown out. The story about how the drugs were discovered kept changing. Then the fact that it was such a small amount and they couldn't link him to it really looked bad so they threw it out. The defense brought up Sammy's records, his expulsion, and the fact that the police were looking for him because of when he hit me in the car. After four days of this the prosecution and the defense were tired. They changed the charge from murder in the first degree to involuntary manslaughter. I exhaled knowing he wouldn't spend the rest of his life in jail if he had to spend any more time than he's spent. I wanted to run and thank the jury personally. As Daddy and I walked out the courtroom someone called my name. I was surprised to see that it was Yvette. She didn't care that I was standing next to my Daddy; she walked up to me deliberate and angry. She stood in my face and asked me if my son was really Malcolm's. I looked around the building; I asked her if she was trying to entrap me in the courthouse. She looked confused. I told her I was under oath, and top of that I was telling the truth. She looked really mad, I told her if she had such a problem with the truth to let me know when and where and we could handle it, but today wasn't the day. Daddy had his hands in his pockets. Her friend told her to come on and to leave me alone. She reminded her that Malcolm and I weren't even together anymore. Yvette sucked her teeth and told me this wasn't over like I was gonna be scared.

Andrew, Momma, Daddy and I went to Gonzalez's for dinner. Momma was so sweet to Andrew; she gave him a ton of hugs and kisses. I sat there wishing she would hug me or even just acknowledge me. But she would just look at me mostly she wouldn't say anything. Daddy said now that the trial was out of the way they needed to focus on Jade's wedding. Suddenly I had something to look forward to. Momma and Jade had been talking and planning since Sonny proposed. Momma said when Jade came out she would tell everyone all the details. I tried to ask Momma questions, but she blank stared at me. When I went home I felt so sad. I didn't want to spend another Saturday hung over. I put Andrew to bed then I stood in the kitchen debating with myself about whether or not to have a nightcap. As I lied to myself saying that I would only have a little my phone rang. It was after ten o'clock, I wondered who was calling me. It was David, and he sound like he had been drinking. He said he was with Patricia and they got into an argument. She left him stranded in Jack London Square. He said he couldn't go home like he was. I told him I would come get him. I went next door, Sophia was up watching TV, Charles and Sasha were already in the bed. I asked her to come sit with Andrew so I could go get David. He was at the train station. When he got in the car I could smell the liquor on his breath. He thanked me so much for coming to get him. He apologized for having me come out so late and for taking me away from Andrew. I told him it was ok, and one day I may need him to do the same for me. When we got back to the house Sophia smiled at us and left immediately. David asked where Andrew was. I told him he was upstairs sleeping. David smiled at me then his smile dropped. He asked me why I hadn't called him. I told him a lot had been going on. He asked me if Malcolm and I got back together. I told him no, and that Malcolm and I were never getting back together. Then I asked why he and Patricia argued. He said he wanted to go to work after high school and she wanted him to go to school. I asked him why he didn't want to go to school. He said he was tired of school and that he wanted to get on with his life. I told him I got into Berkeley and that I was so relieved that it worked out for me. Then he smiled and said so that meant I wasn't going away. I nodded, then he stepped in my face and asked me if I would go out on a date with him. I asked him what about Patricia. He said they broke up, and that he couldn't pretend like they had a future. He said that's why she left him stranded. Outside of going out to clubs with Melvin, and the hook up sessions with Malcolm (those didn't really count as dates to me) I had never been on a real date "date". I told him to sleep on it. I didn't know how drunk he was. I told him if he still wanted to take me out when he was sober we'd discuss it then. Then I made up the couch for him.

Chapter 24

I stood in the mirror taking in my appearance. I didn't want to seem over done or like I was trying too hard. Andrew followed me around all evening. He kept asking why I did everything I did. Why I put makeup on? I told him I wanted to look nice. Why did I put perfume on? I told him I wanted to smell good. Then he asked where I was going? I told him I was going on a date, he frowned his eyebrows like he understood what that meant. I asked him if I looked pretty and he shook his head yes. As I sat there trying on different shoes, Andrew asked me what he was supposed to wear. I told him he was going to go over Sasha's house while I was out. He really didn't like that answer. It was almost six thirty and David was coming at seven. I walked Andrew next door to Sophia. When Sophia opened the door the aroma of her dinner slapped you in the face, she smiled really big at me. She assured me I looked good. I told her I needed her opinion on which shoes to wear. Sophia made Andrew a plate and he suddenly forgot that he was upset that I was leaving. Sophia called out to Charles that she would be right back. I tried on three different pairs of shoes. I was so nervous I couldn't make up my mind. Sophia had to pick the shoe for me. Then she gave me a word of advice, she said no matter what happened not to sleep with David tonight. I assured her I hadn't thought of it. But now that she mentioned it I was even more nervous. David has been nothing but a complete gentleman; I couldn't imagine the evening ending that way. But Sophia said gentleman or not he was still a guy, and I had to be strong. She hugged me and wished me a good time, and then she went back to her apartment. I told myself not to have a shot or even a sip to calm my nerves. At 6:58 David knocked at my door. He was on time and that read as a good sign to me. I opened the door and David's eyes got big he gave me a hug and told me I looked beautiful! After I locked the door he held my hand as we walked to the street where he parked his car. Sophia watched out the window she had the biggest smile. He opened the door for me. Then we drove to Emeryville. I thought we were going to Murphy Carlos, which would've been perfectly fine. But he parked in the Brown Charlie's parking lot. Brown Charlie's was a step up. I smiled but I felt kind of bad, I know David doesn't have a lot of money and this place isn't cheap. I held on to my smile though. David had seven thirty reservations for us. He told me to order anything I wanted on the menu. I could've ordered crab, lobster, steak, but I ordered grilled chicken I over exaggerated my enthusiasm for my order David wasn't buying it though. I smiled an embarrassed smile. David asked what was so exhausting about my week. I figured I might as well tell him everything. If he was gonna run away I rather he did it now. I told him about the break up with Malcolm, the trial all this week, and that sentencing if any would be next week. David took it all in, I waited to see a scared look on his face. But he put his hand on mine and asked how I was holding up with all that. I was relieved that his initial reaction wasn't to run away from me. I told him that there were a lot of things that had to be done. Then I asked him if our date was a rebound date? I told him that he and Patricia just broke up last night, and maybe he needed time to heal. He laughed, he said they had been broken up for awhile but last night made it official. Then he told me that he had to strike while I was single. I smiled, I told him outside of Malcolm no one really wanted me. Everybody was so quick to call me white and steer clear of me. He assured me that wasn't true. I told him that the lawyer's references to me being mulatto hurt. David rubbed my hand; he said people will always be ignorant. I can't let their ignorance cause me to react, he said it is their problem not mine. He told me I knew who I was, and that nothing no one said or did should affect that. David said his family was religious and they believed that everyone deserved love and kindness. He said that's the way he was raised and that was the way it should be. I told him your family didn't have to be religious to think that way. My family on my father's side thought that way at least. Then he asked me if my family was religious and I told him not really. We didn't buy into all the hype. We were good people, and that was that. He was quiet for a minute, and then he said it was time to change the subject cause that one could go on forever and get heated. I didn't know what he meant by that but I agreed. I told him about Andrew's reaction to me going out. He laughed; we both wondered how he would feel once he knew it was David. David got quiet for a minute, then he told me he really liked Andrew and he would hate for Andrew to get hurt behind us. I concentrated on the us. I liked the sound of that. I agreed that I didn't want Andrew to get hurt either. Then he sat back in his chair with a big smile. "I have loved you since the seventh grade!" I blushed so hard. I told him I didn't know why, and I honestly didn't believe him. He told me one day I would understand it. Malcolm was just as twisted as me, but David was good and sweet. How he even knew who I was besides our having classes together was a mystery to me. When we finished our dinner, he took me to a movie theater in Berkeley off of Shattuck. I don't even know what movie we saw. I was so giddy as he continued to hold my hand whenever we walked. He opened the car door for me. In the theater he offered to buy popcorn but I declined, stating we just ate. So he got a soda and offered to share with me. When I took a sip off his straw he told me that was our first kiss. I laughed at the realization of what he meant. Our lips touched the same spot on the straw. He put his arm around me in the theater, and I was gone. I was excited and surprised when I felt my body throbbing. Completely embarrassed I tried to make sure my body language did not portray what I was feeling. David was really into the movie, and I was just happy to be out with someone who thought enough of me to be a gentleman. This was my first real date ever, it was respectable. I wondered if this was how Jade felt with Sonny. It was a shame that I had to be eighteen with a three year old to experience it. After the movie he asked if I felt up to dessert. I shook my head no; I told him I was full. But I really didn't want him to spend any more money on me. He hugged me and then he asked what I wanted to do next. He said he didn't want the night to end. I told him we could walk and talk on the Marina if he wanted. So we went down to the Berkeley Marina and walked along the long pier. He told me his Uncle got him set up for a job on the railroad that he would start right after graduation. He said the money was good and his uncle supports his family through his job, he said he could retire from there. I told him about the school I wanted to open. He stared at me while I talked and when I was done he asked me if he could kiss me. I blushed and asked why would he ask me that. He said he could've wanted to kiss me and I didn't. I told him he didn't have to ask. He kissed me gently and oh so sweetly. It was different from Malcolm's always overpowering but knocking my socks off kisses. David was gentle and sweet. I got goose bumps as I wondered what that meant for how he made love. Crap! My mind wandered, is he a virgin? Maybe that's why he could be so patient and gentle. My throbbing shut down, and I don't know why the thought of him being a virgin scared me. I looked at him in his eyes when we stopped kissing. He smiled and I smiled back I had to ask, I couldn't not ask. I asked him if he was a virgin. He started laughing out loud; I could tell my question embarrassed him. Then he said no, I asked him how many girls had he been with. He exhaled and was completely embarrassed. He told me he had been with two girls. He had to be telling the truth, why would he lie about such a low number. Then he asked me if I was a virgin. We both laughed. I told him I had only been with Malcolm. Then I asked him if he wanted to marry a virgin. He looked embarrassed again. I told him that was all I saw on TV. He told me I couldn't believe everything on TV. We stood out there talking for hours. When he took me home, I asked him if he wanted to come in and he said no. He kissed me goodnight, he took two steps to walk away then he came back and kissed me again. This went on for a minute it was really sweet then he truly walked away. I gently knocked on Sophia's door. She was up watching TV; Andrew was next to her knocked out. I told her all about the night, she smiled through sad eyes. She said she was happy somebody was treated right. I kissed her and told her I'd see her tomorrow. I carried Andrew then I saw David standing on my porch. My heart sped up. He said an embarrassed hi. I said hi and then I opened the door. He took the sleeping Andrew from me I gave him Andrew's pj's then I went in my room. When David came in my room he sat on my bed and watched me take off my shoes and my jewelry. I smiled at him then I sat on the bed. I grabbed his hands then I told him I really liked him. But there was literally a black cloud hanging over my head. We both laughed. I told him I couldn't live with myself if something happened to him because of me. We both knew he would be lying if he said he wasn't scared of Malcolm, only an idiot wouldn't be. We sat there talking and eventually we laid there talking. Next thing I knew Andrew was waking me up to ask why David was in my bed. My heart stopped! We fell asleep fully dressed talking last night. Andrew had a smile on his face, "is David my new Dad?" My heart was beating so fast I popped up. David's eyes opened and then he popped up realizing like I did that we fell asleep. He looked at Andrew who was smiling from ear to ear. He looked at me, and then he apologized. Andrew asked him if he was his new Dad. David asked him if he wanted one. Andrew shook his head yes. David called Andrew up on the bed and then he told him to let him be David for right now. Andrew agreed, I was horrified! David and Andrew went downstairs to make breakfast. I buried my face in a pillow and screamed my behind off. This was bad, this was very bad. What if Andrew told Troy? Troy would tell Malcolm and then something bad would happen. I heard a knock at the door and then surprised laughs. David told Sophia I was upstairs. She came in holding two mugs of coffee. Sophia said, "ooh! You're a bad girl!" As she gave me a evil grin. I told her to shut the door, and then I told her it wasn't like that. We drank coffee and laughed about my freaking out. She thought it was sweet that we slept together without sleeping together.

****

All rise! Malcolm Latour, you have been charged with one count of involuntary manslaughter in defense of others. However, since you have not cooperated with the courts in bringing to justice your accomplices in this crime you are sentenced to four years in a Federal State Prison. The courtroom grumbled in disagreement. Tears poured out of my eyes and Daddy squeezed my hand. I really thought he was coming home today. I couldn't even listen to the rest I felt defeated. Daddy tapped me and said Malcolm was looking for me. I looked up and Malcolm had sad eyes as he focused on me ONLY! I could hear commotion around me, but all I could see is my heart being ushered out of the courtroom. Daddy told me to get up. Yvette was having a crying fit in the lobby. She called me all kinds of whores, and anything filthy she could think of. She said this was all my fault. Daddy was mad and he told me to come on before we all got locked up. In the car Momma explained that his time in the county jail counted as time served and that he could be eligible for parole after a year and a half to two years. So he could be out anywhere from a year to a year and a half from now Momma said matter of factly. Daddy looked at me in the mirror with sad eyes. Then Momma said, "that little boy has been in your head since you were what, twelve or thirteen? I hope you use this time to figure out who you are, instead of moping around like you normally do. The world doesn't stop because your boyfriend got locked up!"

"I do know who I am!" Daddy looked surprised that I said anything.

Momma chuckled, "no you don't. You've been doing as you're told all these years. Malcolm tells you to spread em and you do it! He tells you to have his baby and you do it, shoot you do it twice!" She chuckled sarcastically.

"Are you mad because I sided with him over you? I don't understand why you hate me? I'm sorry I'm not perfect like Jade, or did as good a job keeping my shenanigans away from you as Timothy and Malachi. But I don't know why that means you can't even love me?"

"You're hardheaded and sneaky. You don't listen when I'm telling you stuff. You're just a waste of my energy!" Momma said like she was exhausted.

Tears poured down my face. "Even with all that I don't know when I stopped being your daughter. Worthy of a hello, something you give freely to strangers on the street. But for me nothing!"

"You put yourself in this position. It's time for tough love. I've been there. The bad boy likes you, you risk it all just for him. And in the end what does it get you? Nothing!" Momma said

"You been where? In my shoes? Is that what it is? I remind you too much of you? You hate me because I act like you?"

"SHUT UP AMBER!" Momma yelled

"Annette!" Daddy shot Momma a look. "Talk to the girl!"

Momma folded her arms and refused. "It's ok Daddy," I pushed through my tears to talk. "Now I truly know what it feels like to be her. At least I still have siblings and you. She can hate me forever, I guess I deserve that." I said crying my eyes out. Momma still refused to speak to me.

****

It took everything in me to get out of bed. I got to school at third period, and I couldn't act like I cared. At lunch I cried on Cassondra's shoulder. Bernadette came over and she told me she was going to go see Malcolm this weekend. I tried to put on a strong face, but I was just too depressed to do it. In Ms. Dubois' class I couldn't pulled it together. At one point she just wrapped her arms around me, that made me release the tears I had been fighting all day. I wished her arms were my momma's arms. I wished my Momma didn't hate me.

When I hadn't called David by Friday, he came over. I was outside talking to the new tenants in apartment "A". The Cheng's were a married couple with no children. They were in their late twenties, and really down to earth. I introduced David to them as he approached us. I tried to fake a smile, but I knew it didn't work. David waited patiently while I talked to my new neighbors, and then he followed me in the house. He asked where Andrew was, and I told him he was next door playing with Sasha. He asked me why I haven't called or answered when he called. I told him I've been going through a lot right now. He sat down and got comfortable, and told me to tell him about it. I didn't feel like explaining my family dynamics. So I told him I didn't want to talk about it. I could tell he was trying not to get irritated. Then I told him he and I weren't going to work. He looked irritated; he sat there looking at me. I told him I was bad news and he deserved better. He was too good for me. I told him he needed someone who's done the right things, has good people around her, and doesn't come with all the baggage I got. He told me that he gets to decide what he's too good for. I told him, he at least deserved someone who knew how to love, and that person wasn't me. My own mother didn't love me so how would I even be worthy to think someone else could. He was quiet as I went on and on. I was crying, yelling, and he sat there listening. When I went in the kitchen I pulled a glass out the cupboard. David grabbed the bottle from me, which made me mad. He told me to come and finish talking to him, I got madder. He wouldn't give me my bottle back and all I wanted was a drink. I hit him as hard as I could in the shoulder. He said, "OUCH!" Not something that Malcolm ever would've said. I started crying harder and I apologized for hitting him. I felt like I was acting like my Momma. Then I told him, "see! And that's me holding back. David please just get away from me. Malcolm will be out in a year, and I know he won't take you being in my life nicely. Besides I'm no picnic." I cried my eyes out. He kissed me with snot on my face and everything. He told me he loves me and he's not leaving. He told me I'd have to kill him. I cried harder Malcolm said something like that to me once upon a time. He told me its time to make us official. I asked him if he heard anything I just said. He said, "I want to be with you. Do you want to be with me?"

"No!"

"Wrong answer! We're already a family."

"What about when Malcolm gets out?"

"We'll deal with that when it comes."

"My family's not gonna like this." I said

"It's me and you. Ok?"

"No David! You don't know my family. Malcolm ain't got nothing on my family."

"I don't have to go to family functions. As long as you come home to me."

"David!"

"You're making excuses."

"I'm scared!"

"I know" he kissed me again. "Amber, will you be my girlfriend?"

"Ok, ok, but you can't say I didn't warn you."

"You have to say yes." He said

"Yes" I said. He smiled really big. He kissed me again. Sophia opened the door as David was leaning over the couch kissing me. She grabbed Sasha and Andrew as she gasped. She asked David when he got there, and he said a little while ago. She shot me a look, "I thought you and Cassondra were gonna watch Sasha for me so I could go take care of some family business?" Sophia said shooting me crazy eyes. Her code for going out with Richard. I told her I was still on board. Andrew and Sasha got so excited when they saw David. Sophia kissed my cheek and told me she wanted details when he left. I made hamburgers and French fries while they played go fish. Every so often David would come in the kitchen and kiss me real good. And then he'd go back to playing cards with the kids. Cassondra came over, prom was in a couple weeks and she had filled all her orders. She had saved enough money over the past few years to pay her part through fashion school in the city. The guy she had been crushing on for years finally asked her out and now they were going to the prom together. She was so excited! I asked David if he planned on going to his prom, and he said no. It was assumed that he was gonna go with Patricia but now, he didn't want any problems. He asked me if I was gonna go, I told him I hadn't planned on going to mine either. We spent the rest of the evening reminiscing over old times. Cassondra told us that Rosalind and Benjamin were coming to visit this summer again. Cassondra stayed pretty late, but she decided to go home. Sophia called and asked if it was ok if Sasha could spend the night. I told her yes. I gave Sasha one of my T-shirts to sleep in. Then David and I put the kids to bed. We went downstairs and sat awkwardly on separate couches. I never had to make a move with Malcolm he just came and took over. I didn't have the slightest if it was even a good night to do this. David looked more nervous than me. So I finally said, "maybe you should get going." He thought about it for a minute then he asked if he could spend the night. I swallowed harder then he did. I asked him if he was sure that's what he wanted. He shook his head yes with a huge smile. We cleaned the kitchen together and he started telling me silly joke after silly joke. He definitely lightened the mood. I wasn't nervous anymore. In the middle of laughing he kissed me. David was gentle with everything. His kiss, his touch, and his caress everything was deliberate and not clumsy. He carried me upstairs; I couldn't believe we were going to do this. He closed the door with his foot. He laid me on the bed, as he touched me to make sure I was ready I unbuckled his pants. Then a crying child knocked on the door. "Ambur! Ambur! I had a bad dream!" David collapsed on top of me while he said, "no! No! No!" Just above a whisper. I laughed out of frustration as well. Andrew heard Sasha crying and pleading at my door. When I opened the door both of them were up in the hallway. I tried to get them to calm down and go back to sleep, but Sasha wasn't having it. So we all went downstairs, we took blankets and pillows. David shot me a pouty face from across the room.

****

Jade looked like such a powerful woman when she glided off the plane. She was wearing a simple dress but she looked like a million bucks. Her smile was a mile wide. When Daddy called me and asked me to pick up Jade I screamed into the phone "YES!". Of course I would do it. I couldn't wait to see her. It was the end of the school year, I told my counselor I had a lot going on at home. So she wasn't gonna see me much. Andrew, Sasha, and I went to the airport to pick up Jade and Sonny in Daddy's car. When the kids saw her they took off running. She bent down to hug the kids and pick them up. Sonny followed carrying two bags. He looked so happy; he gave me the huggest hug and said, "THANK YOU!" I laughed so hard. Jade rode in the back with the kids, they were basking in the love of Auntie Jade. Momma's car was gone and Daddy was too, Jade told me they went to the doctors. We put Jade's bags in our old room. Then we took Sonny to his parent's house. I showed Jade my apartment, she said she loved it. She said it was bigger than her apartment at school. I explained the layout of Sophia's apartment next door. Hers was two bedrooms but only one bathroom and one level. I told her that The Cheng's lived in the apartment above. Jade asked how Malcolm was doing. I told her that he was in San Quentin, but I hadn't gone to see him. I told her about the shop, and how Moses acts funny whenever I came down there. He's always got something smart to say and how he's not following Malcolm's process. I keep warning him that if I can't get to the bottom of the disconnect someone else will come. I told her that it doesn't make sense, no matter when I popped up there it's packed. I told her I would take her by to see the space. Then she informed me that she wanted to go see Malcolm as well. Since she was here only for a week that just jammed one more thing into our already packed week. We hung out at my house for a while, she showed me the dresses she earmarked in her Macy's catalog. I told Jade about David and how whenever we've gotten close to making love something happens that stops us. I told her David is great about it and he takes it well. She asked if she was gonna get to see him, and I told her I didn't know because his work schedule is all over the place.

Jade asked how much space each Barber's chair needed? I told her I didn't know. She suggested that after I found out so that we can bring in more Barber's chairs. Currently there was Moses' chair, Malcolm's chair, and Chester's chair. There was a lot of open space. Just looking at the space we could easily get three more chairs comfortably in the space. She said I should bring in someone trustworthy who would not only increase the efficiency, but also be another pair of eyes and ears when I'm not there. I liked that idea but I had no idea who that would be.

****

Malcolm's face was serious as usual. He looked beyond Jade to me, I was sitting back to give them space to talk. They talked for maybe ten minutes, I even saw Malcolm smile when Jade held up her hand showing him her ring. Then she stood up so that I could come talk to him. Malcolm's eye stayed glued to me, I could tell he was reading me. Before I could sit down good he asked who was he? I just looked at him. He said he's heard that I've been seen with some guy. I told him I came to discuss his business and so that Jade could see him. I was not there to go into my personal business. He huffed, I showed him his statements, the interest he was earning. I told him that the economy was shifting and there were rumors that the interest rates were going to drop. I asked what he wanted to do with his maturing accounts. He told me to roll them over anyways. He told me to put his interest into his petty cash for the shop. I told him about Jade's idea about getting more chairs, etc. Malcolm liked that idea. He said he may have someone from in there soon. Then he said I must be happy on some level, I didn't look dried out like I had been looking. I looked at him. Then he asked me if I was still his good girl, I shook my head no. His face turned to stone. He sat there for a minute trying to compose his self. Even though David and I hadn't slept together yet, it was going to happen. So there was no point in prolonging the inevitable. Malcolm glared at me, but he didn't say anything. After what seemed like forever he stood up and walked away. I wanted to cry and I didn't know why. I felt like I hurt him, and until this moment I didn't think anything I did could seriously affect him. Jade's eyes were big. I told her what happened and she put her arms around me and she rubbed my back. Her hug felt so good, I missed her so much. We had lunch together, and then we went back to Momma and Daddy's house. Momma was laying down and Daddy had sad eyes. Jade asked what the doctor said the other day. Daddy said they were running test. Momma's had headaches for years, it's had to have gotten pretty bad if she finally broke down and went to the doctor. Daddy said she was gonna be fine she just needed rest.

The next day Sophia, Sasha, Cassondra, Momma, Auntie Lauren, and I met Nana in Orinda at a bridal dress shop. The lady looked a little surprised when Nana introduced each of us to her. The lady tried not to stare but she wasn't doing a good job of it. Nana snapped her fingers at the lady. She told her to take a long good look at everybody and then she needed to get over it. Her assistant was sort of like a flower child so she just went on and on about how beautiful our family was, and the love in our family should spread across the world. Nana told her to shut up and do her job. Even Momma was trying not to laugh at that. Cassondra and the assistant really hit it off though. Since the wedding was only a few months away Jade needed to pick a dress immediately.

Fortunately there was a dress that looked beautiful on her. It was a timeless style. It was satin and simply elegant. We all cried when she came out in the dress. She had tried on so many poofy princess dresses; Cassondra found this after searching and searching the dress racks. It was perfect! Jade ordered the shoes and under garments

Carey Anderson

that matched what she tried on in the shop. They picked out our dresses, everything
was RUSH ordered. Jade was so happy to have all that squared away. Nana
informed us that it was time to send Andrew and Sasha this summer even though
we wouldn't be able to make it. Sophia agreed quickly, I felt a little sad cause I'd
never been away from Andrew for two weeks. But I knew he'd love it so I agreed,
little Jeff and JoJo would be there too, so I was the only one feeling sad about it.
Since Jade's wedding was happening after Sophia and I's graduation party, Nana
said they'd go camping then. I gave the lady Timothy and Malachi's measurements
to order their tuxes. Daddy, Andrew, the uncles, and Sonny were coming later to be
measured. Then Nana took us to Uncle Frank's house to go over the layout for the
wedding. Cassondra was star struck by the beauty of Uncle Frank's house. Gwen
was there, she looked surprised to have visitors, she was in the pool but she wasn't
alone. She kept trying to keep us away from the area we needed to go in, in the
backyard. Jade and I exchanged looks as we smiled. When we stepped in the
backyard a guy got out of the pool as he got closer he became more familiar. Nana
was mad then she looked at Gwen, Gwen put her eyes to the ground. Nana's slap
could be heard all the way in Oakland. Tag stopped in his tracks, as he didn't know
whether he should come say hi. Nana told him to leave! He looked at me with sad
eyes then he grabbed his stuff and hurried out. Nana yelled at Gwen asking her
what was wrong with her. She just kept saying she was sorry and she didn't know
why she did stuff like that. We went over the details for the wedding. Nana said the
wedding planner would contact Momma as soon as she located the jade accessories
that Jade wanted. Nana told Momma to give me the information in case decisions
had to be made and she wasn't feeling well. I could tell Momma didn't want to but
she wasn't gonna argue with Nana.

****

"Cousin?" As soon as I heard the voice my heart sunk.
I turned around to see Troy and some girl. "Hey Troy" I said as I was holding
David's hand from across the table.
"What do we have here?" Troy said looking David up and down. I introduced David
as my boyfriend to Troy as my cousin, kind of. David shook Troy's hand. Troy
asked what we were up to. I shrugged saying we were just grabbing a bite to eat.
Andrew looked happy to see Troy; he stood up on the seat to hug him over me.
Troy pulled up a chair, the girl said nothing, she didn't seem to mind not being
acknowledged either. He said he didn't want to believe the rumors were true. David
had a question mark on his face. I explained that Troy was Malcolm's cousin. David
nodded with the whole picture. Troy asked David if he knew who Malcolm was. He
told him he did, and that we all went to school together. Troy told him Malcolm
wasn't gonna be happy about this. David shrugged and said that wasn't his problem,
but he wasn't going nowhere. I cringed a little bit when he said that. I looked at
Troy to see if he had a reaction. He looked at David and David was giving him
direct eye contact. Troy chuckled a little bit, and then he looked at me. He asked me
if my family had met him yet. I shook my head no, Troy laughed he said he wanted
to see that. David asked why that was funny, Troy looked at David like he was
reading him. He said Malcolm was the least of my worries when it came to my
family they understood and accepted Malcolm. Then he nudged me he's no Charles,
he said laughing. But he was still a bit clean around the edges. Then Troy looked at
me, "but I guess you'll fix that." I rolled my eyes. I told him David was a gentleman,
and I couldn't help him if he didn't understand what that meant. Troy shook his
head; "he said I better enjoy it while it last." David asked him what that meant. Troy

196

exhaled he said either way when my family found out or when Malcolm got out things were gonna change. David said again that he wasn't going anywhere. Troy laughed; he asked Andrew how was life. Andrew smiled and said good. Troy pointed at David and he asked him if he liked him. He told him if he didn't like him he would take him outside and shoot him. He said it like a joke but we all knew he wasn't kidding. Andrew said he liked David a lot. Troy asked him why, Andrew said he plays games with him and shows him how to play basketball. I smiled at Troy, he looked at David. "You some kind of family man?"
David smiled, "he's a great kid."
Troy sat there thinking, "you might be useful after all." Then he stood up, he handed Andrew money and told him to keep it in his pocket. Then he walked out. David asked me what he meant by useful? I told him I didn't know.

Chapter 25

"What do these flyers mean?" Moses barked at me

"The shop is going to be closing early Friday May 15th and closed all weekend for renovations. We want to make sure everything is everything before the holiday weekend." I said posting the flyers all over the inside. Like I had done outside.

"What renovation? Little girl! What are you talking about? I didn't approve any of this."

"It's not your place to approve anything Moses. Like I said the shop will be closed."

"Little girl you are working my last nerve!"

"The feeling is mutual!" I glared at him

Moses growled! "You need a good pop in the mouth! Don't you know you are talking to a man! You better show some respect!"

"You're a pathetic excuse for a man at best! You're a liar and a thief! I have no respect for you, so I will talk to you any way I please! I wish you would be stupid enough to cross that line right there." I pointed at a tile on the floor. "It'll be the last thing you do."

"Maybe you haven't heard who I am!" He said all huffy.

"I don't care who you are. What you need to do is ask somebody who I am!" I said rolling my eyes.

"You're just some white girl wanna be black girl who was stupid enough to get pregnant by that loser wasting away in jail!" He smiled when he said it. He knew he pissed me off.

I got off the stool and walked over to him, he stood there looking like a wall. Fast as I could I hocked the biggest loogie I could and spit in his face. Moses reared up like he was gonna knock the stuffing out of me. I stood there daring him to do it! He screamed when I didn't back down. "Clean yourself up, I'm opening the door!" I can't stand that man. He's a bully, a liar, and a thief. Somebody should set him up with Momma Shuga. I laughed at the thought of it.

I opened the door and people came pouring in. I signed them in on the sign in sheet that Moses completely ignored. With each person I pointed out that the shop was gonna be closed. Moses was over there grumbling cause he was still mad. I didn't care what he was. Chester came flying through the door apologizing that he was late. He ran to the back and hung his jacket. Chester was average height, medium brown complexion, and he had a huge afro. He was so sweet that after awhile you forgot about his out dated hairstyle. I could tell he didn't know what to do next. Then Chester said he had the next person so I called their name from the list. Moses was over there murmuring telling his customer how much trouble I cause around there. Chester had three people in and out while Moses worked on the same one. He spent most of his time talking. And right now he was bad mouthing me to anyone who would listen. Then Fuzzy walked in the door. When I saw him I rose to hug him, but he put his hand out telling me to sit. So I did, Fuzzy came over to me and gave me his name. He told me he wanted Moses, so I put him on the list. I told him it would be a bit of a wait cause Moses was running his mouth. Fuzzy sat down close to Moses' station and just pretended like he was a fly on the wall. It took Moses a long time to even notice him. The only reason he noticed him is cause I called the person after Fuzzy on the list and Chester asked him if he was ok cause he knew he had been waiting. Fuzzy told him he was fine. Moses looked at Fuzzy and asked him if he was waiting for him. Fuzzy told him he heard he was the best so he was patiently waiting. Moses liked having his ego stroked. He told him he would be right with him. Fuzzy was listening to the things he talked about. When it was his turn to sit in the chair, he put his walkie-talkie on his lap, and Moses covered it with a drape. I don't think he even noticed that Fuzzy had it in his lap. Moses asked Fuzzy where he was from, stuff like that. Moses found a way to work me in the conversation, and he went right back to bad mouthing me. He was so busy talking he didn't see the pissed off look in Fuzzy's face. Fuzzy told him he liked his work when he showed him his hair in the mirror. He told him he was gonna have to come back to see him soon. Then Fuzzy walked out the door. I wondered what that was about. Around noon I went up the street to a deli, I ordered a sandwich for Chester and myself. When Chester finished his customer, I gave him his lunch and told him to take a lunch break. I told him Moses would cover for him. Moses cursed me under his breath. He asked where his sandwich was. I told him I didn't know, and I guessed he'd have to go get it, when it was his turn. He was about to blast me when Daddy walked in the door. Moses got quiet and started busying himself with his customer. I gave Daddy a hug, Daddy's eyes were angry as he fixed them on Moses. Not taking his eyes off of Moses, Daddy asked me how things were going down here. I told him it was the same today as everyday. Chester washed his hands and then he came hurrying back in. He was surprised to see Daddy. "Hey Tim how's it going?" Chester said as he came to shake Daddy's hand.

"I'm hearing some stuff and I don't like what I'm hearing!" Daddy said staring at Moses. Then he looked at me. "How's business today?"

"Good as usual" I said

Daddy asked me how much longer I was staying. I told him I wanted to make it to my last two classes so I would be leaving in a few minutes. He told me to come back before closing. Then Daddy said he was gonna hang around for a bit. He sat in Malcolm's chair and stared at Moses. I told Chester I was leaving the pen for the list, and then I grabbed my purse and headed out the door. Moses suddenly was quiet and working a lot faster.

After school I came back and Moses was ranting to his customer how I went running to my Daddy. If he only knew I didn't have to say anything, he had said it all. I looked at the list and there were only three more names on the list than when I left. The shop was still full of people waiting to get their hair cut. Just before closing Daddy walked in with Andrew. I set Andrew on the counter then I closed the door and put the closed sign in the window. Then I closed the curtains. When the last customer left, I locked the door. "WHAT HAPPENED TO THE LIST?" I asked out loud but everybody knew I was talking to Moses.

Chester said Moses made a scene about him keeping the list up. Daddy looked at Moses. Moses said Chester was wasting time writing down names when he could be working that much faster. I told him that maybe if he didn't spend so much time running his mouth Chester wouldn't have to work so hard. Daddy asked for their takes for the day. I did the math in my head; I was expecting at least two hundred from Chester and a hundred from Moses. Chester handed Daddy two-fifty and Moses handed over fifty. Daddy looked at Moses side ways, "what is this?" Moses threw his hands up like he didn't want any problems.

"WHERE'S THE REST?" I yelled.

"Hey little girl I don't care if your daddy is here or not you will not disrespect me! You better lower your voice!"

Daddy jerked his head, "or else what? You gonna threaten to knock me like you did this morning!" I said

He went to say something back and Daddy grabbed him by the neck. I expected Andrew to be scared or nervous, but he was fine. He watched like this scene was

nothing. "We're gonna change something's around here. My first change of choice is gonna have to wait a minute." Moses was turning red. Daddy released him. "You will not speak to my daughter like this ever again! This is a business, and if you cannot conduct yourself in a professional manner there's the door." Daddy pointed at the door. "Next since daily takes aren't adding up, you're gonna rent your station. It's up to you if you want to pay daily, weekly or monthly. Once you pay your rent anything above that is your bonus. This shop is open eight to five Tuesday through Saturday. If you need to work around that discuss it with Amber."
Chester smiled really big. "I like the sound of that. When will this start?"
"The Tuesday after the renovation." Then Daddy smiled at Moses. "You're getting some new neighbors." Moses had a question mark on his face. "We're adding three more chairs."
Moses blew air, "aw man! It's already crowded enough as it is."
"That sounds like a personal problem to me. Oh and contrary to what anyone may have heard, Amber's running this ship until Malcolm comes back. So if she tells you to jump, you better ask if you're high enough. You will NOT discuss any disagreements with the customers. Act like adults here! Your new contracts will be ready end of the week, think about how you want to move forward. Any questions?"
Moses was mad, but he said nothing.
****

When Rosalind and Benjamin came to visit. Rosalind still had that just existing look on her face. She said she and Benjamin are having a hard time, and that this summer he was going back to the base, and she was going to stay behind. She said she was going to go to night school to get her diploma, but she was going to have a hard time finding a job during the day. As we were putting her resume together I kept looking at Tanisha's hair. Her hair was braided in the cutest little hairstyle. Suddenly I saw that guy from that movie about the school for performing arts with the corn rolls. I asked Rosalind if she could do men's hair. She said she could. Then I told her I had a chair that I needed to fill at the shop. I asked her if she would be interested in renting the chair. She got nervous; she asked me if Malcolm would be ok with that. I told her of course he would be. I told her, that I also needed her to be my eyes on the inside. I warned her about Moses, and then I told her about Chester, and the two new guys. She asked Benjamin if it was ok with him if she worked in the shop. He looked at her funny, and then he told her it was up to her. He looked confused as to why she was asking him.
I took Rosalind by the shop that night just before closing time. I introduced her to the guys. Then I asked Chester to join us in Malcolm's office. You could tell Moses wanted to know what we were gonna talk about. I unlocked Malcolm's office and then I shut the door behind us. I asked Chester for a huge favor. I asked him if he would allow Rosalind to braid his hair. He frowned at me; I could tell he didn't understand. So I told him I would give him a discount on his rent for two months if he wore corn rolls for that timeframe. We had Leon line Chester up then the rest of the guys watched as Rosalind corn rolled Chester's hair. When she was done Chester looked ten times better. As he looked in the mirror, Leon and Rico nodded in approval. Moses sat in his chair watching everything. Rico said he was gonna grow his hair out so that she could do his. Moses asked what she was gonna do until her clientele picked up. I told him that she could assist them around the shop, until she had enough clients to fill her days. I could see the wheels in Moses' head turning, I didn't like that but hey. Chester was still in the mirror admiring himself.

He even started doing a little dance in approval of his new look.

****

David told me that since our schedules weren't linking up, etc. We should just wait until we had the time and space to do it right. I was a little disappointed but he had a point. It seemed like everything was working against us making that final connection. His graduation party was happening directly after his ceremony so he asked me to come. He said I could meet his family, which was the way it should happen anyways. I asked if I could bring my brother since Malachi would be getting in the night before. He said that was fine.

When I picked Malachi up, he was in big brother mode immediately. He asked me how I was doing, how I was getting by, was I ready for college? He shot question after question. I told him I was ok, and then I told him about David. He sat still listening as I talked. I told him that Andrew loves him and that he was a good guy and I really liked him. I told him what Troy said about him not being like Charles and Malachi exhaled. We both laughed, Malachi asked if Sophia was still with him. When I said she was he asked why. I begged Malachi to come with me to David's graduation and after party, cause I didn't want to go alone. He agreed to go; he said he wanted to check David out for himself.

The Richmond Auditorium was packed. An older woman was standing in the lobby watching everyone as they came in. When we walked through the door she smiled and said "Amber?" When I said yes, she hugged me and then she introduced herself as David's Aunt Lorraine. She said David described me to a T. I introduced Malachi and Andrew she hugged and kissed them. Then she led us down a hallway and into a section she pointed to our seats in the middle of the row. We scooted past people who were all almost staring as we walked past. Aunt Lorraine whispered to them who we were. Then they started smiling and whispering. I spotted David in the sea of graduates; he had a mile wide smile. He tapped someone and pointed me out, the guy waved, I waved back. Then the guy gave David five. When they called David Mason it seemed like our whole section stood up to cheer him on. When the ceremony was over, everyone started rushing to their cars. Auntie Lorraine told us to wait for David and they'd see us at the house. David came rushing out of the auditorium. Andrew took off running to David. Malachi smiled real big when he saw that. David picked up Andrew, and then he came over and introduced himself to Malachi. Malachi smiled at me, and that easy you'd swear David and Malachi were old friends. David gave me a big hug and a kiss. He introduced me to a bunch of his classmates. He was so proud of me that was a new feeling. I don't know why I thought he'd be embarrassed to be seen with me. Malcolm never eagerly introduced me to people, but then again he wasn't all that social. When we walked into David's Aunt and Uncle's house he was holding my hand. Everybody was so happy for him and hurrying over to meet all of us. They didn't skip a beat everyone was nice to Andrew as well. I asked David where his parents were, he just said his dad couldn't make it, and I'd meet his mother later. We ate good food, and we met nice people, and danced to good music. It was weird when they prayed over the food, I guess that was because I wasn't used to it. But everyone was so nice; Malachi and I drove home with huge smiles.

****

My graduation party was a lot of fun. I was thankful that I made it to this point. This last school year especially had been so traumatic, at times I didn't think I was gonna make it. Receiving my acceptance letter from Berkeley definitely gave me a second wind. After debating back and forth with Malachi I invited David to come to my graduation party. I explained that we had to be discreet before announcing our relationship to my family. I explained I was with Malcolm so long that everyone's initial reaction would not be positive, and I wasn't ready to deal with all of it yet. I could tell David was trying to understand but he didn't really. He had to work that morning, but he was coming after he showered and changed. Momma was so happy Timothy was home, the way she doted on him, you could tell he was her heart. Her favorite of all four of us, and we all knew who was her least favorite. She cried really hard when he told her he was going with a firm in Chicago. He promised it would only be for a few years and that when he started his own firm he would make his way back to the Bay. Momma told him that he made her heart so proud, and that she could hold her head high because of all of his achievements. Timothy looked a little troubled; Momma was so busy being proud that she failed to notice his face. A little later Timothy asked me if I would mind if he brought someone to my party. Malachi and I smiled big, who is she we asked. Timothy told us he was engaged to a girl named Grace. We paused; Malachi asked how come we'd never heard of her until now? Timothy explained time just kept passing, he wanted to tell Momma especially but he wasn't sure how she would respond. Momma never liked any of his girlfriends in high school. Which is probably why Malachi never got serious about anybody. Timothy was still surprisingly tight lipped about Grace. He had nothing but love in his eyes for her, but he wasn't saying much. Malachi and I exchanged looks, did that mean she was ugly or something?

After the ceremony we came back to the house. Malachi said he saw Timothy but only from afar. When Timothy walked into the backyard he had a beautiful Asian girl on his arm. Malachi and I swallowed hard. I turned to see where Momma was in hopes to distract her. But it was too late she was already locked in. Timothy was introducing her to family along the way to Momma. Momma looked annoyed but you could tell she was waiting for an explanation. Fortunately Nana and Poppa were in the pathway before Momma. Nana and Poppa were really nice to Grace and they chatted for a while. Finally Timothy brought Grace over to Momma and Daddy. Daddy was talking to Uncle Frank so he didn't notice what was happening at first. Malachi and I fast walk raced each other to the punch bowl so that we could get in earshot. Timothy introduced Momma and Daddy to Grace. Momma was actually smiling, and then he introduced Grace as his fiancée Momma's smiled dropped. She looked mad, she told him to say that again and to say it right. Right at that moment Jade looked at me, she was talking to Sophia and Cassondra with Sasha on her lap. I motioned for them to come quick. Jade popped up and Sophia followed. Jade introduced herself, and then Timothy proudly introduced his fiancée Grace. Jade gave her a hug and told her she had to come to the wedding next weekend. Daddy congratulated Timothy, but Momma sat there Stone faced. I came around the table and introduced myself. I asked her to let me introduce her to some people while Timothy and Momma talked. She was nervous, and she seemed a bit relieved to walk away. Everyone was really nice to her, and I liked her. Grace was funny and down to earth, now I understood why he was moving to Chicago. If he stayed out here Momma would ruin this for him. I told Timothy that I liked Grace and I wished him well. He hugged me tight and said, "thank you chipmunk. At least someone could be happy for me." Timothy stayed by Grace's side the rest of the night. When David arrived Malachi and Sonny greeted him I didn't see him until Malachi was introducing him to Uncle Jeff. Jade gave him the biggest hug, and she introduced him to Sonny as her husband to be, and of course she invited him to her wedding. Charles instantly became huffy when he saw David being introduced and received well. Everybody started looking at him instead of enjoying their self. I asked Sophia what was wrong with him and she didn't know. She went and talked to him and he quieted down, but visibly you could tell his feathers were ruffled about something. Momma couldn't fix her eyes right was she gonna stare Timothy or me down. Her evil glare bounced around the party.

When Troy arrived he made a beeline to me. He told me Malcolm wanted to see me. I said ok, David greeted Troy. Troy said hey but he wasn't enthusiastic about it. The boys had been in their own world playing over to the side, when Andrew heard Troy's voice his head popped up. He ran full charge in our direction with little Jeff and JoJo in tow. It looked like he was running to Troy, but he ran past Troy to David. Then he told little Jeff and JoJo that David was his new Dad as he hugged him. Everybody looked at Troy for a reaction. He looked shocked, and then he chuckled. It was a scary chuckle at best. Andrew said hi to Troy then he led the boys in begging David to play basketball with them. David told Andrew to get his ball and they could play for a little bit, but then he wanted to spend time with me. Andrew and the boys ran inside to get Andrew's spare basketball. Troy said David better live it up while it last, then he walked away. David looked at me unamused and asked why Troy kept doing that. We all laughed, and I shrugged. Andrew bounced the ball with the biggest grin on his face. David walked over praising Andrew for practicing, he told him he was getting really good at it. My brothers and cousins all went over to the side of the house where the hoop was. Everyone male from Timothy's age and down were over watching the little ones play ball. Uncle Frank came over and asked who David was. He paused when I told him that David was my boyfriend. He looked at me for a few minutes then he asked me if David was worth it. I asked him what he meant by that. He said point blankly "Malcolm". I asked him if he was still my uncle, and he said forever and ever. Then I asked him why I needed to fear Malcolm. He smiled and then he kissed my forehead. Daddy came over, "am I hearing this right? That's your boyfriend?" I said yes. Daddy asked why I didn't come to him. I told him with the way Momma's been acting I didn't know where he stood. Daddy put his hand on his neck; he said he didn't think it was a good idea. But that I was his baby girl and no matter what I can come to him with anything. Momma's eyes bounced from Grace to David for the rest of the evening. Fortunately for me she decided to focus on Grace.

****

The night before Jade's wedding all the bride's maids spent the night at my house. We sat up talking about our lives and how excited we were for Jade. We talked about when Sonny was just a goofy guy crushing on his best friend's little sister. She told us that she liked Sonny from the first time she met him, but she didn't know what it meant or what to do with those feelings. She told me no offense but she didn't want any part of what I was going through. I told her I didn't either. We had a wonderful evening. In the morning we went to Raynel's to get our hair done. Raynel kept crying saying she couldn't believe how grown up we all were. Momma and Auntie Lauren came a little later to get their hair done. Sasha looked so pretty with all her little curls bouncing and behaving. Sophia and I got our hair straightened and then big barrel curls and flowers around our semi up do's. Rosalind braided Cassondra's hair in long braids that she styled to match the style Jade wanted. Our dresses were dark purple and Nana bought custom made jade jewelry it was so pretty. Even Jade and Momma wore jade accessories. I told Jade I'd forgive her for using my favorite color in her wedding. I said I would make sure my purple was a different shade. We took so many pictures before the wedding.

Carey Anderson

Momma looked beautiful, to my surprise she accepted me telling her so. I hoped
this meant that our relationship would turn another corner. I missed my Momma
and I desperately wanted her back in my life. Sonny got all choked up when he saw
how beautiful Jade looked coming down the aisle. Gwen pouted the whole
ceremony because she wasn't included in the wedding. When I saw Troy sit next to
David my heart sped up. David looked fine with it, I even saw them talking.
Pictures couldn't happen fast enough, I wanted to get over to find out what they
were talking about. By the time I got over there Troy was all smiles, "your boy ain't
half bad. But just so we're clear on where my loyalty lies, it's always with my
family. But you alright." David smiled slightly but I could tell he was thinking.
Afterwards Rosalind and Benjamin, Sophia and Charles, Timothy and Grace,
Malachi and I, and David went back to my house. We kissed the babies goodbye
and sent them packing with Nana. Malachi and I stopped at the liquor store and
bought some drinks for a nightcap. Malachi said he didn't want to be surrounded by
all the couples. He said he was gonna go home, and if he found someone to bring
back with him he would come back. We had music playing and everyone was
talking and enjoying their selves. Everyone except Charles, he kept staring at David
and sulking. When there was a knock at the door we all naturally assumed it was
Malachi, but it was Troy. My heart sank; I didn't know he knew where I lived. He
had a girl with him, he told everybody he wasn't staying but he needed to talk to me
real quick. Suddenly Charles was happy and energetic. He made Sophia get up and
dance with him as Troy and I walked into the kitchen. He gave me some paperwork
to put in Malcolm's safe at the shop. He asked how Rosalind was working out down
there and I told her she was doing well. David was standing by the kitchen with his
back to us, but I knew he was listening. When Off The Wall came on Troy said he
had to dance. He went in the living room grabbed his girl and started dancing.
When David and I started dancing Charles started getting huffy again. Benjamin
asked him what was wrong with him. Charles shook his head to say nothing and he
continued to drink. Malachi came back with a girl that looked familiar but I couldn't
place her. Troy and his friend left and we all continued to drink. Everybody was
tipsy, when Charles asked me if I had any more brandy. I told him where it was but
he acted like he didn't understand what I was saying. So I got up and I went in the
kitchen. As I reached up in the cupboard Charles leaned in to me. I assumed he lost
his balance and I pushed him back a little then I started reaching again for the
bottle. Then he started rubbing my butt and licking his lips. I slapped him hard, but
he kept coming in, his hands were all over me and that fast I had a flash back of
uncle. All I could see was red! I slapped him again and I punched him in the
shoulder. I was aiming for his chest but my precision was off because I was tipsy as
well. He kept coming in talking about he had next after Malcolm and David needed
to get to the back of the line. David grabbed Charles by the shirt and pulled him out
of the kitchen. Charles reared like he was going to do something and David hit him
in the face. Charles bent over holding his nose, and David shook his hand. When
Charles started to stand up again, David drew back like he was gonna hit him again.
But Charles put his hands up. His nose was busted, and that sobered him up. Sophia
asked what was going on but she looked at me, then David, then Charles. She told
him to GET OUT! What a wonderful end to our party. I put ice on David's hand;
clearly he was not a fighter. But I appreciated him defending me all the same.
Sophia cursed Charles from the bottom of his feet to the top of his head. She threw
all his stuff out of the apartment. She told him she wanted a divorce and she never
wanted to see him again. Malachi and Timothy laughed at Charles cause he was

crying and whining the whole time. I watched Grace's face to see if she was shocked or uncomfortable. But she kept talking to Rosalind like nothing happened she was completely fine. Malachi told Sophia he would come and change the locks tomorrow but for now she should sleep at her parents until he changed them. He told her cowards try to sneak up on you. Malachi and his friend took Sophia to her parent's house. Rosalind and Benjamin left when Timothy and Grace did.

David helped me straighten up, and then he grabbed me and kissed me. He carried me upstairs, FINALLY!!!! He kissed me as he gently laid me down. He undressed me like he was unwrapping a present. Then he took his clothes off, when I looked at him I hated to compare, but I only knew Malcolm so I couldn't help it. He wasn't as big as Malcolm but I didn't know what that meant. When he put on the condom it didn't look like it was going to break out immediately. David kissed me and he moaned out loud as he entered me. I chuckled a little I couldn't help it this was different. I could definitely feel him, but I didn't feel like he was going to be bursting through my throat at any second. It was over faster than I wanted it to be, but all of his noises kept me entertained. He held me and he kept kissing me, telling me how much he loved me. Even though I didn't finish, I did feel satisfied.

****

Malcolm's glare stayed on my face as soon as he was in eyeshot. He was mad but I ignored it. He didn't say anything right away he just stared at me. I rolled my eyes he couldn't have called me down here just to stare at me. "So how far is this going to go?" He asked trying to control his tone.

"What Malcolm?" I said unaffected by his anger.

"You've got my son calling him daddy!"

"Your son who you have not mentioned until now calls him David, but he refers to him as his dad."

"Don't split hairs with me! You know what I'm saying!"

"Why do you care Malcolm? You never wanted him. You care about me, but you've never shown a interest in your son."

"How you figure that?"

"Even after I pointed out the simple gesture of cutting his hair, you never did it."

"So not cutting his hair means I don't care?"

"It's one of the many small gestures you could've made in regards to him. You never took him anywhere. You only held him when you came to the house. Andrew hasn't even asked about you. He's more happy to see Troy than he was with you!"

"So let me get this right!" He leaned forward in his chair. "I'm stuck in this prison for another six months to a year behind avenging what I thought was the demise of you and my son. And now you sit there and tell me I DON'T CARE!"

I shifted. "Malcolm I appreciate all that you've done for me. I'm doing my part to take care of your business for you, so you're straight when you get out. I'm taking care of you just like you've always taken care of me. But we are not together, remember we broke up. Andrew calls him David, just David."

He twisted his head as he looked at me. "YOU'RE IN LOVE WITH HIM?" I didn't know how he knew it, but I didn't say anything I just looked at Malcolm. His eyes turned red like he was trying to burn a hole in me. "HOW COULD YOU DO THIS TO ME? I'M GONNA GET OUT OF HERE! I WON'T ALWAYS BE IN HERE!"

"And when you get out you can go back to letting Yvette think you're engaged. Sleeping with married women, and even the ones the courts couldn't find! As for me, I'm with David for as long as he'll have me."

Malcolm looked at me in disbelief. "I knew he was a bug that needed to be squashed a long time ago!"

"Why would you say that? He's never said anything against you. He told Andrew not to call him dad because of you."

He scooted as close to the table as it would let him move. His voice was low and deep. "Amber! You belong to me! You always have and you always will! Your body craves me! I could make you cum right now without even touching you! Have your fun with him now, but things will change when I get out. Whether you wanna play dumb or not, doesn't matter! You will come to me!"

I rolled my eyes, but I had no come back for that. "Why did you call me down here?"

"To remind you! You began with me and you're gonna end with me!"

I tried to hold back my tears and whatever else my body was feeling against my will. "Malcolm, you had your chance. You blew it, and you weren't even sorry about it. You are incapable of being faithful that ruins everything else for me. I'm in love and I'm happy. I will not come down here for anything other than business! I don't need this!"

He smiled, "you don't need what? To remember me? No matter how hard you try he will never be me!"

"And that's the beauty of it. He's not you, I can trust him."

"Trust is irrelevant when you're frustrated. When I get out I'm gonna be looking for you. Bring me my cookies!"

I plugged my ears and tried my best not to reflect the throbbing I was feeling. I hated him for being able to affect me like this. Tears ran down my face, "if you ever want me to come back here, you will NOT do this to me again. Business only! I love David and I don't care about your delusions or fantasies!"

Knowing he was affecting me he sat back satisfied with his self. Then he switched gears. "Jason Palmer is getting out in two weeks. He's gonna come to the shop, write up his contract and have it ready for him. He's gonna use my chair."

Chapter 26

"David's gonna be out of town so I don't see why we can't have some fun." Sophia said snapping her fingers.

She didn't understand why the thought of going to a club made me nervous. The last time I went Malcolm was there, and my whole life turned upside down. Besides I didn't have a sitter, Cassondra lived in the city now. I saw her occasionally, but she had her own life going on now. She and her boyfriend were making good strides; I wouldn't be surprised if her wedding was next. Rosalind has been working hard and hanging with guys all day, she needs a break more than I do.

I asked Sophia is she would mind taking Rosalind instead and I would stay with the kids. Sophia sucked her teeth. She said being with David was turning me into a old lady. She said I never wanted to go out and when I did he was always with me. She said we sat in the house all the time. That wasn't exactly true, but David and I were always together. The only time we weren't together is when we were working, and school was work. My general education classes and then business and then dance. Then I was always at the shop.

Moses tried to pull that bullying crap on Rosalind and I told her she can't show him fear and she had no reason to. If he did anything to her it would be the same as him touching me. I told her not to start nothing, but don't ever back down.

Andrew still takes classes at the center he really likes them. I even got Sasha, JoJo, and little Jeff enrolled at the center. Auntie Lauren drops them off after Jeff gets out of school. Then I pick them up. I do find myself wanting to be under David, but he's so lovable I can't help it. I love the way he is with Andrew, and all the kids for that matter. I love the way he is with me. We don't argue much, more than anything we get on each other's nerves but that only last for so long. Although he doesn't move heaven and earth in the bedroom, I'm satisfied and the intimacy I have with him surpasses everything else. So yes, to someone who's never had what I have with David it will seem like I'm and old lady but I don't care. I'm happy!

Sophia picked up the phone and called Rosalind. Rosalind was so thankful, she said she needed to get out and unwind. I called Auntie Lauren and I asked her to bring the boys over so that she and Uncle Jeff could go out or stay in. I decided to make it a slumber party at my house. Auntie Lauren sang my praises over the phone. She had the boys to me in less than twenty minutes. Sleeping bags and clothes. Andrew was so excited to have all of his cousins over. Even though they all saw each other everyday, every time they got together it was like they hadn't just seen each other. And it was different cause this time they had Tanisha with them too.

As the kids were playing there was a knock at the door. Troy was at the door, I told him he really needed to start calling before he came over. He said I never gave him permission to call. So I took that to mean he had my number he just didn't call me. I invited him in; the kids were enjoying hot dogs and chips. Then I asked why he needed permission to call but didn't need permission to come over. He smiled and told me I had a good point. He brought me more papers for Malcolm's safe. He asked where David was? I told him he was out of town. He whistled, he travels a lot doesn't he? I told him that forty percent of the time he had to travel for work. He asked me how that was working out for me. I told him it was fine, he had to do what he had to do. Then Troy gave me that look, he was about to mention Malcolm. I braced myself for whatever he was going to say next. He started laughing at me; he told me I could stop holding my breath. I didn't realize I was doing that, so I laughed. Then I told him to spill it. Then he said Malcolm wants to see me. I shook my head no. He started laughing; he said Malcolm told him I would react that way.

I've been doing everything in my power to avoid going down there. The last time I was there he got in my head, and it took me a long time to get his voice out of my head. I didn't enjoy being messed with, and all he had time to do was mess with me. I've spent the last year avoiding him best I could. Summer was coming and I was looking forward to no school and no mental trips from Malcolm. I looked at the table and Andrew shifted his eyes like he wasn't listening. But I knew he was. I asked Troy what Malcolm wanted. Troy said we hadn't discussed business, and he needed to know how things were going. I asked Troy if I could give him the information and he could give it to Malcolm. Troy laughed and said he couldn't explain it like I could. Fortunately I had been keeping good records as if it was a school assignment so in my mind I envisioned going in. Showing him everything and then ducking out before he started that other talk. I took a deep breath and I told myself I could do it. Troy gave all the kids money for their pockets, and then he left. Andrew was watching me like a hawk, no like his daddy would. I had no clue what he could be thinking, how much can a four year old comprehend, right?

****

David got home at about two a.m. I heard Andrew bolt out of his bed and down the stairs. He was so excited to see David whenever he came home. David made sure he brought Andrew something even if it was as simple as a piece of candy or as big as a toy. He told Andrew that whenever he was on the road he missed him terribly so he had to collect something that made him think of Andrew and that would help him get through the week. Andrew would tell him about his week, and even though David would be whooped from driving eight plus hours sometimes he would sit there and patiently listen to Andrew and even carry on a conversation with him. It didn't matter how tired he was, he'd hop in the shower and wash all the railroad dirt off of him, and then we'd make love, slowly but passionate love. Then!!!! Then we'd both fall asleep satisfied and in love. This morning when I woke up, he was staring at me with a smile on his face. Then he told me he had something for me too. I smiled, and then he sat up, so I did the same. He handed me a letter. I looked at him with a question mark. Then he called out to Andrew and told him I was reading the letter and to come quick. Andrew bolted up the stairs, he had his hands behind his back, and his smile was a mile wide. David told me to read the letter out loud if I wanted to. So I did:

To my dearest Amber,
As I sit here trying to put my thoughts down on this paper there are no words to express what I feel for you. You are the love of my life, and I thank Ms. Blevins everyday for sitting you next to me. This past year together has almost been exactly as I imagined it all my life. I go out, work really hard all day, and I get to come home to you. I wish you could be me for one day just so you could know how good that feels. You are God's gift to me. Don't roll your eyes cause God is real, and you are proof of that. I don't know what the next fifty years will bring me, but as long as you're by my side I know that my life will be more than ideal, it will be heaven on earth. As you are reading this I have asked Andrew for his permission to ask you a very important question. So when you're ready for the question look me in my eyes.

Loving you forever with all my heart,
Your loving and faithful David

I was in complete tears! Andrew looked surprised that I was crying, David smiled at him and told him these tears were good tears. I looked David in the eyes and he asked me to marry him, and then Andrew held out the ring box. David opened the box and there was a solitaire ring in a gold setting. I cried harder as I said, "YES! With all my heart!" David and I kissed while Andrew danced on the side of the bed. We all got dressed and then we went over my parent's house. Daddy wasn't surprised, but Momma was. She hugged me for the first time in two years! I was on system overload. Momma said she was so afraid for me because my life was spiraling out of control. She thanked David for loving me like he does. She told him he has been a calming affect on my life, and she was thankful that he found me. I stayed under my Momma all day; she could barely go to the bathroom without me following her in there. I was so happy! I had a good man in my life that loved my son as if he was his own, and he brought my Momma back to me. I woke up in the middle of that night crying because I was so happy.

Feeling recharged I entered the prison sure that nothing Malcolm could say or do could mess with me. His eyes got really big when he saw me. I wasn't wearing anything special, but I was wearing David's love all over me like it was my new fashion. Malcolm told me that I looked really good. I smiled and said thank you. I pulled out the paperwork to show him his financials for the shop. He sat up happy and ready to hear me. I pulled out the binder with everything in it. I pointed to a number on his statement. "STOP!" He shook his head like something was wrong in the statement. I looked at the statement and then at him. "WHAT IS THAT?" He barked. He looked like he was about to start foaming at the mouth.

I didn't know what he meant, "I'm going to explain everything, but your profits have only gone up."

"NOT THAT!" He pointed at my hand, "THAT!"

I swallowed hard, I forgot in all my rushing around to take my ring off. I smiled a clumsy embarrassed smile. "Surprise! I'm engaged!" I said with a goofy smile.

"WRONG AMBER! WRONG!"

"Excuse me!" I said looking at him crossly.

"YOU WILL NOT!" He grabbed his composure as people started to look at us. He stood up, paced in a circle for a minute then he sat down. "I'm only going to tell you this once. Unless you want to end up a widow right after you say I do, there will be NO WEDDING!"

"What?" I sucked my teeth. "Malcolm! Come on DON'T be ridiculous!"

"I don't make idle threats." Malcolm said, the look in his eyes was just as crazy as when I went to the police station.

I burst into tears, "why Malcolm? Why can't I be happy?"

"You belong to me. I'm sorry if that makes you unhappy, but that's the way it goes!"

"This isn't fair! He makes me happy, and he's the only man to want me forever on my terms. How could you take this from me? From your son!"

He shot me a nonchalant look, "sorry". He said as he shrugged.

I sat there crying in disbelief. "Would you really hurt me like that?"

"It would hurt me more to let it happen!"

"Can't we talk about this? Be reasonable Malcolm!"

"Oh trust me! I am being reasonable. You can stay engaged as long as you like, but you can't marry him!" Then he leaned forward, "DON'T TEST ME!"

Chapter 27

"I understand you're upset, but he's not threatening you. David seems like a nice respectable young man, but how does it benefit me to protect him? What does he do?"

"He works for the railroad." I said sounding completely defeated.

"Do you know how much money, and how many connections the family would lose just so you could have love in your life? As long as he's not threatening to harm you, I can't be in it." Uncle Frank said matter of factly.

"So what am I supposed to do?"

"I asked you in the beginning or at least when I found out about him if David was worth it. Why didn't you understand this was gonna happen?"

"How in the world was I supposed to know?" I cried my eyes out. I couldn't believe this was happening. Everybody was washing their hands of the situation like it was a personal argument between Malcolm and I. The fact that he was threatening the love of my life didn't matter. No one cared!

When I came home that night I went straight to bed. David and Andrew were playing dominos when I came in the door. I couldn't even look at them; I went upstairs and climbed into the bed. I didn't even take my shoes off. As soon as my head hit the pillow my tears came flying out again. Andrew came upstairs; he asked me what was wrong. I told him nothing, I just didn't feel good. He told me he was going to bring me some tea. I thanked him, and then David came in the room. He rubbed my back, and asked me if there was anything he could do. That made me cry harder! He sat there looking at me; he wanted to ask me what was wrong. But we both knew I wasn't gonna talk about it.

I woke up to David taking my shoes off. It was dark in the room. I thanked him, and then I got up. I went down stairs; the clock said it was almost eleven. David followed me downstairs; he stood over to the side watching me. I looked at him; he's never looked so perfect to me. I couldn't allow myself to tell him. I couldn't tell him how my past was affecting me. "David I love you so much!"

"I love you!" He said

"I just need you to know that in your heart!"

"Amber, what's going on?"

I started crying, "I can't even talk about it!" He came and sat next to me. He put his hand on my back and he rubbed my back. I laid my head on his shoulder. He kissed my cheek, I made him kiss me. I unbuckled his pants, when he attempted to move like he was going to go get a condom I looked him in his eyes, as I didn't let him get up. He had a question mark on his face. I mounted him, and he exhaled like I was taking all his power away. He grabbed me by my hips, exhaled "Amber!" He was trying to be responsible, do the right thing. I shook my head, and kissed him. I took his hands off my hips. He was trying his hardest to be quiet, but his eyes were crossing and he was virtually powerless. His body tensed, and he buried his face in my bosom. I didn't stop until I knew he had nothing else to give me. I kept kissing him while he sat there trying to gather his thoughts. "I love you David!"

****

"We need to set a date." David said

"Baby I can't even focus on a wedding right now. Takes too much planning, and it's too much stress." I said rolling my eyes.

David shook his head, "I don't understand. Every time I talk about the wedding you have an excuse. You don't want to marry me?"

"Of course I do!"

"Then why can't we set a date?" David asked

"I can't talk about this right now! You're gonna stress me out! The doctor said no stress!" I said pointing to my stomach. This pregnancy was so different from Andrew. This belly was really small compared, and the baby didn't move as much as Andrew did. This baby was stubborn, and moved when it wanted to. I continued to dance and exercise as much as possible. Whenever I went to the shop I wore big shirts or whatever I could to cover my stomach. My face didn't really change, it was a miracle. I didn't tell anyone about the baby unless I felt they knew for sure. So a lot of the people at school knew, I couldn't hide my stomach in my dance clothes. David's family knew about the baby and they were really excited. Andrew knew about the baby but we made him promise not to say anything to anyone. When we got home he would talk to my stomach, and kiss the baby. Whenever Troy popped up at the house I found a reason to be sitting at the table or on the couch with something covering me.

When Momma told me she knew I told her the whole story. What Malcolm promised and how I needed something to hold on to. She told me I needed to talk to David. But I didn't know how. I told her it would hurt too much. I told her he would either leave me or insist that we marry anyways. Either way I would die! I told her I was hoping for a miracle.

****

"Welcome to Drew's! How may I help you?" I said as I answered the phone from behind the counter. The person on the phone hung up. A customer walked in the door, I asked who they came to see. He didn't have a preference; I told him the wait would be about ten minutes. Rosalind came over and asked me how I was holding up. I told her I needed to go take a power nap in the office. I told her if I wasn't back in twenty to send in reinforcements. I unlocked the office door, and I locked it behind me. I sat at the desk, opened my legs, and laid my head on the desk. I was out in like five point two seconds. I awoke to a familiar touch on my shoulder. When I sat up I screamed when I saw Malcolm standing in front of me. He smiled at me and apologized for scaring me. My heart wouldn't slow down; I asked him when he got out. He said he's been out for a couple of weeks. Then he told me to get up and hug him. My eyes turned evil, "I HATE YOU!"

He jumped then he smiled. "We're going straight there? Ok well..."

"Malcolm! I gotta tell you something!" I said interrupting him. He looked at me. I stood up and I showed him my stomach through my shirt. His body flinched, but he didn't move. We sat there quiet for a long time. Malcolm was furious! "You said I couldn't marry him. I found another way to keep him forever!"

Malcolm sucked his teeth, "you think you're so smart don't you!" He sat on the desk like he was losing his footing.

"No, I was desperate!"

"How far are you?" He asked. I told him I was eight months. He stared at my stomach like it was a disease. Then he focused on my face. I couldn't read the look on his face, he opened his mouth then he closed it. He watched me as I walked over to the safe. I opened it and started to explain what I was taking out. He put his arms around me; I jumped cause I didn't realize he had gotten up. He kissed my neck and said he had been waiting for me for a very long time. As soon as he said in my ear that he needed me I started throbbing. I was confused by my body's betrayal especially in its current state. I pushed away from him and told him to stop. His eyes pleaded with me as he moved in slowly. I slapped his face and I hit him trying to keep him away as he moved in closer. He picked up my left hand; he looked at

211

my engagement ring. He asked me how did I tell him that there would be no wedding? Tears came to my eyes; I said I couldn't tell him. I was hoping Malcolm would change his mind. His hands started wandering all over my body, as he told me nothing could change his mind. Feeling desperate again I asked him what I could do to change his mind. Then there was a knock at the door; I hurried to the door as he sat down in his chair. Rosalind was at the door; she asked me if I was ok. She looked at Malcolm, his face was still angry. I told her I was fine, and then I thanked her for checking on me. As I looked forward into the shop and it seemed everyone was trying to see what was going on. I closed the door, and then I told Malcolm I had to go. He shook his head and told me he wanted to see his son. I told him I would bring Andrew before the shop closes.

When I got to Auntie Lauren's I was in tears. The kids were in the backyard playing as usual. She looked surprised and asked me what was wrong. I told her that I just saw Malcolm. She sat down then I showed her my belly. She wasn't surprised when I showed her. She said I wasn't dressing the same and I was always tired. I told her how he had me trapped in a corner and how I felt helpless. She said being in this family does that to you. She asked me to never tell Sophia, so I promised. Then she shared with me some of the drama that she's endured being married to Uncle Jeff. She said there's such a huge gap in Sophia and little Jeff's age because they fought so much. She said they both cheated and everything, she said they moved to Oakland for a fresh start. She said being close to Momma and Daddy really helped them grow. She said our situations weren't the same, but she understood the feeling of being trapped. She told me like Momma told me, to talk to David. I told her I couldn't do it. I didn't want to break his heart. She told me in this situation it was impossible for him not to get hurt.

I took Andrew home, cleaned him up and put on some nice clothes. He asked me what was wrong twice and each time I tried my best to pull out a smile and tell him nothing. After that he kept quiet and watched my face. Herb coughed really hard before starting up like I asked him to. I needed a new car especially with the baby coming. But I never told David about all my money I couldn't very well just show up with a brand new car from nowhere. So we discussed getting a new car, but we hadn't made a move yet. Andrew looked around quietly, but he was mostly watching my face. When we pulled up to the shop there was a crowd of people inside. Mostly customers, Moses was working like I've never seen him work before. Jason kept giving Moses the eye, but Moses was so busy working he didn't catch it. Everyone said, "Drew!" When Andrew and I walked in the door. Andrew generally waved but he didn't say much. I grabbed his hand and led him to the back office. I knocked on the door and Troy answered. Troy gave me a funny look as he opened the door to let us in. Troy asked where my stomach was. When I put my hand on the top of my belly, his face looked so surprised. Then Andrew and I walked in the office. There were two other guys in there with Troy and Malcolm. One guy got up offering me his seat then he introduced himself as Juan. Juan seemed really sweet, but something told me if he was back here right now there was more to him than meets the eye. I had Andrew sit in my lap. His eyes stay glued to Malcolm, and Malcolm watched him. They had the same expression on their faces. The other guy asked Malcolm, "when do you want me to pay him a visit?"

Malcolm gestured to Troy, he told him to ask Jason to come in for a minute. Jason was kind of short, caramel brown with a serious expression most times. But he did smile, and seem more normal than Malcolm. He did not like Moses he would put him in his place all the time. Chester was the peacemaker constantly trying to get everyone to get along. Leon and Rico were just about making their money. Jason walked in the room, he nodded at me and then he looked at Malcolm. Troy shut the door and leaned against the wall. Malcolm said he was looking over the books and it just didn't look good. Jason nodded but didn't say anything; Malcolm said he was sure that "he" was still trying to find a way to under cut him. Jason said he didn't doubt it, Jason started telling him about the various regulars that Moses had. He said he's sure Moses has his own plan to execute. Then Jason nodded at me, and told Malcolm how he keeps hearing about how I spit in Moses' face. Malcolm smiled at me, and then he asked me what happened. I told him what happened, and then he asked me why was he just now hearing about it? I told him Moses was a royal pain, and that was only one of many run ins with him. Malcolm sat back, he looked at Juan "he continues to threaten my Queen" he said calmly. I shot Malcolm a look like he was crazy cause I was no longer his queen. Juan put his hands up, he told Malcolm that he needs a visit but they needed to do a little more research first. I asked what kind of research. Malcolm looked at me then he looked at Andrew who hadn't taken his eyes off of him. He put a finger up to me, and then he told Juan to let him know what he found. Then he asked Jason did he want to do it. Before he could finish his question Jason was saying YES! Malcolm said a few more things then they all left except Troy. Troy asked Andrew why he was being so quiet, Andrew shrugged and then he looked back at Malcolm.

His face was very serious, "do you know who I am?" Malcolm asked. Andrew nodded yes. "Can you talk?" Andrew nodded yes. "So speak"

"Yes" Andrew said

"Who am I?"

"Malcolm" Andrew said

"Who is Malcolm?" I asked

"My father" Andrew said

"You've gotten so big. You start school yet?"

"No" Andrew's tone matched Malcolm's, no excitement just matter of factly.

"I was looking at the books, I didn't see you on the payroll." Malcolm said to me. "Was I supposed to be?"

"You've been running this place for the past two and a half almost three years. You don't think you should be paid for your services? How have you been surviving?"

"I have David, besides I have savings if I truly needed something."

He looked at me. "You still should've been on the payroll." Then he took out the checkbook, I put my hands up in protest. "Look Amber! Either you take this check or I will deposit it myself. It's almost tax time, I gotta account for everyone. This isn't personal, you've been handling business and quite well. I have to pay you." He said continuing to write the check.

"What research?" I said taking the check without looking at it.

Malcolm told me he will not relive the night that got him locked away ever again. He said he's starting a temporary employment agency. I frowned at him cause that sounded random to me. He said he's structuring it so that he can have people do what he needs when he needs them to do it. He said Juan is in charge of that venture for him. Then he told me he needed to know that both of us are safe at all times. I frowned at him cause I didn't get it. Then he asked me if I ever wondered how Troy knew where I lived? I looked at Troy and he smiled real big at me. Malcolm said first task was to make sure I was safe and it was Troy's job to make sure I stayed that way. I asked him who was a threat to me? He said Momma Shuga for one; he asked me if I really thought she would stop at one attempt to get at me. I asked him why she wanted to hurt me. He told me not to even worry about it. He said Renee's gonna take over the house, then I could go see the kids if I wanted to. But not until he told me it was ok to go over. His voice was matter of factly, I looked at Troy and he looked away. I told him I couldn't believe he could talk about his grandmother like that. Malcolm's face turned to stone, "a real grandmother would not do the things she's done. She only cares about money, the things she's done have gone on long enough. Leonard and Sterling are gone..."

"WHAT?" I yelled!

"You didn't tell her?" Malcolm said to Troy.

Troy shook his head, "I couldn't tell her."

"TELL ME WHAT???" Tears pouring out my eyes.

Malcolm shifted in his chair. "She was trying to deal from the house. Her setup was..." He was trying to think of a word. "Very thrown together to say the best about it. The house got sprayed." Then he shifted again. "The kids were outside. Sterling got hit."

I grabbed Andrew, and started balling my eyes out. Andrew rubbed my head; he told me it was ok. Malcolm shifted in his chair a few times refusing to show emotion. Troy walked out the office, and then he came back and told Andrew to come with him. Andrew hesitated; I told him I was ok. He reluctantly walked out with Troy, Troy shut the door. Malcolm moved closer to me and sat on the edge of the desk. I was trying to pull back my tears, but it's not easy when you're pregnant. "No one called me! No one told me!"

"She didn't make arrangements for him, she didn't care. Tiffany and Penny have been staying with Troy cause she was trying to put them out there like she had Renee. You started something unifying them like you did. Momma Shuga hates you for it. Tell me what kind of grandmother that is?"

I was still trying to calm my tears, but I couldn't stop crying. So Malcolm went on with his point and why and how he was setting up his agency. As I read between the lines that also meant he was watching everything with David and I.

Then he went back to business. He told me he was going to open a second barbershop, and that he wanted to have a few chain shops in the Bay Area. He asked how school was going, and then what was my plan after the baby was born. I told him school was coming along fine, and I hadn't discussed the baby outside of my Momma cause I didn't want him finding out about it until I was ready to tell him. He told me he needed to know what my plan was cause he was gonna need me. I rolled my eyes, and asked him why. He said I did a wonderful job with the shop, and the expansion was just going to be more work. He said my idea to add Rosalind was genius, and he wanted to add a couple more braiders in the new location. He told me that once the second site was up and running he wanted to expand this space. I sat there listening to him talk about all the business plans he had. All that downtime had done him some good, but I really thought I was going to be able to bow out gracefully once he got out. I wondered if this was going to be ok with David. But it wasn't like Malcolm was giving me a choice. As I finally calmed down from my crying fit, I got a tissue off of his desk. As I started to sit down he grabbed me by my shoulders and raised me to kiss him. I tried to fight it at first, but I found myself giving into his kiss. When I realized that I gave in I pushed him away and I wiped my mouth. He sat there staring at me. "You miss me don't you?" He almost had a grin on his face. I shook my head no, but I kept my eyes on the floor. Against my will my body was on fire! I sat there staring at the floor. He got up and locked the door. My heart started beating really fast. He sat on the desk directly in front of me. He put his feet between my feet and forced my legs open, and then he bent over staring me in my eyes and started rubbing me. I told my body not to respond, I told my body not to feel anything. But my body disobeyed me; his face was stone while he stared in my eyes. I argued with my body not to respond, not to feel anything but my body started shaking against my will. Then he pulled his hand back and licked his fingers, "hhhhmmmm just like I remembered" then he kissed me. But I wouldn't give him my tongue. "I've waited all this time for you. I'll wait a few more months."

"I'm not gonna sleep with you!" I said

He smiled, "you always say that".

****

When David came home I was sitting on the couch. I told him Malcolm was out before he could put his bag down. David asked me if he should be concerned and I told him no. Andrew came downstairs; he gave David a huge hug. He told him about his week, and then he got quiet. He said that I took him to see his father, and that his father made me cry. David looked at me with a huge question mark. Andrew told him that he rubbed my head just like David did and he told me it was gonna be ok. David asked him if that helped me, Andrew said it did. Then he said that Troy and Malcolm gave us a ride home because Herb needed rest. David pulled out a hot wheel car, and Andrew got excited and started driving it around the living room. David gave me a peck on the cheek and then he said he would be back. I heard the shower water running, I looked at Andrew debating whether to scold him or not. But I let it go, they tell each other everything, and I liked that Andrew had that with David.

David sat next to me on the couch and he put my feet on his lap and started massaging them. Then he asked why I cried. I rubbed my belly and exhaled deeply. I told him as fast as I could about Sterling. That didn't stop me from crying again. Andrew asked who Sterling is and I told him he was his big cousin. I told David about Momma Shuga, Renee, Tiffany, and Penny. David sat there listening while he massaged my feet. He asked how did Malcolm take the news about the baby. I told him he wasn't happy about it, but what could he do. David just listened, and then he asked how Malcolm responded to me being engaged. I told him Malcolm's not happy about it. Then he asked me if I got closure. I asked him what he meant. He said that he thought maybe I couldn't set a date because I needed closure with Malcolm first. I told him that I had to ask him a question, why did we need a piece of paper? Why couldn't we just be committed to each other and live the rest of our lives that way? He said he wants to be married and he thought that's what I wanted too. I told him I did want that in the beginning, but we already live like we're married so I didn't see the point. He asked me how long had I felt this way. I told him that I've been feeling like this for a long time. Lying the whole time! I knew this conversation was hurting him, and I wished I didn't have to have it. David put my feet on the couch then he started pacing. "So you don't want to marry me?" I looked at Andrew who was standing like he was in shock. David stopped and he looked at Andrew as well. He went over and hugged him. Andrew started crying, he looked at me and he told me that I said yes. David told him, we're just having a conversation and maybe it would be a good idea if he went upstairs so that David and I could talk. David said he would come up and tuck him in, in a minute. Andrew cried all the way up the stairs. I felt horrible! David quietly repeated the question, "so you don't want to marry me?"

"David I love you more than anyone in my entire life. I love you with my heart and

215

soul! But I can't marry you right now." It broke my heart to say it. And seeing that devastated look on his face hurt worse. "Why can't we just live together?"

"I want all of you or none of you!" David said

I started crying really hard. "Please! Please don't leave me! I want you! I do! You're a good man, a wonderful father! I just can't marry you right now."

"Why are we having a baby?"

"Because I love you! I wanted to carry the man I love inside me. I love you!"

"But if you don't want to marry me, why did this have to happen?" He asked searching for the truth in my eyes.

"I do want to marry you. Just not right this second." I said through tears.

"Why?"

"Just because" I said

"You know I hate that. Because what?" He said getting the maddest he's ever gotten with me before.

"David!" I pleaded.

"Amber! You're not making any sense!"

"Baby! I know! I just need you to understand...." It felt like my wind was taken from me. A big contraction hit me. I bent over holding my stomach.

David's eyes got big as he rushed to me. I started breathing as it started calming down. David asked if I was ok, I shook my head yes. Just then I remembered why I wasn't in a hurry to have another baby. I got scared knowing those pains were going to come back. David threw his hands up and said we didn't have to discuss this right now. That night once every two hours I would have a big contraction. About eight am my contractions went away and I was good for the rest of the day. David's family came over in droves bringing food and cakes.

I talked to Jade over the phone. I finally told her about the baby and everything. She cried with me over the phone.

Nana came over; she asked me why I didn't tell her about the baby. I told her I moved impulsively, and then I was embarrassed. She said there was nothing I couldn't tell her. I told her what Uncle Frank said when I went to him for help. She told me she knew about that, her eyes were sad. Then she laughed and said I definitely took a different route.

She asked where my car was. I told her it wouldn't start at the shop. She went downstairs and told David she and I were going to get a new car, she asked him if he wanted to come. He came upstairs and asked me if I wanted him to go, he didn't look enthused about going. I told him I wanted him to go if he wanted to. Then he said he and Andrew were gonna go play basketball. When I got in the car, I started crying hysterically. I told Nana he was going to leave me. She put her hand on mine and said that was for the best. That wasn't what I wanted to hear. I wanted to hear that we were going to be together forever, that I would get to spend my life with the man who gave me everything I needed. Nana asked me if I wanted him to live or die? Of course I wanted him to live. She said as long as he stayed with me he had a target on his back. She asked me how did I think he'd respond to being rejected? I didn't know, she said every man has his limits. She said right now he's sweet as pie, but it wouldn't last in these circumstances. She said either way he was gonna have to leave.

****

I was down on my knees cleaning the kitchen floor busying myself, when another contraction hit me. The doctor said it was gonna happen any day now. I had been having sporadic contractions all day. I told myself to breathe through it, and I tried but I really wanted to tense up. That one was so big I was instantly covered in sweat. When it was over I stood up and before I could take two steps there was another contraction. I stood there trying to catch my breath. My hand was shaking as I reached for the phone. Andrew ran inside like he was coming for some water. He stopped in his tracks when he saw me. He asked me if I was ok? I told him I needed to get to the hospital. He didn't panic; he picked up the phone and called my Momma. "Hi Grand Momma, I think my momma's ready to have the baby." He said calmly, but his face conveyed his true feelings. "Ok I will, David went to the store. Ok. Ok." He said. Then he looked at me. He put my arm around him as if his little body could support me. He made me laugh. He led me to the couch. Momma was there just as I sat down. Andrew ran upstairs and brought my hospital bag down. Momma asked if my water broke yet and I told her no. She led me to the car. She was squinting; I asked her if she was ok. She said she was laying down when Andy called. When we got to the hospital Momma gave them my name and she told them my fiancée would arrive shortly. These contractions hurt worse than I remembered. When the doctor checked me he told me I was completely dilated. My water broke right after that. David came flying in the room. Momma went out in the waiting room with Andrew. They told me to push, and four good pushes later the baby was out. "Congratulations it's a boy!" They laid the baby on my chest. David was excited, but I could tell he wasn't completely happy. I was happy that it was over faster this time. But I was on fire and they were stitching me up again. Seven pounds even and twenty-two inches. Once I was cleaned up they moved me to my shared room and then Momma brought Andrew in to see his little brother. Andrew asked what his name was. David said Derrick, I looked at him cause we had discussed naming the baby David jr. if he was a boy. He looked at me with sad eyes, but I didn't say anything. Derrick was fine.

Chapter 28

Malachi was so surprised when he came home to find me with a baby. With everything happening so rapidly I didn't have it in me to tell him about the baby before he met him. Malachi kept asking why I didn't wait until after the wedding. When I finally broke down and explained everything, he said he wondered how Malcolm was handling all this. He felt sorry for me but again he had that "I told you so" look. I was getting so tired of that look or tone. None of that was helping me today. My whole world was falling apart and no one cared.

Derrick is totally different from Andrew. Andrew's basically one of the very few people who can make him smile and laugh out loud. The rest of the time he looks at people like he's trying to figure something out. He's not much of a crier either. There has to be something really wrong otherwise he doesn't cry.

When I took Andrew for his kindergarten shots, he said he wasn't gonna cry so he could show Derrick how to get shots. Then when I took Derrick to the doctors for his shots he never cried, but he did frown at the doctor like he wanted to get him. Derrick is a lot browner than Andrew, that's genetics for you. When it should be in reverse according to the complexions of their fathers. I keep snapping pictures of David and the boys. I keep looking at the pictures of us before the engagement and even just after. Sometimes I click my heels together hoping that would bring back the days when I could show my true feelings.

David has been quiet, and I could feel the breakup coming. He's been drinking more at night. Never to the point of sloppy drunk, but tipsy. And then his personality changes. He would switch from sweet and gentle to rude and rough. That's when the arguments would happen. It didn't even really have to be about something important or meaningful. The arguments would get so bad that he's even pushed me a couple times. Fortunately Andrew was at Nana's or fast asleep, whenever David would start drinking. So to avoid arguments I've started going to bed when Andrew does. A couple times I wasn't sleep when he came in my room but I pretended to be. We haven't slept in the same bed since the baby was born. When David looks at me all I see is pain on his face. I keep bracing myself for the out of town trip that doesn't end.

****

"I love babies!" Rosalind said kissing Derrick.

"Are you and Ben gonna have anymore?" I asked with my feet up.

Rosalind said she didn't think it was possible. She said she thinks Ben was seeing someone on the base. She started crying; she said she couldn't care about it anymore. She said at first she was fighting for Benjamin and their family. Then she sighed, she said when she suggested that she come home to get her footing almost two years ago she pretty much knew then that it was useless to fight to hold on. She said his calls home have become less and less. She said Tanisha used to cry for her daddy, but now she doesn't even get happy when he calls. Ben's family still remains very involved in Tanisha's life, but sometimes that isn't enough.

When the knock hit the door my heart sped up. David answered the door; he stood to the side so that Malcolm could enter. They acknowledged each other, but neither one of them spoke to the other. Rosalind waved hello to Malcolm while holding the baby. Malcolm came over to get a closer look. He had no expression as he looked at Derrick, at that moment I wished I could read his mind. David called Andrew downstairs. Little Miss Sasha came down first. She had her hands on her hips as usual. When she saw Malcolm, she paused in her spot. His face was serious as usual, and Sasha's sass was no match for his demeanor. Sasha ran over to me and laid her head on my shoulder, her little heart was beating so fast. Malcolm didn't say boo or anything, just looking at him had her scared. Tanisha and Andrew came down together. Tanisha had met Malcolm before at the shop so she had no reaction to him, not that our little soldier would've had one if she hadn't. Andrew was dressed in his Raider gear that Malcolm had bought for him. They looked like two billboard posters for the Oakland Raiders. Andrew hugged me and David goodbye then he walked out the door with his little hands in his pockets behind Malcolm. Malcolm was taking Andrew to his first Raider game. They had a box and Andrew was going to meet a lot of Malcolm's family. David said he was going to his parent's, and he left without kissing me goodbye or anything. I tried to put on a I don't care face, but Rosalind knew better. When she reached out to touch my hand the tears just fell. I did not want Malcolm; all he ever did was break my heart. David was a good man, and it hurt me to be forced to hurt him like this. I took a deep breath, and then I handed Rosalind the keys to my car I asked her to go get boxes for me. It was time to pack up David's things. She asked me if I was sure and I told her yes. Rosalind took the girls with her; I took the baby with me upstairs. I told myself to suck it up and do what had to be done. I took all his things out the drawers. Every time I felt myself breaking down I told myself to suck it up. I looked at Derrick and he just laid there watching me move quickly. I folded David's clothes in the closet. When Rosalind came back I had majority of his things packed and by the door. I asked them to put that stuff in boxes. I had all his things packed in no time. When Sophia and Richard came to get Sasha, Sophia asked me if I was moving. I shook my head no. She hugged me and asked if I needed her to stay with me. I shook my head no. She told me she would be right next door if I needed her. As Rosalind and I were saying goodbye David walked in the door. He had been drinking, I instantly knew this wasn't going to end well. Rosalind hurried Tanisha out the door.

David looked at the boxes then he looked at me with disgust in his face. It hurt to see him look at me like that. He stood there looking at me; I could tell he was wrestling with himself. Then he told me he should've never fooled his self to believe that I actually cared about him. I stopped myself from telling him the truth. I stood there staring at him. Derrick was sleep on the couch. David pointed at Derrick and asked me if I was going to stop him from seeing his boys? I shook my head no. Then he got mad and asked me why I wasn't talking to him. I shrugged, but I didn't want to beg him to stay so I kept quiet. Before I realized what he was doing he rushed me and slammed me into the wall. The wall felt like cement behind me, I was in shock. Then he slapped me HARD! He was screaming and crying the whole time. I knew this was all my fault, so I didn't scream. I just stayed on the floor holding my face. As if he was someone else when he hit me, and now he was back to his self, he looked at me in complete surprise. That made two of us, I never thought of my gentle giant as someone who would ever strike me. He started apologizing immediately, he tried to help me up, but I wouldn't let him touch me. That didn't just happen I kept telling myself. I got up and opened the door, I started throwing boxes. He kept flickering between personalities; I could see him fighting with his self. But I didn't care, if he hit me again the shock value was gone and I would have to defend myself. Once all his boxes were out I screamed at him to get out! Sophia and Richard came to the door. The Cheng's asked me if I was ok. Sophia was watching at first but then she rushed over to me and asked me what was wrong with my face. I ran to the bathroom with her on my heels. I looked in the mirror and my cheek was bruised, he must've hit me harder than I realized. Sophia started to go off and run to the door. I beat her to the door and put my now tender back against it. I begged her to calm down. She was irate and she couldn't understand why I was stopping her. I told her I fell while we were arguing. I told her I jumped on him and while he was getting me off I fell and hit my face on the stair. She looked at me like that was the dumbest lie she ever heard. I told her who would lie about something so dumb, I told her it was the truth, and I begged her not to tell ANYONE! I could tell she didn't want to believe me or agree but she did. I asked her if she had any witch hazel. She went to her apartment to go get it I tried to look at my back in the mirror, but when I heard her coming back through the door she was still mad. She said he was gone.

When Malcolm brought Andrew home, I had my hair down on the right side of my face and I kept him on my left. I was bouncing the baby on my right. I ask Andrew if he had fun and he said a calm yes. Malcolm looked at Derrick and I, he reached out and touched Derrick's hand. Then he asked me where David was. I shrugged and said he wasn't home. Then he asked me when I was coming back to work. I told him I wanted to take Andy to and from school his first week of school. And I wanted to get settled in my own classes first. He knew I wasn't in a hurry to be around him, so he smiled at me and said that was fine and to let him know when I was ready.

****

Sophia and I took all the kids to school then she and I went out to breakfast. She was telling me a funny story about something Sasha said to Richard when a woman walked up to our table. She very rudely interrupted our conversation asking if my name was Amber. My hand started flexing, I asked who wanted to know. She started getting loud and I couldn't understand what she was talking about. Sophia got up and asked her what her problem was, but the woman just kept going on and on but I couldn't understand what she was talking about. I scanned the restaurant trying to figure out where this woman came from. That's when I spotted Momma Shuga who looked pissed off. Remembering what Malcolm said about her I stood up. Derrick was in a high chair next to me at the end of the table I felt completely vulnerable because she was by my baby. I doubt this woman was supposed to be doing all this talking. Our waiter came rushing over trying to defuse the situation. The woman huffed back to Momma Shuga's table wiggling her neck and waving her hands. The look on Momma Shuga's face told me that did not happen the way she wanted it to. We paid our check and then we walked out the restaurant. I held on to Derrick, as I didn't know if she had somebody outside or what. Sophia was beyond livid and trying to take in what I was telling her. I was telling her to be cool cause we could be walking out into a set up. When we stepped into the parking lot Fuzzy was there. He said "hey cousin!" As he gave me a big hug. My heart kind of sped up cause I hadn't seen Fuzzy in a long time. We never had any problems, but I wasn't sure if his resolve had changed on account of the fact that Momma Shuga was his grandmother. He had the biggest smile on his face as he said hi to the baby who looked at him. Then he waved hello to Sophia. I looked around to see if anyone else was around. Fuzzy looked at my face and asked me what was wrong. I pointed at the door and all I could say was Momma Shuga. That woman walked out and Fuzzy said, "Pam?" The woman stopped then she recognized Fuzzy. Fuzzy moved me to the side then walked to meet her. He pulled out his walkie-talkie, and he said "Pam's here". She frowned looking at Fuzzy's walkie-talkie; she asked him who he was talking to. He didn't answer her question; he asked her when she got out. She tried to ignore him and walk towards us. Fuzzy grabbed her by the waist and asked her where she was going. She got mad at him and started yelling talking about her momma told her to do something. He picked her up and wouldn't put her down. Momma Shuga came out of the restaurant yelling at Fuzzy to put Pam down. Someone was asking Fuzzy a question over the walkie-talkie, but he couldn't answer because he had Pam in his arms and she wasn't a small woman. Fuzzy was trying to stop both of them from coming. I handed the baby to Sophia and I told her to take him to the car. Sophia started to argue with me cause she didn't want to leave me; both of those women were bigger than me. I told her I needed her to take the baby and my stuff, I was preparing myself for whatever was coming next. Sophia backed away slowly with Derrick but I know she didn't want to. I could tell Fuzzy was trying to decide which one was the lesser of two evils. Pam was kicking and screaming trying to get loose. And finally Momma Shuga came around him and she started coming at me. I could not believe this old woman was coming to fight me. I almost thought I couldn't fight her, but she was coming so I had to. The person on the walkie-talkie kept asking questions but Fuzzy couldn't reach around to his back pocket. As Momma Shuga came at me I prepared to hit her as hard as I could in the face. I remembered how that stunned her when Momma did it. When she stepped inside my circle I swung but she ducked, I missed, then she picked me up by my legs and threw me on the trunk of my car. That knocked the wind out of me. When she stood up I kicked her, which made her stumble back, and I rolled off the car. I was trying to catch my breath, but my back hurt and then my adrenaline kicked in. She grabbed me by my hair and started pulling with all her might. It seemed like all sound disappeared and I was moving in slow motion while everyone else moved normal. Sophia sucker punched her in the eye, and she released my hair to grab her eye. I couldn't hear anything but I was beyond mad when I saw some of my hair in her hands. I charged at her determined not to miss again, she tried to duck again but I was aiming lower so my fist still connected with her face. I could see movement happening around me but all I could see was red, this woman not only threatened me with my baby, my hair was on the ground. I kept hitting her; she kicked me in the stomach after she fell. I was about to dive on her when Juan caught me by the arm and spun me around. I almost fell, but I caught the car to balance myself. Juan picked Momma Shuga up by grabbing her shirt. He did that effortlessly, and then he kneed her in the stomach and slapped the mess out of her. Pam started screaming at Fuzzy asking him why he was letting him do that to his grandmother. Fuzzy looked upset but he didn't respond. Momma Shuga's lip was busted, and she looked crazy. The people in the restaurant were in the window all looking. Another car pulled up that I didn't recognize and Daddy got out the front passenger seat. He was mad and his face was stone, he walked over to Juan and he told him to go deal with "them" pointing at the restaurant. Juan let Momma Shuga go, she stood still as Daddy approached her. Daddy looked me up and down then he looked at the hair blowing on the ground. "Barb!" He grabbed his composure then he started again. "We've been looking for you! I was actually lobbying to save your life. But you don't respect what's mine!" Momma Shuga started to say something and Daddy growled at her. Pam was yelling to her momma asking her who Daddy was, but Momma Shuga was stuck. Daddy told Fuzzy to let Pam go. Then he told Pam if she knew what was good for her she'd stay over there. Pam stood there staring at Momma Shuga while she stood there visibly shaking. Juan came out and gave Daddy a thumbs up. Daddy asked Fuzzy who Pam was. Fuzzy said she was Malcolm's mother. My neck whipped over at her. I had never even seen a picture of her. She looked like once upon a time she could've been pretty, but life had dealt her such an ugly hand that she was hard and bitter. I could see Malcolm had her nose and eyes, but she wasn't as dark as him. She was a chocolate brown, but her complexion was dull and lifeless. Daddy asked Fuzzy does she go with Momma Shuga? Fuzzy hesitated, Daddy growled and asked again. Fuzzy exhaled hard as he shook his head yes. Pam started screaming asking where she was going. Juan said something to her, and she started crying saying she didn't want to go. Momma Shuga started talking real fast, she was telling Daddy there had to be something that they could agree on. Daddy looked disgusted, "Barb! Don't make me!" He barked. Fuzzy pulled Pam towards Juan's car, she was pleading and screaming. Daddy walked away from Momma Shuga he asked me if I was ok. I shook my head yes then he turned me around. He started moving my hair around. I felt the cool morning air hit my scalp in the middle of my head. I heard daddy telling her to get in the car his voice was angry. He asked Fuzzy what happened. Fuzzy stammered saying seeing Pam caught him off guard. Daddy told Sophia to take Derrick to my Momma, stay there until it was time to pick up the kids. Daddy told me to come with him. Momma Shuga got in the car with Juan, Pam, and the driver. Daddy opened the back door to the car he rode in. I was surprised to see Uncle Jeff driving, this car wasn't his car. Uncle Jeff asked Daddy if I was ok. Daddy said yea, but he was mad. We went to the shop; Malcolm was talking to Chester when we walked in. He looked at Daddy and Uncle Jeff, and then he looked at me. He gestured towards his office and we all walked to it. Daddy sat in Malcolm's chair, Malcolm stood by the door. Daddy was trying to remain calm. Daddy told Malcolm that Juan had Momma Shuga and Pam. Malcolm frowned as he repeated "Pam?" Then he looked at me and asked what happened. I told him what happened, he nodded. Then he looked at Daddy and asked him if he was gonna make the call. Daddy took a deep breath like he was wrestling with himself. Malcolm walked over to Daddy; he put his hand on his shoulder. He picked up the phone, dialed a number, when the other person answered Malcolm said, "do it".

Chapter 29

I went to the bathroom, I looked in the mirror and my hair was all over my head. As I ran my fingers through my hair it was coming out. I closed my eyes and told myself to breathe. All my life women have made such a big deal about my hair; this was the first time I was making a big deal as well. I was yelling having a fit. Rosalind came running to the bathroom. I asked her for a comb. I took a deep breath and then I started combing. I looked at the hair on the floor and started cursing. Rosalind moved my hair around, she told me I was missing a few patches but the hair on the ground looked worse than it actually was. She started braiding my hair for me. Daddy came in the bathroom he asked me if I was ok. I exhaled and said I was going to be. Daddy asked Rosalind if she could give me a ride to his house when she was done. Of course she agreed. Daddy and Uncle Jeff left; I cleaned up the hair while Rosalind went back to her customer. When I came out the bathroom I looked out on the floor and everyone was working and it seemed like business as usual. I knocked on Malcolm's door, he didn't answer. I opened the door slowly; he was sitting back in his chair staring at the ceiling. I closed the door and I sat in the chair in front of his desk, I started turning my engagement ring as I fidgeted. He blew air; I didn't say anything I just sat there looking at him. Then he said he didn't even know she was out. Then there was a knock at the door. He lowered his eyes to the door and told the person to come in. Fuzzy came in and he was an emotional wreck. I jumped out the chair and I threw my arms around him. Big ole Fuzzy broke down in my arms. I couldn't help but cry with him. I thanked him for protecting me. He squeezed me and cried harder. Malcolm sat there watching us looking annoyed. After he had enough he told Fuzzy to take his hands off me. Fuzzy put his hands in the air as if he was surrendering, and I slowly released him. I wiped the tears from his eyes, and I kissed his cheek. Malcolm asked Fuzzy what he wanted besides getting on his nerves. "I'm out man! I need a break." Fuzzy said

Malcolm blank stared at Fuzzy. "You know how she is."

"Which one?" Fuzzy asked

"Take your pick, both of them are on the same level."

Fuzzy was trying to compose himself. "But she ain't done nothing." He was talking about Pam.

Malcolm looked at Fuzzy irritated. "Blindly listening to her mother is what got her locked up in the first place. Look at where she was, what she was doing."

Fuzzy shook his head. "I know man, but she didn't know what she was doing."

Malcolm looked at me then at Fuzzy, "so you tell me."

Fuzzy shook his head. "I know, I know." He exhaled, "that's why I told them to take her." Tears leaked from his eyes. "I need some time."

Malcolm nodded at him, but you could tell he viewed his tears as weakness. "It's a waste of time crying over someone who could care less about you."

Fuzzy wiped his face. "I ain't crying. My eyes are leaking." Fuzzy said trying to make a joke.

"Juan's gonna call you. After it's done you can go for as long as you need."

Fuzzy thanked him then he slipped back out the door.

"Are you ok?" I asked

Malcolm looked me in my eyes. "Of course I am, why wouldn't I be?"

"This is a lot to have happened in the course of one morning." I said

"We've been looking for Momma Shuga for a minute now. Everything has been set up we just needed her." Malcolm said in a matter of fact way, with his eyes still locked on me.

"Do I even wanna know what that means?"

"Immediate death is too good for her. Your Poppa set it up, she's going to prison for the rest of her life however long that may be." Malcolm shrugged, "that's not the way I would've handled it. But Poppa's the boss."

"What about Pam?"

"What about her?"

"She's going too?"

"I don't know, don't care." He said nonchalantly.

"You care Malcolm."

He sat there quiet for a minute. "Where's David been?"

I sat back down. "Working." I said turning my ring again.

"Yea, but he hasn't been coming home to you. Trouble in paradise?" He smirked

I rolled my eyes, "I don't want to talk about it".

"Oh come on Amber, tell me how great he is one more time." He said mocking me.

"He is great! I love him very much, I still want to be his wife." I said defensively.

"Whatever Amber. Nobody is perfect, and with the way he's been throwing them back. I bet you're starting to see the other side." I couldn't say anything to that. "When are you coming to me?"

I sucked my teeth. "That's not why I came in here."

"Did you think you were going to have some kind of emotional conversation with me? Then you wouldn't feel guilty about giving in? I've been waiting, but my patience is growing thin."

"You want me to want it don't you?" I shifted in my chair. I couldn't even believe I was having this conversation or that, that easy my body started throbbing at the thought of it. "I need more time."

"You really like playing this cat and mouse game don't you. I don't care about what you're going through with David. He's irrelevant to me. Don't sit there and lie to me telling me you don't want me. You've wanted me this whole time. I bet you're over there swimming in your panties trying to act like you don't want me." I looked at him with a question mark on my face. "You're body is tuned to my station, I know you."

"I'm still with David." I said in a defeated tone, "I love him."

Malcolm exhaled walked around the table. He bent down in my face, "not like you used to. But ask me if I care about your little crush. You love me!" Then he stood me up, "and it's time for you to show me."

I felt defeated anyways, so why care any more. My body seemed to have a mind of its own anyways. Then Rosalind knocked on the door. She said she was going to lunch and she could drop me off. I told her I would be right out. Malcolm looked like he wanted to kiss me, but he didn't. I backed away from him, and I walked out. I told Sophia and Momma what happened with Daddy at the shop. Momma kept saying she should've went with us to breakfast. We picked up Andrew and Sasha from their first day of kindergarten. We took lots of pictures of them and made a big fuss about it. When little Jeff and JoJo got out of school, we took them all to Bob's for a after school snack. The kids were so happy. Then we drilled them about the route they would walk to school everyday once the first week was over. Little Jeff was very serious about his responsibility of watching over everyone. JoJo liked the idea of being second in command.

That evening I kept zoning out. I wondered what David was doing, how different our lives would be if Malcolm didn't care. I wasn't mad at him for hitting me. I know he didn't mean it. He just felt out of control in that moment, if I didn't see it coming I know he didn't know he was about to do it, right? Andrew asked me when David was coming home. I told him that David loved him very much but he didn't live with us anymore. Andrew's eyes were very sad, he asked why. I told him it was my fault, but as soon as I could I was gonna fix it and we'd be a family under one roof again.

Sophia had an early appointment so I took all the kids to school. I thought about going over Momma's house. But I decided to go home, Derrick was knocked out. As I laid him in his crib there was a knock at the door. I knew who it was by the knock. I took a deep breath; I didn't have any more fight left in me. I opened the door and Malcolm walked in. I locked the door and walked up the stairs. When my foot hit the first stair, I was mad at my body for instantly being excited about what was about to happen. I tried not to show it on my face, or seem too eager. I barely got the door closed, before Malcolm was all over me. With that initial contact he looked me in my eyes and asked me what his name was. I forgot how deep he went, I gasped and said "Malcolm". Clearly I had forgotten what being with Malcolm was like. I didn't have to ask for anything, or give permission. He knew what I wanted before I realized I wanted it. He kept asking me what his name was. Every time I uttered his name he'd down shift on me, OH MY GOD!!! It was so insane, so passionate, so fulfilling that I fell asleep from exhaustion afterwards. I woke up to him reviving the fire in me that I thought he just put out. I couldn't pretend like I didn't love this, or him. I laid there completely speechless. My mouth and throat were completely dry. Malcolm laughed at my completely surprised expression. Then he told me not to ever choose someone else over him again then he stared at my ring.

"Malcolm can we please have a moment of truth?"

He looked at me then he sat up. "Ok, shoot."

I didn't know where to begin, but he sat there patiently waiting. "You took Andy to a football game. That was great, but please don't stop there. He doesn't know you like he knows David." Malcolm nodded. "I don't love you like I love David."

He looked at me, "you may actually love David. He seems like a good guy, family man and all that. But he's not nor could he ever be me. He may have the market cornered on the family stuff, but you need more than just that."

"You're saying I don't want a family guy?"

"I'm saying you want me. You were happy with me until the other females. You don't mind the lifestyle, and you would end up bored stiff with David. I waited for you. Didn't touch anyone else until I touched you. I'm too young to promise you it would even stay this way. You're my Queen Amber. But you gotta get him out of your system. And I got some things to get out of mine."

"Every testimony hurt Malcolm. I had to sit there next to my Daddy listening to female after female confirm what I finally come to terms with. You can't love me like you say you do. You say whatever you want about David, but I was enough for him. He loves me, and he treated me good."

"But was he enough for you?"

"I love David." I said defensively

"Answer the question Amber."

"I thought he was."

Then he kissed me, "but now you know better. I hope you get him out of your system soon for his sake."

"What does that mean?"

"That when I'm ready for all of you, I will have all of you again no matter what."
"I hate when you make it seem like I don't have a choice. I don't have to choose you."
"You already did, you just don't understand why."
****
"How was basketball?" I asked
"GREAT!" Andy said
"If it's ok with you, I want to take the boys to the beach before it gets too cold."
David said trying not to look at me. As if his whole resolve would melt if he looked at me.
"Of course that's ok." I said with a smile.
"You have plans tomorrow? I gotta drive to San Luis Obispo Monday morning, so I'd like to go early, if that's ok." He said still not looking at me.
"No plans, that's fine." I said
"You could come too, but only if you want to." He glanced at me to see my reaction.
Andrew got so excited. He started jumping in place showing his approval and anticipation of my yes. "I would love to." I said
David looked surprised by my acceptance of his invitation. His presence became more energetic. "Ok, I'll come at 8 so we can have breakfast before we head to the city."
"Sounds like a plan." I said reaching out to hug him.
David seemed awkward like he was in the beginning when we first started dating.
"Why are you going home? How come you don't sleepover?" Andrew asked
David looked embarrassed and like Andrew put him on the spot. "Um.... I don't think your momma wants that." He said still searching for a better answer.
Andrew got excited. "She doesn't care! Do you momma?"
"You guys could have a sleepover on the floor." I said
David stood there. "Only if it's ok with you."
"David it's fine. The boys miss you."
"Momma tell him you miss him too." Andrew said with a smile.
"Andy!" I said totally shocked.
"She cries to Sophia all the time telling her how much she misses you." Andrew said like he did his good deed of the week.
"Andy! It's not your place to repeat ANYTHING you hear me talking to another grown up about."
David gave me a busted smile. "Give me five Andrew." Andrew gave him five. "My man!"
Now that I was embarrassed I walked away. I just didn't know where I was going. I started towards the stairs then I went to the kitchen in the opposite direction. "I need to get clothes, is it ok if Andrew comes with me?"
"It's fine," I said.
I picked up Derrick who clearly wanted to go too. And we waved goodbye. About fifteen minutes later my phone rang. It was Malcolm he asked what I was doing, I told him I was making dinner. Then he asked me why Andrew left my house with David. I told him they went to run and errand and they would be right back.
Malcolm sounded annoyed, but I ignored it. I asked him what he was doing and he said missing me. I pretended to gag, I told him he was never cheesy like that and it was too late to start now. He laughed, and then he said he wanted to see me. I told him it was kind of impossible right now and that he needed to call one of his stand

ins. He said he wanted the real thing. Then I said the wrong thing. I told him my man was coming back, so I couldn't entertain him. Malcolm lost it and started screaming into the phone, "DON'T YOU EVER IN YOUR LIFE PLACE ME AS SECOND BEST TO THAT IDIOT!"

I sat there quiet for a minute not knowing how to respond. "What do you want me to say?"

"That you will be here in a hour!"

"Malcolm I can't do that." Then I took a breath. "Even if I wanted to, I have kids I can't just fly out of here whenever you want."

"We'll see about that." He said irritated.

"Malcolm I've always asked of you what you ask of me. I can't show up to your house expecting you to drop whomever just because I want you."

"Yes you can!" He started laughing. "Doesn't matter who the stand in is."

I smiled, "I'm gonna hold you to that." Then I told him I had to go.

When Andrew and David came back we had dinner like we used to, at the table like a family. I gave them blankets and pillows and then I went upstairs. I was working on homework when David came upstairs. He knocked on my door. I didn't know whether I should cover up or not. I only had on a big nightshirt. I told him to enter; I was sitting on my bed with my back against the headboard. First thing I looked for was whether he was sober or not. I was relieved to see clarity on his face. His eyes went up my body from my bare feet, legs, t-shirt, and then face. He thanked me for letting him stay. I told him he did me a favor cause he gave me more time to study. He told me the kids were sleep then he asked how my classes were going, and then how I had been. I told him classes were fine. And that I had been best as could be expected. I asked how he's been. He said he's been horrible. He said he didn't understand why we broke up exactly. I didn't exactly realize we broke up, but I didn't mention it. Cause how could I justify sleeping with Malcolm if we were still together? I said that it was my fault for changing the plan. Then he asked why I still wore my ring? I touched my finger, and I told him that the man who gave me this ring gave it to me with all his heart. I told him that made me feel more loved than any man has ever made me feel. I said whenever I look at that ring I remember the love he showed. David sat there speechless for a minute. Then he apologized for hitting me. I didn't say anything, I didn't want him thinking it was ok or that I was ok with it, I just looked at him. I told him I had to get back to my homework. He stood up and then he asked how Malcolm was doing. I told him not to ask questions he couldn't handle the answer to. He frowned and asked what that meant. I told him he always falls apart when Malcolm comes up. Then he came over and gave me a gentle but passionate kiss.

In the morning we had breakfast at Merritt bakery. I saw guys walking around with walkie-talkies. I didn't recognize any of them, but David and the boys were blissfully unaware.

We had a good time at the beach, running around in the sand. We tried to build a sand castle, but we didn't go far enough in to escape the tide, and or building skills were horrible. Andrew and Derrick had fun stomping the castle as the ocean water erased it. David snapped pictures all day of all of us. He even had who he thought was a stranger snap a picture of us. Juan told David he had a lovely family. David stood there all prideful as he said thank you. I shook my head at Juan as he engaged David in conversation. On the way home David held my hand like he always used to. I looked back at Andrew who had a huge smile on his face as he looked at our hands. We brought a pizza home and I left them to their visit while I got some last minute homework in. At bedtime I bathed both of the boys who seemed so happy about the day. They said good night to David and then they went to bed. David and I straightened up, and then I walked him to the door. He told me he missed me, and how he had such a wonderful day. I told him I enjoyed the day as well, but I had to get back to studying. He put everything he could into his kiss goodbye. He told me he wanted to get back together. I kind of liked living alone, so I told him we could talk about it. He kept kissing me and hugging me. Then we heard someone clear their throat. When we both turned around it was Malcolm. He had a briefcase in his hand. He pretended to apologize for interrupting. I asked what he was doing here. He held up the bag and stared at David. David looked so irritated; he asked Malcolm why didn't he call first. Malcolm stood there looking at him. I knew that look, I told David to go and to call me when he got back. Malcolm walked past me and went inside. I watched David walk out to his car. Then I shut the door, I was irritated with Malcolm. I asked him why he did that. He didn't care; he took out the books from the shop. Then David knocked on the door. I begged Malcolm to be cool, Malcolm agreed to nothing. I opened the door; David said he forgot something upstairs. He went upstairs and Malcolm looked annoyed by his interruption. David came down with his work jacket; he kissed my cheek and told me he would call me. Malcolm sat at the table, when I closed the door he told me to come over. My body started responding to what wasn't even indicated yet. I stood next to Malcolm, and he tapped his lap and he told me to sit on it. I sat on his leg, and then one hand went under my shirt while the other pointed out the small salary I had or at least that's what he was calling it. He said I wasn't getting paid enough. Then he asked what we were going to do about that. He started kissing my stomach. I told him we couldn't do it down here cause Andrew could come down. So he said lets focus on business, although his hands stayed all over my body. He showed me potential locations for the next shop. He showed me his business plan according to the demographics of each location. Everything he had was very impressive. After going back and forth he decided on a Richmond location. He said he'd hang on to the other locations as potential future locations. There were two other Oakland locations, and three Berkeley. He mentioned San Francisco and I started stammering. He rubbed my back and said it was ok. Then he asked me how I was able to go to the beach etc. I told him every time I cross the bridge I get really nervous. I told him that since we only ever stay on the Golden Gate Park side I'm ok once we get there. He asked me if David knew anything about all that and I told him no. I told him I didn't tell him much about my family except the basic information. He asked me how long I was going to keep stringing David a long. I told him I wanted to marry David. He stopped touching me, he looked irritated. He asked me why I wanted to marry David but not him. I told him it was very simple, David was a good father, and for me he didn't ask for anything from me that I wasn't getting from him. Malcolm huffed, and then he stood up. He started to say something then he pulled it back. Then the phone rang I got up to answer it, it was David. Malcolm told me to tell him I would call him back cause we were discussing business. When I hung up the phone, Malcolm took it off the hook. He sat on the couch and asked himself what he was gonna do with me. I told him there was nothing for him to do with me; I did not belong to him. Then we got into the petty argument of "no I don't!" And "yes you do!" We were going back and forth like kids. I started yawning, and he asked me if I had classes tomorrow. I told him I had one in the morning, and then I picked Andrew and Sasha up before I went running. He smiled, and told me he didn't know I still did that. He told me he wanted to go. I said that was fine then I asked him why the walkie-talkie men were following me again. He said "Momma Shuga is a ignorant somebody!" He said there's some things going on that have to be dealt with. He exhaled; meanwhile they need to make sure we were safe. He said Juan was so good at his job that he has complete confidence in him, and that's why he's on me most times.

When we pulled in front of Troy's apartment, I had a flashback of Leonard sitting there waiting for me daily. My eyes watered up for a moment. I missed him, and I wondered how Fuzzy was doing. Andrew looked out the window with no expression, he asked me why this place looked familiar, and I told him we used to live there. I could see his brain computing things. Malcolm walked out the building and Sasha gasped. Andrew asked her why she always did that and she said because Malcolm was scary to her. Andrew said no he's not, I was happy to hear Andrew say that. Malcolm said, "Drew! Sasha! Hello." They both said hi, then Malcolm kissed my cheek. Sasha gasped again, Andrew was not happy about that. When we got to the field Andrew and Sasha stretched with me. Malcolm watched me bend over more than he stretched. I had Andrew and Sasha warm up like Tag used to do with me before we began our runs. Then we ran, Andrew was a lot faster than Sasha so I always hung back with her. Andrew would finish and then go to the water fountain. When Sasha and I finished our four laps we stopped for water as well. Malcolm told Andrew he was pretty fast, Andrew smiled. Then Malcolm told him to race him. I knew it wasn't a fair challenge, but I said nothing. Sasha told them to go, Andrew took off like a bullet. Malcolm stayed on his side, then when they were half way through the lap Malcolm left Andrew in his dust. Andrew kept running hard until he finished. I told Andrew he did a good job, and I was proud of him. Malcolm told him to try to beat him next time. Andrew got mad and said he did. Malcolm told him to catch his breath and then they'd try it again.

Andrew said he was ready they got on the field, Sasha told them to go. Andrew took off like a bullet again, you could tell his little body was giving it all he had. Malcolm stayed by his side and as soon as they hit the half way point Malcolm left him behind again. Malcolm asked him why he beat him. Andrew said it was because Malcolm was bigger than him. Malcolm told him size wasn't everything. He said that Andrew was so focused on winning that he forgot to check his opponent's abilities. When I hugged Andrew and told him I was still proud of him. Malcolm told me not to encourage him to settle for second best. Then our argument started, he said I've been babying Andrew since he was born. He said if I keep babying him like I do he wasn't gonna be a man capable of handling anything. I told him I didn't want my son being hard and desensitized like he was. I told him I wasn't trying to raise a thug, I wanted a man. Sasha was nervous, I told Andrew to take her to the side while Malcolm and I fussed. Andrew comforted Sasha telling her it was ok and not to cry. Malcolm watched them, and then he blew air. We argued for a good hour back and forth. He was so set on being right so I gave up. He gave me a funny look when I gave in. Then we argued about me giving in, he said I was changing and he didn't like that.

****

Sophia and I checked ourselves in the mirror. I had butterflies in my stomach, my first club in years. After lots of convincing Sophia convinced me to go out especially since it was now legal for us to actually be in the club. She convinced Cassondra to come watch the kids for us. Cassondra and Rosalind were downstairs catching up. We were going to meet David and Richard at a club in Berkeley. When we came down stairs the three of us posed for pictures. Then we took pictures with and of the kids. Then the three of us piled into Sophia's car and we were off. We waited in line to get in the club. When we got to the door the bouncer hollered "OH YES JESUS YES! WE ARE BLESSED TONIGHT!" Everyone laughed; the bouncer pushed us through and told us we didn't have to pay the cover charge. We were excited. We found a table towards the back. David and Richard joined us shortly. David and Richard left to get us drinks; Sophia and I said at the same time that we'd have the house special. We laughed at our inside joke. When they returned we downed our drinks, a guy asked Rosalind to dance so she was off. Sophia and Richard took off to the dance floor. I asked David if he wanted to dance, and he said maybe next song. Then someone touched my shoulder. When I turned around I screamed as I thought I was seeing a ghost. It was Melvin. I popped out of my seat and threw my arms around his neck. I was so happy to see him. I introduced him to David. David didn't look impressed by Melvin, and Melvin gave him the same look. Then Melvin asked me if I could dance or if I was chained to the table. I asked David if he mind, but I admit the way I asked him I didn't really give him the space to say no. Melvin and I went on the dance floor, and Sophia and Richard said hey to him as well. Melvin and I danced song after song together. Melvin still had it, and he and I danced so well together still. When we went back to the table there were fresh drinks for everyone. I asked David if he bought the drinks and he said no. I knew that meant Malcolm was somewhere in the club, but I couldn't spot him. I asked Melvin to dance with Rosalind as I sat there feeling a little uncomfortable. David looked angry; he asked me who Melvin was. I explained that he was my dance partner in high school, and that he was just a friend. David didn't seem convinced. I downed my drink then I asked David to dance. David refused, as he sat there drinking his drink and brewing. I told him I didn't come out to sit around; if he wasn't gonna dance he should've stayed home with the kids. That statement didn't help him get out of his funk. As I walked back to the dance floor, I saw Troy walking to meet me there. I asked him if Malcolm was here. He shook his head no and said not yet, but he was coming. I asked him if he bought the drinks, and he smiled and said you're welcome. We danced to a song, and then Rosalind started to walk past us to go back to the table. Troy grabbed her arm, he was drooling. He asked her where did her body come from. Rosalind blushed he asked her to dance, so I turned to walk away but Melvin was there his eyes locked on Troy. I asked him if he was ok. He said yes, I told him that Malcolm was coming, then I asked him if he was gonna be ok. He shook his head and said yes, and then we started dancing. After a few songs we went back to the table. A fresh drink was waiting, I promptly drank it. I asked David again to dance. I had to kind of beg him to get up. ANNOYING! I told myself I wasn't inviting him next time. Once he got on the dance floor he did loosen up some. Rosalind danced with Troy all night; I kept asking her if she was ok. She kept promising she was fine, but I was kind of worried. Troy isn't anything like Benjamin, and I didn't want her to get hurt. When David and I went back to the table I saw Malcolm sitting in the VIP section, and Yvette was sitting next to him. Both of their eyes were locked on me. I waved hello with a big smile then I continued to my table. I downed my drink and then Melvin snatched me up to go back out on the floor. When Malcolm saw Melvin he leaned forward. Melvin didn't notice Malcolm he was focused on me. This was all too overwhelming, but I decided to stop drinking so that I could make sure Rosalind was ok at the end of the night. Malcolm brought Yvette on the dance floor right next to us. She was fuming and she kept looking at Malcolm like what was he doing. When Melvin noticed Malcolm, he stopped in his place. I asked Melvin if he was ok, he shook his head yes. Then Malcolm reached out to shake Melvin's hand. Then Malcolm pushed Yvette to Melvin and he pulled me towards him. Yvette looked so hurt as she reluctantly danced with Melvin while she shot me daggers. I asked Malcolm why he was starting mess, he smiled at me then he kissed me on the cheek. He said what everyone here needed to understand is that it's about me and him, everything else was nonessential. I looked back at David who wasn't looking, but he was drinking. I started getting a sinking feeling. I asked Malcolm to let Melvin leave without messing with him. Malcolm smiled and said he NEVER started it. He said Melvin always tried to flex at him. He promised me that he wouldn't do anything to Melvin as long as Melvin didn't try to flex. Then I told him I needed to get back to David. His grip got a little tighter, he told me not to start. I told him I didn't feel comfortable cause Yvette was still shooting me daggers and I didn't want David to see us. He told me not to worry about the inconsequential. I relaxed and enjoyed the dance. Melvin was having a good time with Yvette, but she was not happy. I could tell David was drunk without looking him in his face. I knew that meant he was going to be mean, and I didn't want to go home with him. They gave a last call at the bar; a lot of people went to the bar. Troy and Rosalind danced next to us; I asked Rosalind if she was ok. She had a very big smile as she said yes. Sophia and Richard were having a great time in their own world. When they called out last song of the night, Malcolm still wasn't letting me go. I asked him not to front Yvette off like this. He shrugged and said she needs to remember it's not about her. It didn't help that the last song was The lady in my life. Malcolm was feeling the song, and singing it in my ear. He said this was our song. I didn't say anything I was trying to keep the clarity needed to get Rosalind away from Troy. And then convince Richard why he needed to take David home. Malcolm kissed me at the end of the song. My heart sped up, and I pulled away from him. David still wasn't looking thank goodness. I grabbed Rosalind and pulled her off the dance floor and then we went to the table. Sure enough David was drunk. I asked Richard if he could drop David off at his house. Richard wanted to get Sophia home. So we were debating back and forth. Richard tossed me his keys and told me to take his car, and then he led Sophia out of the club. Melvin asked what was going on. I tried not to act uncomfortable as I told Melvin that David had drunken too much. Melvin volunteered to help us help David out. David was rambling about things I didn't understand. When we finally found Richard's car, I had Melvin put him in the back. Troy came over and asked Rosalind if she wanted to come with him for a nightcap. I didn't mean to scream "NO!" But I did. Everyone looked at me, I apologized, and then I told Rosalind I needed her to ride with me. Rosalind asked Troy for a rain check. He looked disappointed, but agreed. We gave Melvin a ride to his car; I gave Melvin my number I told him we needed to catch up. When I handed him my number he stared at my engagement ring.

David was in the back fussing about everything and me. He told Rosalind how I broke his heart, and I keep playing games with his emotions. When we got to his apartment he asked why we were at his house. I told him he needed to sober up before he came around the kids. He opened the back door. I put the car in park he opened the driver's side door and pulled me out by my hair. Rosalind hopped out the passenger side so fast. I put my hands out; I told her its ok. He's drunk he doesn't know what he's doing. She was ready to fire on him, but I kept telling her it was ok. I reached in his pocket and pulled out his keys. I asked him which one opened his front door. He started rubbing all over my body begging me to stay. I wanted to keep him calm until I got him inside. Rosalind started following us ready to fire on him if he grabbed me again. I asked her to go to the car. She argued with me I told her the key was still in the ignition and the last thing we needed was to get stranded in Richmond cause someone stole the car. She ran back to the car, but I knew she was coming back. I tried to find the key as fast as I could. The fourth key unlocked the door. He had a studio apartment; it looked like he tried on everything in his closet before he chose his outfit. I sat him on his bed. I put his keys in the cupboard in a bowl just in case he decided to try to leave. Rosalind was back in the doorway waiting. He barked at her and asked her what she wanted she rolled her eyes at him. Then he got irate accusing me of leaving him. I begged him to sit down. I started taking his shoes off when he hit me in the back of my shoulder, which made me fall. Rosalind flew in the apartment she hit him in the face, and he asked her what was wrong with her. She started yelling at him. I took his other shoe off. I made him look at me. I told him I was going to the bathroom and then I was gonna come back and do him up good. He smiled and then he closed his eyes. He said I did love him, and that statement hurt worse than my shoulder. I told him to lay down. He was snoring before his head hit the pillow. I locked the door and then I closed it. Rosalind was pissed; she asked me why I let him hit me. I told her he was drunk and didn't know what he was doing. She told me that in a drunken state a person's truth comes out. I made her promise not to say anything. I begged her, she wouldn't agree. She said when my Daddy finds out David's dead meat. I explained everything the whole story to her, even with all of that she said it wasn't right and I needed to open my eyes. Finally she let it go and told me she wouldn't say anything but she didn't like him anymore. I told her that was fair.

Chapter 30

"Little girl you need to take that sass somewhere! I've about had enough of you! You walk around here like you own the place. You may run them, but you don't run me!"

"Moses, you know your rent is due on the 1st, I've been letting you slide to the fifth. Today is the sixth! If you can't pay, pack up your stuff and get out!"

He got mad and acted like he was gonna charge at me. Chester opened the door and ran to the back to put his stuff down, he didn't see that anything was going on. Moses was still coming he didn't realize I already had Jason's razor behind my back if he got too close to me.

This man gets on my nerves, and I can't believe he's even trying to pull this on me. The door opened again as Leon and Rosalind walked in the door. Moses got in my face. "I'll pay you when I'm good and ready! There's nothing you or nobody else could do to change that! I run this shop!"

"Your delusions of supremacy continue to alter your perception of reality to the most amusing degree!"

Moses got mad at me, "SPEAK ENGLISH!!!!"

"Doesn't matter how I say it you will never get it! Now get out my face, pack your station and get out!" I said

"What is going on in here?" Rosalind asked taking my side.

"Moses you need to calm down before Malcolm finds out." Leon said

"Somebody needs to teach this little girl some respect! I'm sick of her BS, Roz if you wanna go down with her be my guest!"

Rico walked in the door, "Moses! Come on! It's too early in the morning for this." He said walking by

I fanned my nose, "somebody needs to give this fool a mint. His breath!"

Rosalind laughed which made him madder. He swung to slap me, Rosalind and I both moved to the side. I sliced his finger. Moses screamed right as Jason walked in the door. Moses raised his hand again, "MOSES YOU HAVE LOST YOUR MIND!" I didn't even see Jason move and he was in front of me so fast! "TODAY MUST BE A GOOD DAY TO DIE!"

"I'm tired of her!" Moses said

"Who cares what you're tired of! You know better, you always testing limits."

"Oh so you gonna let the white man run you too!"

"Moses you've got issues! What difference does it make what the color of your employer's skin is. You got a job man! Or at least you had one. Now if I have to tell you again it ain't gonna be pretty, BACK UP!" Moses was WAY taller than Jason, and clearly he was stupid enough to think this gave him an advantage. He swung like he was gonna clobber Jason, but Jason grabbed his arm and twisted it behind Moses. Still twisting his arm, he kicked him in the back of his leg, which made his knees buckle. Jason snatched the razor out of my hand and put it at Moses' throat. "The bigger they are the harder they fall you idiot!" No one said anything. "Roz, take Moses' cards give one to each of the customers outside waiting, tell them to bring that card back in an hour and I'll give them a free haircut. Apologize and tell them we have a mess we need to clean up in here. Make sure you lock the door when you come back. Amber, go call Malcolm and tell him it's time!" Rosalind and I did as we were told. When I came back on the floor Rosalind said she gave out six cards. Moses was red and the quietest I ever heard him be. Malcolm got there in no time. He sat in Moses' chair, then told Chester, Leon, and Rico to go take a walk and to come back in an hour. Malcolm told Jason to release Moses.

Moses shook his hand like it was going numb. Then Moses stood up, he looked at me. "Poison!" He shook his head, "white girls ain't nothing but poison!"
"She ain't..." Rosalind stood up to defend me.
I put my hand up. "It's ignorant people like you who are poison. I'm probably just as black as you are Moses, I know who I am and I don't have a problem with it. I love my Daddy dearly and I will not apologize for who I am! My skin isn't the issue, you are the problem! I've been trying to work with you, but you're always trying to get over!"
"What happened?" Malcolm asked. I told him about the rent. "Where's my money Moses?"
"Man! I'd rather deal with you than her. She..."
Malcolm put his hand up, he didn't wanna hear it. "I put her in charge, disrespecting her is disrespecting me. This is the last time I'm gonna ask you, where's my money?"
"I don't have it." Moses said matter of factly.
Malcolm glared at him. "You're fired Moses! Pack your stuff and go." Then Malcolm stood up, he told Jason to come with him. They went in the office and closed the door.
Moses walked over to his station mumbling under his breath. He took out his duffel bag and slammed all his personal belongings in it. He packed up his stuff in no time. Then he stood in the middle of the floor cursing me out from the top of my head to the bottom of my feet. I blew him kisses. Malcolm opened his door and asked him why he was so stupid. When Moses opened the door Rico, Chester, and Leon came back in. Malcolm told Rosalind to let the customers in. Then you heard somebody say, "shut up Moses you always talking smack!"
Jason came out the office and asked who had cards. The six men stood up. Malcolm had his clippers in hand as he prepared to cut from Moses' station. Then you heard a big BOOM! Everybody hit the floor. Then you heard screaming. Chester crawled over to the door and locked it. Malcolm told me to call 911! I grabbed the phone next to the front station.
"911 what's your emergency?"
I gave them our address and said there was some kind of loud boom outside. The police and fire department got there fast. Moses' car blew up, and the screams we heard were from Moses. Uncle Frank, Daddy, Uncle Jeff, and Poppa got there so fast. Everyone in the shop had to give statements about the events of the morning, the staff and the customers. The police report said that there was a mechanical and operator mishap that caused the explosion. Malcolm closed the shop for a week. On the following Monday night I got a phone call from Momma she said Drew's was on fire. Sophia stayed with the kids while I rode down with Daddy. Malcolm was talking to the fire department; they reported the fire as arson. I went to the pay phone and called the insurance agent. He came first thing in the morning. Malcolm called a meeting at Troy's place. Daddy and Uncle Jeff came as well. Malcolm asked everyone to tell him what they were taking home weekly, and he'd make sure they were compensated during this down time. When everyone left Malcolm roared! He told me for now it wasn't safe for the kids to walk to and from school. Fortunately they only had a week left in school, so we collectively decided to pull the kids out of school. Daddy said it wouldn't be a bad idea for all of the women and kids to get out of town for a bit. My heart was beating out of my chest. I didn't exactly understand what was happening but they were definitely fighting someone. Daddy told me to drive casually to my apartment, he told me to only pack important

stuff. Not to even worry about clothes, then for Sophia and I to go to Uncle Frank's. He specifically told me not to call David. I did as I was told, we told the kids we were going on an adventure. Gwen put us in a huge room with its own bathroom. When Momma and Auntie Lauren came in the middle of the night, Momma said she sent Malachi a ticket to spend the summer with Jade and Sonny. When Nana came she said Walnut Creek wasn't far enough away from the madness in Oakland. Then she called her travel agent and booked a flight and hotel for us to Southern California to go to take the kids to all the tourist attractions. We washed the clothes we were wearing, and then a limo came to take us to the San Francisco airport. As I went through my normal Bay Bridge anxiety, I realized Momma was going through her own anxiety. I moved next to her and I held her hand and we both cried a little. Nana looked at us but she didn't say anything. Nana checked us in, the cashier who checked us in she asked if we were celebrities cause Nana bought out the First Class section.

First Class was amazing and I told myself from now on First Class was the only way to fly. As soon as we landed we went shopping. Nana told us to get what we needed to cover two weeks. My mind kept drifting to the men, wondering what they were going through. My natural assumption was that the fire was retaliation from Moses' people. But what if the fire had something to do with Momma Shuga? Or could it be someone else? I didn't understand all the details or why only we had to leave. There's other cousins and family around the area.

After three weeks and we had seen everything we could see in the extremely hot Southern California sun, from a random pay phone Nana called home. We expected her to say the coast was clear and it was safe to go home. But instead she said we needed to go somewhere else.

Of course Momma suggested that we go visit Timothy and his family. I hoped the suggestion meant she was going to be on good behavior as well. We hadn't seen them since the wedding. Timothy III was about Derrick's age and they just had a little girl Tina who was so precious! Timothy was doing very well at his firm, Momma kept putting on pressure. Asking when they were moving back to the bay. Timothy was dragging his feet about answering, which was only getting him in trouble with Grace. So finally Grace spoke up and said it would be a long while before they came back to the Bay to live. As a compromise she said they would make more of an effort to visit more often. Momma looked like her head was gonna spin right off. Then Timothy stepped up, he told Momma that more than likely they weren't going to move back to the bay. I thought Momma was gonna hit him, but instead she started crying. They went in his office to talk it out. The rest of us sat there in shock.

We shared just a few of the not as bad as she could get stories about Momma. Grace's eyes got big, but then she shared stories about her momma. Both of them ran to Chicago to get away from their crazy families. Momma and Timothy were in there for a long time. When they finally came out Timothy looked drained and Momma clearly had been crying.

After another week and a random pay phone call home we headed to Atlanta. Jade looked GREAT and so happy. Looking at her made me think of David. Jade had a good guy and she was happy. That's what I wanted, a good guy and a happy life. She didn't look stressed about the company Sonny keeps, and I didn't have to worry about that with David either. He was a great father, kind and gentle. Well he was kind and gentle as long as he hadn't been drinking. And he didn't start drinking until I started distancing myself from him. I started drinking heavily mainly at clubs, when you're out you party, right? It just got heavy and hard to deal with when I had that miscarriage. At first I was upset about how it all happened. But seeing Malcolm excited about our child did make me want it. For the first time in a long time it felt like he loved all of me. I get it; it was hard to deal with how Momma cut me off, just like it's probably hard for David to deal with my change. I don't want him to die, I'd rather that he be mad at me than he die for trying to stand up to Malcolm. Ok, ok so I love Malcolm. But he's so focused beyond me, beyond Andy. He may slow down to remember me, but the child he never wanted... He lacks parenting skills to give Andrew what he needs.

Jade saw me lost in my thoughts. She told me she wanted to take me on a tour of the campus. She asked Momma to watch my kids, and then we snuck out the door before anyone could see us walking out. As soon as we were in the clear she told me to spill it. I told her everything that was happening. How I felt torn when it came to Malcolm, but I did love him. About that night in the club, Malcolm sang to me he's never done that before. How he kissed me in front of Yvette and how angry she was and how he didn't care. I told her about the change in David when he drinks. She stopped walking when I told her about the first time he hit me. Her face instantly became angry. I felt like I wasn't explaining the situation right, so I kept repeating myself. Then I told her about the second time, and she folded her arms. She started rocking waiting for me to finish. I dropped my eyes when I couldn't think of anything else to try to justify David's actions. She didn't raise her voice but by the way her voice shook I could hear the anger in her voice. She told me no matter what the situation, NO MAN had the right to put his hands on me. She told me it may be difficult to understand with the way we grew up, but we are not punching bags. I tried to explain that David is really a good man, and how it's just hard on him right now because things have changed. I hadn't slept with him since before Derrick was born. She put her hands on my shoulders, and told me that didn't matter. Then she asked me what was gonna happen once our family found out about this. My heart sank, I asked if she was gonna tell. She said she won't have to, if I continued to see him eventually it would come out on its own. She begged me to stop seeing him before it came to that. I told her she didn't understand. We went back and forth for a long time; I didn't feel like she understood everything. We stood in the same spot for hours. Jade told me that I was idealizing David too much. I needed to look at him for who he is showing me he is. I told her she couldn't understand because Sonny was perfect. She interrupted me and told me no one is perfect, you have to choose which flaws are liveable and which ones aren't. She shared some of her issues with Sonny, like when they argued he was quick to assume that she was done with him just because they argued. Sonny felt like Jade was too good for him, and that left him insecure about their entire relationship most times. But she assured me that the day that his insecurities led to him putting his hands on her, she shook her head. Her eyes went far off, she wasn't with me anymore. "I HATED the way Momma came after us. She would've had Daddy's neck if he even thought about spanking us like she did. Cleaning your little legs and back after Momma beat you is more than any person should have to see or go through. It wasn't until I started reading these psychology books that I understood that she did love us in her own way. But I promised that no one would do that to me at will." Tears were streaming out of her eyes. She hugged me and begged me to get away from David. Now I just felt dumb for not agreeing with her. I know David doesn't mean it, but he won't do it anymore.

In the middle of the night Jade called our hotel. She said Daddy called and that

Nana and Auntie Lauren needed to call immediately. When they called Auntie Lauren immediately burst into tears. As soon as Sophia heard her mother cry she ran to the bathroom and threw up. Nana called the airline in complete tears. She booked a ticket for Auntie Lauren immediately. Sophia wanted to go, Gwen was the only person who could calm Sophia down. Uncle Jeff had been shot, he was gonna be ok. But he was asking for Auntie Lauren. The children were fast asleep so we did our best to keep our sobs to low tones. I couldn't understand what was going on at home. I wanted this nightmare to be over. Malachi drove Auntie Lauren to the airport first thing in the morning. Because we were so out of it, I found myself overly energized. I was worried about Daddy, Malcolm, Uncle Frank, and Poppa mostly. Malachi and I took the kids to the park. We ran them around until their poor little legs seemed like they were going to fall off. Little Jeff kept looking at my face. He said he could tell something was wrong even if I didn't tell him. He was a miniature version of his daddy; I hugged him as much as I could. I promised when it was time I'd tell him, but for today I just wanted him to enjoy being a kid. He made me promise which made me cry. Auntie Lauren called and said that Uncle Jeff was fine. We cried tears of joy. We had been gone for just a little over two months. She said we would be able to come home soon. The next day she called as our eyes on the ground. She said there was another fire and Sophia and I's apartments were gone. She said a few of Uncle Frank's businesses were hit as well. That's when I knew Momma Shuga definitely had something to do with this.

****

Stepping into Oakland airport felt like we were home. Nana and Poppa embraced in a tearful embrace. Momma and Daddy were in tears. Auntie Lauren, Uncle Jeff, Sophia, little Jeff, JoJo, and Sasha. Uncle Frank and Gwen. Malcolm! Malcolm put his hands out and Derrick came running. Andrew lagged a little behind me as I threw my arms around Malcolm and kissed him over and over. He had Derrick in one arm and me in the other. Andrew stood by us, but he didn't want to hug. It was such a three-sixty in personality. Andrew had been happy to come home; I guess he was hoping for David instead of Malcolm. Malcolm didn't seem phased by Andrew's indifference towards him. I held Andrew's hand as we walked through the airport. I asked him if he was ok, and he tearfully told me he wanted to see David. I told him we would call him as soon as we could. Malcolm looked at Andrew although he didn't hear us I could tell he knew what was wrong with Andrew. He held Derrick who was perfectly content with him and didn't say a word. On the car ride to Uncle Frank's, Malcolm told me he missed me so much. I glanced back at Andrew who just stared out the window. I stared at Malcolm until he saw me then I nodded in Andrew's direction to tell him to say something to him. Malcolm gave me a lost look, and then he asked Andrew how his vacation was. Andrew said a very dry "fine". Then he told Andrew he was happy he was back and he was hoping that they could go back to the track just the two of them. Andrew asked him a skeptical "why"? Malcolm told him that he was impressed with how fast he was and how he couldn't stop thinking about that. Andrew perked up, "you think about me?"

Malcolm looked at him in the rear view mirror, "of course I do! You're my son!" Andrew smiled flashing his dimples, "thank you Malcolm!" He continued looking out the window but with a smile on his face.

I felt like I was gonna burst seeing Andrew's response to Malcolm. I leaned over and kissed Malcolm's cheek, Malcolm smiled and Andrew lost his. Andrew looked at me with evil eyes, I reached back before I even realized what I was doing and I slapped him. I told him to never look at me like that. He rolled his eyes and went back to looking out the window. Malcolm said that peace was short lived, as he chuckled. When we got to the house I asked Malcolm to take Derrick inside cause I needed to talk to Andrew. I grabbed Andrew by the hand and we walked around the house to the backyard.

"Boy! What is wrong with you?"

"I want my dad!"

"Malcolm just went inside."

"Not my father, my dad! I want David!" Andrew said with Malcolm's glare.

"We just got off the plane. I haven't had a chance to call him yet." I said

"Why didn't he come to the airport?"

"Grand dad told me not to call him yet."

Andrew looked at me like he didn't believe me. "You haven't talked to Grand dad in a long time."

"Boy! I know, when we were leaving Granddad told me not to call him. Or else I would've, I know he's probably worried sick."

"Can we call him as soon as we get inside?"

I exhaled, "Andrew let me see what's going on first. I promise I will call him as soon as I can."

"Ok" Andrew said, and then he hesitated. "Do you still love my dad?"

I felt like I was going to be sick. "Yes"

"Then why did you kiss Malcolm?" Andrew asked

Ok now I felt like crap, how do I explain to a child what doesn't exactly make sense to me? "Baby, it's hard to explain. I love your dad, but we are not together anymore. He will always be special to me; he's shown you so much love. And he gave us a beautiful baby."

"But you don't want to be his wife anymore." Tears rolled down his cheeks. "But why?"

"It's too hard to explain baby. But please believe me when I tell you it's for the best."

"But I don't understand!"

"Most times I don't either. I'm sorry baby, it's all my fault."

Andrew hugged me, "can I talk to him when you call him?"

"Of course you can. Matter of fact let me see what the adults are talking about and then we will call. Deal?"

"Deal!" Andrew said sounding happy again.

When we walked in the house everyone was in stitches looking at Malcolm and Derrick. I asked what was going on. They said Malcolm was talking to Daddy, Derrick saw the serious face on Malcolm's face and he stared mimicking him. Then they looked at each other and they've been staring each other down ever since. I walked and took Derrick who then complained cause he wanted to go back and stare at Malcolm some more. I asked Daddy if it was ok to call David. He told me to wait until the morning, he said David was gonna be pretty upset so I might as well sleep well tonight.

****

It was weird being back in my old room. That teddy bear Malcolm bought me was in the corner, all my important stuff was still here. Nana said the insurance on the building was going to rebuild, but it would probably be in my best interest to look for a house. She said that process would move along faster.

I took a deep breath and I dialed. Andrew was looking at me with anticipation in his eyes. The phone rang and rang. I told Andrew, David was probably at work. Andrew was just happy I called. I wrote the number down for him, and whenever he thought David could answer he'd call. After two days, Friday morning I heard "DAD!" Andrew was talking so fast I doubt David got a word in edgewise. I rolled over smiling, I peeked my at the crib and Derrick was staring at me like, "woman you better get up and feed me!" I smiled at him, and he got excited! I drug my tired bones out of bed. I played with Derrick for a minute, changed him. And then I made my way to the kitchen. Andrew was still talking, then he said, "momma's up". As he handed me the phone he told me he had to go get in the shower cause David was coming. When I said hello into the phone, David proceeded to curse me out in the worst way. Daddy warned me that he was gonna be upset. I kept apologizing, and trying to explain that the whole situation was beyond my control. But David was beyond upset, and then he hung up in my face. I quickly made breakfast for the boys and I got them ready. Daddy asked Andrew where he was going. Andrew very excitedly told Daddy that David was coming. Sweat trickled down my back at the thought of David even looking at me sideways in front of Daddy. I was hoping that Daddy had somewhere to go, but he was so happy to have us home that he hung around as much as possible. Before I wanted it to happen David was knocking at the door. Daddy went to open the door with a overly excited Andrew on his heels. David respectfully acknowledged Daddy but it was clear he was upset. He gave Andrew a huge hug, and then he took Derrick from me. He asked me if I was gonna be home later. I shook my head; I told him there was a fire. He looked annoyed, I told him a lot has happened that he didn't give me a chance to tell him. He said he'd be back in a few hours. Daddy watched my face, as I said nothing while David left. When he was gone Daddy asked me to take a ride with him. He took me to the shop, I hadn't realized before that the fire affected the adjacent offices. The first thing I noticed was that the parking lot was bigger. Malcolm bought out the other two businesses and expanded the shop to almost three times the original size. Everything was brand new and bigger. Daddy explained that Malcolm figured it made sense to bring everything to code so that they could not only barber and braid, but he added shampoo bowls and sit under dryers to process Jheri curls. There was now a break room slash lunchroom in the back. Customer bathroom and a separate employee bathroom. Malcolm's office was bigger with its own bathroom, separate entrance, and space for a table with four chairs and a couch. His new safe was huge and not so obvious. He had blinds up instead of curtains. He said the shop was going to reopen in a couple weeks. I asked who decorated the shop? It was nicely put together, this time there were details in the shop that made everything more modern eighties style. Daddy said Uncle Frank's interior decorator picked a lot of things out. I shot Daddy a look when he said that. I asked him if that meant she brought some of her friends around. Daddy put his hands up and said it wasn't like that. I cut my eyes at him, all these men were happy we were back, but not one of them seemed overly frisky etc. kind of like their extra energy had been spent. Daddy and I had lunch, and I enjoyed having this special alone time with him. But I also got the impression that he was making sure he was around when David came back. We got my mail from the apartment. I could tell the fire was pretty big; Sophia's car, which was in her garage, was also burnt to a crisp. I asked Daddy what happened to the Cheng's. Daddy said they got out of the building just in time. I asked Daddy what happened. He said everything kept dominoing. Malcolm's fire was retaliation from Moses' family. He said as they were dealing with that, Sammy's family struck at them with inside help from Momma Shuga. He said they were fighting two families at once. I asked how she was doing this from jail. Daddy said she can't do anything anymore.

When we pulled up to the house David was playing with the boys on the lawn as they waited for us. David still looked angry when he looked at me. Daddy sat on the porch to give us space but he stared at David. David came and stood by me next to the car. He said he was loosing his mind trying to find us. I apologized and explained that I wasn't able to call. I knew he didn't understand as he didn't understand who my family was. Eventually I stopped talking cause there were certain things I couldn't explain. He said Andrew told him that we went a bunch of different places on an airplane. I nodded but didn't say anything. He told me to never do this again, he was so worried. And when he came to my parent's no one was home. He didn't realize my Momma was with us. He was still visibly angry, but he pulled it back on account of Daddy.

****

"Welcome to Drew's!" I said greeting each customer as they entered the shop. A lot of the old regulars gladly filled in. The original crew was all here Chester, Rico, Leon, Rosalind, and Jason. They had first pick of their stations the week before. Then the new people were going to pick according to hire date. I hadn't met all of them yet, but I had their paperwork ready for them when they showed up. I kept looking at the one name and I couldn't place why it looked familiar I kept saying the name out loud Camille Caruthers. Maybe I went to middle school with her, I couldn't remember. The originals were still under rental contracts, and the new people were employed by the shop.

Tiffany walked in the door and she got so excited when she saw me. Penny was a few steps behind her. We did a happy to see each other dance, and then we all hugged. Tiffany and Penny were going to split the front desk responsibilities before and after school, while I was in school. They were going to handle scheduling for Rosalind and the other braiders. I told them whenever I wasn't there they should go to Rosalind if Malcolm wasn't there. Apparently while I was gone Rosalind and Troy had gotten quite cozy together. So the girls knew Rosalind and Tanisha very well. Malcolm completed his probation so he was looking for a new place. He was leaving the apartment by the lake to Troy. I hadn't seen Malcolm much, he said he was busy working, but I knew there was more to it than that so I waited. Malcolm emerged from the back with a few boxes full of donuts. He told the girls to pass them out. As he was kissing my cheek saying good morning she walks in. We locked eyes on each other and fire turned in my stomach. She rolled her eyes at me and looked at Malcolm. Malcolm frowned at her and asked what was that. She shook her head and asked him which station was gonna be hers. He told her I would give her, her orientation. I looked at him like he had to be crazy. Malcolm told her to wait there then he asked me to come to his office. All the men were drooling looking at her, and Rosalind had a "oh no he didn't" look on her face. When Malcolm closed the door he was trying to read my face.

"WHY IS SHE HERE?" I was pissed and insulted.

"She's a really good braider."

"So are fifty million other hookers in Oakland, why did you bring her here?"

"I just told you why."

"Are the other two girls part of your harem as well?"

"I knew you would feel some kind of way about this. But this is business!"

"Whatever Malcolm, maybe you don't have a problem messing with a married woman..."

"She's not married anymore." He interrupted in his defense.

"Like that matters! If you didn't want me down here anymore you could've said something. This is just tacky!"

"Amber! You can't fall apart just because you don't like the way I conduct my business."

"That's right! This is your business, not mine! I don't have to be here."

I reached for the door. He asked me where I was going, I told him I had better things to do with my time, then waste it chasing him around. I took my purse out the locker, I hugged the girls and I headed for the door. Camille grinned and evil grin at me, I wanted to punch her in her face, but I kept going. She was there because Malcolm wanted her there. Even if I hit her it wasn't gonna change anything.

Chapter 31

My dance instructor says my form has vastly improved. My style was still kind of raw and edgy, but it flowed better.

I saw Cassondra for the first time in a long time. She just had the most precious little girl that she named Nihjia. She was going to Vegas to get married in a couple weeks. She was so excited. I didn't even know she was pregnant so I was completely surprised. We told each other that we had to do a better job of keeping in touch.

After my initial nervousness about David's anger dissipated, I slowly started coming around David. He was angry at first and he grabbed me a couple times, but when I attempt to leave he would do his best to calm down, and apologize thoroughly. But the more I was around the calmer he would be. When I wasn't hanging out with David and the boys I hung out with Melvin. Melvin and I cleared the air about everything that happened between us. He finally owned up to being bisexual. I told him I didn't care, but I didn't view him as anything more than a brother. He said he was fine with that, but he didn't like David even more than he hated Malcolm. I tried to assure him that David was a good guy but Melvin wasn't going for it. Melvin would flash me looks whenever he came around and we were arguing. David was calm as long as Malcolm wasn't around. He even became my sweet and gentle David again. We started spending more and more time together; eventually I was spending nights with him again. It made Andrew so happy to be around David all the time again, Derrick didn't seem to care one way or another. Eventually Melvin brought his self around to hang out with David and I. Once David picked up on some of Melvin's ways, he completely relaxed about Melvin. He didn't even care when I went out dancing with Melvin as long as I came home to him at night. David had gotten a bigger apartment once we started hanging out at his place more often. It was nice to be away from Oakland sometimes. It started to feel like everyone knew who I was.

****

Nana asked me when we were going to go house shopping. I told her I wasn't ready yet. It was kind of nice living carefree. Neither Malcolm nor David were just gonna pop up on Momma and Daddy like they did me when I was in my apartment. If I didn't feel like being bothered I could just go home. Sophia, Nana, and Auntie Lauren were already looking for a house for Sophia. I figured they should focus on one house at a time anyways.

Upon graduation Malachi was hired as an design engineer for Japan's T car. His office was in Fremont close to the N plant where the cars were actually built. His job paid him very well, and flew him all over the world on a regular basis. He loved his job, he came out to see us whenever he could, but since he was so busy it wasn't too often.

Jade and Sonny are still in school. Sonny is in law school, and Jade is going for her Ph.D.

****

David's family came over a lot, which was fine, but they would make him feel guilty about us not being married. They would ask him if he wanted to come back to service and he would say yes quickly. Then everyone would look at me like they wanted to know what the hold up was. I just told them I wasn't ready yet. So the last time his aunt asked me if I loved David and I told her I do. She asked me if I wanted to be with him and I assured her I did. She said she couldn't understand what the hold up was. I told her I would leave David alone so that he could get his life together. Out of nowhere his temper spiked as he told all of us that I had to be in his life. Auntie Lorraine told him he was acting like his father when he acted like that. Then she looked at my face. I didn't say a word, she got mad at David. She said no woman wants to marry a man who beats on her. I looked at David with a question mark on my face. I didn't want to show a reaction cause I knew that would only make him mad.

He was quiet for a minute, which only made Auntie Lorraine angrier. She told him she was so disappointed in him. He would open his mouth to defend himself and then he'd stop. I looked out the sliding door windows at the boys outside with his uncle having a good time. Then Auntie Lorraine apologized to me; she told me they tried to raise him better. Then she told me I needed to get away from him. His face turned evil when she said that. He told his aunt she needed to leave. She gave me sad eyes as she called his uncle to leave with her. She hugged me goodbye and whispered that I needed to get out while I still could.

David was angry when they left. I sat there waiting for him to calm down so he could talk to me. He told me about his parents, they had a very volatile relationship. He said his dad beat his mother up regularly. He assured me he would get help. So I finally asked him why he ever hit me in the first place. He said things got too out of control. He said that's why he doesn't drink as much anymore, and he's really trying to be more patient. I told him I appreciated the effort. I didn't want to start anything by saying the alcohol was no longer the excuse.

The rest of the day he seemed agitated though. Like his aunt pricked a nerve relating him to his father. That night he wasn't gentle at all! He kept grabbing my hair and being rowdy. When he was done I told him I didn't like him like that. He put his arms around me but he didn't apologize. I had gotten used to not being satisfied by David. I hate it when Malcolm is right, although tonight instead of being only unsatisfied I was hurting.

****

Seriously????? My period was late and I was freaking out! I didn't want to have another baby I was just fine with the two kids I had. I couldn't even say when this happened. I didn't want to say anything to David cause he was gonna start talking about marriage again. Even though I hadn't seen or spoken to Malcolm in ages (it felt like), I doubted that his resolve had changed. Richmond wasn't far enough to hide from Malcolm. I told myself to relax and it was probably just a scare like last time. A little after David and I got back together, we had a pregnancy scare. It didn't scare me enough to get back on the pill, but enough to freak me out. David wasn't mad, but he started talking marriage again. Which is why I couldn't let on until I knew I was in the clear. But just like with Andy I had that sinking feeling my period wasn't coming. Sunday morning I felt like I couldn't breathe. I put my head between my knees and as soon as a regular thought would enter my brain I felt like I was gonna suffocate again. David asked me what was wrong; I told him I needed to go see my Nana. He asked me if I wanted him to come, I told him no. I gave him the number to her house in case he needed to call me. But to also show I wasn't lying about where I was going. It was barely light out, but I couldn't wait any longer. As I walked up to the door Nana met me. She was still in her nightgown. She looked disturbed and she looked at me with wide eyes. I didn't say anything, she just held me and asked me why I always have to be so hard headed. I didn't know how she knew, but I was glad she didn't make me say it. She asked me what I wanted to do. I sat there devastated not knowing what to say. I did not want another baby, Momma was gonna flip out on me. I didn't want to do this again. But the alternative was

Carey Anderson

worse to me. Who am I to say who gets to live and who doesn't just because it inconveniences my life? When Nana asked me I told her I couldn't do it. She told me to stop being so hard headed. I was fertile and knowing that, I couldn't be so careless with myself. She told me we had to get my house right away. I asked her if she thought Malcolm still cared, maybe I could finally marry David and Malcolm wouldn't care. She laughed at me; she said a promise like that did not have an expiration date on it. Then she picked up the phone and made her voice sound very sweet and grandmotherly. "Hello Ava, did I wake you?" She laughed, "oh dear. I keep losing track of the days." She winked at me. "Oh well I'll try to remember to call you tomorrow dear." She smiled, "oh well, I was talking to another one of my grand daughters about buying a house." She shook her head. "Un huh, yes.... Oh but she will need at least a three bedroom... I guess we'll go drive around her neighborhood and look for open house signs... You will?" She faked a surprised voice. "We're just about to have breakfast we can be ready in an hour... You will? Well aren't you sweet! Ok see you then." She hung up the phone. She told me to make Poppa breakfast while she got dressed. I said ok mimicking her old lady put on. She laughed.

Ava came prepared with listings. Of course it was the last house she had to show me that I absolutely loved! Andrew wouldn't have to change schools and there were so many possibilities. It was a four-bedroom three-bathroom house. It had an upstairs and a downstairs. The master bedroom had its own bathroom, I loved that. Three bedrooms upstairs, and one downstairs. The kitchen was huge, and there was a basement. The attic was good size but I only peeked in there. Nana was buying the house for me, but my name was on it. She was putting ninety percent of the loan balance down. She told me I was responsible for the monthly note and the taxes and insurance.

I left class early to go sign the loan documents with Nana. When I came home, I told Momma about the house. Momma was listening then she looked me up and down. She sucked her teeth, she told me she was too tired to even deal with me. I didn't say anything cause I knew what she meant. Then she said maybe I'd get the little girl I was chasing. I told her that I lost my little girl. I would love to have a little girl but I wasn't gonna set my heart on it.

Nana called to tell me the loan funded and we went together to get the keys. Poppa changed a lock showing Andy how and then he had him do the others. Derrick ran from room to room hooting and hollering. He was having too much fun. Andrew asked me why we were moving here instead of staying with David. I told him we would talk about it in a little bit. Poppa was out talking to my next-door neighbors. Mr. & Mrs. Hall who's house was on the left. They were a retired couple and they hit it off with Nana and Poppa right away. Mrs. Hall did a double take when I introduced her to Andrew and Derrick. The boys instantly liked her, she told them they could drop by whenever they wanted.

I had all the utilities put in my name, Daddy brought over the beds from my old room. I had him put one in Andrew's room, and the other one in Derrick's room along with the crib. That was my way of telling Daddy. He looked disappointed but he didn't say anything. He told me it would be best to keep this from Malcolm as long as I could. I nodded in agreement.

That night Andrew and I tucked Derrick in to his bed. Then I tucked Andrew in to his. I told Andrew that I couldn't marry David. When he asked why I told him that I couldn't do it. I told him I couldn't explain it to him in a way he could understand now. I told him I needed his help tomorrow. I told him it was top secret so he

244

couldn't tell anyone. He smiled at me giving me his dimples. I knew he didn't understand, but I had to change the subject. We dropped Derrick to Auntie Lauren, and then Andrew and I had breakfast. We went to the doctor, and when the doctor said I was pregnant I watched the surprised then excited look flash on Andrew's face. I smiled at him and tried not to act scared. I was tired of being pregnant, but Andrew was excited enough for the both of us. I told him it was a secret and he couldn't tell anyone. He looked like he was gonna burst but he agreed.

****

David called early Saturday morning; he wondered why we weren't there. I told him I needed to talk to him. His voice got low, I gave him directions and I told him to come once he was up. So of course he was there in less than thirty minutes. He came while my bedroom furniture was being delivered. He didn't look happy. I told him my grandmother bought me a house. He looked me in my eyes and asked why. Andrew walked into the living room with a mile wide smile. I told him it was ok to tell him. "MOMMA'S GONNA HAVE A BABY!!" Andrew screamed completely excited.

David's face twitched a couple of times. He hugged Andrew and he asked him if he was excited. Andrew said yes. Then David said he wanted to talk to me. Andrew took Derrick out back to play. He said he didn't understand why my having a baby would be a secret unless the baby wasn't his. My heart plummeted into my chest. I told him I didn't tell him right away cause I needed to verify that it was true first of all, and second I knew he was gonna start pressuring me to marry him and I didn't want to open that can of worms.

"So I'm good enough to sleep with but not to marry?"

I didn't want to argue. "David don't be ridiculous. Let me show you the house." I said walking away.

He grabbed my arm. "Don't walk away from me! I need to understand what's happening here."

"David you're hurting me!" I said trying to get my arm back but he kept squeezing harder. "Ok, I'm sorry what don't you understand?"

"If that's truly my baby prove it." He was beyond livid.

"David please let go!" I said trying to get my arm back. "Who's baby could it be?" Asking that made his grip tighter. "Don't play dumb with me! You been back sliding?"

"No! David please calm down the boys will hear." I said flinching cause I just knew he was getting ready to hit me.

He let me go when he saw Andrew and Derrick standing in the doorway. Andrew's expression broke my heart. Andrew's little eight-year-old body seemed two times bigger. He had his daddy's presence in that moment. He looked at David like he was a stranger. He walked up on David and told him to get out. David looked shocked and heartbroken. Andrew told him one more time to get out! David hung his head and walked out the front door. Andrew asked me if I was ok. I shook my head yes, but I was in shock. Little Derrick was right there behind him following Andrew's lead. Andrew came and looked at my arm, he gently touched my bruises. Then he looked me in my face, "momma is that why?" I shook my head yes. He hugged me and cried.

****

For the next seven months David was doing everything he could think of to try to get in Andrew's good graces. David never tried this hard to get on my good side after he pushed me, or threw me up against the wall, or worse. Whenever David came around Andrew wouldn't leave my side. If Andrew had to go with Malcolm, he would make sure I had plans with Sophia, Melvin, or someone. So far Malcolm didn't know about this baby. His head was so far up Camille's behind that he completely forgot about me. Not that I was exactly complaining, but sometimes I would miss him.

****

I woke up in the middle of the night to contractions. I had an overwhelming sense of urgency. Andrew my little protector was at my door checking on me and I thought he was fast asleep. He picked up the phone and called my parents. He had my hospital bag, and the bag I packed for him and Derrick ready when Momma and Daddy came. From the hospital Momma called David, who got there in no time flat. I didn't labor long at all. Daddy stayed out in the waiting room with the kids. This baby seemed to come out on his own; I didn't really have to do too much. And of course they said, "congratulations it's a boy". I could see the confirmation on David's face. The baby looked like another version of Derrick. David kissed my cheek and he apologized in my ear. Momma watched David but she didn't say anything, she looked angry. I could tell she was holding something back. When Daddy came in with the boys to see the baby, Momma studied Andrew. Andrew's eyes were locked on David as he walked in the room. He stood on the opposite side of the bed looking at David then he smiled at the baby. Andrew asked me what the baby's name was. David and I hadn't discussed names; we didn't really have a chance to discuss much. I looked at David and he shrugged, I asked Andrew if he had any suggestions. He told me he wanted to name him Darryl after this boy who could do anything in this movie his father just took him to see. I told him it was done.

I was in a lot of pain like I was having contractions still. I called the nurse; she explained to me that I was having after birth pains. When the doctor came to check on me the next day, I asked her to put me on birth control. I told her I didn't want any more children. She couldn't write the prescription fast enough.

Darryl was such a silly baby. Again totally different from his brothers. But he seemed like he was always laughing about something. Andrew and Derrick would have him cracking up by being silly.

****

I called down to the shop because Rosalind sent word through Sophia that she missed me and hadn't seen me in forever. Penny answered the phone, "Drew's how may I help you?"

"Yes, is Rosalind available?"

"One moment, may I ask who's calling?"

"Is this Penny?"

She paused for moment. "Yes"

"It's me, Amber!" I said

She got so excited. She asked me where I've been. And how come I hadn't come down there in forever. I told her I had been laying low. She said real low, no one's seen me in forever. I told her I had a few things going on. She said Malcolm was out of town and I should come by tomorrow if I could. I told her I'd think about it. Then she put Rosalind on the phone. Rosalind was so excited to hear my voice. I gave her my number and then I confirmed with her that Malcolm was out of town. I told her I'd come by tomorrow.

I waited until Andrew got out of school and then the four of us went to Drew's. When we walked in the door everyone said hey to Andrew, they paused when they saw the two month old in my carrier. I saw Jason literally counting my kids. Then he made a whistling sound with his mouth. Rosalind ran over screaming asking who's baby Darryl was. When I said he was mine she looked me up and down. She told me I didn't look like I just gave birth. I thanked her, and then she said hi to Derrick. He didn't remember her but he was only three, and it had been over a year and a half since he saw her last. Tiffany came and took Darryl from me. Andrew was telling Tiffany and Penny all about Darryl. His silence had been wearing on him. We had a nice long visit with Rosalind. Camille's station was set up, but she wasn't there. I assumed she was where ever Malcolm was. After our visit, I drove home. Then the boys and I walked over to Sophia's. Sophia was talking to Nana on the phone. Andrew and Derrick went out in the back to play with LJ (that's what he told us to call him instead of little Jeff), JoJo, and Sasha. When she got off the phone she said she had an idea. She told me she wanted to open a restaurant. As soon as she said it I could totally see it. It was time to put our degrees to work. I needed to come up with my business plan.

In the morning I took Andrew to school, and Derrick to preschool. When I got home Malcolm was sitting on my porch. His face was stone, he watched me as I pulled Darryl out the car. He rolled his eyes and started shaking his head. I walked to the back of the house instead of using the front door cause I didn't want to even walk past him. He pressed on the doorbell, I thought I could ignore it but ten minutes later I opened the door screaming at him. He was mad, and for the first time I was scared of him. When I realized I was scared it made him madder. He sat on the couch. "So you've been busy!"

"No more than you have been!" I said standing across the room from him.

"Did you marry him?"

"That's none of your business!" I said

He looked at me, and then he stood up. "You must've thought I was kidding with you!" He reached around his back and pulled out his gun. He took the safety off. "I told you!"

I felt like I was going to pass out. "Malcolm!" I yelled

"Woman! You are killing me! How you gonna have another baby? I gave you a pass on Derrick, but this is too much!" Malcolm was unglued. "Did you marry him?" When he walked up on me I flinched like he was going to hit me. He squinted his eyes; he put the safety back on his gun. He sat the gun on the mantle. "Since when do you flinch?"

I tried to talk over my tears. "YOU HAVE A GUN!"

"So!"

"YOU WERE POINTING IT AT ME!"

"No I wasn't!" Then he looked me up and down. "What's up with you?"

"Nothing!"

He stood there staring at me. I moved to escape his stare. He frowned at me. "Something is up with you."

"I thought you were out of town?" I said not knowing what he meant, but not wanting to find out.

"So?" He shrugged

"So why are you here?"

"You came by Drew's yesterday. I told Juan he must've counted your kids wrong! Why did you do this?"

I heard Darryl cry. I turned on my heels to go get him. Malcolm grabbed his gun and followed me. My heart kept beating out of my chest. Malcolm looked around as he followed me. When I picked up Darryl, Malcolm stared at him for a minute. Then he asked me again why I had another baby. I told him I didn't do it on purpose, and that I don't even really know how he happened. Darryl smiled at Malcolm, Malcolm frowned at him. Then he asked me again if I married David. I shook my head no. Then the doorbell rang, I walked to the door with Malcolm on my heels. Malcolm sat on the couch while I went to the door. It was Melvin he looked at my face when I opened the door. He walked right in the door; he asked me what was wrong with me. I pointed with my head trying to give him a heads up. When Melvin walked around the corner, he jumped and said whoa when he saw Malcolm. Then Melvin went over and shook Malcolm's hand. He told Malcolm that he must've just found out. Malcolm nodded, and then he asked Melvin what was up with me. Melvin looked at me and he shrugged, I swallowed hoping Melvin wouldn't tell him anything. Malcolm made himself comfortable on the couch. I wanted him to leave especially before David stopped by on his way home from work. But he got comfortable engaging Melvin in conversation and watching TV. After a bit I told them I would be back, I took the baby upstairs to breast-feed him. I closed the door to my room and I got comfortable. I could hear Malcolm and Melvin downstairs talking about a video they were watching on the soul video. I looked at my baby wondering how I could've ever felt anything other than blissful about him. Malcolm knocked on my door as he opened it. He stopped in his tracks looking at Darryl eating. Then he looked around my room. He asked what did I name the baby, I told him. He nodded his head as he peeked his head in my closet. I could tell he was making sure David didn't live here. That would make it harder to convince him that we weren't married if he did. He asked me why I haven't come around. I looked at Darryl then at him. He said I stopped coming around long before the baby. So I told him, "I wanted to be with you. As usual you were distracted. I couldn't continue to go through that with you."

"How did I get distracted?"

"Hello? You brought Camille into the shop. Who knows whom else you brought in there. You let your other head do your thinking too much."

He smiled at me. "Why do you let them bother you? They don't mean nothing."

"They meant enough to keep you distracted for two years. If I hadn't gone to see Rosalind would you even remember me right now? I'm just the little girl you knocked up years ago. You don't have to act like you still care." I said keeping my eyes to the floor.

Malcolm stood there looking at me. "What happened to our eye contact? Why are you looking at the floor?" I heard his question but I couldn't bring myself to do it. Looking at the floor is something I do without realizing it. I shrugged as I kept my eyes on the floor. "Seriously Amber, what's up with you?" He said lifting my chin with his finger.

Darryl was finished eating so I stood up to burp him. "Lets go downstairs." I said walking out the room.

He asked to see Andrew's room, so I pointed it out. He walked in shaking his head and nodding. Then he peeked in Derrick and Darryl's room. I walked downstairs and Melvin gave me a look. Melvin had the biggest smile on his face. He would always say to me that the day Malcolm found out about David would be the day of total satisfaction for him. I was standing in the living room when Andrew and Derrick came home. Andrew was saying hi to Melvin before he rounded the corner. Andrew stopped in his tracks when he saw Malcolm. "Where's your car?"

"It's out there. How was school?" Malcolm said

Andrew blew air, "I got suspended again."

"WHY?" I said

"Same reason different day." Andrew said matter of factly.

"And what reason is that?" Malcolm asked

"Fighting, JoJo got suspended too."

"Why were you fighting?" Malcolm asked

"They keep calling me white boy, or thinking that I'm gonna be scared of them. Or they try to pick on Sasha, take your pick." Andrew said sounding exhausted. Malcolm sat back, "I can tell you how to fix that."

Andrew sat on the floor in Indian style, Malcolm had his full attention. "How?" Derrick sat next to Andrew and mimicked him.

Malcolm had everybody's attention. "You have to make an example out of someone. People need to see what will happen to them if any of them think of messing with you again. You may have an occasional fight here and there, but most people will leave you alone. Every fight you have, don't hold back, I guarantee you will have less of them."

Andrew nodded his head like he was following Malcolm's logic. "But what do you mean by example?"

"You tear into someone without holding back." Andrew nodded his head. "Remember what I told you. Pay attention to your opponent's ability then you destroy them!"

"Malcolm! I don't want Andrew walking around here like a monster scaring people."

"You want him getting suspended every other day?"

"No, but..."

"Ok then, he's gotta nip this in the bud! Stop babying him."

I walked out the room in a huff. I hated whenever he accused me of babying Andrew. I didn't want my son walking around angry all the time like I did. As I walked back towards the front room I saw David's truck pull up. I started sweating, I shot Melvin a look. And he looked at me but he didn't understand my panicked expression. The doorbell rang; Malcolm's eyes followed me to the door. David didn't even say hi to me. He was barking out to Melvin that he was tired of seeing his car outside whenever he came over. When he rounded the corner he stopped dead in his tracks. "What are you doing here?" David asked in a deep voice.

Malcolm smirked, "I heard about the baby. I was coming to put a bullet in your head! But Amber said you aren't married, so you breathe for another day!" Malcolm said matter of factly in an equally deep tone.

David was taken back by Malcolm's frankness. "What?"

I asked Andrew to take Derrick and the baby upstairs. He didn't want to leave, but I didn't give him a real choice.

Malcolm stood up. "My promise hasn't changed. And I guess I need to add a new addendum to it."

"What promise?" David growled

Malcolm looked at me. "You didn't tell him?"

"Tell me what?" David barked at me.

I kept my eyes on the floor and shook my head no.

Malcolm's breathing got heavy. "Why are you putting your eyes on the floor? Look at me when I'm talking to you!"

David pulled me by my arm and put me behind him. "I know you guys have a child together, but this is my woman!"

Melvin flinched on the couch. All you heard was breathing. "Your woman?" Malcolm was clearly irritated. "Don't get on my nerves!" Then he inhaled and exhaled. "When Amber, I guess it was an accident, told me about your engagement I told her you would die IMMEDIATELY afterwards! How did she explain her change of heart?" Malcolm said with a smile.

David looked at me. "Why didn't you tell me?" I shrugged, "ANSWER ME!" He barked at me.

"Hold on!" Malcolm walked around the coffee table. Melvin rocked in his seat with a smile on his face as Malcolm walked up on David. "Who are you yelling at?"

"This doesn't concern you Malcolm! I'm talking to her!" David said ignoring Malcolm and turning his back on him to face me.

Malcolm punched David in his kidney. David went down. "If you're smart you'll stay down!" Malcolm said pointing at David. Then he looked at me. "Amber what is going on here? What's happened to you?"

"Nothing Malcolm! Please leave!" I said crying.

"You want me to leave?" Malcolm sound shocked.

"Yes! Please!" Then I looked at Melvin. "You too!"

Andrew came running down the stairs. "Why do they have to leave?"

"Because!" I said pointing at David on the floor.

"Can I go with Malcolm?" Andrew asked.

I gave Andrew a pleading look as I said ok. Derrick ran down and asked if he could go too. Malcolm told them to grab their jackets. David was in pain, so I helped him on the couch. When I went upstairs Darryl was laying in his crib looking at me. I picked him up and then I went back downstairs. I sat on the love seat and I peeked at David. He was crying, "you did love me?" I nodded my head yes. "I wish you would've told me. I've been so mad at you. I thought you were taking pleasure in hurting me. I thought you didn't love me!" He cried a deep and mournful cry. "I'm sorry! I'm so sorry!" He came and threw his arms around me.

I told him he had to leave before Malcolm came back. I could tell he didn't want to, but I begged him to leave. I spent the next few hours crying my eyes out.

When Malcolm brought the boys home, Andrew was carrying Derrick who was knocked out. Malcolm waited until the boys went upstairs. Then he looked me in my eyes. "Is he hitting you?" I looked at Malcolm and I blank stared at him. "The day I find out he's ever laid a hand on you!" He hugged me then he left.

Chapter 32

"Hello, we just moved next door. My name is Connie."

"Hello I'm Amber, nice to meet you."

"Is your mother home?" She asked

I looked confused, "my mother?"

"I noticed your little brothers out back, so I wanted to come over and introduce myself."

"You mean my sons?"

She put her hands over her mouth. "Oh honey! I'm so sorry! You look so young I assumed they were your brothers. I'm so so so sorry! This is your house isn't it?" The lady looked totally embarrassed.

"Yes it is." I smiled

"Can we start over? I need to get my foot out of my mouth."

"It's ok." I said

Connie was newly divorced and she had two boys. Conrad who she called Hubby, Carlos who she called Dude. They were both about the same age as Andrew. Hubby was a chubby little boy, I wondered if they called him Hubby as a guise for his appearance. Connie worked for the city of Oakland, and she moved next door to be closer to her job. I invited them in and then I called Andrew and Derrick inside. We introduced the boys; Andrew looked both of the boys up and down. Then he asked Hubby, "why you so fat?" I gasped.

Hubby and Connie started laughing. "Cause I like to eat." Hubby said still laughing.

"For real, then you guys need to meet Mrs. Hall next door. She always makes cookies, cakes, and pies. Me and Derrick go over everyday helping her around her house." Then Andrew rubbed his stomach, "then she gives us the good stuff."

The boys got excited. I told all the boys they could go out back. I took Darryl out of his high chair and I brought him in the living room. I chatted with Connie for a little bit. I told her it was ok if her boys came over after school during the week. I told her about the dance school I was looking to open in the near future, but as it stood, I was home in the afternoon.

Sophia and Rosalind came over together. I introduced them to Connie, and we sent the girls in the backyard with the boys. Sophia was excited because she had her business proposal ready to shop around to banks. Connie told us she admired our ambition. We told her it was kind of mandatory in our family. We told her about the architects, doctors, lawyers, engineers, entrepreneurs, etc. in our family. I even told her that Andrew's father owns a barbershop chain.

David knocked on the door pushing it open. When Darryl saw him, he took off running to him. As soon as Rosalind saw him she rolled her eyes and blew air. David still said hello to her anyways. I introduced Connie to him as my new neighbor. He said hi to Sophia, she spoke but she lacked enthusiasm about him. I took him to the back and I introduced David to the boys. Andrew stood over to the side watching David, but he didn't say anything.

Ever since that night David has been like the original David I fell in love with. I still haven't given in and slept with him though. I've been done with him since that rowdy night, but he hasn't pushed the issue either. He said he needs to work on himself and get reconnected to God. I'm fine with that as long as he doesn't come at me like there's something wrong with me for not going. I think the hardest part has been Andrew's reaction to him. Andrew has noticed his change, but I think he's holding out for the moment he flashes backwards. I don't blame him for being cautious because I am too.

David told Andrew he had something for him out in his truck. Andrew didn't say anything he just looked at David. David gave Darryl back to me then he went to his truck. He pulled a big box off the bed of the truck. Then he drug it to the backyard. David looked around the backyard. He set the box by the furthest wall, and then he got his tools out of his truck. He opened the box pieces fell out. But the backboard was undeniable. Hubby and Dude cheered, Andrew said an unimpressed thank you. But you could see that David was wearing him down. Before long the girls were up in my room playing in my clothes and makeup while the boys were helping David put the hoop together. You could tell when they were done, cause all you could hear was that basketball bouncing.

That night long after Hubby and Dude had gone home David and Andrew were still out there playing. After nine o'clock I had to tell them to come inside before they irritated the neighbors. When the phone rang I thought it was Mrs. Hall calling to say she had had enough. But it was Daddy, he was crying. My heart dropped instantly I thought it was Poppa or Nana. He could barely talk, he told me to come to the hospital and that it was Momma. I screamed to the top of my lungs. "WHAT DADDY? WHAT IS IT?" He wouldn't say, he just told me to get there. I dropped the phone, my heart was stinging me! David and Andrew came running in the living room! I couldn't really talk! All I could say was "my Momma!" And "hospital". Andrew ran and got the diaper bag and my purse, while David grabbed jackets for the boys. We were in my car, kids strapped into car seats, and on our way to the hospital in no time flat. I couldn't think straight, all I knew is I had to get there. David pulled up to the door so I could get out before he parked. I didn't wait for him to come to a complete stop when I opened my door to get out. I went to the desk and asked for Annette Wallace's room. The woman at the desk tried to tell me that visiting hours were over. I did my best to remain calm, I told her my father called me down there. She and I were going back and forth when Uncle Jeff came and told them I was the niece he told them was coming. He asked me where the kids were. I told him David was parking and that he'd bring them. Uncle Jeff said, "lets try this again! Anyone asking for Annette Wallace BETTER get sent up, or else whether or not you still have a job will be the least of your worries!" The girl looked scared. Uncle Jeff put his arm around me as tears started pouring out of his eyes. I asked him what was going on? But he couldn't answer me, he didn't really know. When we got off the elevator Uncle Jeff pointed me in the direction of her room. When I went in Daddy was sitting next to the bed crying his eyes out. He gave me the tightest hug. I asked him what was wrong and all I heard was cancer. If Daddy was still talking after that I didn't hear him. Momma was laying on her side with her back to us. I walked over to her; she was laying in a pool of her tears. She didn't raise her head to look at me; she kept rubbing her finger on the pillow in front of her eyes. I grabbed her hand, and she squeezed my hand. Daddy said Malachi should be here any minute and Jade and Timothy were arriving in the morning. Momma took a deep breath, and then more tears spilled out of her eyes. Andrew walked in the room slowly. He looked at Daddy, and then at me. He studied our faces as he came to my side. Momma reached for him and he held her hand. Then he bent over and kissed her, he told her he loved her. She started crying harder as she patted his hand. The door opened again Malcolm walked in he stopped in his spot when he looked at Daddy. He swallowed then he took a few more steps. He stopped when he looked at me, he swallowed again. Then his eyes dropped to Andrew, that's when tears started pouring out of his eyes. I moved out the way so he could get closer. He reached down and touched her hand. When she grabbed his hand Malcolm broke down, he kept saying "Momma No!" Daddy came over and they hugged while Malcolm held on to Momma's hand. Momma's body shook from her tears, Malcolm sobbed out loud. Andrew hugged Malcolm; they embraced for a long time. Then Malachi walked in the room. He looked startled by seeing Malcolm in his current state. Malachi hugged Daddy, then me, he hugged Malcolm and Andrew. I couldn't take seeing one more person break down. I walked out the room on the right I could see Uncle Frank talking to Uncle Jeff they looked like they were crying. So I went to the left, I didn't know where I was going but I needed air. I ended up in the stairway crying my eyes out. I was there for a while. When I came back I passed Momma's room and I went to the waiting room. David was there with Derrick and Darryl in his arms, they were both sleep. David and Malcolm were engaged in a good ole fashioned stare down. Andrew was sitting next to Malachi; they weren't talking but just in their own depressing thoughts. I told David and Malcolm to stop it. They both looked at me. Auntie Lauren and Sophia left, Auntie Lauren could barely walk. She and Sophia kind of held each other up as they left. I told David I didn't know how long we were gonna be there. I asked him to take the boys with him; they were too little to be there. David hesitated cause he didn't want to leave but he knew I was right. Andrew and I walked him out, David told me to keep him posted. I agreed and then I hugged him goodbye. As Andrew and I walked back towards the hospital the sun was coming up and Malcolm was standing in the doorway. He asked me where I went when I disappeared. I told him I needed some air. We rode the elevator in silence. As we exited the elevator I saw a woman go in Momma's room, I stood in the doorway of the waiting room and I asked Malachi who the woman was. He didn't see her, so he followed me. I told Andrew to go have a seat. When Malachi and I walked in the room the woman was talking to Daddy. She had sad eyes then she looked at Malachi and I, she had Momma's eyes. Momma's snore was unlike anything I had ever heard come from her before. Even though she was sleep she was fighting for us. The woman walked over to Momma and rubbed her hand. I looked at Daddy; he whispered that she was our Auntie. I didn't know how to feel about seeing her. Malachi and I looked at each other and then we watched her. I had no memory of this lady other than she was the one who called to tell Momma when her momma passed away. Daddy kind of nudged us to go over to her. I pushed Malachi in front of me; he's the social one. Malachi put his hand out to her and introduced himself. She shook his hand and said her name was Emma. I shook her hand as I told her my name. She looked at me and then she said I was the one that acted just like Annette. She asked where the others were, we told her they were on their way. Then I told her I'd give them space. I went back in the waiting room. Andrew had his legs crossed in Indian style and his head leaning back against the wall. When Malcolm saw me, he patted the seat next to him. I sat down and rest my head on his shoulder. I saw Poppa and Nana walk past the waiting room to go to Momma's room. Malcolm rested his head on my head. I closed my eyes for a minute then I heard hurried footsteps, I caught a glimpse of Jade, Sonny, and Timothy rushing past the waiting room. Nana and Poppa came in the waiting room. They were both crying so hard, Andrew woke up and went to hug Nana. Then I heard Daddy asking the nurse for something for Momma's pain. Malcolm, Andrew, and I popped up and went into the room with Momma. Jade was crying really hard holding Momma's hand. Momma's breathing was really heavy and she was fighting to hang on. I went to Jade's side. We told Momma that everybody was here; that everyone got to say goodbye and that she could go to sleep. We told her we loved her and we were gonna miss her, but it was ok. She had been fighting all her life, now she could finally rest. Momma looked at us with sad eyes, and then she closed her eyes. Daddy started crying really hard as her breathing slowed down. We all kept telling her we loved her. It looked like she was sleeping but her chest wasn't moving. Jade almost passed out on top of Momma. I caught her and pulled her into me. Timothy was crying on Daddy's shoulder. I don't know when everyone made their way in the room but everyone was in there crying their eyes out. Time seemed like it stopped moving, instantly I thought of all the things I wanted to make right with Momma before it came to this. I wanted to apologize for every time I made her mad, for every time I disappointed her, for every time I got smart with her in my brain and she didn't catch me. There were so many things I wanted to say.

We went back to Daddy's house. Andrew and I rode with Malcolm in complete silence all you heard were our sniffles cause we were all crying. When we got to the house there was a ton of food laid out. Sophia and Auntie Lauren had been cooking all morning. LJ, Sasha, and JoJo met Andrew at the door with tears. The four Amigos went to the backyard to console Andrew. I called David and I told him to bring the boys and my car to Daddy's house. He got there fast and Derrick went outside with the big kids. Sasha eventually came and got Darryl. David sat over to the side out of the way.

The house was full of Daddy's family. Then I looked at Emma sitting in the corner by herself crying. I sat next to her and she hugged me. Emma apologized for not being around. She said so many things were complicated in her family. She told me stories about her and Momma when they were growing up. Before long she had a big audience. And the next thing you know we were all sharing stories about Momma. Most of them involved her beating somebody up. Malcolm even shared how he knew Momma loved him when she threatened to kill him. He smiled, "I knew she loved me when she threatened my life". Everybody laughed. We all had stories about how Momma didn't take no stuff. Listening to the stories started putting wind underneath my wings reminding me of who I am, and where I came from. I remembered how no one could put fear in me like my Momma did, after her everyone else was a walk in the park. I looked at David who was politely sitting over to the side listening to everyone's stories. Ok so maybe he didn't fit in with my family. I wanted to have a good guy in my life so bad that I didn't stop to think about whether this good guy was the good guy for me.

Daddy called the four of us in the room. Momma had her obituary all planned out the only thing missing was the sunset date. Looking at all the pictures were amazing. Some of them I had never seen before. Pictures of Momma when she was a little girl, pictures of Momma and Emma. Tons of pictures of Momma and Daddy over the years. Momma and Daddy looked good together and they knew it. Pictures with them with each of us after we were born. Family pictures with all of us. Pictures of Momma and Andrew, Momma and Derrick, Momma and Darryl. Pictures of Timothy's kids. Pictures of Momma and me jumped out at me. I'm sure my siblings all felt the same way about their pictures. But even though I look like Daddy, I promise it was like I was looking at twins when I looked at Momma and me. Twin souls for real. We all sat there crying our eyes out looking at everything. Timothy asked why Emma was here, and Daddy explained how Emma was the only one that Momma kept in contact with. They didn't speak very often, but they kept in contact. We asked Daddy why they didn't tell us Momma was sick. He said Momma didn't want to tell us. We asked how long they knew, and he said since just before Jade's wedding they knew for sure. I asked Daddy if the only reason Momma stopped shutting me out is because she was sick? He told me that Momma felt betrayed when they found out I was pregnant, and it took all those years just for me to think to apologize. He said, "I'm sorry goes a long way". I sat there searching my memory bank. He was right, I didn't apologize. I didn't think that would help me, but that was no excuse. I should've apologized right away. Maybe I wouldn't have lost all that time. Maybe Momma could've told me about David right away. I know she saw it, I could tell she saw it. But she didn't say anything, why?

Auntie Lauren knocked on the door, she said she had the mortuary on the phone and she wanted to know if Thursday worked for us to have Momma's services. Daddy said that was fine. Timothy left to make arrangements for Grace and the kids to come out. Malachi said he wished he would've gotten married before this. He said getting married now just wouldn't feel right. Daddy told him not to worry about it and when he found the right girl, none of that would matter.

I walked Emma out to her car. She had the date and time. She said she would tell family about Momma and whoever wanted to come would. I told her as long as she was there we didn't need the others. She hugged me really big, and then she got in her car. Malcolm came and put his arm around my neck while we waved goodbye to Emma. He asked me how I was holding up. I told him this felt like a horrible nightmare. I told him I was waiting for someone to wake me up. Malcolm said he couldn't believe she didn't tell us, that us included him. I looked at him, I knew he loved her and looked up to her. But I had no idea that he looked at her like she was his mother too. I told him he needed to update the beneficiaries on his accounts. He took a deep breath and agreed. Sasha brought Darryl to me she said she had to go help her momma. Malcolm took Darryl from her; he looked at Darryl real hard. Then he asked me why my kids with David looked more like they could be his sons than Andrew did? I told him I had no idea. Then he said it was probably because I was missing him so much each time. I didn't say anything. Then he asked me how things were going with David. I shrugged and said they were going. I asked how things were going with Camille. He frowned and said they were never together. I gave him a knowing look and he smiled and said in a relationship. I asked him how Yvette was, he blew air. He said she doesn't even know him. Then he said she was fine. I asked him how long he was in the doghouse after that night at the club. He smiled at the recollection, then he said she doesn't have the power to put him anywhere, none of them do. I told him I've put him in the doghouse multiple times, he smiled at me and said he knew. Then Darryl started cracking up laughing at Malcolm. Malcolm chuckled and asked me what was wrong with him. I told him Darryl was just a happy baby. I told him it was a surprise since I was so miserable when I was pregnant. I felt eyes on me and when I looked up at the house David was watching us in the window. Malcolm followed my eyes up, and when he saw David he smiled at him and held Darryl up to him. I rolled my eyes and told him to stop that as I took Darryl from him and walked back into the house.

Andrew was gonna walk home with Derrick, LJ, and JoJo. He told them about his new friends and his basketball hoop. So they decided to walk together to my house. Derrick wanted to be everywhere Andrew was, and Andrew always wanted him around. I was so thankful they got along in that regard. David was quiet on the car ride to the house. I knew he was bothered by Malcolm's presence; I waited for him to say something. I just hoped he'd keep it together and let me mourn my mother in peace.

I ran a bath for Darryl, and then I put him in the tub. David stood in the doorway watching; I could tell he was struggling with himself. I appreciated the effort so I pretended like I didn't notice. Darryl liked splashing the water, so I just let him go to town. We heard the basketball so I knew that meant the boys were out back. David confirmed the start time for the services. He told me he was really sorry about my Momma. I thanked him; he asked me if there was anything I needed him to do for me. I told him no, then I thanked him for everything he did for me today and last night. He said he had to get on the road soon, but he'd be back in time for the funeral. I thanked him, but he was still lingering. I asked him if he was waiting for something. He blew air, and then he said he had to say it. He felt like he was leaving me in a vulnerable state and that Malcolm was gonna pounce on me as soon as he turned his back. I could feel my face turning red. I told him my Momma just died! I wasn't worried about anybody's underhanded plots and schemes. I told him if he was that worried about it then he should stay close by. He was trying to control his temper, then he said if we were married he could've taken the time off as bereavement and still gotten paid, but he couldn't afford to take a whole week off unpaid. I told him I didn't know why he brought it up. Either he was staying or he wasn't, but I didn't have time for the pettiness! He stood there clinching and un-clinching his jaw. I stood up and looked him in his eyes, and then I told him to go to work. He growled at me real loud then he left. Darryl sat there smiling at me like he approved. Just after seven Mrs. Hall came over. I thought the ball or the noise from the boys was bothering them. But she told me that Nana called, and she was calling on me to come check on me. I tried to open my mouth to say I was ok, but my wind left me and tears poured out of my eyes. Mrs. Hall put her arms around me and she really comforted me. She told me it was gonna be a long hard road, but I would get through it. She said not to worry about the ball; she said they could go all night long if they needed to. When little Derrick came staggering in the house cause he couldn't hang with the big boys anymore Mrs. Hall left and I gave Derrick a quick bath. He was knocked out before his head hit the pillow. I sat on the couch in the living room completely tired but unable to fall asleep. Finally the boys came inside all them were red and sad. I called Auntie Lauren and told her the boys were gonna sleep over. Then we all kind of sat there in a state of shock. Not saying anything just existing. At midnight there was a knock at the door Andrew answered it and it was Malcolm. His eyes were sad just like all of ours. He sat on the couch next to me. He didn't say anything he just put his arms around me. We all fell asleep where we were.

****

Wednesday night I didn't sleep, I laid in my bed with my mind going fifty miles per hour. When the sun started coming up I told myself I might as well get up. I laid out the boy's clothes. Malcolm took all of them to get black suits and crisp white shirts. He said Momma deserved to have everyone looking their absolute best on her day. He had Jason cut Andrew and Derrick's hair at the shop. Jade and I went to Raynel's to get much needed trims and I had her put my hair in an up do, I didn't even want to deal with it. Getting myself ready seemed like a chore. I laid my dress on the bed, exhaled, put my stockings on the bed, exhaled, and took my shoes out the closet, exhaled. Then I sat on the bed looking at it. I heard the doorbell, and then I heard David's voice. He came up the stairs and knocked on my door as he opened it. He looked surprised to see me just sitting there. He closed the door behind him and then he dressed me. I thanked him, he kissed my cheek. He changed the heels I chose to flats. He said my feet were gonna hurt in the others, and this way I could be more comfortable. I shrugged, I didn't really care if my feet hurt or not. I couldn't really feel too much right now. Andrew knocked on the door; David opened it while he put my shoes on. Andrew looked so handsome and so much older than my nine-year-old baby boy. As usual Derrick was right there on his heels. Andrew came and hugged me then he thanked David for helping me. David went and got the diaper bag ready. Andrew held my hand and told me to come on. Everyone was quiet and serious on the car ride over. When we got to the funeral home Daddy and Malcolm were outside talking. Both of them had shades on and serious expressions. I hugged and kissed them both then I grabbed David's hand as we walked inside. We sat in the first row, next to Sonny and Jade. I held on to David's hand for dear life. When it was time for the program to start, Daddy sat between Jade and I. Malcolm was going to sit next to Nana, but Daddy stood up and told him to come sit next to him. Daddy scooted closer to Jade, which put Malcolm next to me. I didn't think anything of it until David's grip got a little firmer. I rubbed his hand without looking at him. I couldn't tell you how the service went. My eyes stayed glued to the casket, when people came up to pay their respects it was so many people I couldn't tell you who came and who didn't. Andrew had a steady stream of tears and he didn't care who saw them. I hugged him tightly, and he squeezed me as well. David tended to the baby mostly I was really no help all day. David followed in my car with Darryl while the rest of us rode in the limo following the hearse. No one said a word all you heard were sniffles and soft sobs. At the gravesite a few words were said, then Timothy read a poem Daddy wrote Momma when they first started dating. I knew my Daddy was sprung on Momma from jump but hearing that poem made EVERYONE break down. Even though Malcolm had shades on everyone could tell he was staring at me the whole time. Like Daddy was speaking his thoughts. I tried to pretend like I didn't notice, but everyone noticed. Afterwards we went to a big community center to eat. Daddy and Malcolm stood over to the side talking and obviously drinking something. They both still had shades on so people were mostly offering their condolences and leaving them alone. At the table we were sharing Momma stories, Andrew and the boys were sharing as well. We were all laughing so hard at the stories we shared. We'd laugh then we'd cry the whole day was draining. Derrick and little Tim ran around outside burning off energy. David stayed outside with them. He couldn't really relate to our stories, as he never really spent time with Momma. When he came inside I was sitting with Daddy and we were talking about Momma's stuff. David said the boys were really tired and he wanted to take them home to put them to bed. I went to my purse and gave him my keys. He looked disappointed that I wasn't going with him, but how could he ask me to leave, ESPECIALLY in front of my Daddy. Daddy waved his head around like he was Stevie Wonder and not paying attention to our conversation. But I knew that meant that he was irritated with David and was doing everything in his power to be cool. Then David asked me where Andrew was.

"Andrew stays! You wanna take your sons, be my guest! But Andrew STAYS!" Daddy exploded. Daddy's reaction triggered Malcolm's attention.

"Mr. Wallace I meant no disrespect. I was just trying to consider all the boys." David said trying to mask his irritation.

"Don't get me started on disrespect with you!" Daddy took a sip of his drink. "I'm gonna...." Daddy blew air. "This is not the time or the place!" Daddy said shaking his head and turning in his seat to put his back to David. Now Uncle Frank was looking as well.

David shot me a look and I hopped out my seat. I never went over Momma and Daddy's with any showing bruises, so who knows what Daddy knows. But today wasn't the day or time to find out. I told him to come on. David looked like he was gonna snap, and since he doesn't know my family he had no idea how lucky he was to be walking away from Daddy untouched in this moment. David asked me how long I was gonna be, and I told him I couldn't tell him. I hugged him, and ducked when he tried to kiss me. I squeezed his hand and said thank you. Then he watched me walk back inside. Daddy was talking to Malcolm and the uncles when I walked in. They all looked at me, my face started stinging. I put my hands up and asked them what the looks were for. Uncle Frank asked me where David worked again. I told him that David worked for the railroad. Uncle Jeff said, "he has no idea who you are does he?" I shook my head no. "Well it's not like knowing saved Charles." Then they all laughed. I looked at them not liking what they were getting at. I walked away from them and sat next to Jade, she had a cup full of something. All I saw was brown and I took a big gulp. She smiled at me her eyes were droopy from crying and drinking. A few more gulps later Andrew asked me where David was. I told him that he went ahead to the house to put the boys to bed. Then Andrew asked if he could spend the night at Uncle Jeff's, I told him that was fine as long as it was ok with them. Auntie Lauren shook her head yes from across the room. Andrew gave me a hug and asked me if I was ok. I smiled and I told him I was, I asked him if he was ok. He shrugged, kissed my forehead and took off. I stayed with Jade and finished off her cup. I hadn't had a drink in so long I forgot how good it was. I asked Jade where I could refill her cup and she pointed at Malcolm. As I walked towards Malcolm with the cup he shook his head no. When I asked for a refill he told me no. I told him it wasn't for me it was Jade, he still told me no. He said I had enough, I told him he wasn't my daddy and to stop it. Malcolm said no again and then he walked away from me. I looked at Jade and I shrugged. Jade waved at me to tell me it was ok. But I wanted more so I followed Malcolm. He started shaking his head when he saw me coming. He walked out the door and I followed him. I kept begging him; he gave me a small splash more. When I complained about the amount he said he wasn't sending me home to David drunk. Then we both got quiet. He was going to say something but I walked back inside. Rosalind, her mom, Troy, Melvin, Cassondra, and her husband all hugged me goodbye as they left. The facility staff came and started cleaning up. I told everyone who felt up to it to come back to my house. I rode with Jade and Sonny. When we got to the house David was very comfortable with his shirt unbuttoned, pants unfastened, shoes off. When we walked in the door he jumped up and fixed his clothes. When he saw all my family coming I could tell this wasn't gonna be his scene. He hung out for an hour and a half. Once he felt comfortable that Malcolm wasn't coming, he kissed me on the cheek and said he'd see me later. Twenty minutes after he left Malcolm came over. We were watching some movie, and one by one we all fell asleep where we were. My head started on Malcolm's shoulder, but it ended up on his chest sleeping to the sound of his heart beat.

****

Ever since the funeral, my family pops up more randomly at the house. And whenever they do, they don't leave until David's been gone a good thirty minutes. David tries to remain calm but it's wearing thin on him I can tell. He's been working really hard on his temper, but I've also stopped holding back so I know it feels like a double whammy sometimes. I don't start stuff, but if I don't like something I speak up again. I don't show him fear anymore, so sometimes he grabs me, and then he catches his self and lets me go. I still may haul off and hit him for grabbing me but he leaves immediately. Andrew has opened back up to him. They play basketball a lot, it helps both of them burn off energy. Hanging with us has made Hubby drop most of his chub; he's still a little husky, but barely.

The doorbell rang just after breakfast. Malcolm was so excited. He was telling me about the recording studio he just opened. He was mid-sentence when David barked at him asking him why he never calls before he comes over.

"I see someone has eaten their courage cereal this morning!" Malcolm glared at David. "She is the only reason you still breathe!"

Andrew asked Malcolm about the studio, changing the subject. Malcolm told him to go get his jacket and he'd show him. Derrick got up and followed Andrew. They both came back with their jackets.

"Where are you going?" David said to Derrick

"With Malcolm"

"How are you going to leave when I'm here to see you?"

"I always go with them." Derrick said in a nonchalant tone.

"David it's ok, they'll be back soon." I said shooing them towards the door. David was standing up when I came back in the kitchen.

"DON'T YOU EVER DO THAT AGAIN!!!! IF I'M TELLING HIM HE CAN'T GO SOMEWHERE YOU BETTER NOT TELL HIM HE CAN!"

"Excuse you! I don't make Andrew stay home when you wanna take him somewhere real quick and we all know his dad is coming. What's the difference? You want them to feel like they're separate and different?" I said picking up the dishes from the table.

"I'm getting tired of you disrespecting me!" He said

"David please! Nobody's disrespecting you, you're just not looking at the big picture."

David huffed and went in the living room. Darryl came out the bathroom celebrating his victory over the potty. He asked me where Andrew and Derrick were. I told him they went with Malcolm and they'd be right back. Darryl huffed then he went in the playroom and started playing with his toys. I started washing dishes then David came in the kitchen he put his arms around me, he apologized for being grumpy. I asked him what was wrong. He took a deep breath, and then he said, "I think we should get married!"

I froze in my spot. I turned so red, "David you know...."

"Amber I'm a man, and no other man can dictate to me how I express my love." Then he kissed me gently on my lips. "Besides there's only so long I can be around you without wanting to tear your clothes off!" He laughed. "What do you say?"

"David, he wasn't joking."

"We don't have to stay in Oakland. There are open positions all over the country. We could just move away, take the kids."

"What about Andrew?"

"He'll have me." He said

"You would have a fit if the shoe was on the other foot. I couldn't do that to Andrew."

"To Andrew or to Malcolm?"

I sucked my teeth, "seriously?"

"He's always around." David said irritated.

"He's Andrew's father."

"Yea but your family is already bonded to him. They don't give me a chance."

"Yes they do or they did before you started acting like they're the plague."

"Amber seriously! Lets do it! Me and you! I love you!" He said kissing my neck.

"David, I can't. What about my Daddy? My grandparents are getting older. If I left with you I couldn't ever come back."

"AMBER!!! Well what am I supposed to do? Live the rest of my life suspended like this? I think three years in is being a good sport. I want to move on with our lives." He lifted my chin. "Just say yes! Show me you love me!"

"What do you mean three years in?"

"Three years of no sex is a long time!"

"Has it been that long?" I was trying to remember.

"Yes, you cut me off when you found out you were pregnant. Darryl is two."

"Oh" is all I could say cause I hadn't missed sex. Plus I didn't wanna remind him of when the last time was exactly; I had no desire to relive that. "If this is just about sex, you can get it from anywhere."

He dropped his arms. He looked me up and down. Out of nowhere he grabbed me by my hair. "Have you been getting it from somewhere?"

I had a flashback of Momma Shuga pulling my hair. I punched him in the face. "Take your hands off of me!"

When I swung again he backed up. Darryl started crying I didn't know how long he had been there, but his cry let me know this was real and not a dream. David put his hands up, "I'm sorry! I'm sorry!"

I stood there ready to fight. He caught me off guard. I was not expecting him to change up like that. He hadn't done that in years. "And you wonder why I won't marry you! I was HEART BROKEN when I couldn't marry you! Now I won't even if I could!"

My words hit him like a ton of bricks. I wanted to take them back seeing how badly they wounded him but I couldn't do it. "So then why am I here Amber? Every free moment I spend it with you. I've worked very hard to make us a family. I worked my butt off to regain Andrew's approval. What am I doing it all for?"

"David! I will not marry you! If that means you stay on the porch when you come to get your boys then so be it. But you have to get out, and you have to move on."

"I'm sorry! Please, let's talk about this."

"David you've got to go! Get out!"

"I'M SORRY! HOLD ON!" He was trying to calm down.

"No! No! No! I'm not going through this with you again! Get out!"

David walked past Darryl who was standing there crying. I picked Darryl up, he was hysterically screaming. I was trying to comfort him. David got in his truck and left. It took Darryl a long time to calm down.

When Malcolm brought the boys back Darryl had just calmed down to that sporadic breathing you do after you've cried your eyes out. They were all smiles, but Andrew and Derrick's smiles dropped when they looked at Darryl. Derrick asked Darryl what was wrong while Andrew asked me where David was. He walked towards the kitchen, then the downstairs bathroom. Malcolm was looking at the change in the boys. I told Andrew he left, I tried to say it matter of factly. Andrew and Malcolm had the same expression on their face as they tried to read me. Then Andrew asked me why David left. I didn't appreciate how he was trying to draw me out in front of Malcolm. I told him we had an argument and Darryl didn't like it. Then I put Darryl down and told him to go play. Derrick followed Darryl into the playroom. Andrew asked me if I was ok, while his eyes danced all over my body, Malcolm's eyes were doing the same. I sucked my teeth and told them to stop being silly. Just as their faces were starting to relax Derrick walk back in the room and asked me why David pulled my hair. I scrunched up my face, Malcolm told Darryl to come to him.

Darryl's face was mad, a dead give away cause he was my happy baby. Malcolm picked him up and asked him if he was ok. Darryl shook his head yes while he rested it on Malcolm. "Mommy and daddy had a fight?" Malcolm asked. Darryl shook his head yes. "What happened?"

Darryl said, "daddy did like this to mommy" and then he pretended like he was pulling hair. "Then mommy did like this" and he made a little fist and pretended to hit his face.

"Then what happened?" Malcolm asked

"Mommy said get out! Daddy said sorry, sorry."

"Did he do it again?" Malcolm asked looking at me. Darryl shook his head no. "Has this happened before?" Malcolm asked the boys.

"Malcolm! Stop it! I don't go prying in your relationships."

Malcolm eyed me then he looked at the boys. He shot Andrew a serious look. Andrew huffed, then he told Malcolm that he saw David grab my arm before, but that was it. Malcolm asked Derrick, Derrick said he saw David push me before. Just like everyone else I was surprised, I had no idea Derrick had seen that before. Malcolm looked at me with angry eyes. "He hits you?"

"No!" I said real fast.

"Malcolm, it's not like that. He doesn't hit her and I make sure he doesn't grab her anymore." Andrew said defending David and I.

"Is that kind of behavior ok?" Malcolm asked Andrew, his tone was deep and piercing.

"I guess not," Andrew said thinking about it.

"I can't believe this! This is who you choose over me?" Malcolm yelled, everybody jumped.

"It's not like that Malcolm." I was trying to calm him down. "My relationship with David hasn't been perfect, but it has gotten better." I said in my defense.

"I've never hit you!"

"No, but you've picked me up before." I said reminding him

Malcolm thought about it. "Amber, mark my words. This isn't gonna go away. The next time he even tilts his head at you he's done!"

My eyes filled with tears, "Malcolm what about the kids?"

He looked at Andrew his eyes were big, and then at Derrick who had no expression, and Darryl who was still calming down. He squinted his eyes, "you don't bully women! Sometimes things happen where you may have to handle a female. But men do not bully women! Walk away! NOBODY HITS YOUR MOMMA YOU HEAR ME?" They all shook their heads. Malcolm looked at their little faces then he groaned. "Amber, I've exhausted just about all my patience."

"Malcolm please! He won't hit her, he's not crazy!" Andrew said

Malcolm looked at Andrew, "careful about how much faith you put in a person like this son."

I went back to washing dishes. Andrew and Derrick went out back followed by Darryl. Andrew was teaching Darryl to play just like David had taught him. When there was nothing left to clean in the kitchen I finally came out. Malcolm was on my phone discussing business with someone. Melvin came over, he wanted to go out dancing that night, but I wasn't feeling much like dancing. Malcolm even got on the bandwagon, as he invited his self to go out with us. I tried to use the kids as an excuse. But Malcolm countered with asking Tiffany and or Penny to babysit if I'd go. I still wasn't sure, when I went in the kitchen I could hear them whispering. Then Melvin came in the kitchen, "you know if Malcolm goes we pay for nothing,

and we get VIP treatment no matter where we go. Why you dragging your feet?"
I whispered and told him about the morning I had. I told him I didn't feel much like
partying. Melvin wasn't sympathetic. He told me that's the reason he didn't like
David. Melvin never saw David do anything to me, but he said he could tell. I didn't
feel like arguing about it and clearly they weren't gonna leave me alone until I
agreed to go. So I agreed to go if the girls could come to my house, and if Sophia
could go that they'd be willing to watch Sasha too. Melvin had a bag with him when
he came; he said he had his clothes already. Malcolm said there was a spot in
Hayward he wanted to checkout, someone told him it was a nice spot to chill. The
thought crossed my mind that David has family out there, but what are the odds
they'd be at this particular club just because they lived out there. Sophia said she
was in, she and Richard had a fight and she needed to get out.
"Hey Ms. Connie" Malcolm called out; "I'll be back".
When I walked in the living room Connie was exaggerating shivers. "GURL!!!! I
don't know why you have David around when you could have that one!"
I laughed, then I shared that David and I broke up this morning. She said she was
sorry to hear that. Then she told me that she didn't really care for him. She said
there was something mean in his eyes. I rolled my eyes as I suspect everybody was
gonna start coming with these stories.
Sophia was super excited when she got to the house. Sasha went straight to the back
with the boys. Sophia said she wasn't driving cause she was gonna have fun tonight.
I told her that David and I broke up, she and Connie high fived. Their celebration
irritated me. Then Melvin came in and added his two cents. I sat there looking at
them all in disgust. Malcolm came back at around a quarter to eight with Penny and
Tiffany. Connie gasped when he walked in the door. She kept nudging me like I
wasn't looking at him. He did look good, but I saw him she didn't have to point it
out. I introduced the girls to Connie in case they needed anything. Then Sophia and
I ran upstairs while Melvin dressed in the bathroom. Of course in that moment I
couldn't make a sound wardrobe decision. Sophia went downstairs to order pizza. I
settled on a dress that I had completely forgotten about. I turned around in the
mirror admiring how this dress clung to me. I pulled my hair kind of up in a banana
clip. I put on simple makeup, and then I went downstairs. Troy and Rosalind were
all snugly on the couch when I came down stairs. It was still too weird seeing her
with someone other than Benjamin. I asked where Sophia was and Melvin said she
was outside talking to Malcolm. Troy studied my face to see if I had a reaction.
That was weird, but I didn't care. Sophia looked a little upset when she came inside,
but she didn't say anything. Malcolm stopped in his tracks when he saw me, then he
started nodding his head. Sophia told me she needed something strong before we
left. When we walked into the kitchen Penny and Tiffany made a big deal out of my
outfit. They told me I looked good, I thanked them. Hubby and Dude sat there with
big eyes not saying anything watching my every move. Andrew asked them what
was wrong with them and they just shook their heads. I asked Sophia what was
wrong, and she told me nothing. I eyed her, and then she told me to stop looking at
her like Auntie Annette. I smiled I liked anything about me that referenced
Momma. But I didn't stop watching her. Malcolm came in the kitchen still admiring
me. Andrew shot him a look like he didn't like the way Malcolm was looking at me.
Malcolm said our ride was outside. There was a limo waiting for us. The kids ran to
the window, they were oohing and awing over the limo. I kissed my babies,
Tanisha, and Sasha bye. Malcolm held my hand as I stepped in the limo. Melvin
was really excited; it was his first limo ride. When we got out the limo Malcolm

held my hand and then he didn't let go. We bypassed the line and went straight inside. We went straight to the VIP section. This club had a kitchen so Malcolm ordered one of each appetizer and he told them to keep the drinks coming. Juan was there he came over said hi, and then he told Malcolm he needed to talk to him. They walked over to the side and talked for a few minutes. We ordered the house special. I looked around, everybody was throwing back drinks. I didn't feel up to being hung over tomorrow so I sipped slowly on my drink. Sophia downed three drinks before she was ready to dance; she and Melvin were in a zone. I thought Melvin only danced like that with me. Rosalind and Troy went out on the dance floor, I told them to get a room. Malcolm was still talking to Juan. I didn't really feel like being there anyways. Malcolm came over and sat next to me. He asked me how I was holding up. I told him I was fine, he pointed at my drink, and asked why I was still on the first one. I told him it's been a long day. I told him peer pressure brought me out tonight, but I don't feel much like celebrating. He watched my face, and then he moved closer. He put his arm around me and he asked me to be honest with him. I had no idea what he was gonna ask me, so I told him I'd try to be. If he asked me about David hitting me I couldn't be honest I knew better. Malcolm asked why I was so ready to marry David but I wouldn't marry him. I grabbed his hand, I told him David's package was wrapped differently. I told him that David took a personal interest in Andrew right away, and he was always faithful to me. I told him amongst our problems I never worried about him cheating on me. I told him that things took a turn for the worst when he told me I couldn't marry David. David changed when I changed my tune about our future together. I told him I wonder how different my life would be right now if I hadn't forgotten to take off my engagement ring. Malcolm said there's no possible way David could love me like he does. It made me feel good to hear him say that, but my mind doesn't accept it. I told him my heart wants to believe him, but my mind doesn't. We sat there going back and forth for a long time. Then I asked him where he told Yvette he was going tonight. He exhaled, "I don't love her!" But I told him he feels something for her they've been together all these years. He kept searching for words to try and explain, but he couldn't. We spent most of the night talking which is something we hadn't done in years. Everyone came back and forth to the table, while Malcolm and I talked. I worked my way up to two and half drinks for the entire evening, tipsy enough to not drive, but coherent enough to know exactly what was going on around me. The last song of the night the DJ played The Lady in My Life. Malcolm told me I had to dance with him to our song. So I did, being that close to Malcolm did send energy through my body. Being in his arms is where I wanted to stay, but remembering his wandering eye threw cold water on the fire that almost started to burn in me. That song seemed to go on forever.

On the way home Malcolm and I realized that everybody was drunk. But there's something about seeing police cars with lights on at your house that sobers you up FAST! I couldn't get out of that car fast enough. Connie and Mr. & Mrs. Hall were in the living room with the girls and all the kids. It was after two o'clock in the morning and all but Darryl were wide-awake. I asked what was going on. Connie said she came over to collect her boys and a slice of pizza when some guy named Charles showed up. She said he was drunk and demanding to see his daughter. She told him he had to leave. I asked Sophia how he knew where I lived cause he never came to my house before, she said she didn't know. Connie said the boys really roughed him up, and Andrew told him to leave. I looked at Andrew and he had no expression on his face. Connie said it was quiet for a while and then the doorbell rang again only this time it was David. I looked at Andrew again and his face turned sad. She said he was looking for me and he had been drinking too. She said he kept asking Andrew where I was, but Andrew wouldn't answer him. Derrick told him he had to leave, I looked at Derrick and his little face was stone. I asked Derrick why he felt the need to tell David to leave? Derrick said David made Andrew cry. Everybody looked at Andrew cause he wasn't a crier, my heart sank. I asked what did he do? Derrick said David was calling me all kinds of names and he lost it when he found out I was with Malcolm. When Andrew wouldn't tell him where we went, David kept screaming at Andrew. Connie called the police and everyone made David go outside. Connie said Charles came back and he and David started fighting. They stopped by the time the police came. The police made them leave, and it was quiet for a few hours. The Halls came over to check on everybody. Connie said she decided to stay at my house until we came home cause something didn't feel right. The police came back asking Andrew all kinds of questions about David, and then we pulled up. And officer took Sophia to the side, she started crying. When I went over to comfort her she said Charles was dead. I thought she heard the officer wrong I asked if he was sure it was Charles. They said he was wearing the same clothes as earlier and he still had his identification on him. They said he had been beaten to death. They were looking for David for questioning. I told them David wasn't a murderer. Malcolm and Troy were very quiet, they just listened. Andrew told the officer that David would get mad sometimes, but he didn't believe that David could kill anyone. The officer asked if David had ever become belligerent when he drank before. I hesitated, everybody was looking at me. I kept saying um, um, um. I asked the officers if I could talk to them in the kitchen. Sophia yelled out that I had a bruise on my cheek once after he and I argued. It looked like Malcolm lost his balance for a second, he sat in the chair next to him and he clasped his hands together. I looked at Sophia with tears in my eyes. Then Melvin said sometimes we would be fighting when he came to my house, and every once in awhile he'd see a bruise on me and I would have some stupid excuse for it. Malcolm started rocking in his seat. The officer asked Sophia and Melvin if they ever saw David hit me, and they both said no. I started to walk them to the kitchen, and then Rosalind called out that she had seen him hit me and pull me out of a car by my hair. Andrew looked at me in disbelief, and then he looked at Malcolm. Troy was asking Rosalind why she never told him. I gave the officers David's address and I told them to go find him. Sophia and Rosalind took the kids upstairs to go to bed. Andrew wouldn't take his eyes off Malcolm. Malcolm was unglued but he was trying to keep it together while the police were still there. Troy was visibly angry as well, but he was calmly talking to Malcolm in a low tone. The Halls went home, and Connie took her boys home. As soon as the police left Malcolm picked up my phone, he called someone and said there was a change in plans. I was begging Malcolm not to do it. "This Nigga has been beating you up! Why are you even talking to me right now?" Malcolm said in a cold tone.

I pushed through tears, "what about the kids?"

His eyes were cold, "they have me. Now go to bed, I'll deal with you later." Andrew was still in the living room. I told him to go to bed, Malcolm was yelling into the phone. Andrew had tears going down his face. "Momma save David!" "I'm trying baby".

When Malcolm got off the phone he roared at me. "YOU LET HIM HIT YOU!!!!!" "Malcolm it wasn't like that!" Andrew said

Then he looked at Andrew. "WHAT ARE YOU CRYING FOR? HE HIT YOUR

MOTHER!!!!"

"Malcolm he didn't mean it. That was a long time ago, he's not like that anymore. Please!"

"I CAN'T BELIEVE THE BOTH OF YOU! HE MAY NOT KNOW WHO YOU ARE, BUT HE KNOWS WHO I AM! HE'S DEAD!"

"Malcolm please! I broke up with him this morning please." I reached out to touch him, but he pulled away from me.

"Malcolm, PLEASE! I don't want him to die!" Andrew said

Malcolm walked up on Andrew. "Did you hear anything that was said tonight? It's not like he did it one time. Why are you pleading for someone who didn't care enough about you to keep your mother safe? You think he cares about you? He's been using you to get at your momma this whole time! If he really cared about her he never would've laid a finger on her. I'm done talking about this. IT'S DONE!"

(To Be Continued in Part 2)

MORE FROM THE AUTHOR

Thank you for allowing me to entertain you. I hope you have enjoyed reading my current release. If you have not read Volumes I – VIII of the Wallace Family Affairs series, please do so. Click here for a list of all the background stories. Once you have read the background stories, please checkout the current date series Together We Are Strong. Stay tune for more to come shortly.

Wallace Family Affairs
At Last (Click here)
Tracy's Complications (Click here)
Distorted Mirrors (Click here))
Sometimes Love Isn't Enough
Love Is Just Enough (Click here)
Just A Friend (Click here
Invisible (Click here)
Look Beyond Your Eyes (Click here)
No Regrets (Click here)
First You Laugh Then You Cry (Click here)
A Heart That's Taken (Click here)
Abandoned (Click here)
Last Words (Click here)

Together We Are Strong
Season 1 Present (Click here)
Beyond The Wallace's ~ I Knew You When (**TBD**)
Season 2 What Comes Next (Release **TBD**)

Standalones
Secrets & Lies ~ (**TBD late 2016 release**)
Anthology **Short** Story (Where Love May Find You Collection) ~
(Click here)
Waiting (**TBD**)

Hopefully you've enjoyed all of the background stories for our lovely Wallace's and Latour's. Please tune in for more from the "Together We Are Strong" Wallace & Latour Family Episodes on Amazon